ALIKA

ODYSSEY OF A NAVY DOLPHIN

DONALD E. AUTEN,
CAPTAIN, USN (RETIRED)

ISBN 978-1-64003-736-6 (Paperback)
ISBN 978-1-64003-737-3 (Hardcover)
ISBN 978-1-64003-738-0 (Digital)

Covenant Books, Inc.
11661 Hwy 707
Murrells Inlet, SC 29576
www.covenantbooks.com

Praise for *Alika: Odyssey of a Navy Dolphin*

I've just had the pleasure of reading *Alika: Odyssey of a Navy Dolphin*, by Donald E Auten, and cannot recommend it highly enough. The story centers around an Atlantic bottle nose dolphin, named Alika, that is orphaned and found stranded in the mudflats of Florida by a young girl and her brother. After his rescue, Alika is shipped to San Diego for treatment and rehabilitation, then entered into the Navy Marine Mammal Program, where he is taught to locate mines and patrol the waters for enemy divers. His training is at the hands of Brent, a naïve young cowboy from Wyoming, and the two quickly become inseparable.

The setting for the novel is the period leading up to the second Gulf War, and as Alika's training reaches completion, storm clouds gather. At this time, we are reintroduced to Katie, a marine biology student. Katie is the young girl who saved Alika seven years previously. The reunion between Katie and Alika will have you reaching for the Kleenex. And the budding romance between Katie and Brent smiling with the simpatico of it all. However, the world isn't always a perfect place and darker days are ahead.

Mr. Auten's naval background predominates in the storytelling and although his novel is rich in detail, extensively researched and quite technical at times, with his smooth writing style at the controls it never comes across as overbearing or condescending. In fact, his attention to detail in creating and building the characters within the story works so well that the finale will have you wiping away a tear and hugging your family pet, or your neighbor's - if pet-less - in admiration.

Neil A White, Readers' Favorite – 5-Star

I LOVE ALIKA. What a fabulous story. I laughed and cried. It is a hard-to-put-down read. I loved the tender way (Auten) captures the horse training, the dolphins and the men who work the ranch, the trainers and their superiors. What a movie this would make!

Karen Dwinell, Director of Animal Welfare, Coronado
Animal Care Facility, President, PAWS of Coronado

While listed as fiction due to the incorporation of a story line involving fictional characters, *Alika: Odyssey of a Navy Dolphin* by Donald E. Auten reads more like a non-fiction account of animal training and the use of marine mammals in war-time maneuvers. Beginning with the rescue of the baby dolphin by a teenage girl in Florida, and his eventual admission to the Navy Marine Mammal Program, this story not only details the amazing ability of these mammals, but also the special mental focus and sensitivity required for a person to successfully interact with animals.

The focus then switches to a horse farm in Wyoming where Brent Harris is introduced. Brent has a special way with all animals, and his ability, along with instruction and oversight from his father's master horse trainer, allows him to successfully train a horse another rancher was ready to put down for being too dangerous. Wanting something more out of life after visiting family in California where Brent is introduced to the sea and the intelligence of dolphins, he enlists in the Navy. A great amount of detail is included regarding Brent's training for and activity as a Special Warfare Combatant Craft Crewman. Brent hears about the Navy Marine Mammal Program and switches specialties, and the majority of the book is then devoted to his work there and eventual deployment for active duty in the Middle East.

Dialogue and the interaction of the crew members with one another as well as with their dolphins make this story easy to follow and more enjoyable to read than a simple non-fiction account of the activities related in the text. With the added love interest when Brent meets Katie, the girl who saved Alika, there is even more of an emotional pull to add appeal and excitement. Well written and extremely informative, Alika: Odyssey of a Navy Dolphin covers a tremendous amount of information, but following Brent and his relationship with the orphaned dolphin ties it all together and keeps you engaged. Donald E. Auten has certainly researched all the material in the book extensively and provided a wonderful story that will make you laugh, cry and experience the wonder of these amazing mammals – dolphins.

Melinda Hills, Reader's Favorite – 5-Star

Petty Officer 3rd Class Brent Harris had a dream; one that, until recently, he had thought impossible. Since the age of sixteen he had wanted to work with dolphins, but he never thought he would be fortunate enough to become involved in the Navy's Marine Mammal Program. His life had shaped him for this, twisting his path and increasing his love for dolphins, and he developed an affinity with these creatures. Training Thunder had stirred something within him, and from that moment on he dreamed of such work. He felt a pull to them, yet instead he found himself rising through the ranks of the Navy. Now it seemed that, as he had envisioned, joining the Navy had not only taken him back to the sea where his experience with a pod of dolphins had forever changed him, but it was guiding him towards his dream. Follow his adventure in Donald E. Auten's Alika: Odyssey of a Navy Dolphin.

Alika: Odyssey of a Navy Dolphin by Donald E. Auten is a historical fiction story focusing on the Navy's Marine Mammal Program. Written at a steady pace, readers will find this to be an interesting, insightful, and immersive tale. I thought this was a beautiful read, a heartfelt story about loyalty, love, and kinship. I really enjoyed watching Brent's growth, from the moment he first discovers his passion to his introduction to Alika and a seemingly destined encounter with Kate. You will easily lose yourself in this wondrous and insightful tale, and you may even learn a thing or two about not only the nature of animals, but that of people as well.

K.J. Simmill, Readers' Favorite – 5-Star

Raves for *Roger Ball! Odyssey of a Navy Fighter Pilot*

"His only deficiency lay in his reluctance to acknowledge that he was not bulletproof."

"In Roger Ball!, Donald E. Auten chronicles why John "Hawk" Smith is so worthy of such a tale and the adventure rings true with the promises in the early pages. ... a fast and fascinating read. However, the readership shouldn't stop with those who love a good military read. Teens with a fascination for the military or aviation will find a new hero within the pages, one more worthy and interesting than those found on the big screen."

—*Pacific Book Review*

"*Roger Ball!*" makes for an exciting story and Don Auten does one hell of a job immersing the reader in all aspects of naval carrier aviation and keeping him engaged throughout a very compelling, true story. So, strap in and enjoy a great read and one hell of a ride!"

—*Leighton Warren Smith, Admiral, U.S. Navy (Retired)*

"This biography recounts the life and career of Navy pilot, John Monroe "Hawk" Smith. While it is a tribute to one particular naval aviator, it reads like an homage to the courage and bravery of all military men and women who strap themselves into fire-breathing fighters and tear through treacherous skies to keep others out of danger. Auten's tale of Smith's strength, character, and resolve repeatedly illustrate why he was eventually made Commanding Officer, Navy Fighter Weapons School—more familiarly known as TOPGUN."

—*US Review of Books*

"… author Donald E. Auten does an outstanding job of putting the reader in the cockpit. His descriptions of flying Navy aircraft in both aerial combat and carrier environments are without parallel. His knowledge of the Navy has allowed him to write with an authority usually not seen in a biography of this type."

—*U.S. Naval Institute, Proceedings*

"'Duck' Auten has crafted a masterpiece in *Roger Ball!* This can't-put-down saga is a perfectly focused look into the heart and soul of a great American and outstanding leader."

—*Mike Denkler, Captain, USN (Retired), TOPGUN Instructor*

"Author Auten, himself a former Naval Aviator, tells the story of CAPT John Monroe 'Hawk' Smith, a colorful and highly regarded fighter pilot. … the narrative aptly captures the very nature of a career in Naval Aviation with all its ups, downs, challenges and achievements. …an enjoyable read for those who 'have already been there', and for the youngsters who aspire to join that special cadre of aviators, the ones who fly from the flattops."

—*Wings of Gold Magazine*

"The story of Monroe "Hawk" Smith, wonderfully told by Donald Auten, is a classic tale of challenge, disappointment, and triumph, set against the action-packed backdrop of carrier aviation. *Roger Ball* captures the heart-pounding sweaty-palmed episodes and the result-ing exhilaration of having cheated death one more time."

—*Frederick Hamilton "Rick" Hauck, Captain (Retired), USN, NASA Astronaut.*

Soon to be published: *Black Lion ONE*

GOD'S BLUE MARBLE

We come to this universe as denizens and share in the splendor of this world as one among all God's creations.

While God's beasts rejoice for their part in the cosmos, man—too innovative, too clever, too naive, too brutal, too narcissistic to gaze into crystal blue waters and see anything but his own reflection—defile and foul our paradisiacal planet...now less perfect, less pure, smaller.

Had we the character of the dolphin, the humility and harmony to take our rightful place among all things and be happy in the knowledge we are a rightful part of a vast community of life, had we enjoined them in the celebration to swim, to leap, to rejoice in the passion of life, had we embraced the simple magnificence of life as was God's design, ponder then the exquisiteness of God's blue marble.

D. E. Auten

Photo provided by Space and Naval Warfare
Command, Public Affairs Officer Navy

Dedicated to the memory of
Makai – Mk-7 Dolphin, USN

Oh, what tales he would tell.

In 1974, off the shores of Mississippi, a young Atlantic bottle-nose dolphin was caught for the U.S. Navy. Mammal experts estimated that he was three-years old at that time. He was given the name "Makai". Little did he know that he had joined an elite group—the Navy Marine Mammal Program (NMMP). Thus began the adventure of a lifetime and an amazing story about a dolphin who served the Navy and the nation.

Early in his career, Makai was stationed in Key West, Florida and made multiple deployments to Mayport, Florida and Hawaii. From 1993 to most recently, he was reassigned to San Diego, California, North Carolina, Camp Pendleton, Hawaii and finally San Diego again.

Makai was the first dolphin to complete the Buried Mine Readiness Certification. He was a stalwart dolphin—his ardor, diligence, and dependability made him a mainstay in mine warfare exercises, training missions, and real world mine counter measures. However, it was his character—a nexus with the human species and genuine enthusiasm to work with his handlers that catapulted Makai to rock star status within the NMMP community. He was just a very likable dolphin. When it was time to go to work, he set the standard. But Makai also had a sense of humor and élan about him which impressed everyone he worked with and, most certainly, made an impression on the young dolphins who learned from him.

By the late 1980's and in the years that followed, demand for mine detection and clearance operations increased world-wide. In response, the United States Navy deployed Makai to many overseas theaters including Canada, Denmark, Korea, Kuwait, Germany, and Norway. His achievements, and those of his dolphin and sea lion compatriots, elevated the reputation and the standing of the NMMP internationally.

In his long career Makai racked-up an impressive list of "firsts", but undoubtedly the most significant was his assignment to Task Force 55 as part of the NMMP element which conducted Mine Countermeasures (MCM) operations during Operation Iraqi Freedom in 2003.

During that conflict, Makai and eight other dolphins went aboard USS *Gunston Hall* (LSD-44) in Manama Harbor, Bahrain in early March 2003. On the 20th of March, USS *Gunston Hall* cast lines and sailed north up the Khawr Abd Allah waterway and into the deep water of Umm Qasr, Iraq. There the dolphins conducted mine countermeasures clearance operations as U.S. and coalition forces engaged elements of the Iraqi Republican Guard during the battle of Umm Qasr. Live fire was exchanged as close as 500 feet from the piers in which they were housed. During this kinetic exchange, Makai was the first to enter the water for mine clearing operations during yet another first—the first time Navy marine mammals were used in mine clearing operations during military action.

Through the rest of March and into April 2003, Makai participated in dozens of sea-lane clearing actions which expedited the entry of the HMS *Sir Galahad* (T226) into the port of Umm Qasr to deliver desperately needed humanitarian aid to the Iraqi people. In the years that followed, Makai's echolocation system and eyesight degraded to the point that he was unable to continue operational or training assignments in open water. The story in the pages of this work tell of Makai's unsinkable enthusiasm to continue to try to board the boats and head to sea with his handlers. Even in his declining years his effulgent spirit and depth of character enamored him greatly in the hearts of his humans.

Like all Navy marine mammals, Makai was treated to a life of luxury and comfort in his retirement years and was allowed to fraternize with the female dolphins when young dolphins were needed. Owing to his extensive experience and maturity, Makai not only sired a great number of young dolphins, he assisted in their socialization and in the development of their mission skills.

For forty-three years Makai lived an adventure, an odyssey really, working with humans in a mission which saved lives and served our nation in peace time and in war. On 11 April 2017, Makai, the most celebrated dolphin of OIF and perhaps the most beloved and respected mammal in the history of the Navy Marine Mammal Program, with immense sadness and upmost reverence, was lovingly and mercifully put to sleep at Pt Loma, California.

It was a great loss to the program and a gut-wrenching passing which left an immense vacuum in the hearts of those who knew and loved him.

I have no doubt that Makai's spirit will live on, not by this simple dedication, not by this unworthy paean, but by his illustrious achievements and by his unbreakable bond with those he worked with.

If Makai was with us today, if he could talk, if he could describe his adventures, what he saw, the wondrous things he did, if he could describe for us those intimate bonds he forged with his humans, if he could tell his story … oh what tales he would tell.

Fair winds and following seas, shipmate!

CONTENTS

Preface...21

Prologue...27
    Intro to a Tiger...27
    The Pod...29
    Contact...32
    The Attack..33

Chapter 1: Sanctuary..37
    The Savior..37
    The Cavalry...44

Chapter 2: The Fork in the Road..................................50
    The Decision..50

Chapter 3: Home on the Range...................................54
    Star Valley..54
    The Harris Ranch..56
    The Harris Clan...57

Chapter 4: Brent Harris—Cowboy..............................68
    A Boy with a Gift...68
    Thunder..72
    The Breakthrough...82
    Heading for the Big Show..................................86
    Origins of Cutting Competition...........................88
    The Gridiron...89

Let's Rodeo...97
At Last—Freedom..102
Into the Big Blue..103
Twenty-One Miles Across the Sea........................106
Epiphany...110
Hitching Up...112
Boot Camp 113
Special Warfare Combatant Craft.........................115
The Fork in the Road 116

Chapter 5: Exordium 118
Leaving the Team 118
Checking In 121
Foxtrot Platoon..130
Marine Mammals—The Basics............................136

Chapter 6: The Plan of the Day............................144
A Day in the Life of a Navy Dolphin Handler......144
Tony's Fish House 153
Meeting Alika...155
High Cover 160
The Day America Stood Still 163
Standing Ground 166
Uniform Code of Military Justice.........................169
Perp Walk...173

Chapter 7: Prep School 175
Cram Session..175
Training Progress..184
War Drums—SITREP-CENTCOM 185
Overview of the Persian Gulf War 189
Safe for Solo 192

Chapter 8: Fleet Recert..196
Marine Mammal Systems Operator and
Maintenance Course 197

Introductions and Coursework..................................201
The Reunion 203
Midcourse Progress..207
Trials and Tribulations..217
The Council 223
Pins and Needles 225

Chapter 9: The Home Stretch 227
False Positives..227
A Bond Forged...228
Breaking Records..236
Homecoming...238
Fish Cake for One 239

Chapter 10: Adventures in Dolphin Land....................242
The Mobile Unit THREE Boys 242
Hatching a Scheme 244
The Phone Call 248
Happy Days 254
First Contact 257

Chapter 11: The Making of a Mark 6 Handler 260
Mark 6 First Operations..268
The Threesome—Roger, Bilbo, and Bruiser.................269
Class in Session 272
Mk 6 Dolphin Handler—Under Training.....................276
Learning the Ropes..279
On to the Big Show..281

Chapter 12: The Blue Team 284
Mixed Emotions..284
Naval Base Kitsap Overview 285
Gearing Up 286
Day One—COMEX..290
Red Force Contact 291
A View to a Keelhauling..294

Bruiser—Coloring Outside the Lines 296
The Debrief...300
Reflections...302

Chapter 13: A Field Trip to Foxtrot 306
Prepping for the Visit..306
Welcome to Foxtrot Platoon..309
The Grand Tour 317
Touché 325
Departing...329
Rhapsody Under Starlight 331

Chapter 14: Storm Clouds...340
Tough Sledding 340
Caught Off Guard and Taken by Surprise 342
The Short Road to War...345
When It Rains, It Pours..355

Chapter 15: Xanadu in the Eye of the Tempest...........358
Bouquets and Carousels 358
Chivalry 101 362
The To-Do List...364
Beer Call 368
Warning Order...370
Rapture 375
On Silver Wings...376

Chapter 16: DEPORD...378
Spinning Up...378
Deployment Order..380
Stressing the Heartstrings 382
Preparation and Staging...383
The "Go" Brief 385
Breaking the News 388
Climbing to Flight Level 230 392

Chapter 17: Riding to the Sounds of Gunfire 396
    Recce Runs...396
    The Battle for Umm Qasr...401
    Into the Lion's Den 403

Epilogue This Day Shall Gentle His Condition 415
    The Black Maw of Despair 415
    Katie's Promise 420

Notes 431
Glossary 441
Dolphin Anatomy..445

PREFACE

In 1987, I was on an adversary detachment to Naval Air Station (NAS) Key West working with VF-101, the F-14 Replacement Air Group. The oil pump on one of our A-4 Skyhawks failed during a routine sortie and the pilot ejected. He was quickly picked up by some local fishermen and returned to us looking humble and soggy but none the worse for wear.

As the Officer in Charge of the squadron at that time and on-site, it was my job to locate the wreckage which, according to witnesses, went in shallow water about a mile north of the NAS. I made a dash to a Navy small boat unit near the NAS and requested assistance in locating the airplane. While the boat unit scrambled to put together a crew and make ready a boat, I was treated to a short tour of the facility. The main attraction was the Navy Marine Mammals they worked with.

A polite, young petty officer was kind enough to let me visit the dolphin pens where I met my first dolphins. There was a big bull with scars forward of his dorsal fin which outlined a huge set of jaws from some earlier brawl with a very large predator. He really wanted nothing to do with me. As I think back to that time, laying on the edge of his pen, he approached me with more interest than an offering of friendship. He allowed me to stroke his flank as he slowly glided by, but there was no real connection. His name was Makai. Little did I know that years later he would play such an important part in the development of this novel.

The second dolphin, a much friendlier little cow by the name of Mako, was a different story entirely. She was a delightful muse of a dolphin. After I slapped the water for a few minutes, she approached

21

me, slipped her rostrum into my hand and, with inquisitive, bright eyes, bored deep into my eyes and, as it turned out, into my heart. She flashed all the mannerisms of managing a big smile. She spent several minutes cruising past me, sometimes just out of reach, as if she was enticing me to join her. She was strikingly gorgeous. If she had been equipped with eye lashes, I swear she would have batted them at me. It was a most unnerving and startling encounter. Never had I experienced the attraction or the magic of a gaze such as hers.

Fast forward to 2012, my active duty Navy career behind me and my assignment on the staff of COMNAVSPECWARCOM, the SEAL headquarters at Coronado, California, just ramping up, I met a gentleman by the name of Chris Harris at one of the Porsche club's autocross races. Chris ran a Porsche 914 which, with less than half the horsepower of my old 911, was disturbingly quick and placed consistently in the top times of the day vanquishing me on a regular basis. Chris was one of those people you like on first introduction. Friendly, engaging, and when he had something to say, you listened—it was always interesting stuff.

As the conversation developed we got around to our jobs. It was quite a surprise when he explained he had been training animals for a number of years to include elephants, sea lions, Orcas, and dolphins. Chris's experience as an animal trainer began at an early age working as an exotic animal trainer and care giver for various oceanariums and zoological parks since the early 80's. Chris has amassed over 30 years' experience connecting with and nurturing our non-human counterparts. He's a walking encyclopedia of the characteristics and behavior of large animals and truly captivating to listen to.

I proceeded to share my very limited experience with the two Navy dolphins at Key West. When I mentioned their names he said, "Do you know," he beamed, "… the Navy still has those dolphins and they're doing great."

I was happily shocked—it was twenty-five years ago that I had met them, but the chance meeting with Chris rekindled those wonderful memories.

I had read and enjoyed many stories of the military working dogs—those brave and stupendously loyal war dogs who, day in and day out, lay their life on the line for their handler and their team. I had been quite captivated by the stories, but they were always about dogs. I had read, and heard many stories of dolphins assisting humans and, in some cases, saving their lives. Why, I asked, were there so few books or novels similar in genre but whose main characters were dolphins?

I just couldn't put the idea on the shelf and soon found myself in the clutches of a concept for a story about a dolphin. My objectives were to: build an exciting and heartwarming adventure which captured the reader's imagination and introduced them to the Navy Marine Mammal Program (NMMP) and the life of a Navy Dolphin; show the reader the care, concern, and consideration the men and women of the NMMP hold for their charges, and avoid divulging any classified or sensitive information. The story would be based on facts with the elasticity and license ensured as a novel.

With Chris's help I began to fashion a story board for a novel about the NMMP dolphins and sea lions using a fictitious Bottlenose as a main character. The story is oriented around a small wild dolphin who loses his mother and is stranded on a beach in west-Florida. He is then saved by a young girl, adopted, and rehabilitated by the Navy and inducted into the NMMP.

Enter my own personal experience (though very limited) and the adoration (in abundance) for dolphins and soon I had a story unfolding which perhaps strayed, to some degree, from the actual *professional* relationships of handlers and trainers with their mammal charges, but captured many of the real-life adventures and tales of dolphin-human relationships.

In order to keep the story as faithful and accurate as possible I was fortunate enough to be assisted by several people in leadership and command positions and many handlers, trainers, and bio-techs in the program. One of the reviewers described my affection for the dolphins as anthropomorphic. To that I unabashedly plead guilty. With his guidance, however, I rewrote several sections of the story and revamped others that he believed would reflect poorly on the Navy and the program. These changes should not dampen the plethora of anthropomorphic thrills but should provide more accuracy, greater fidelity, and work more closely within the constraints, procedures, and guiding principles of the Navy's Marine Mammal Program.

That said, in the interest of full disclosure, I must attest to the fact that I have, on occasion, breached the boundaries of Navy standard operating procedures, handler etiquette, and, in some cases, common sense, which would neither be condoned nor tolerated by Navy leadership.

There remains, however, several stories that contribute to the light humor and mood of this heartwarming fable. Duffus, a California Sea Lion, is described as a close friend and pet of the command master chief of Naval Special Clearance Team ONE and effectively has the run of the facility; consumption of spirits within the confines of Foxtrot Platoon, and allowing a civilian to swim with a Navy dolphin are a few of the stories in *Alika* created out of whole cloth from my fertile imagination and in no way reflect the policies, actual events in the history of NMMP, nor portray the practices of NSCT 1. For these occasional romps down the rabbit hole, I accept full responsibility and attribute them to an over stimulated mind and a run-away story board.

There are a great number of people who assisted in developing this story and many more who helped contain it, heightened the realism and provide accuracy and details where there was little to be found.

My most humble thanks to Chris Harris for assisting in the development of the story line and for sharing with me his astounding knowledge of marine mammals. I have met only a few people with the same compassion, concern, and respect for animals of all species as Chris. Anyone who can quote Henry Beston from memory must have a bit of St. Francis of Assisi in their blood. Commander Jon Wood had been assigned as the Executive Officer of Explosive Ordnance Disposal, Mobile Unit 3, led the Fifth Fleet staff planning effort during Operation Iraqi Freedom, and then was assigned as Commanding Officer at Naval Special Clearance Team ONE. Mr. Jeff Haun had a long and intimate association with the NMMP from January 1972 through June 2006. His career included assignments as a trainer, head trainer, program manager, branch head, and division head in charge of the Marine Mammal Program. Mr. Ed Budzyna is the Public Affairs Officer for Space and Naval Warfare Systems Command and assisted in coordinating my research efforts with the right experts within the NMMP; he proved to be very helpful. With a critical eye and a flair for literary composition, I thank Alan Weiss for his contribution in enhancing the story flow and ferreting out my silly mistakes. I thank these gentlemen for their time, effort, expertise, and for their valuable assistance in making this book far better than it would have been without their help.

'Mamas' don't let your sons grow up to be cowboys.' This is the title of a song by Willie Nelson and Waylon Jennings released in early 2011. There's a counter point to this popular song in the form of Mr. Phil Wilson—practicing preacher for the Wyoming Cowboy Church in Jackson Wyoming, director of the Jackson Rodeo, an authentic American cowboy, and a man any mother would be proud of. In the early chapters of Alika, there is a section on raising, socializing, and training horses and preparing both cutting ponies and riders for rodeo competition. Mr. Wilson was kind enough to take time out of his very busy schedule to help me in building these stories. His assistance in imparting his knowledge, experience, and gentle training techniques in these sections proved invaluable.

I owe a debt of gratitude and thanks to my aunt, Ellen Rogers, whose many years of teaching helped keep the story line on track, whose line-editing skills were most helpful, and whose encouragement was always inspiring. To my wife, Katie, my own Navy nurse, who kept me pointed into the wind and spent countless hours making readable (and I hope enjoyable) my scripted chatterings, thank you.

To the many men and women in the Navy Marine Mammal Program, these everyday heroes, who give far more of themselves than their time—thank you! It is a job for which few have the patience, the kindhearted character, the commitment, or the remarkable alchemy to transform wild mammals into partners to humans performing a vital job in challenging environs.

The dolphins of the Navy Marine Mammal Program are an enchanting species whose vast cognitive abilities remain uncharted.

Until one delves into the depth of their glimmering eyes, succumbs to the allure of their beauty, and revels in the mirth of their perennial smile, one cannot truly appreciate their uniqueness. They willingly abdicate much of their right to self-determination by virtue of their trust, confidence, and sense of faith in their human handlers and perform a vital, strategic, life-saving mission for our nation. To those wonderful and majestic beasts that prove that God enjoys a lighter side and without whom, there would be no story—my eternal gratitude.

PROLOGUE

There is witchery in the sea.

—R. H. Dana Jr.,
Two Years Before the Mast (1840)

Intro to a Tiger

September 1995
Cape Cod, Massachusetts, eastern seaboard

She weighed in at just over eleven-hundred pounds. From nose to the tip of her tail, she was ten feet, four inches long. Not particularly large for her species, the female tiger shark, *Galeocerdo cuviera*, can reach lengths of fifteen feet. One female was caught off the coast of Australia, which weighed over three thousand pounds.

Although more common to the central Pacific Islands and those areas with tropical waters, this particular tiger had followed the warm currents of the Gulf Stream as far north as Cape Cod until early September. As the water cooled, she reversed course and headed south. She was in no hurry. Hunting was good.

Although she was a deepwater macropredator, she stayed relatively close to the coastline and navigated southwest between Nantucket and Dukes Islands, turned farther south direct to the Virginia coast, and rounded Cape Hatteras. She cruised just off the coast of South Carolina and Georgia until finally entering the Strait of Florida. Prey was in abundance as she transited the coastline. She'd had her fill of skipjack, devoured scores of bluefish when she happened on a feeding school, scored an injured bluefin tuna, went to deep water to dine on squid, and even found a lone turtle whose shell was no match for the tiger's powerful jaws and rows of razor-sharp teeth.

Tigers, the largest member of the order Carcharhiniformes, are identified by five gill slits, a fore and aft dorsal fin, as well as an anal fin and a nictitating membrane that covers and protects the eyes when needed. Tigers are more commonly referred to as requiem sharks and are cousins to many other powerful medium-sized sharks to include the blue shark, lemon shark, and the bull shark.

Three characteristics make the tiger one of the most feared and successful hunters in the sea: extraordinary sensor systems, eye-watering maneuverability, and aggressiveness.

Through thousands of years of evolution, the tiger has developed a system of sensors that greatly aid in detection and tracking of prey.

The *tapetum lucidum*, a reflective layer behind the tiger shark's retina, aids in capturing visible spectrum light and greatly enhances vision in low-light conditions. *Ampullae of Lorenzini* are small electroreceptors, tiny pits, arrayed linearly along the snout. These enable tigers to sense electric fields, even weak electrical impulses, generated by other marine animals. Finally, a sensory organ, *the lateral line*, extends down the flanks on both sides of the tiger's body. This very sensitive array of sensory cells improves detection of minute vibrations in the water.

The combination of these sensors has enabled the tiger to become one of the most extraordinarily lethal apex predators in the sea, especially at night.

Tiger sharks conserve energy through use of strong, steady, and graceful tail and body movements. Pitch, planing, stability, and turning maneuvers are aided by the tiger's stout pectoral fins. A long upper tail flexes when the posterior section oscillates from side to side. This action provides enormous acceleration and assists in attaining the shark's remarkable top speed of about twenty miles per hour. Its high back and dorsal fin provide the surface area to allow the shark to pivot—to spin very quickly on its vertical axis.

Like most sharks, their teeth are set in rows. As teeth are lost or broken, they are replaced continually by new teeth. They are also serrated, which assists in slicing through flesh, bone, blubber, and other tough substances such as turtle shells.

The female tiger mates once every three years. She is the only shark in the species that is *ovoviviparous*—her eggs hatch internally. Gestation may take up to sixteen months. When the pups, sometimes eighty in a litter, are fully developed—they are born live.

In effect, the tiger was designed to do three things extraordinarily well: swim, hunt, and make little tiger sharks. As she cruised north along Florida's western coastline, she was in her hunt mode.

The big tiger was getting hungry. She'd spent the last four hours tracking a medium-sized pod of dolphin. Cautious and stealthy, she carefully formed a picture of the number of dolphins in the pod, their sizes, and their defensive posture. She wasn't particularly worried about a single dolphin, but she knew from experience that these animals hunted and defended their members as a team, often to the death.

Ordinarily, she wouldn't have pursued an adult dolphin pod, but she had sensory input suggesting that there were a number of smaller dolphins in this group—that's what she was interested in.

The Pod

Saturday, 9 September 1995
Near Turkey Point, Florida; northeast of the Apalachicola Bay

The pod that the tiger was shadowing was a group of Atlantic bottlenose dolphins (*Tursiops truncatus*), members of the Cetacean order. Owing to a highly developed cognitive process, dolphins, porpoises, and whales are fully sentient beings and considered to be some of the most intelligent of all mammals. The dolphin's brain size is proportionally second largest only to humans. Bottlenose dolphins, grouped together in pods, exhibit a complex matriarchal society, strong cultural order, and durable pod bonding. Behaviors are acquired through social learning.[1] The adult females assert leadership, maintain order, give live birth, wet-nurse, engage in other nursery duties, and transfer knowledge and shared behaviors to the daughters. This group activity strongly suggests some level of *culture* among dolphins long thought to be a characteristic unique among humans and some other primates.

Adapted through thousands of generations, dolphins have developed a communication system that is described as *whistling*. Within months of birth, each dolphin develops their own unique *signature whistle*.[2] It is this whistle that provides communication to each of the dolphins on some level. This acoustic transmission is omnidirectional and is used to convey information to the pod to include identity, relative position, and possibly, emotional state of the transmitting dolphin.

Another one of the keys to their hunting success is the dolphin's amazing *echolocation* capability. Clicks—also described as squeaks, trills, creaks, and buzzing—are generated in the nasal passage. This acoustic signal passes through the melon,[3] which serves as an acoustical lens to focus the outgoing sound waves into a beam. This acoustic beam is then focused and projected in front of the dolphin. In receiving the returned acoustic signals—or, in the case of multiple clicks, a *click train*—the dolphin acquires information on the target's size, shape, speed, distance, and in some cases, the internal structure of the target.

The fluid dynamic shape of dolphins is a triumph of natural design and evolution. They are equipped with a dorsal fin located on the back midway between the fluke[4] and the rostrum.[5] This appendage serves to stabilize the dolphin. The pectoral fins, located on the lower side of the dolphin and aft of the head, assist in stopping, rolling, turning, and also act as planing devices. The fluke or horizontal tail is the source of the remarkable power that can produce enough thrust to speed the dolphin up to twenty-two miles an hour.[6] But unique among dolphins, especially the Atlantic bottlenose, is their stupendous turning ability. While most fish turn by pivoting about their dorsal fin and using their tail to change direction, dolphin will actually roll, much like an airplane, and use their massive fluke to generate both pitch and thrust at the same time. The combined effectiveness of the dorsal, pectoral fins, and fluke produces a stunning turn capability that allows the dolphins to outmaneuver everything in the ocean except other dolphins and, perhaps, the nimble sea lion.

Adult females give birth, usually a single calf, every two to three years. Normally, the mother will deliver the baby's tail first, often with the assistance of another female,[7] an *auntie*. The baby is immediately guided to the surface and assisted in breathing until the baby breathes on its own. At birth, the baby weighs between twenty-two to forty-four pounds and averages about three to four feet in length. At three months of age, the baby nearly doubles in length, and many grow to be nearly as long as their mother in that time.

The relationship of mother to baby is extraordinary in its tenderness and remarkable in its intimacy. While young, there is considerable physical contact and persistent tactile reinforcement between the mother and baby. For up to eighteen months, the baby nurses, and it's not until the age of six—until they've developed their own hunting and survival skills—that the calf leaves its mother.

When transiting, the baby drafts on his mother for both protection and to conserve energy. A baby will often be assisted by several aunties who help in a number of nursery tasks and, in some cases, will lactate to assist in nursing duties as well.

Interestingly, the female calf matures at two to three years of age while the male might extend his childhood until ten to twelve. When the males reach adulthood, they will join the other males in bachelor herds and ordinarily stay on the periphery of the main pod of females and calves unless circumstances dictate that they join the inner sanctum of the pod. Unlike the females, the adult males will play with one another, mock fight, and engage in what might be viewed as aggressive behavior toward one another. Often, the marks of this practice are evident in the raking scar tissue on the bodies of the males. In the dolphin matriarch society, adult males are relegated to less-dominant roles of protection, regeneration, and pack hunting for the pod.

This particular pod consisted of nineteen dolphins: seven males, nine females, and three baby dolphins, all born five months earlier in April. The pod had been hunting near Alligator Point, east of Apalachicola in the Gulf of Mexico, for some time, pursuing a large school of mullet.

Using one of several techniques for feeding, the dolphin herded the mullet together in a tight ball and then took turns barreling through the bait ball to feed. By this time, the dolphins were fairly well satiated; and the mullet, on the other hand, were fairly well decimated.

Contact

Saturday, 9 September 1995
Near Turkey Point, Florida; northeast of the Apalachicola Bay

The adult dolphins in this particular pod, through intermittent echolocation, were aware of a large contact in their vicinity, one that had been in their area for quite some time. On this day, information on this specific target generated considerable concern for the pod.

The adults were now double-tasked, hunting the mullet and maintaining contact with the object that seemed to maintain constant range just outside their field of vision. Ordinarily, Atlantic bottlenose dolphins are not concerned about many threats. They are apex predators, growing to nearly ten feet in length and weighing nearly five hundred pounds. The only two animals that would threaten them are humans and larger apex predators—sharks.

The composition of the pod, in sheer numbers and the ability to coordinate and synchronize movements of the entire group, is in itself a proven defense mechanism, but the astounding maneuverability and speed of each individual dolphin both enhanced hunting and improved individual survivability.

The pod, now well satiated on hundreds of pounds of fresh mullet, continued moving west along the coastline, remaining in shallow water, partly to herd the remaining mullet but also in an attempt to shake off their unseen trailer. Owing to the growing concern for the unidentified threat shadowing the pod, four of the females kept the pod in a tighter group than usual through whistles. Two of the bigger males detached from the pod and carefully cruised toward the source of the return in an attempt to identify the intruder.

The Attack

Saturday, 9 September 1995
Near Turkey Point, Florida; northeast of the Apalachicola Bay

As dusk approached, visual acuity advantage shifted to the tiger. She was getting bolder as the light failed and gradually moved closer to the pod.

Ordinarily, the dolphins would have begun their sleep mode. Dolphins are reflex breathers; they must be conscious to breath. But the amazing ability to let one hemisphere of their brain lobe sleep while the other lobe continues to maintain vital functions allows dolphins and several other marine mammals to sleep while respiring. This evening, only the baby dolphins would be awarded this pleasure.

As full darkness set, the tiger closed the distance to the pod. Her posture and her cruising pattern had changed now. Her swimming became more aggressive, her speed increased, and she adopted a definitive arch to her back. As her range to the pod decreased, she began to visually acquire many members of the pod with her enhanced night vision, but the tiger was beyond the visual range of the dolphins. They relied more on their sonar apparatus only at this point. And what their sonar was telling them made them very anxious.

The two big male outriggers finally ventured close enough to the ping return source to get a positive visual identification, and what they saw forced them to return to the pod. Whistles were emitted to tighten up the pod and ensure all members were accounted for. This allowed the dolphins to reduce the defensive area, consolidate their defenses, and maintain better contact with the intruder.

A half-moon and clear water allowed the tiger to finally locate what she had been searching for—a small dolphin. She could handle an adult dolphin if she held the element of surprise, but surprise in shallow and clear water did not facilitate a surprise attack. No, she wanted a quick kill with no conflict with the larger dolphins.

The tiger swam in half circles trying to stay deep and sort things out. All the while, she maintained visual contact with the small dolphin, now swimming on the opposite side and tight against its mother. That was now the tiger's designated target.

The tiger made a turn away from the pod and, with a series of powerful tail thrusts, increased her speed and dove for deeper water. When she turned back to the pod, she was fast, deeper, had good situation awareness, and visual contact with the little dolphin and the mother. The tiger wanted to maneuver around the mother and hit the smaller dolphin.

As the tiger quickly closed the gap, two events took place that she did not anticipate: The two protector dolphins emitted a series of clicks, broke away from one another, spurted to over twenty knots, and pivoted to put the tiger directly on their nose. The second event that came as a complete shock was that the mother dolphin, having matched her click-train return with now a visual sighting, emitted a series of frantic clicks and then also turned hard into the tiger.

The baby dolphin was now fully alert to heightened tension within the pod, but not to the specific threat. He was completely caught off guard when, unexplainably, his mother emitted a shrill warning, spurted ahead, and then turned away from him.

The tiger and the mother dolphin closed with a combined velocity of nearly forty knots. The mother successfully blocked the tiger with her own body, but as they passed, the tiger, eyes rolled back and mouth full agape, sliced a large chunk of flesh from the mother's flank, opening a three-foot gash of muscle, bone, and entrails from her abdomen.

A second later, the two protector dolphins, closing from two different directions, converged at nearly the same instant and hit the tiger before she even knew they were upon her. So focused was she on the small dolphin she never saw the two shapes that converged on her. They rocked her world.

Over eleven thousand foot pounds of energy converged upon the tiger from two vectors, nearly folding the eleven-hundred-pound shark as if it were a jackknife.

The hit by the first dolphin was massive and well-aimed. He impacted along her flank just above the trailing edge of the tiger's right pectoral fin. The dolphin delivered so much energy to the abdomen the shark's liver was effectively pureed. This would have terminal effects: failure of normal bodily functions and buoyancy.[8] Destruction of the liver allowed squalene oil to pour out of the liver and into other abdomen cavities, causing loss of the hydrodynamic balance needed to maintain proper swim trim. This condition would force the tiger to expend significant energy just to maintain a trimmed position and avoid sinking to the bottom.

The second issue was the devastating effect of the loss of the liver as a functioning vital organ. It may take some time, but this was a death knell for the tiger.

But it was the hit by the second dolphin that more immediately altered the roll of the tiger from attacker to casualty.

The second dolphin arrived at the point of attack with colossal speed and struck the tiger just aft of the dorsal—a tremendous blow, but it would have not caused any lasting damage. As if for good measure, the second dolphin also slapped the shark with his powerful fluke as it completed the pass. While less spectacular in terms of energy transfer, this impact lit solidly on the tiger's gill plates, an organ of high vascularity. The contact caused immediate massive hemorrhaging and impeded the shark's ability to respire. This caused death to the tiger in a matter of minutes.

The defender dolphins broke off the attack and quickly regrouped around the mother dolphin. Three female dolphins raced to the injured mother. With great gentleness and care, they braced against her, nudging her to the surface.

Their efforts were in vain. So much lost blood and tissue damage had the mother sustained she passed moments after the attack. She may have lost the battle, but in her last breaths, she could take solace in knowing that her last conscious act was in saving her baby.

For the big tiger, the attack was over. Her blood was now mixed with that of the mother dolphin. In the dim light, it appeared as a spreading cloud of dark crimson and marked the battleground where the lives of two of nature's most highly evolved and most proficient predators ended.

The baby dolphin was in full panic. He heard the signature whistle from his mother and finally realized the critical nature of the situation when he saw his mother's flank being ripped open by a monster the likes of which he had never seen.

The last acoustic message from his mother was a command. This, he executed: he swam using every gram of energy his small body could produce.

The little dolphin had never swum so hard, had never been without his mother, and had never been so afraid. He lost all contact with his family. He could hear the high frequency emissions but tail-on to the pod as he was, he could process no specific navigation information. For nearly a minute, he swam on the same course with all the strength he could muster.

The small dolphin stayed close to the surface and blew air often. Sheer terror, the image of his damaged mother, and her last command drove him well beyond the point of exhaustion. He was only slightly aware of the decreasing depth of the water—he drove forward still when his belly hit the mud and continued his tail flapping even when most of his body was out of the water.

He writhed, thrashed, struggled, and continued his effort to swim but made no further progress. He was in a new and frightening world, one without water, one without his mother.

The little dolphin was encased in mud, and even the magnificent engineering design of his fluke and fins would propel him no farther.

He was stuck, exposed, alone, and very, very afraid.

CHAPTER 1

SANCTUARY

The Dolphin is a friend to seamen, a creature of good omen, of size and strength, but quite weak, when out of its proper element.

—Herbert Pierrepoint Houghton, Amherst, Mass, Carpenter and Morehouse, "Moral Significance of Animals as Indicated in Greek" (1915)

The Savior

Sunday, 10 September 1995
Turkey Point, Florida; northeast of the Apalachicola Bay

She rode like she did everything—with complete mental focus and physical commitment. Katie, a lanky fourteen-year-old golden-haired, green-eyed native Floridian was conflicted with a compelling need to explore everything on the beach and in being hampered by the constraints of time—there just wasn't enough of it in a day to get everything that needed doing done.

They'd just ridden nearly three miles from their home west of St. Teresa, Florida, on an unimproved road headed toward Turkey Point, a place of mystery and enchantment and teeming with wildlife.

"Hurry up, Troy."

Troy, her twelve-year-old, brother was clearly not in her class when it came to energy level, exploratory skills, or interest in the great outdoors.

"Hey, what's the rush? Why are you goin' so fast anyhow? We got all day!"

"No, we don't, Skippy." She was usually sweet as spring corn, but she had an edge to her when things weren't falling into place, especially when her little brother impeded her progress.

"We told Dad we'd be back by noon, and we're running late 'cause you don't know how to ride, Skippy."

Troy was so used to his moniker that he didn't even bother responding to the nickname that was awarded due to his fondness for peanut butter.

"Hey, I'm faster 'n you. Just try to keep up with me!" He quickly put his back into it, strained against the handlebars, and managed to close some of the distance to Katie. With a bit of amusement, she let Troy pull alongside. As soon as Troy caught up with her, she flicked her gear lever twice, dropping her chain into a larger rear sprocket, then jammed down on the pedals and leaned over the handlebars. In a dozen hard strokes, she'd passed Troy and was quickly opening the distance. Dust from the unpaved road traced her progress.

"Butthead," was Troy's only comment, and that was said in a whisper. Girl or not, he'd experienced the misfortune of antagonizing her, and he didn't want to do it again—not today.

Katie was already off her bike and leaning it against a big maple when Troy finally skidded to a stop. He was still trying to catch his breath while Katie had pulled her small backpack off the front bike basket and wiggled into it.

Her pack was loaded with everything a modern explorer and naturalist would need for a day's adventure: four bottles of water, rain jacket, field glasses, two granola bars, a small mirror, fifty-feet of light line, sunblock, floppy field hat, an old German made Beier Beirette, K100 35mm camera, six plastic bags for collected trash or specimens, two pencils, sketchbook, and her prized possession—bought second-hand at the bookstore—a well-used copy of *The Audubon Society Field Guide to North American Birds*.

Troy had his entire load-out of survival gear stuffed in the right front pocket of his shorts: an old Swiss army knife with a broken screwdriver blade handed down to him by his father.

Troy was still leaning over with his hands on his knees, breathing deeply, when Katie announced, "Let's go, Troy. We're burning daylight!"

"Jezzo. How 'bout a break!" Again, a whisper was the safest tone.

Katie had already plotted her course and objectives for the day, and this being early fall, it was a grand opportunity to see many of the early migrators.

"Troy, we're after some shots of red-cockaded woodpeckers. I saw where a few were nesting last week. Also on our list is the yellow-rumped warbler. But the prize would be some shots of chuckwill's-widow. I've seen the photos of these birds in my bird book, but I'll be darned if I ever saw one. These are the biggest nightjars in the country. They're said to have dappled brown plumage, and that helps them blend in with their surroundings…maybe too well. They look like a chunk of bark, and unless they move, you ain't gonna see 'em. But your eyes are better than mine, so keep 'em peeled."

Notes and a few photos of these birds would be a boon to her collection. Her *Audubon* guide identified this area as home to these and a whole host of other birds. She lugged her trusty 35mm and her bird logbook along just in case.

They marched nearly due west over rough ground and turned south when a small freshwater stream joined the broken trail. This would lead them to the beach, almost a quarter mile distant.

"You ever see so many pretty trees, Troy?"

"They're trees, Katie. Ain't no big thing."

"Ah, but what kind of trees, and how'd they get here?"

"Don't know and don't care!"

"Ignorant and arrogant, Troy. How do you ever expect to learn anything?" Katie stopped, spread her arms wide, her head up, and twirled in a 360-degree arc. "Just look at all this, Troy! It's beautiful even now, but not far from here, there were trees 120 to 250 years old. These were old-growth trees, and they were over 100 feet tall.

But in the late 1880s, they were nearly all cut down for lumber. A lot of the pine trees they didn't cut down were tapped for gum and turpentine."

Katie started down the trail again with Troy in tow. He was beginning to enjoy the guided tour.

"It wasn't until the mid-1930s that the Forest Service took control of a bunch of the clear-cut areas. We're in one of those now. Any ideas what national forest we're in?"

"Ah…" A moment's deep effort of recollection resulted in, "The Applea, the Apalachoi, ah heck…the Apalachicola National Forest?"

"Not bad, Troy. It was declared a national forest about 1936. The Forest Service was supposed to take care of the land, keep it as a natural habitat for all the animals, and make sure the public could use it. But then came World War II. With all the building going on then, and even after the war, I guess wood…er, timber was in demand, so they went right back to clear-cutting the forest— again!"

They continued south toward the beach. Katie could smell the saltwater and hear the waves brush against the beach now, and although she hadn't seen one bird or animal, she felt compelled to take photos of about everything. She just knew something big was about to happen.

Troy was gradually becoming interested in this outing, partly because of Katie's storytelling ability—she was always able to read something once and recite it verbatim—but now he realized she had an uncanny ability to put him in the middle of what was becoming a mental state of discovery. And he'd never tell his sister, but he was really starting to enjoy their "adventure"—so long as he didn't see any snakes.

"Well, the Forest Service started to replant the clear-cut areas with slash pine. Some of the older pine trees have grown all on their own from stands that had been cut way back in the early 1900s. If I remember right, about 25 percent of the land that was native longleaf pine is now slash pine.

"If you keep your eyes open, you might see longleaf pine, slash pine, black gum, and red maple trees. And as far as animals go, this place is loaded with stuff. We could see wood storks, herons, swallowtail kites, alligators, and maybe an eastern indigo snake. They're a threatened species, ya know. And if we're really lucky, we might come across a bald eagle or two."

The correct response from Troy would have been, *Gee, a bald eagle right here. Wouldn't that be something!* But what Troy said instead was, "All I wanna come across is a double bacon and cheese Whataburger, a chocolate shake, and large fries." He knew at once this would provoke some return fire, but it was too late to take it back.

"You need to cut down on the fat pills, Skippy. If you'd come with me more often, your butt wouldn't be hanging out of your shorts so much."

"Katie, I'm warning you. Knock it off er—"

"Or what, Troy? You gonna fall on me and break my foot!"

"One of these days, sis!" A whisper.

"Heads-up, Troy. There might be gators in the area, and Marsha said she saw a moc in the water last Saturday."

"I heard all about that sis!" Troy was not much into the reptilian life-forms, and though he was enjoying the guided tour much more than he thought, he was always edgy anytime they got into the boonies, especially where slithery things hung out.

"Just wanted you to get your head on business and remind you, if you get bit by a moc, you're a dead man, Troy. I ain't suckin' nothin' out of you!"

Troy whispered to himself, "Some sister you are!" Her comment begged a response, just not one she could hear.

"Don't think I've ever seen so many raccoon prints. If you look over there to your right, close to the palmetto plant, you'll see a bunch of monarch butterflies. Now, how do you figure—" Katie stopped so suddenly Troy almost ran into her.

She was still as stone and straight as a pool cue. Her sharp green eyes locked on something up sun in the distance. She shielded her eyes with her hand, and for a moment, even her breathing stopped. When she did exhale again, she formed two words, "Run, Troy!"

She took off as if she were hit by lightning. Troy didn't know if he were running from something sinister or running to something exciting, but he wasn't asking questions—not yet.

The distance between them opened. Tall with long twitch muscles, she was far more suited for a sprint over broken ground than was Troy. Katie was fifty yards ahead of Troy heading toward the mudflats when finally, she stopped and dropped to her knees in the muck. The image Troy saw as he approached was bewildering. It had the shape of a small torpedo, nearly as long as Katie was tall, caked in mud, but a flat horizontal tail protruded from one end. And it was moving up and down. Clearly, this was a life-form treasure of some sort, but what? Whatever the species, it was alive, completely encased in mud, and struggling to breathe.

"It's a baby porpoise,[9] Troy. I think a bottlenose, but what's it doing here so far from the water and, where's his mom?" Troy was still trying to fashion an answer to one of the two questions when Katie directed, "Quick, Troy, give me your shirt."

Troy finally did have a response, "Hey, use your own shirt! This is my Dan Marino shirt and—"

Katie, now splattered with mud from her sneakers to her elbows, lifted her mud-encrusted right forearm—fist clenched. Troy knew at once the significance of his favorite shirt was of no interest to his big sister. Mumbling to himself, Troy wiggled out of his shirt and reluctantly handed it to Katie. Katie snatched it from his hand, jumped up, and wadded into the stream. She immersed the shirt in clean water then returned to the dolphin, knelt, and as good as she could, carefully cleaned the area around the dolphin's blowhole and eyes, all the while speaking in gentle and reassuring tones.

The dolphin continued to writhe and flap his tail for a few moments, but at her tender touch and soft voice, a frequency high enough for a dolphin to register, some of the frenetic activity abated slightly. By this time, there were very few areas of Katie's skin that wasn't encased in mud. In fact, the porpoise was now cleaner than Katie.

Troy watched his sister carefully run to the deeper part of the stream yet again and rinse his shirt, return to the dolphin, and with comforting words, carefully laid Troy's wet shirt over as much of the dolphin's body as possible. "We need to keep him cool and the sun off him," Katie said to ensure Troy understood the value of his contribution. "Troy, now listen, and I don't want no back talk."

Troy was about to do just that, but one look in those crystal-green eyes told him to hold his tongue.

"I want you to run back to the bikes as fast as you can. Ride back to the Jenkins' house and ask them to call the sheriff. Tell the sheriff we found a little baby porpoise on the beach, and if we don't get some help, he'll die fer sure. Wait for the sheriff there and then lead him back here. Ya got it?"

Troy knew there was something he should protest, but he sensed the determination in his sister's voice and knew the outcome of his challenge would not be favorable.

"Okay!" was all he could muster.

"And Troy...watch for snakes."

Troy really didn't need a reminder.

Katie watched Troy jog away. For once, he showed some interest in doing something. Katie continued to coo to the little dolphin and stroke his flanks.

While she waited impatiently, an interesting thing happened: the little dolphin emitted a series of whistles, then stopped, then whistled again. Katie, after a few rookie trials, finally roughly replicated the dolphin's whistle. The dolphin immediately tensed for several seconds, then responded with his own whistle again. When Katie returned the whistle, there seemed to be a slow release of tension from the little dolphin. Clearly, this was a breakthrough of some form because much of the agitation and the fear he had shown just moments ago seemed to disappear. Katie continued to pet the dolphin's sides and alternately spoke softly and whistled. The dolphin finally had a few moments of repose.

The Cavalry

Sunday, 10 September 1995
Turkey Point, Florida, northeast of the Apalachicola Bay

It was nearly an hour before Katie could make out images of people breaking out of the foliage next to the stream. But there were five people in the group, not the two—Troy and the sheriff—Katie had expected.

By this time, the little dolphin had settled into a rhythmed breathing but was startled into tail flapping again when Katie stopped talking and suddenly stood up.

Troy broke from the group and sprinted back to Katie and the dolphin. Someone had lent him another T-shirt. It was two-sizes too large, but at least it would keep the sun off his back.

"Who are all those people, Troy?"

"I called the sheriff, and he called the Florida State Fish and Wildlife Conservation Commission guys. They even have a stretcher to carry the dolphin back if we have to."

A tall, slender tanned gentleman wearing the uniform of a Florida state ranger was suddenly beside Katie and the dolphin. "We may not need to bring him back. Let's take a gander at the little critter."

In mud-splattered slacks and hiking boots, the ranger didn't hesitate a second. He plopped down on his knees in the muck and spoke softly to the dolphin.

Changes in his environment and new voices agitated the dolphin. His wiggling and tail action had flipped off the shirt covering his dorsal area and splattered mud everywhere and on everyone. No one seemed to mind.

While the sheriff and the other two rangers stood and watched, the ranger kneeling next to the dolphin placed his hands on either side of the dorsal fin, looked into his eyes, and inspected his blowhole. Noting the increased activity and agitation of the dolphin, he looked to Katie. "Miss, would you do whatever you were doing before to keep him calmed down? We've startled him pretty good, and he could use some reassurance and contact from you."

Katie brightened and responded, "Yes, sir, if you think it'll help!"

"Oh, it'll help plenty. Just watch."

Katie began stroking the dolphin's side, leaned down toward the dolphin's head, whistled twice, then spoke softly. In just a few moments, the dolphin seemed to relax again, much of the agitation dissipating.

"See, told you. And…why did you whistle?"

"Well…" Katie paused, "that's what he was doing. And he kinda liked me to whistle back."

"Smart girl," the ranger returned.

The tall ranger pulled his own small backpack from his shoulders and set it on the ground. From it, he produced a stethoscope. He adjusted the earpieces and then gently pressed the diaphragm against the latter aspect of the dolphin's rib cage. He looked at his watch for a time then moved the diaphragm forward to a new location then stopped and—head down, concentrating—listened again. After a moment, he placed the diaphragm in a position over and slightly forward of the dolphin's left pectoral fin and listened intently.

When the ranger leaned back on his heels and pulled the earpieces off, he showed relief. He looked at one of the standing rangers and said, "Ted, we need to roll this little guy on his side to check for injuries and sex him." Without a word, the ranger kneeled in the mud next to the dolphin.

The tall ranger looked at Katie. "I think your brother said your name is Katie, right?"

"Yes, sir! Katie Donavan."

"Okay, Katie Donavan, we're going to roll him on his right side. I'll need you to keep his rostrum and melon—his head—out of the mud and be sure to protect his eyes. We don't want any mud or anything gettin' in them."

"Yes, sir!"

"Ted, help me roll him to the right. Keep his pectoral pressed against his flank."

"Got it, Matt," Ted replied.

"On three…one, two, three." And with that, the three, in unison, smoothly rolled the dolphin on to his right side. Matt worked quickly, using his hands as much as his eyes. He moved his fingers from the dolphin's rostrum, down the anterior region to his ventral area, and stopped near the genital region, then continued to the fluke.

Katie watched in open-mouth wonder. The delicate but purposeful and efficient movements of this tall man as he made a field assessment on the dolphin was indeed fascinating. She'd never seen a dolphin up close, but clearly, this man had—and she was guessing—seen many. And it was not just that he was comfortable around the dolphin, he seemed to know a whole lot about him. In fact, he seemed to know everything about him.

In truth, the tall ranger was a graduate of the University of Hawaii, Hilo, with a BS in marine biology. U of H was one of the ten most heralded universities for marine biology in the nation—in the world, for that matter. Matt could be in another line of work making far more than a Florida state employee, but he was consumed by the challenge of helping marine mammals, especially dolphins. This was his calling. He felt completely "self-actualized" with his chosen profession.

When Matt finished, he heaved a perceptible sigh then said, "Now let's get him back on his tummy. Gently now…roll."

Matt stood, pulled a towel from his pack, cleaned his hands as well as he could, squinted against the sun, and looked toward the beach then back to the group. "He's amazingly calm for what he's been through. Katie and Troy, what we have here is a little boy Atlantic bottlenose dolphin, about six to ten months old and still nursing. He has no external injuries that I can see. No bruising or cuts, and based on a quick triage, no internal injuries. The lungs seem to be clear. No signs of aspiration of anything foreign and no indications of pneumonia. Both the systolic and diastolic cycles of the heart are synchronized, and the beat is strong. Good respiration rate, about six breaths per minute, and good heart rate, about sixty beats a minute. That's a little fast but understandable, considering the trauma. As I mentioned, he's anxious, but he has plenty of reason to be. I don't know what you did, Katie, but you may have saved his life!"

The ranger reached into his backpack and removed another towel. He then pulled a jackknife from a leather case on his belt, opened it, and cut a one-foot slit in the center of the towel. He extended the towel to Troy and said, "Son, would you kindly get this wet? But don't wring it out."

"Yes, sir," Troy replied. He trotted off to the deep part of the stream and returned with the towel soaking wet.

The ranger took it from him and delicately placed the slit over the dolphin's dorsal fin, extended the rest of the towel to the tail, and laid Troy's favorite shirt just forward of the blowhole to the dolphin's rostrum. He then turned his full attention to Katie. "Katie, sorry for the late introductions. We had some things we needed to do first. I'm Ranger Matt Patterson. This here's Sheriff Johnson." Matt pointed to a well-built black gent in his early thirties, who then touched the rim of his hat and nodded. "A pleasure, Katie."

"And these two are Florida State Fish and Wildlife Conservation Commission rangers Barbara Bishop and Ted Parker." They both politely nodded.

"As near as I can figure at this point, this little dolphin's in pretty good shape. He's dehydrated, slightly sunburned, and clearly shook up. Physically, he seems strong, but he ain't out of the woods yet. Barb and Ted, would you hike down to the beach and see if you can find the pod this little guy belongs to? And look for his mother too. If they're still in the area, she'll probably be the one closest to the shoreline."

"On it, sir!" Barbara responded.

As they stepped toward the beach, Matt's full attention returned to Katie. "Well, Katie Donavan, we may need to take him to a marine mammal medical team at Gulf World in Panama City, especially if we can't find his mom or the pod. The med team is very good at taking care of stranded dolphins. I called ahead. They're standing by in the event we need them. If we need to take him, I'd like you and your brother to come with us. We can call dispatch and ask them to call your parents if you think they'll let you come with us."

"Thank you, sir. I think our parents would let us go for something like this. I'd be grateful if we could be with him. I need to tell you, my brother helped a lot, and really…I didn't know what to do."

Matt noticed a slight tremor in Katie's lower jaw and definite moisture forming under her eyes. "Look, Katie, he hasn't been out here too long. You kept the sun off him for the most part, and somehow you kept him pretty calm. I think he's going to be okay."

Katie squinted, took a deep breath, and with a courage that was more show than substance, looked up to the tall ranger, and said, "Okay, sir. What do we do now?"

"Sheriff J, can you grab that stretcher for me?"

"Got it Matt," the sheriff replied.

Handing Troy the towel he was holding, he said, "Troy, take this and the towel on the dolphin and get both of them good and wet. And, Troy, we might just as well use your T-shirt again, so get that wet too."

"Yes, sir," Troy responded, carefully lifting the towel and his shirt from the dolphin, and wadded into the middle of the stream again.

At this time, Barbara and Ted hiked up to the group. They both looked disturbed.

"What'd ya find?" Matt asked, seeing the concern in their eyes.

"No sign of the pod." Barbara paused and then gave a side glance at Ted.

Ted picked it up. "We did find a female bottlenose, about eight feet long in the tide line. She was lactating. She had fatal injuries, and it looked like she got hit by something pretty big." Ted glanced at Katie and realized that he didn't need to elaborate.

Katie's head went back down, stroking the baby dolphin. She stopped for a moment, her shoulders heaved slightly.

Troy returned with two soaked towels and one ex-favorite T-shirt.

"Okay, gang…Barb and Ted, we're taking this little guy to Gulf World. It'll be the best for him, and we've got to get this guy on the stretcher. We're going to carefully roll the dolphin on his right side as we did before. Ted, remember his pectoral fin. Katie, unroll the stretcher, and when he's on his side, I want you to slide that stretcher as close as you can to the dolphin. Then we'll carefully roll him over to his left side and extend the stretcher so when we roll him back onto his tummy, he'll be centered on the stretcher. Any questions?"

There we none.

"Okay, team, let's do this. On three again. One, two, three!"
And it was done.

The dolphin was placed on the stretcher and, except for his
blowhole, was covered from rostrum to fluke with wet towels and
Troy's shirt. Once the stretcher straps were adjusted, Matt, Ted,
Barbara, and Sheriff Johnson grabbed a handle at each corner of the
stretcher and, on "three," lifted.

The hike back to the road took less than twenty minutes. The
stretcher was carefully placed on a length of thick, soft foam in the
rear of Matt's Fish and Wildlife pickup. Katie, Troy, and Barbara were
seated in the bed of the truck on either side of the dolphin with the
bikes secured along the sides of the truck bed. Katie continued to coo
to the dolphin and stroke his flanks.

Sheriff Johnson started his pickup, lit up the gumball lights,
and with Matt's truck in trail, they were soon barreling down the
dusty road on a fast track to Gulf World marine mammal rescue
group in Panama City, a two-hour and twenty-minute trip.

They were still bouncing along the dirt road on the way to join
Highway 98 when Katie yelled something over the buffeting wind.
It was tough to hear, but Troy thought she said, "You did really good
today, Troy. I'm proud of you!"

CHAPTER 2

THE FORK IN THE ROAD

When you come to a fork in the road, take it!

—Yogi Berra

The Decision

Tuesday, 14 August 2001
Special Boat Team TWELVE, Navy Amphibious Base, Coronado, California

"Master Chief, I know what you've got invested in me. I love my job. I'm dedicated to the team. I owe you and the guys a lot, and I know I still have a year left on this stint. But this thing was just announced and well...I think I can do some good there. And...it's what I want to do."

Master Chief Madrigal of Special Boat Team Twelve was the command master chief, senior enlisted noncommissioned officer of the command, and—to the enlisted personnel of the boat team—the right hand of God.

Right now, he looked at Petty Officer 3rd Class Brent Harris's request chit and scowled. This was not something he needed at this point.

Elbows on his desk, hands pressed against his buzz cut, he lifted his head, looked at Brent, and scowled some more. "Brent, you're what…twenty years old? You have a home here. You've made a name for yourself, a place for yourself. And while no man is irreplaceable, we've built a squad around you. You've come up through the ranks faster than anyone I've ever seen. You have natural leadership skills that others will never have. I'd like to keep you on the team. What can I do to convince you to stay with us?"

Petty Officer Harris looked down at his highly polished low-quarter dress shoes and thought, *This hurts. I never thought it would be so tough.*

He was torn between his allegiance to the team and a powerful desire to achieve a dream he'd had since he was sixteen—working with big marine animals, namely dolphins. For the longest time, Brent thought it was just that: a dream.

Brent, of course, had heard of the Navy Marine Mammal Program (NMMP). And he had it on good authority the NMMP worked with both dolphins and sea lions, but he had little understanding of what their missions were. Information on the program was scarce as hen's teeth. And besides, he didn't figure there would be an ice cube's chance in hell that he'd ever get orders to the program.

The announcement appeared to be a sign—a disturbing and powerful clarion call he'd had since his family had taken a trip to Catalina, and he had that very first contact with a big open-water Pacific bottlenose dolphin. That was four years ago, but the calling had lost none of its power. This might be Brent's only opportunity to make that dream a reality.

Brent thought quietly, *But then there is the problem of allowing a special boat team guy to cross over to the NMMP. The Navy is mighty touchy about letting special ops warriors change their warfare specialty after they had put so much time, energy, and money into building one of us. But why not? They'd taken SEALs before, and they were close cousins to the special boat team guys and in higher demand than the boat team sailors.*

"Nothing, Master. You and the team have given me everything, every opportunity. Everything I've ever wanted to do in the team, you and the skipper have allowed me to do."

"Brent, I'm not pissed. I know exactly how strong the pull of chasing a dream can be. I—well, we—were just hopping your dream was right here on the team. I'll get over it if you think you have to leave, but Skipper Lear is going to go through the overhead. He had big plans for you."

The master chief stood and walked to the window. Hands on his hips, he looked out at the brilliant crystal-blue day. Although this vista provided him with a million-dollar panorama of the San Diego Harbor, the Coronado Bridge, Glorietta Bay, and many of the boats assigned to the team, his mind was far from the magnificence of the view.

The master chief turned to face Brent. "I'll tell you what, Brent. Today's Tuesday. I'll give you two days to think this over. Dig down deep into your gut and think long range. Think big picture. Do you want to be a special boat warrior, or do you want to clean up sea lion crap all day? I'm not going to speak a word of this to the skipper. He's got enough on his plate, and losing you…well, he just doesn't need the additional stress right now. So the crack of jack Thursday morning, come see me. And for now, let's keep this between us girls, okay?"

"Aye, aye, Master."

"Now get out of here, sailor!"

With that, Brent Harris came to attention, took one step to the rear, executed a crisp about-face, and stepped out of the command master chief's office and made a beeline past the quarter deck to the command exit.

Brent stopped on the sidewalk just outside the entrance, took a deep breath, and surveyed the day. The temp was a comfortable seventy-four degrees, light wind from the southwest, and except for the ever-present seagulls patrolling the skies, there wasn't a thing aloft to blemish the perfect sky. It was a day that elicited the San Diegan phrase "another day in paradise."

What have I got myself into? Brent said to no one. For the second time that day, Brent stared at his shoes and cogitated his future. *My life was all so simple before! How did I get in such a hot mess?*

There were two components to this question: how Brent came to find himself in one of the most elite and respected combat units in the world; and second, how he came to the decision point of leaving Special Boat Team Twelve for the unusual profession of working with marine mammals.

For each component, there was a predominant, life-changing event in Brent's early years that would have titanic influence on his decision and, ergo, his life.

CHAPTER 3

HOME ON THE RANGE

For the animal shall not be measured by man. In a world older and more complete than ours they move finished and complete, gifted with extensions of the senses we have lost or never attained, living by voices we shall never hear. They are not brethren, they are not underlings; they are other nations, caught with ourselves in the net of life and time, fellow prisoners of the splendour and travail of the earth.

—Henry Beston, *The Outermost House*

Star Valley

Star Valley, Wyoming

Forty-five miles south of Jackson, Wyoming, lay the northern end of the Star Valley. It sits at six-thousand-feet elevation, is forty-two miles long, and is nestled between the Caribou Mountain Range of Eastern Idaho and the Salt River Range of Western Wyoming. It is a land of utter beauty, breathtaking serenity, magnificent wildlife, and at times, cold indifference to all who live there.

Aspen, blue spruce, fir, and many other evergreens abound and give nourishment and cover to an array of animals to include moose, elk, mule deer, bear, mountain lion, geese, ducks, sandhill cranes, trumpeter swans, osprey, grouse, golden and bald eagles, and many more of God's creatures.

While late spring through early fall is usually quite comfortable—a celebration for the body and spirit—the winters can be devastating. Entire herds of elk and deer have been wiped out during cold winters and heavy snowstorms. Mother Nature shows no deference to humans.

In early times, Shoshone Indians were one of the primary human residents of the valley. During the spring through the autumn months, they hunted the lands, harvested food and nature's materials from the forests, and fished the great rivers. Not until 1812 did white adventurers and explorers travel through the valley, mapping new routes to the West and the Pacific. Trappers followed in the 1840s, and immigrants and settlers began to make the valley their home decades later.

Three world-class trout rivers converge at the northern end of the valley and pour into Palisades Reservoir: the Salt, the Gray, and the famous Snake River. Cutthroat trout, German browns, brookies, rainbows, and mackinaw thrive in these rivers, which are considered Valhalla for practicing and recovering fly fisherman.

At the northern entrance to the valley is the town of Alpine, population eight hundred[10] and change. Here, the Wyoming Game and Fish Department feed a herd of nearly a thousand elk in the winter months.

By the mid to late 1900s, dairies, creameries, construction, home services, farming, tourism, guided hunting and fishing expeditions, and ranching were the primary sources of employment throughout the valley.

While some ranchers choose to herd cattle with more current equipment: snow mobiles in the winter and all-terrain vehicles (ATVs), motorcycles, and off-road vehicles in the warmer months, the traditionalists stick with the original all-terrain, all-weather, all-season cattle mover—horses.

A road trip down Highway 89, the main thoroughfare in the valley, on any given day may present the adventurer with a great opportunity to view in real life the image on Wyoming's license plate: a cowboy on a bucking bronco. Horses remain part of the mystique of this lush valley and came on scene decades before their air-polluting substitutes of the twentieth century.

Horses—Morgans, pintos, Thoroughbreds, broad-chested Clydesdales, American Quarter Horses, and even Appaloosas—are at home in the valley and are used for trail riding, big-game hunts into the high mountains, equestrian events, large pets, and sometimes for that activity for which the Wild West is best known: roundups, herding cattle, and rodeos.

The Harris Ranch

1990s
Harris Ranch, Star Valley, Wyoming

Eight miles south of Alpine sits the small town of Etna with a population under two hundred. It consists of a community center, a grade school, and a small general store with an attached section that serves as the town's post office—the Etna Trading Company. It's a quiet little town whose residents raise families, work hard, enjoy the environment, and have the grit to brave the elements year-round.

Two miles south of Etna, just off Highway 89, is a horse ranch. It occupies a quarter section, 160 acres, of flat farm and ranch land with nearly a quarter mile of Salt River frontage. It is known as the Harris Ranch. It had been in the Harris family for three generations, and the grand plan was to keep it in the family from generation to generation, always improving the horse bloodlines, the training services, and the productivity of the ranch.

The ranch had been growing steadily in terms of size and revenue generation since it was built in the late 1920s. In 1990, Ron Harris, head of the Harris family, took over the operation and management of the ranch.

By 1996, the ranch had expanded to eleven structures. It included one large main family house, an expansive barn with birthing area, an equipment storage structure with attached mechanics shop, a bunkhouse for a dozen men, the boss's quarters, three pump houses, a feed storage shed, a large second barn for quartering horses of other families who couldn't or didn't want to take care of their own animals, and finally the newly built house for Ron's mother and father, who were living comfortably and fully retired from responsibilities of the ranch.

The Harris Clan

1996
Harris Ranch, Star Valley, Wyoming

Ron Harris and his wife, Jean, were blessed with four children, all boys, ranging in age from the youngest, Brent, age fifteen; Kurt, sixteen; Scott, eighteen; to the oldest, Jeremy, age nineteen. These young men were in good health, strong, and coordinated from long hours working the ranch and playing on any number of high school sports teams. While they were blessed with high moral standards, they paradoxically inherited the Harris propensity for mischief and competition. High on their fun list were tractor races, outhouse tilting contests, road-pie tossing championships, bull-tail pulling trials (which never went well), pumpkin-busting events, and a favorite of all the boys—farting contests.

One such event three years earlier nearly burnt down the barn, which also wisely ended the farting contests. One might make the argument that Jeremy, the oldest, age sixteen at this time, should have been engaged in something less callow and more mature, more sophisticated. He should have been setting the example for his younger brothers. In truth, Jeremy did set the example for being accountable for his actions, hard work, honoring their parents, and for the most part, staying out of trouble. Sometimes, however, Jeremy's sense of responsibility took a second seat to his zest for buffoonery.

At the base of the problem was that the boys were not only brothers but best friends as well. In the spirit of adventure, competition, or for the thrill of the moment (and sometimes just to see if one of the boys were just dumb enough to do it), they would occasionally goad one another into doing something they all knew they shouldn't.

This all came to a head on one chilly November evening after supper when the boys assembled in the barn. Relaxing in a deep haystack, it was Kurt's idea to have a farting contest. This was quickly seconded and passed.

Kurt felt fully confident that this would be his moment in the winner's circle. For most of the day, he'd been snacking on hardboiled eggs and broccoli just for this occasion. So gaseous was his current condition that he was concerned that he was going to suffer a catastrophic GI detonation during school.

Now, some teenage boys seem to have a flare for producing GI gases on a whim. The Harris boys, through diet, luck of their genetic coding, or persistent practice, each had this unique ability.

Kurt began the competition and duly impressed his brothers with a whopper. The other three boys joined in with their versions, but none could top Kurt's exposé. The air grew foul, and the laughing began, which, in a serious state of competition, may degrade the volume of release and the tonal quality. The boys were in a raucous state, and when Kurt suggested they ramp the competition up to a higher level, say a fart-lighting contest, all agreed it was a good idea. But this was shortsighted.

Before anyone knew it, Kurt produced a Bic lighter and, lying on his back, threw his legs over his head, lit the lighter, and positioned it near his posterior region. Instantly, an enormous blue flame was released, which not only ignited Kurt's Levis but torched off some of the surrounding hay. A quick-thinking Jeremy grabbed the horse's watering bucket and doused the growing inferno and Kurt's jeans. Both were left smoldering.

With the crisis passed, the boys joined in on a body-jarring laughing spree—all except Kurt, that is. His Levis, now soaking wet, had a distinctive charred part at the seat area, and he believed he would soon suffer the pain and embarrassment of a few blisters as well.

All agreed, Kurt won the contest hands down. Learning from Kurt's mistake, none of the other brothers competed. They all vowed to never speak of the event, especially not to their father.

To the casual observer, the four boys had all the ingredients of a band of hoodlums, but this was the rare exception rather than the rule. Ron and Jean were God-fearing Christians with good hearts and giving members of the community and their church. Ron, as a successful small-business employer, was well respected throughout the valley as a savvy ranch owner and a fair and benevolent employer. He had no conflicts with anyone in the valley, no criminal record, not even a speeding ticket. Only once was Ron ever questioned by the local constables, and that involved a confrontation between his ranch hand boss and three out-of-town bikers in the parking lot of the Bull Moose Saloon in Alpine.

One afternoon, Ron came out of the adjacent market with his arms full of groceries. He noticed an argument escalating between Bill Washakie[11] and the three leather-clad bikers. Bill was Ron's ranch boss, a full Shoshone Indian and descendant of the famous Chief Washakie. Ron and Bill were bound together by far more than just an employee-employer relationship. They were best friends with a long history of training great ranch and rodeo horses.

Dumping the groceries in his pickup, Ron turned and leaned against the side of his truck to assess the situation. When it was apparent that things were not improving, he walked slowly toward the men. "Hey, gents, what seems to be the problem?"

"Boss, no issues here. I was just leaving," Bill said.

The tallest and maybe the drunkest of the three slurred, "You may be leaving, but you ain't walking away from here. You dissed us in the bar. You're an Injun and should be back on the reservation, not here in a white man's bar drinking white man's whiskey. Now you're going to pay…Injun!"

To Ron, who had grown up in the valley and had many friends who were Indians, had hired many and was, in turn, accepted by them as a man of integrity and loyalty. This situation was like a bad cowboy-and-Indian movie—those rarely went well for the Indians.

Although Ron tried his best to defuse the situation with friendly talk, he could tell this approach was not going to be successful.

From out of the blue, a right roundhouse was thrown by the man standing to the left and closest to Ron. It was not a complete surprise. Ron ducked underneath the punch. The drunk, thinking he was going to make contact with Ron's face, unfortunately followed through with the swing and, in so doing, pivoted to his left. Ron easily extended his arm under the drunk's right armpit, wove his hand behind the man's neck, and then quickly mirrored that motion with his left arm, resulting in a near-perfect full nelson, a move that vanquished many a boy during Ron's high school wrestling days.

At this point, the other two bikers entered the fray. The man standing in the center, realizing that Ron had his hands full, cocked and launched a powerful left hook. Ron had anticipated this and nudged his trophy first to the left and, as the man resisted, spun him quickly to the right and into the oncoming punch.

The air was punctuated with grunts, a scream, and the sound of breaking bones as the man Ron held took the force of his drunk friend's swing full in the face. Ron released him. He dropped like a barbell.

Bill, by this time, was also fully engaged and, though smaller in size, had the advantage of endurance, speed, enormous strength, and sobriety. The biker clumsily rushed the Indian. Bill gave way initially then did something completely unexpected. He quickly stepped toward the man. To the towering drunk with a forty-pound advantage on the Indian, this was something he had never seen before and certainly didn't expect. In the past, he had always been able to cower his victims, usually picked for their smaller size, and used his mass and meanness to overpower them. Bill did the exact opposite of what he expected and realized too late that something was amiss.

Although the drunk's left arm, and a sizable arm it was, had already been brought back in preparation for a punch, Bill was inside the radius of swing. He quickly brought both hands together in a tremendous clapping motion with the man's head as the center of impact. Acting as two cymbals, Bill's hands came crashing down on the man's ears and temples. The man instantly aborted the swing, staggered back, and put his hands on either side of his head. Eyes clenched, mouth open, he dropped to his knees. Bill reared back and was ready for a second strike, the weapon of choice was a knee to the man's nose, but Bill realized the fight was out of the guy.

Now, there was just one drunk left in the fight. The biker may have been drunk, but he could still count, and the odds were heavily in favor of the Indian and the cowboy. The drunk took three steps backward; raised his hands, palms forward; and said, "Hey, I got no issues with you gents. This was all Fred's idea. What say we just call the whole thing a learning experience?"

"That would be fine with me, but I think you're going to have to explain this to our local peace officers." Ron nodded in the direction of the street entrance to the Bull Moose Saloon as a sheriff's black-and-white braked to a stop twenty feet from the standing men.

"Shit! Not again," was all the biker said.

It took two days for word of the skirmish to get to the boys at school. There's not much distance separating Etna from Alpine, and news of this sort, involving one of the most-respected men in the valley and an honored Shoshone leader, traveled fast.

The boys were anxious to ask their father about the incident, but they agreed to ambush him after supper so their mother could hear the story also.

That evening, Jeremy sprung the opening line, "So, Dad, how was your trip to the Alpine market on Monday?"

Ron eased his coffee cup down, leaned back in his chair, and took a sideways look at Jean. Jean, who was in the process of gathering plates from the table, gently set the stack back on the table, lifted her apron, wiped her hands, then said, "Boys, I know all about this, and it's a serious matter. Your father was standing up for Bill. Bill is family, and you always protect your family. Now, I don't for a moment condone fighting, but in this case, your father did the honorable and right thing."

With that as the icebreaker, Ron added, "I don't know what you heard, and the details aren't important, but I leave you with this: fighting takes place when people stop listening to one another and reasoning fails. Never walk away from a fight if you're right, but never fight if you can solve the problem using your wit and the power of persuasion. It's a potent force."

The boys were at first gravely disappointed with their father's retort. They were expecting a gruesome detailed, blow-by-blow account of a fight between their heroes, their dad and Bill, and three drunken bikers. What they got was a two-line philosophy session. But as their father's words set in, quiet disillusionment turned to immense pride in the wisdom and character of their father.

The boys didn't need a lecture about the tribulations of fighting, but the simple words of their mother and father struck a chord in each of them. They'd each had their share of scuffles at school—they were boys and cowboys as well—but fighting was not at the top of their list of things to do, nor did any of them consider fighting a skill they needed to develop. No, their skills were adapted and then honed to support and complement all the activities and projects on the ranch.

They were all cowpunchers at heart, by family tradition, and by necessity. They roped, branded, herded, fed, and looked over the health and well-being of their cattle, dogs, and their horses. In the spring, summer, and early fall, they either led or assisted in pack-in trips into the remote areas of Western Wyoming for rich trophy hunters and devoted fly fishermen. Each of the boys could sit a horse as well as they could operate any of the ten-plus pieces of motorized equipment needed to keep a ranch at peak efficiency. But each of the boys seemed to have cultivated a second specialty as well.

Jeremy had taken an interest in the overall operation of the ranch. As a youngster mounted on his filly, Sarah, he'd tagged along with his father around the ranch. He took special interest as his father worked with the ranch hands, talked to the owners of the horses they stabled, and helped his father mend fences, repair breaks in irrigation pipes, weld heavy gauge steel frame barns and other structures, branded cattle, and helped train horses. By age nineteen, Jeremy was shaping up to be the next and rightful heir to the ranch by chronology and by skill set.

Jeremy spent two semesters at University of Idaho. He selected the operations management curriculum but realized, none too soon, that he could learn nearly the same lessons taught in the university right on the ranch. He may not have the same polish, but how much academic refinement does one need to train horses and help manage the operations of a ranch?

This, as it turned out, was a valuable lesson for the other three boys. Ron and Jean didn't push any of them into higher formal education. They figured if they wanted to go to college after high school, all the boys had to do was apply and be accepted. Certainly, as staggering as college tuition and the living costs would be, the Harrises could come up with the money.

The primary takeaway for Jeremy and then communicated to Scott, Kurt, and Brent was that the ranch—for all the hard work, long hours, inherent risks, and intermittent monotony—was their heritage, their parents' dream, their home, and the best place to learn a practical trade.

This lesson made mounds of sense to Scott. If there was a scholar amongst the Harrises it was Scott. Although less athletic and slightly smaller in stature, Scott was a whiz when it came to school. He spent less time studying and made better grades than any of his brothers. He had a knack for math and science and a mystifying comprehension of all things structural.

Two years previously, when Scott was but sixteen, Ron was reviewing commercial plans for another barn. The blueprints caught Scott's attention. Scott had taken design courses in high school and from that developed a working knowledge of material stresses, load distribution, and architectural design. With some hand-scribbled drawings and basic load calculations, Scott was able to design a slightly bigger footprint, add an elevated hayloft, and design a system of pulleys and overhead tracks that would greatly enhance the efficiency in stacking and stowing hay and bundled grains. He just had a natural calling for engineering and design, something that would be most useful on a spread the size and complexity of the Harris Ranch.

There were ten pieces of rolling farm equipment on the ranch, everything from Case tractors, to Bobcat front loaders, snowblowers, a John Deere row-crop tractor, a Hesston baler, an old not-much-used

New Holland combine harvester, and an array of smaller wheeled equipment—jeeps, cars, and an old Ford 1978 F100 pickup. The truck was well used and had fallen from grace, but even with a new 300-cubic-inch V6 engine, it didn't have the power to get out of its own way.

For reasons unexplained, brother number three, Kurt, had a keen interest in things mechanical. After studying a piece of machinery, Kurt could imagine the kinematic relationships of the parts, understand the transfer of energy of the drive components, and pretty much figure out what all the parts did. This interest extended to the internal workings of about every piece of equipment on the ranch. But in his younger days, Kurt proved far more efficient in dismantling things than he was reassembling things. In fact, there were parts of at least two Briggs & Stratton–powered lawn mowers stored in the garage that were still in boxes. They would likely never be returned to working order.

Over time, however, Kurt enhanced his mechanical aptitude. He took a year of auto shop in high school and became a bit of a gearhead. Through trial and error and a gifted imagination, he honed his skills at repairing engines, gearboxes, transmissions, and pretty much everything found on a piece of farm equipment.

The ranch had a full-time mechanic, Bob Wilson; and while Kurt was not quite in the league with Bob, together, there was nothing on the ranch that stayed out of commission for long. In fact, some equipment slightly modified by Kurt and Bob ran even better than it did when it was new.

One day, Kurt responded to an ad listing a 1967 Ford Fairlane GTA that had been totaled on Highway 89 near Thayne, just south of the ranch. Interested, Kurt visited the owner. If Kurt was right, sitting under the hood was a treasure. A 390-cubic-inch V8 brute that could easily produce over 450 horsepower with the right dose of love and mechanical attention.

At first sight, Kurt knew he struck gold. The GTA obviously had spun backward into a telephone pole, apparently at moderate speed. The driver had walked away from the accident but made a mess of a once highly collectable Motown beauty. Thankfully, everything forward of the front seats were unscathed and intact.

There, under the hood, sure enough, was the beast of an engine Kurt had only read about in *Hot Rod* magazines. Kurt offered the owner two hundred bucks just to take it off his hands. Clearly, the owner had had enough of this car and, without bickering, took the money and signed over the title.

Kurt and Bob returned with a flatbed and towed the project car to the ranch. In the garage, they hoisted the engine out of the GTA, ensured the mounting points and transmission would match up with the old Ford F100 pickup—an anemic excuse for a ranch truck engine if ever there was one—and began the task of swapping engines.

In three weeks—after school, after work, and over the course of the weekends—with Ron's tacit permission, Kurt and Bob tore the engine down to parade rest; replaced all essential components to include racing pistons, connecting rods, valves, valve guides, and springs; rejetted the carburetor; and fabricated all the parts necessary to wedge the monster 390-cubic-inch engine into the F100 engine bay. They completed the rebuild with a high-volume air intake and, to allow the acoustics to testify of its muscle, installed a set of big-throated glass-pack mufflers.

When the job was complete, they primed the carburetors, checked the battery, and crossed their fingers. The monster cranked several times then fired. When it did, it was more like an explosion than an engine start. Things rattled off the shelves!

The engine continued to idle while Bob made several small adjustments to the carburetors and the timing. For a moment, Kurt and Bob looked at each other; neither could help the stupid ear-to-ear grin on their faces.

"Wait 'til Dad sees this," Kurt yelled over the noise of the mighty 390.

Up until this time, it was interesting and rewarding work but still work. What would happen next would either make or break their day—either the event of the year or a sad and giant waste of time.

While Bob backed the F100 out of the garage and positioned it in the center of the long straight driveway heading to Highway 89, Kurt gathered his brothers, Bill, and invited his dad to *check out the old truck*.

With everyone assembled, Kurt threw his dad the keys, smiled, and said, "Crank it up, Dad!"

Ron caught the keys, stuck his hands in his jeans, looked quizzically at his son, and slowly walked around the old muddy truck. "Wadja do?"

"Replaced the spark plugs. It runs a lot better now."

"What? You two spent nearly a month replacing six spark plugs? I'm paying you too much!"

"Dad," Kurt chirped, "you've never paid me anything."

"Yeah, well, it's still too much!"

Bob responded, "Two of the plugs were stuck, and we didn't want to break 'em off. It took a while."

Ron reluctantly opened the driver's door and pulled himself into the seat, inserted the key, looked at Kurt suspiciously, and cranked the engine. It lit off instantly.

Chickens scattered, the goats bolted, both Australian sheepdogs hightailed it for the house, and Brent's horse, Domino, repositioned himself behind Brent.

And the boys grinned and nodded their heads.

Ron slowly looked outside the passenger window at Kurt and Bob; no telltale expression was obvious.

Kurt and Bob, for a moment, held their breath.

"Nice!" was all that Ron said.

Victory! High fives all around.

Ron thumped the throttle a couple of times, checked all the instruments, pulled the door closed, smoothly engaged the clutch, and dropped it into first gear. He added throttle, a lot of throttle, popped the clutch, and leaned harder on the gas pedal. There was thunderous acoustics but little movement. However, the truck did appear to lower some.

The tires, with more than four hundred pounds of torque, spun in place and dug themselves into a hole of their own making. All at once, the tires finally bit, and the old truck took off like it was shot out of a cannon.

Ron was halfway down the quarter-mile driveway when he finally came to a stop, marked by an enormous plume of dust. He executed a three-point U-turn and crept back to the starting point, beaming! He shut down the engine and looked squarely at Kurt and Bob. "Pretty good spark plugs."

Ron climbed out of the truck, tossed his son the keys, started to head back to the house, but then turned and, looking at both Bob and Kurt square in the eyes, followed up with, "Don't touch any of the tractors!"

CHAPTER 4

BRENT HARRIS—COWBOY

We need another and a wiser and perhaps a more mystical concept of animals. Remote from universal nature, and living by complicated artifice, man in civilization surveys the creature through the glass of his knowledge and sees thereby a feather magnified and the whole image in distortion. We patronize them for their incompleteness, for their tragic fate of having taken form so far below ourselves. And therein we err, and greatly err.

—Henry Beston, *The Outermost House*

A Boy with a Gift

Summer 1997
The Harris Ranch, Star Valley, Wyoming

Brent showed none of the special interests or intrinsic skills of his older brothers. He sat a fine horse, though, and of the fifteen ranch hands and siblings, only Bill was as accomplished when it came to the refined arts of horsemanship and training horses.

But his talent was much deeper than simply controlling a bronc and pushing the animal through the training routines. Brent had the very rare instincts of one who seemed to actually communicate with horses and many animals on a nonvocal level. He seemed, in fact, to be able to make eye contact with most animals, horses in particular, and understand what was going on in their noggins.

To many who watched Brent work with horses, dogs, and cattle, it was almost as though it was reciprocal. Animals responded better to Brent than other cowboys. The animals almost gave the impression that they wanted to work for Brent, and in a horse way, they seemed to enjoy Brent's company.

Brent had a gift that no one really understood, but none would deny this special sense existed after having seen him work with animals. Not to solve the riddle but at least to validate the existence of this gift, Brent was nicknamed the *horse whisperer*.

Interestingly, only Bill Washakie held a similar gift. Neither Ron, nor the brothers, nor the ranch hands ever developed that same sensitivity, that same ability to communicate, to see into their eyes and into the hearts of the great beasts.

It was during Brent's early years, mimicking his father, that sparked and then nurtured Brent's philosophy on human-animal relationships. Ron took each of his boys aside at a very young age and instilled in them the magna carta for training horses and working with farm animals. This was ranch scripture practiced and improved by both Ron and Bill Washakie. By Ron's thinking, no farm animal should ever suffer the wrath of a human. Certainly, none of his ranch hands and absolutely none of his sons would ever bring harm to one of their animals.

His constitution on training animals was, "You did not break them. You inspired trust and confidence, and once that was gained, you trained them."

The positive results of Ron's approach to training were much more immediately apparent in training their family dogs, most currently their two Australian shepherds: Martha and Heather.

"Dogs are quite a bit more intelligent," Ron explained to his sons. "Usually, they're more eager to please, and that gives you more leverage than with horses. But the techniques applied to dogs also worked well with horses. You just have to work a little harder. And because of that, you need to be more patient with horses," Ron confided to his sons.

The Harris's ranch colts, those born on the ranch, began human socialization on the day they were born. Bill, a horse vet, and one of the boys were always at the foal. Shortly after the dam delivered, after she had time to introduce the baby to his new world, one of the Harris boys or Bill would make initial *human* contact with the foal, not in an attempt to imprint the foal on a human but to begin an association with the foal.

In addition to a medical evaluation by the ranch's horse vet, that first joining with a human included lots of physical contact and much gentle vocal reassurance. Both of these actions had enormous rewards in building bonds and trust and expediting the foal's socialization process. But that first contact only took place if the mother allowed it and then was always secondary to the contact, affection, and duties of the dam.

As the foal matured, one of the boys, normally the one present at the birth, visited the baby and mother each day. The foal was monitored for medical complications, but mostly these daily visits enhanced bonding. Calm reassurances were uttered nearly continuously while the colt was lavished with physical contact.

Ron Harris was a stickler for respect and proper treatment for all ranch animals, and the boys were true to his rules. Many horse owners believed that these animals were stupid, inferior, and slow to learn. Unfortunately, too many believed the way to speed the training process was to mistreat and abuse them, commonly termed *breaking* the animal.

That was flat wrong according to the Harris clan: cruel at best and criminal at worst. Horses are social herders. They look for strength and leadership, and in a training setting, they respond best to patience, positive reinforcement, and friendship. They respond to negative reinforcement also, but over time, they learn quicker with the positive aspects of the Harris approach.

A trainer can force a horse into learned behavior, and most will react as expected, but they won't do it because they want to; they'll do it in an attempt to avoid pain, discomfort, and anxiety. The Harris approach was all carrot, no stick. This produced a trained horse, not a broken horse, and one who will learn faster, not because he's afraid but because he wants to. He will learn more, quicker, and form a stronger bond with his trainer in the process.

Brent adapted well to his father's approach, but even in his early years, his father, brothers, and the ranch hands began to notice that Brent was not simply following the script; he was writing new chapters.

Horses, dogs, cattle, even the sheep and goats seemed to approach him whenever and wherever he came into sight. Horses and the family dogs clearly socialized and learned quicker, and no one could dispute the relationships he'd developed. Brent's own horse, a rather small, fourteen-and-half-hand black-and-white pinto named Domino, acted more like a puppy around Brent than a nine-year-old filly. When not in her stall, Domino would actively hunt for him; and when found, she'd follow him around the ranch as if they were best friends.

At the age of twelve, when Brent was first asked about this special gift, he simply replied, "It's not special. Everybody has it. I think I'm just more patient. I listen to them. I look in their eyes unless they don't want me to. I put my hands on them and try to feel if they're nervous or afraid. Sometimes they don't want to be touched, and sometimes they're scared. You can feel nervousness and tension in their skin and in their muscles. You can see it in their eyes, the way they flick their ears, hold their head, snap their tail, and the way they stand. If they don't calm down when I talk to them, when I stroke them, or look in their eyes, I back off. They're not stupid. They'll always tell you what's going on. You just have to listen closely and show you care."

Thunder

Summer, 1997
The Harris Ranch; Star Valley, Wyoming

In the summer of 1997, when Brent was sixteen and heading into his senior year of high school, a horse breeder of some note and a close neighbor, Mr. Pearson, trailered a rather expensive three-year-old Morgan to the Harris Ranch. Ron, Bill, Brent, and many of the ranch hands were at the corral when Mr. Pearson pulled up, towing a large horse trailer.

"Good day to you, Mr. Pearson. How does it go with you?" Ron said, tipping his hat and walking toward Mr. Pearson.

Mr. Pearson's normal jovial demeanor had left him. "Not that good, Ron. This damn horse is driving me off the deep end. He cost me a ton of money. I had four trainers try to break him, and not a one of 'em will even get in the pen with him now. He's wild, and he's crazy, and I'm thinking he's damn dangerous. He's yours if you want him, but let me tell you, he could hurt someone real bad. You and Bill are the only cowpokes I could think of that would stand a fighting chance of breaking this damned colt.[12] If you don't want him, well…I'm going to put him down before he kills somebody."

Ron thoughtfully peeked inside the horse trailer. The horse was wild-eyed, twitchy, and quite anxious. "Mr. Pearson, can you back your trailer up to the corral? We'll let him out and have ourselves a look-see."

"Can do."

One of Mr. Pearson's ranch hands expertly maneuvered the trailer into the corral area. Mr. Pearson, with the assistance of two of Ron's hands, unlocked the trailer ramp. No sooner had they released the latch on the trailer door than there was a commotion inside, and the door burst open. Both hands made an impressive leap over the top rail of the fence. Mr. Pearson, aging and a bit overweight, dove through the split-rail fence with the elegance of a rhino.

The massive Morgan backed himself out of the trailer without the aid of the ramp. He was big, well-muscled, and at this instant, quite annoyed. In a quick canter,[13] he made a tour of the entire training corral then returned to the vicinity of the trailer. In a flurry of dust and debris, the big beast came to a complete stop with the definitiveness of a NASCAR racer. He snorted loudly, pawed the ground, and looked around contemptuously at the cowboys as if to see if any were up to the challenge.

"See what I mean?" Mr. Pearson huffed as he picked himself up, brushed off his trousers, and slapped his hat against his thigh.

Ron, Bill, Brent, and five of the hands were there to assist and, in truth, watch the unloading. They all had the same reaction: they looked down at their boots, looked at one another, those who chewed spat out a wad, smiled, and shook their heads. What a show.

Ron leaned on the fence, chin on his hands. Quietly and with admiration, he stared. Before him was one of the finest animals he had ever seen—big powerful chest, broad rump, thick corded neck, and a massive straight back. He was a buckskin, the color of summer wheat, with a jet-black mane, tail, and socks. Exquisitely marked and well contoured, his flank shimmered as light played off the form of his withers and rump. A handsome head with a small muzzle suggested some Arabian heritage. He stood and scanned his surroundings, pawed the turf, and looked in defiance at the humans as if to say, *I've broken your best. Send the next.*

Ron was dazzled. Bill was cautiously hesitant but very impressed, which, for a full Shoshone Indian, was saying something.

Bill stood next to Ron. For more than nearly two decades, hardly a horse in the winner's circle at Jackson's annual rodeo had not been trained at some stage of their education by Bill. Barrel riding, calf roping, breakaway events, cutting ponies, and everyday workhorses—it didn't matter. Bill had developed an impressive reputation in Star Valley and all points on the compass as one of the best horse trainers around. Like Ron, he was patient, reinforced good responses, and built trust. He never punished horses in training.

Ron and Bill looked at each other. Thoughts were exchanged; heads occasionally swiveled to the horse, who continued to stare, big brown eyes smoldering.

Bill finally nodded, and Ron turned to Mr. Pearson. "Mr. Pearson, we'll take him. I'm not much on taking something for nothing, though. I'll pay you a fair price. What're you asking for him?"

"Ron, knowing I tried everything to salvage his black soul is payment enough. He doesn't know this, but you're his last hope. I hate like hell to even think about putting so fine an animal down, but I just don't trust the son of a bitch. He's a handsome brute and smart. Why, I actually think he comes up with things to do just to piss me off, and that's for sure, but he'd just as soon kick you over the fence as look at you."

"Okay, sir. We'll do our best."

"I know you will, Ron. That's why I brought him here."

The ranch hands quickly closed the gate as Mr. Pearson pulled his truck and trailer forward. As he was about to leave, Ron yelled, "Mr. Pearson, what's his name?"

"Right now, his name is Shit. But you can change it if everything works out."

That earned a tenuous grin from everyone.

The question was, would everything work out?

Bill, Ron, Brent, and two of the ranch hands watched the brute closely as he surveyed his new surroundings. Then a concerned look came over Ron. He looked at Brent and said sternly, "Brent, you stay away from him. This is not a horse for you. You're not going to smooth him over like you do the other horses. This guy has a mean streak!"

"Dad...," Brent began a retort.

"I'm very serious, son. This guy could hurt somebody. We need to go slow with him. You leave this horse's training to Bill. You can watch Bill and learn from him, but your magic will not work on this guy. He won't listen to you. You understand me, son?"

Head down, Brent kicked at a dirt clod and said, "Yes, sir!"

Turning to Bill, Ron said, "Fine animal. But he's gonna need some work. Whatdaya think?"

"Good horse," Bill responded. "He's not happy."

"I can see that. He doesn't trust anybody. You need any help?"

"No." Bill's single-syllable reply was typical, a man who believed in economy and moderation of everything, including conversation.

"Okay. I'll be mending the fence down by the Salt. You coming, son?" Ron asked Brent.

"If it's okay with you, sir, I'll stay and watch."

"That'll be fine, but stay out of Bill's way, and don't turn your back on that horse!"

"Yes, sir!" said Brent.

For nearly an hour, Bill just watched the big horse. The colt made several laps around the training pen but always returned to the same spot nearest the gate. Glances were exchanged between Bill and the colt, but Bill generally broke eye contact if it persisted. He did not want to communicate that he was a threat nor give any indication of intimidation.

Then Bill spoke softly as he slowly ducked under the upper rail and entered the training pen. Brent inhaled and watched intently.

Bill slowly approached the colt but not in a direct path, he closed slightly from the side so as to appear nonthreatening, and he did not make eye contact. Bill stopped about ten feet away. The horse's ears flickered, his flank twitched, and he snorted. Then his ears folded back, and he pawed the ground, head down, menacingly. Bill gave no ground but no signal of aggression. He just continued to speak in soft, calming whispers. This went on for fifteen minutes, then, "Brent, would you get me an armful of alfalfa? And on your way, make sure the trough is full." And as an afterthought, Bill added, "Brent, move slow."

"Yes, sir!" Brent walked slowly past the trough—it was full. He walked to the barn and returned a few moments later with an armful of fresh alfalfa. "Here ya go, Bill."

"Fine," Bill said as he took the grain from Brent.

Bill piled most of the alfalfa in the feeding bin but withheld a handful, walked halfway to the horse, and dropped that on the ground. He slowly turned his back to the beast and walked back to the fence and exited the training pen. "That's enough for him today. We'll let him get used to his new home. Tomorrow, we'll make introductions."

The sun was just rising over the Salt River Mountains to the east the following day. Jean and Jennifer, a cute twenty-three-year-old raven-haired Mexican girl who had worked for the family for years, had fed all eight hands and was clearing the table. Bill grabbed his hat and turned to Brent on the way out the door. "You coming?"

"Sure, if it's okay."

"You ask your dad?"

"Yep. He said learn everything I can from you."

Bill put on his hat, nodded, then walked toward the training pen with Brent close in tow.

The horse had been circling the corral since early morning, but at the sight of the two humans approaching him, he stopped and lifted his head. His ears straightened, his flanks twitched, and his tail fluttered. Good signs compared to the day prior.

Bill slowed his pace somewhat, and still twenty yards away, he began speaking to the horse. In return, the horse whinnied and strode slowly toward the fence. His eyes were still afire and focused on Bill, but today, his posture was far less menacing.

"Brent, how 'bout fetchin' some alfalfa for our boy?"

Brent turned and walked to the barn. He returned with an armful of alfalfa and passed it to Bill. Repeating the routine from the previous evening, Bill placed most of the alfalfa in the bin. He kept a large handful and crossed under the upper railing, walked halfway to the horse, speaking to him all the while, and laid that portion on the ground. He paused for a moment, turned around, and exited the training pen. Then he watched.

The colt took a couple of steps to the alfalfa, sniffed at it, then began eating. When most of that was eaten, he walked to the bin, in close proximity to Bill and Brent, seemed to appraise both humans, and without hesitation, began eating that alfalfa also.

"He seems a bunch calmer and interested this morning," Brent noted.

"Yep. Sure does."

While the colt ate, Bill spoke to Brent in the same soft-spoken tone as he used with the colt. All his observations and assessments were communicated to Brent. And seamlessly, Bill often switched to Shoshone when he spoke to the horse. That was about the only clue to discern to whom he was speaking.

When the horse had finished eating, he started a slow gait around the perimeter of the training pen. After two trips around the corral, his gait changed to a trot and then to a fast canter. He whinnied, snorted, and shook his head, and seemed to be having a grand time of it.

"He's just loosening up his muscles and burning off some of his excess colt energy. White men call this *feeling his oats*. The more he exercises, the less aggression he may direct at us, so we'll just watch him and let him burn off some steam."

"Gosh, what an animal," Brent said admiringly.

Bill smiled in approval. "He is that!" Then added, "I think he wants to be a good horse, but he's been mistreated. He just doesn't seem to trust us, not yet anyway. We need to change that." A few more moments of quiet observations, and then Bill said, "Well, it's time for introductions."

Bill headed for the tack room, and Brent continued watching the big colt.

The colt had finally come to a stop near the gate where Brent stood. When Bill returned, he was carrying a coiled lariat and a thin rod with a ten-foot length of line connected to one end. Attached to the free end was a small yellow flag.

The colt didn't know what to think about the equipment, but he didn't like it one bit. Bill entered the training pen and approached the colt from the side.

"Brent, tell me what you see, and then tell me what it means."

"Well...he sure isn't having much fun. His head is down, he's pawing the ground, ears are folded back, and his tail is swishing all over the place. I think he's kinda unhappy, and he's challenging you. You're getting real close to his space. I think he's about ready to tell you so."

"Good. If I kept moving into him, he'd probably rear up on me. He's just trying to establish dominance and define his space. So, our first lesson is to explain to him those threats are not going to work. We're going to redefine roles. He doesn't like the rope, and he really doesn't like the crop, so we're going to use them to get his attention. I'll never strike a horse with either, but I will use them to remind him of what is acceptable. First, we'll get him running around the pen in a circle. This will tire him out a bit but will also help him understand who's boss. When he's got that figured out, we're going to start doing some bond building."

For the next several hours, Bill worked the big colt around the training pen. Occasionally, the colt approached Bill in a threatening posture, trying to assert dominance. Bill would step into him, snap the crop, or wave the lariat, relinquishing no ground and reinforcing the new roles. Progress was slow initially, but by the end of the day, the horse lowered his head a bit; and when Bill changed positions, the horse would pivot to face Bill—a sign of respect.

"You may notice that he's not lowering his nose to the ground, which in horse talk means, *Pay attention, I'm about to tell you something*. He's also keeping his eyes on me now. There's no turning away from me. He's occasionally licking and chewing, and even better, he's yawning now and again. This is good. We're about to break through. He's finally realizing that we are no threat to him, and he's beginning to accept the new roles."

Bill had approached the colt and extended his hand slowly. Initially, the colt fidgeted and tried to push his nose into Bill's space, possibly in preparation to nip Bill. Elevating the rope and slapping it against Bill's thigh ended that notion. The colt moved his head away and then lowered it again, licking and chewing.

"Now we're going to see how much progress we've made today. I'm going to move to his side and turn my shoulder to him and then start walking. If he follows me, that's good. It means he's accepted the new roles, and he's allowed me to take the lead. Here we go."

Whispering a steady stream of Shoshone, Bill moved to the colt's side and again extended his hand; but this time, the colt smelled Bill's hand and then his arm. Bill carefully reached farther and gently rubbed the horse's forelock then moved down his jaw-line and scratched it. It was a tense few seconds, but gradually the colt accepted the contact, and then he appeared to even enjoy Bill's touch. Bill rotated slightly so his right shoulder was closest to the horse; then he took the first couple of steps away from the colt.

To Brent's immense surprise, the colt followed Bill, taking care not to push his head into Bill's space. Bill practiced stopping and starting several more times to ensure the colt understood the relationship and the activity.

It seemed to be a very elementary accomplishment, but it signaled the establishment of roles—the dominant man and the submissive horse. Further, it set the first needed step in place to build trust and, from there, form a bond.

It was a major tipping point. Now the real training could begin.

Bill and Brent spent a couple of hours with the colt each morning and after supper. The goals were to reinforce the progress they had made, allow him to realize that humans were not all bad, and continue strengthening the bond they had established. This process went on for four days.

On the fifth day, there was an additional event that marked an unexpected achievement, and it was not at Bill's initiative.

Brent leaned on the fence where Bill entered the pen. Bill had walked away several times and reapproached the horse coming slightly closer each time. Finally, when within two feet of the horse, the bronc leaned toward Bill, sniffed then tasted his hat, smelled Bill's hair, his shirt, and then, most remarkably, eased his forehead into Bill's chest. It was a small thing to the casual eye, but it was a major leap in signaling a growing trust and a welcome indicator of just how far they had come in forging the relationship. It was momentary, but that may well have been the only extension of friendship and trust the big colt had ever shown a human being. It was so startling and so unanticipated, knowing the history of this brute, that even Bill was, for a moment, without words.

Bill smiled and scratched behind the big colt's jaw and beside his ears.

Brent could hardly control himself. He felt like his whole body was plugged into an electrical socket. He wanted to jump and shout and run circles around the barn, but for the sake of propriety and horse protocol, he restrained himself.

Brent half-expected some outward sign of accomplishment from Bill, but Bill was not like that. Still, Brent couldn't help but notice the restrained smile etched on Bill's face, probably the one sign of emotion Brent could remember.

Following that encounter, Bill and Brent went their separate ways, Brent to help his dad mend fences and Bill to supervise the ranch hands.

The day went slowly. Brent's mind was not on work; he was distracted and could think of little else but the progress Bill had made with this giant horse. He was eager to get back to the beast to watch the next session unfold.

It was just before dinner when Brent got back to the barn. He saw Bill drive one of the jeeps to the house. He parked and got out. Brent rushed to the barn, but on the way, he noticed two developments: a line of tall thunderheads building over the Caribou Mountains west of the valley; but what caused him to stop in his tracks was the sight at the training pen. The colt was there at the gate apparently waiting for Bill. Brent simply smiled, shook his head, and continued to the barn.

When Brent returned with an armful of alfalfa, the horse was within a few feet of Bill, listening, as it were, intently to Bill's melodic Shoshone words. It was as if Bill was singing in his strange language to the colt, and the colt seemed to be enjoying the melody.

Brent slowed as he approached, and Bill gathered a handful of grain and offered it to the horse. And then the horse did a funny thing: he smelled the alfalfa and then nudged Bill's outstretched arm as if to say thanks. Equally as surprising was Bill's physical gesture. He slowly extended his left hand and scratched under the colt's jaw and stroked his forehead and poll. The horse made no aggressive responses and, in fact, clearly enjoyed the contact.

Is this the same horse?

No one was ever late for Jennifer's Southern fried chicken, and with eight hands and family members to feed, there were never any leftovers.

As the ladies cleared the table, Ron pushed his chair back, crossed his legs and, with his coffee cup in his hand, looked at Bill and asked, "So…how's the horse training going?"

"Okay." Typically underplayed by Bill.

Brent was ready to jump out of his chair to trumpet the great news. A sideways glance from Bill silently told Brent to do otherwise.

"Ya think we have a keeper?"

"He is a good horse. He is smart. He is weary. He has great spirit. I think he has been mistreated. He needs some friends. We have made progress. And yes, he is a keeper."

Ron nodded in agreement. "He's damned beautiful and strong as a bull. I think he knows it too. Any ideas for a name yet?"

"I will leave that to Brent."

"Me?" Brent exclaimed. "You're the one working all the miracles."

"I leave the name to you. We already have a greeting for each other in Shoshone. You name him."

Brent, not entirely sure that this would work out, had never given it any mind. Brent looked down and thought, *Big, powerful brute force and dazzling strength, what would a good name be?*

At that moment, the heavens opened up. The cumulus cells that had mounted over the Caribou Mountains had entrenched itself firmly over Star Valley. A bolt of lightning lit up the sky and flashed brightly throughout the kitchen. Within two seconds, it was followed by a tremendous crack that rattled the old house.

Brent grabbed the side of the dinner table, looked at his father, smiled, and said one word, "*Thunder!*"

The Breakthrough

Summer, 1997
Harris Ranch, Star Valley, Wyoming

In the days that followed, with the establishment of the new roles, Bill and Brent worked as a team to begin a more advanced training regimen for Thunder, a name deemed to be quite appropriate for the colt. Training went quickly. Bill, as a master horse trainer, ably assisted by his protégé, Brent, were suitably challenged with his number one pupil, Thunder, not because Thunder was slow to learn, thickheaded, or defiant but rather because this colt's capacity for learning was much higher than even Bill had anticipated. Finally, Thunder had found humans he trusted, and his herding instinct allowed him to accept his position within his new pack.

Bill initially kept the training objectives simple, but when he came to the realization that, one, the horse was steady and quite smart, and two, he was surprisingly quick to absorb the lessons, Bill increased the learning tempo.

When Ron was apprised of Thunder's amazing turnaround and progress, he gave Brent permission to assist Bill with the training at a hands-on level. Now Thunder had two trainers, and in truth, both Thunder and Brent were under the tutelage of Bill.

In less than a week, Thunder had learned to accept lunge lines, lead ropes, saddle blankets, a halter, and even being leaned on by Bill or Brent as they walked around the training pen. The next steps involved circle training.

Circle training teaches the horse to transition through the various gaits—walk, trot, canter, and gallop. Thunder became quite tolerant of both the lunge line and the lead rope. Even the coiled rope brushing across his flanks was accepted. The halter was gradually replaced by a bit. Thunder initially shied away from the bit, but with constant praise and reinforcement, he gradually accepted his bit without protest.

Bill and Brent took turns introducing Thunder to a saddle. First, they let him smell it. They brushed the saddle across its flanks, shoulders, and hindquarters. Initially agitated, it was the trust Thunder had for Bill and then Brent that set the stage for the next major leap in training.

For most of a day, Bill and Brent presented the saddle blanket and saddle to Thunder; gradually, they alternated setting it across Thunder's back. His tail switched, and his flanks twitched, but he took no aggressive action. After hours of this, Bill slowly set the saddle in position and then reached under Thunder's chest, grabbed the cinch strap, and speaking calmly to Thunder in Shoshone all the while, ran the end through the cinch ring.

Thunder turned his head to get a better look at Bill and sniff the saddle. He remained unruffled but became more interested. Bill walked him around the training pen, and gradually, as Thunder became more comfortable with all the equipment, Bill occasionally stopped, put his left boot in the left stirrup, and very slowly, lifted himself and leaned across the saddle.

Thunder seemed more interested in the growing number of ranch hands and family that had quietly migrated to the corral. Something was up, and they were forming to watch what certainly would be either calamity or a major victory.

Ron was among those in the crowd and watched as Bill stepped out of the stirrup. Bill and Thunder made two more circuits around the pen; this time, Bill jogged beside Thunder and continued leaning into him to allow Thunder to sense the physical contact. When next Bill brought Thunder to a stop, he whispered in Thunder's ear—Shoshone speak. Thunder was completely calm as Bill put the toe of his left boot lightly in the left stirrup, lifted himself up, slowly swung his right leg over the cantle, and eased the tip of his right boot into the right stirrup.

No one spoke. No one moved. No one breathed.

Thunder, placid and still taking it all in, bent his neck to sniff Bill's pant leg and the saddle, then looked up at Bill with big brown eyes as if to say, *What's next, boss?*

The natural reaction to such a climactic achievement would be for the crowd to go absolutely nuts—yelling, screaming, and hopping around like a bunch of jackrabbits in a brush fire. But these were ranchers and cowboys, and they knew better. But no one had the discipline to remain completely stoic: ear-to-ear smiles were glued on everyone's face.

With a light rein, Bill gently tapped Thunder's flanks with his heels. As if this was an everyday event, Thunder stepped forward into a walk. After one complete circuit around the training pen, a second tap, and Thunder broke into a slow trot. Bill gently reined Thunder to the left across the fence line and kicked Thunder into the next gear—the canter. Bill eased back on the reins and spoke something to Thunder unintelligible to the fans. Thunder geared down to an exquisite trot with his head high, chin tucked in close to his chest, ears up.

After another circuit around the perimeter and in full view of the fans, Thunder almost pranced. Bill, back straight as a rifle barrel, tipped his hat. And at that point, all semblance of discipline was utterly lost. The roar of cheers and whistles could have been mistaken for a touchdown at a Super Bowl game.

Thunder hardly noticed. He was so locked into sensing the inputs of his rider—the subtle touches of his body movements and his soothing words—he was nearly oblivious to the rowdy whooping. Even Ron, usually so in control, so reticent, caught himself in the hoopla and quickly realized his hat was missing. He looked around and saw it hit the ground ten yards away. This would become one of those events that Harris ranch hands would be telling around the campfire for years to come.

For another month, with the basic learning objectives achieved, Bill and Brent considered expanding the program to train Thunder as a workhorse with special emphasis on development as a cutting pony. This was a specialty in which Brent was more comfortable. Brent could not have taken Thunder so far, so fast in the basics of training as did Bill, but in the regime of ranch-horse and cutting-pony training, Brent was effective, if not at par, with Bill.

Bill and Brent approached Ron for his approval.

They sat on the front porch. A slight breeze pushed water-laden cumulus clouds to the northeast, the hint of rain in the air.

Bill slid into a bench seat against the house. Brent seated himself on an aged barrel in front of an ancient wood table and placed his elbows on his knees. Ron, at ease in an old wooden rocking chair that creaked with each rearward rocking motion, asked, "What's up, Bill?"

Bill started with the easy sell first. "We're doing good with Thunder. He might be the smartest horse I've ever worked with. It would be a shame to keep him just as a ranch horse. I think he'd be a good sire and would command a big breeding fee especially if he got a few wins in the rodeos as a cutting pony."

There was pause as Ron gazed at the puffy clouds then, straight-faced, said, "I like the idea. Let's do it." Then Ron offered, "You know, the annual Star Valley rodeo kicks off in October. That's nearly four months from now. Why don't you give some thought to entering Thunder in the cutting competition?"

"That's a thought," Bill responded. "But I don't know if we can have him ready by then. And to be honest, I'm a bit rusty myself."

"Hell, Bill, two months ago, Mr. Pearson was going to send him to the glue factory, and look what you two did with him. And as for you being rusty, don't think I need to remind you that you were the barrel-riding, calf-roping, and cutting champion of the entire valley for three years running."

"Yes, I know, but that was long ago. Besides, my back has been giving me fits. I don't want to take any chances of busting anything."

There was a moment of deep silence, and then Bill continued, almost as if he had this entire conversation designed to lead to the solution. "How about letting Brent ride Thunder in the cutting competition?"

Brent's elbow slipped off his knee, and he followed through by bouncing his chin off the table. He straightened up, rubbed his reddening chin, and looked expectantly but said nothing.

"An idea, Bill, but Brent's only sixteen. He's done a lot of range riding, but he's never ridden the rodeo."

"How old were you when you rode your first rodeo?" Bill countered. "And besides, no one ever rode their first rodeo until their first rodeo."

Ron pondered that. Finally, he figured out that he'd been worked into a corner. It was as though he was a spring calf and was now corralled by one of Bill's cutting ponies. There was no maneuvering room, but in truth, Bill's argument made a lot of sense.

Ron's gaze shifted to Brent. "What do you think, son?"

Brent sat up straight, hesitated, then said, "I know Thunder could pull it off, but I'm not the horseman Bill is."

"We have four months to make you and Thunder a team. You showed me a lot out there. You can do it," Bill retorted.

Ron closed the conversation with, "Well then, it's done. We have four months. Get cracking, gents."

Heading for the Big Show

Autumn, 1997
Harris Ranch Star Valley, Wyoming

Four months is a lifetime for those in general population, but for Bill and Brent, it went by in a flash. Each day for over one hundred straight days—all day on weekends, holidays, and after summer school on weekdays—Bill instructed Brent in advanced horse control, the basics of cutting competition, and trained Thunder as a competition cutting pony.

Thunder, being a horse with surprising *cow sense*,[14] was a quick study. In fact, Bill reckoned he was one of the most adaptive cutting ponies he had ever had the pleasure of working. He was startlingly quick, agile, powerful, and radiated a kind of domineering presence, a trait cowboys called *draw cattle*.[15] It seemed as though Thunder could read the cow. This was an attribute found only in the most exceptional cutting ponies. There were moments when Bill suspected there was some Australian sheepdog DNA lurking in Thunder's genes.

Brent had years of riding experience, true, but that entailed working the ranch, trail riding, moving cattle, and running pack trips in the high country during hunting season. Harris ranch ponies were more a mode of transportation than a trained and tuned athlete used in a competitive event.

Brent discovered that cutting competition was a brave new world full of its own language, techniques, and riding etiquette. Bill's challenge was to acclimate Brent in the arena of cutting competition, but even before that, there was the greater test of bonding the two—melding the horse with the rider so each would physically and mentally join and act as a single entity focused exclusively on cutting two cows out of a herd for a two-and-a-half-minute run.

A cutting pony, far more than a trail or ranch workhorse, takes input from the rider's knees, toes, heels, reins, and the way he sits the horse or balances himself in the saddle. In cutting competition, once the rider and the horse had designated the target cow, it was nearly a hands-off affair. The pony must watch, anticipate, and then respond quicker and more decisively than the calf to keep him separated from the herd for the allotted time.

Many horses have all the necessary traits to be good cutting ponies, but it takes a great trainer to maximize those and produce a champion pony. And it takes a rider with a tender hand and a gentle touch to bring that learned behavior to the rodeo.

The Harrises had a winning combination: a young cowboy who started riding a few years after he began walking, a master horse trainer and rodeo champ, and the third member of the team—a massive horse with demonstrated spirit and agility, who could become a rodeo great.

They had all the makings of a formidable team.

Origins of Cutting Competition

1800s
Western United States

Cutting competition was born of necessity in the late 1800s. It harkened back from the days of the Wild West when American cowboys worked the open range. Often cowhands were required to separate specific cattle from the herd in need of branding, vaccinating, castrating, or deworming. The cowboy and his horse, working as one, pushed, guided, and rounded up cattle in open country and woodlands.

The transition from the open-range cattle herding to the competitive disciplines exhibited in public arenas, as in today's modern rodeo, was a natural evolution. It followed that cutting competition was just one of those activities that had grown into a widely recognized sport across the country.

Cutting competitions were held among ranchers and cowboys well before the 1900s. Horsemanship, technique, proficiency, and heart earned bragging rights at the initial meets, but it wasn't until 1898 that the first cutting-horse sanctioned competition was held in Haskell, Texas. Twenty years later, in 1918, the Fort Worth Stock Show held a national cutting-horse competition as one of the events in the very first indoor rodeo exhibition.

With steady growth of cutting-horse contests, competitors and cutting-horse owners scripted rules and regulations governing the organization, conduct, and awarding of points in cutting-horse events. In 1946, the National Cutting Horse Association (NCHA) was founded as the governing body for cutting-horse competition.

In accordance with the rules, judges evaluated the ability of a rider and his horse to work as a team to "cut" a cow from a herd of young steers and heifers. A rider and horse were required to make at least two cuts from the herd and maintain separation for a two-and-a-half-minute *run.* One of the cuts was required to be a cow from deep inside the herd while the other could be peeled from the perimeter of the herd.

Once the rider and horse had selected a cow, the rider would *commit* his horse by freeing rein to the horse, dropping the rein hand, and giving the horse his *head*. From that moment on, it was pretty much up to the horse to keep the cow separated from the herd. Exceptional cutting horses respond nearly instantaneously, mirroring the target cow's sometimes frantic actions to return to the herd. The best cutting ponies match almost synchronously the cow's hard stops, turns, sprints, and rapid direction changes all in an effort to keep the cow separated from the herd.

The judges score a *run* on a scale from sixty to eighty points based on their assessment of a lengthy list of attributes including dominance, focus, agility, courage, presence, cow control, and team-work. In every way, an exceptional cutting pony must demonstrate an extraordinarily high degree of athleticism and discipline, not unlike human athletes in high-end sports.

The Gridiron

August to September 1997
Harris Ranch, Star Valley, Wyoming

After several days of dry work,[16] Brent and Thunder mastered the finesse of toe, heel, knee, and rein commands. The fundamentals were laid, and while they were a long way from the big event, Bill figured it was time for the next step—to introduce real calves into the crucible.

Ted Petty, one of the more senior ranch hands, and Colleen, his little paint cutting pony, rounded up seven hardy six-month-old calves. On deft tiny feet, the little filly efficiently herded the calves into a holding pen adjoining the arena. She made it look so easy.

Brent and Thunder watched intently from a position near the railing some distance from the gate so as to avoid spooking the cattle.

Brent was all set, gloves on, chaps tied loosely, hat pulled down snuggly, toes of his boots centered on the stirrup, his body loose and balanced aboard Thunder.

"You ready, Brent?"

Brent only nodded. Thunder, head up, ears forward, was totally zeroed in on the claves. He didn't twitch.

"Let 'em go, Ted!"

With that, the ranch hand pushed the gate open and slapped his lariat against his chaps. The calves tentatively trudged out of the holding pen but remained packed in a tight group close to the fence.

Brent and Thunder slowly eased toward the herd. With Brent using rein, toe, heel, and knee commands, Thunder responded well in moving through the herd and, under Brent's control, was success-ful in separating a small heifer from the herd for a few seconds. When it bolted, inputs from Brent only succeeded in confusing Thunder, and the little cow successfully rejoined his group.

This first training session with real cattle went on for two hours. Initially, there was enough misunderstanding and mixed signals to go around. Thunder didn't understand that there was still work to do after he cut the cow from the pack, and Brent had trouble explaining that to Thunder through his feet, knees, and hands. The only one that didn't seem to be frustrated was Bill. He'd been through this drill scores of times. He warned Brent of expecting too much too soon and offered sage advice: "Talk to Thunder. He still doesn't under-stand that he needs to keep the cow separated from the herd after he makes the cut. Tell him what he needs to do. He'll start to connect your words with your body inputs. I think he's about to have a big breakthrough. And when he does, you will be amazed."

With the calves watered and rested, Brent and Thunder went back to training. Brent and Thunder cut a fair-sized brindle[17] out of the herd. Brent spoke to Thunder continuously and synchronized his words with foot, knee, and rein inputs. Thunder finally began to respond to Brent's physical inputs now reinforced with Brent's voice commands.

The breakthrough that Bill had anticipated came early in the afternoon.

Thunder had tried to keep a cow separated from the herd by running in front of the cow and using his flank to block the cow's path. Thunder was making half-turns as quickly as he could by turning his entire body and then attempting to sprint in front of the cow in an effort to cut him off. The fact was, he was a big horse, and trying to turn his whole body 180 degrees to match the directional changes of the cow was taking too long. He couldn't hope to change direction as fast as a little cow.

Finally, Thunder realized that it was far quicker to face the animal and pivot on his hindquarters to change directions.

Now Thunder began to face the cow and sidestep to head off the cow during slow turns and reversals. When the cow tried to break and make a run for the pack, Thunder began to *sweep*—he leaned back, extending his forelegs, squatted down on its massive hindquarters, and pivoted to change direction. This posture also allowed Thunder to launch himself if the cow attempted a fast end run.

This was the breakthrough that Bill had foreseen. Brent was appropriately amazed.

To ensure that Thunder now had his *sweeps* and *pivots* ingrained into his maneuvering routine, they had five more runs, each more impressive than the previous run.

The sun was sinking behind the Caribou Mountain Range when, finally, they called it a day. The calves were greatly relieved, but less so was Thunder, who wanted to continue the game.

Brent had had little sleep when the Harris clan was rousted just before sunup. He skipped breakfast and had Thunder watered, saddled, and in the training arena just as Bill stepped from the house. Ted was pushing a group of now ten young cows into the holding pen when Bill walked up to Brent and Thunder.

Thunder whinnied and nuzzled Bill's chest, begging attention. Bill scratched his forelock, rubbed his ears, and said, "Well, we made some progress yesterday. Believe it or not, most cutting ponies don't pick up that kind of cow sense and maneuvering techniques for weeks, and some never do. I know you were getting frustrated, but Thunder did well."

"I know what I was supposed to try and teach him, but I just couldn't coordinate the inputs clearly enough. When he started sweeping, pivoting, and sidestepping, well…I think he learned that on his own."

"Maybe. There's a lot more to him than meets the eye, but I'm thinking it was a team effort."

Bill didn't mention it because he felt Brent knew intrinsically that melding the horse with the rider was still a task in progress. Thunder hadn't quite mastered the horse art of collecting or balancing his rider, but much of that was Brent's responsibility. This stemmed from the issue of a divergence of opinion of which calf to cut. They needed to work on that.

"This morning, I want you to reinforce everything you two learned yesterday. Talk to him. Give him voice commands at the same time you're giving him physical inputs. Pretty soon, he'll be able to respond to you by your voice alone. One of the big things to learn—and the earlier, the better—is to start synching up your minds. Tell him what you want him to do. Talk to him about which cow you want to go after. Do that in coordination with your knees, toes, heels, and reins, and always stay balanced in the saddle. You two are not together yet, but it's early. It'll come. Any questions?"

"Nope. Not a one."

"Then git on that brute and show us what you two can do!"

Bill strolled over to the fence and climbed on the top rung and took a seat. Brent whispered to Thunder, stroked his neck and under his jaw, then tossed a leg over the saddle. Thunder was very ready for day two.

"Kick 'em out, Ted!" hollered Bill. Ted opened the gate, and ten young heifers and steers waddled into the training arena but remained tightly packed. Thunder, twitching with excitement and loaded with adrenaline, pushed a little too aggressively into the center of the herd, scattering the cattle.

Brent tried to speak softly to him and eased the reins back, but Thunder was having none of it. Brent was interested in a likely target calf, a baldy[18] to the left, and positioned himself for a quick left pivot. But Thunder, full of vinegar and purpose, had other ideas and bolted after a calf on the right.

There was an enormous flurry of activity, and rider and horse parted company. Thunder had quite successfully separated a calf from the herd. He had hardly noticed he was riderless.

It took but a few seconds for the dust to settle. Brent picked himself off the deck, grabbed his hat, and slapped it against his chaps. All eyes shifted to Thunder.

Thunder—head down, front hooves spread, shoulders, withers, and flank tensed like a coiled spring, chest nearly touching the dirt—had the little calf stuck near the railing and well away from the herd.

Brent looked at Bill. Bill stared at Thunder. Thunder glared at the little calf. The little calf looked for an escape route.

Thunder rolled his head around to look at Brent and snorted some horse obscenity. His intelligent brown eyes said, *What the hell are you doing over there? The cow's here!* Then Thunder returned his glare to the calf.

"That's some horse ya got there, Brent!" bellowed Bill.

"Lordy! What just happened?"

"I think Thunder had a difference of opinion on which cow to cut from the herd."

"How could he have done that? He's never even seen this before yesterday!"

"Don't know, but I'll bet you're thinking this is harder than you thought."

Bill, a large smile planted on his face, hopped off the railing and strolled over to Brent, who was now back with Thunder. The little calf had rejoined the herd.

"I've got a couple of thoughts," Bill remarked.

"I'm all ears. I don't like the gymnastics. And besides, I think I broke my butt."

"You are young. You will live. Here is what I want you to try..."

Bill strode alongside Brent and explained the new plan. Thunder watched patiently as they approached. Thunder immediately pushed his forehead into Bill's chest; Bill rubbed his neck, forelock, and jaw.

Half under his breath, Brent said, "Don't blame you, Thunder. I wouldn't pay attention to me either."

What followed was a very detailed debrief. Bill stressed the need for Brent to maintain control of Thunder, keep him calm, and avoid sudden movement that might alarm the cattle. Together, though, they would commit on a target cow. Once the cow was designated,

Brent needed to ease tension on the reins and allow Thunder to do his cutting-pony stuff. While this was happening, and to maintain balance aboard his mount, Brent needed to anticipate Thunder's moves, who was anticipating the cow's moves.

"It all makes perfect sense," Brent said. "Sure hope it works. The ground is a lot harder than it looks."

Now all Brent had to do was make it happen.

In the course of several hours, they went through the same activity nearly a dozen more times. There were no more involuntary dismounts, but Thunder occasionally ignored control inputs and went after his own targeted calf. Thunder's footwork, the way he crouched down, pivoted, and sprung like a tiger using those monstrous hindquarters to cut off the cow's intended escape path, was nothing short of remarkable to Brent and fairly well astonishing to Bill also. There were times Brent thought he was just along for the ride and 160 pounds of ballast that Thunder didn't seem to notice.

The lunch bell rang at the house. Brent dismounted, this time on his own, and led Thunder to the water trough. He was pulling the saddle and blanket off and removing his bit when Bill sauntered up.

Brent asked, "You ever seen anything like that? It was like he's done this before."

"I said he was smart, but I'm thinking he's got this in his blood."

"Huh? What do you mean?"

"You ever watch Martha and Heather when they were puppies, the first time they pushed sheep around? I know they're Australian sheepdogs, and they're supposed to do that, but—"

"Yeah! I was little when we first got them, but how could anybody forget that?"

"They picked it up all by themselves. Anybody teach them that?"

"Nope. Seemed like they had some kind of instinct thing to herd sheep. What are ya saying?"

"Some great horses have an instinct to do what you just saw Thunder do. My people believe in reincarnation. Now, do not act like a paleface and laugh this off, but some spirits return to earth in different forms. I think Thunder was something else in a previous life. He has done this before in a different life maybe, but watching him work today...I have to believe he has done this before!"

"Let me get this right. You're saying Thunder was an Indian in another life?"

"Maybe. Maybe a cowboy, maybe a sheepdog, maybe an Indian. Ever wonder why he understands Shoshone?"

Brent pulled his hat off, stared at the ground deep in thought, and rubbed the back of his neck. He lifted his gaze to Bill. He had no answers and was fresh out of intelligent questions.

"Curry Thunder down. We're coming back after lunch. I have an idea," Bill said and then headed for the house.

With lunch complete, Bill and Brent grabbed their hats and headed back to the arena. No sooner had they stepped off the stairs than Thunder saw them and trotted toward the gate, tail high, nose tucked closely to his chest. He approached the two men as if he were joining the huddle. Bill leaned across the fence and rubbed his ears, crest, and under both sides of his jaw. Thunder almost purred.

"So...you goin' to tell me what your plan is?" Brent asked.

"Brent, been thinking about this all morning. Thunder has a skill, a special gift. Let's use it."

"Ahh...okay." A pause. "What do you mean?"

"Let Thunder pick the calf. Don't tell him anything. Just let him run with it."

"Yeah, but he's supposed to pick one cow on the outside of the group and then make a deep cut on another. How do we make that happen?"

"The order is not important. Let him figure that out. Long ago, during my rodeo days, I heard of a couple of stories kinda like what we have here but never put much stock in 'em. Let's try it anyhow and see how it works. All you need to do is get him near the middle of the pack and let him go."

"I'm game. At least this way he won't toss me!"

"Mount up. I'll get Ted to bring fresh calves in."

Ted and Colleen had the calves in the holding pen ten minutes later. Brent and Thunder were positioned near the side of the training pen so as to minimize the appearance of a threat. Bill was inside the pen now standing twenty yards away from Brent and Thunder. "Remember, Brent, let Thunder make the cut."

At the sound of his name, Thunder snapped his head toward Bill as if he understood each word.

Brent leaned forward and whispered in Thunder's ear, "Show me your stuff, Thunder!"

Thunder whinnied. Head down, he pawed the ground, and his flanks quivered.

"Let 'em rip, Ted!"

Ted opened the gate and eased a dozen calves into the arena. When they had cleared the gate, Brent made a small pressure with his heels, lightly touched the reins, and spoke calmly, almost a whisper. With uncharacteristic composure and coolness, Thunder quietly eased into the sea of cattle. Clearly, Thunder had a calf in mind, and this was a deep cut from the middle of the pack. Initially, Thunder gently eased the little frosted steer, white markings on the tips of his ears out of the pack; but the farther he was pushed away, the more agitated the little steer became and the quicker he moved. Now with some fifteen yards of separation, the cow made several frantic runs; and each time, Thunder, now looking much more like a crouched tiger than a pony—huge chest just inches above the turf, front legs extended—pivoted on his rear haunches and sprang so quickly and with such fury he cut the cow off from escape faster than Brent could believe. It was all Brent could do just to stay balanced and hold on. The steer tried six times to end-run Thunder, and each time, with stunning agility and lightning speed, Thunder blocked him. Finally, the cow, recognizing the futility of the effort, stood in place and bleated mournfully.

Brent eased back on the reins, Thunder's signal to let the cow rejoin the herd.

Brent leaned over Thunder's neck, rubbed his crest, and whispered, "You are something special, Thunder. Now let's go pick out an easy one."

Thunder stepped lightly into the pack and waited for the cattle to settle down. As the fidgeting subsided, Thunder shouldered a little brindle heifer from the edge of the pack.

Ten times that afternoon, they made runs and cut two cows from the pack, one on the periphery and one from the center of the group. Timing varied from five minutes to just under three minutes—well over the two-and-half-minute mark the judges look for. Bill was unperturbed and explained, "Brent, first, we meld the horse and rider, get our game plan smoothed out, then we'll work on getting the time down."

While Brent noodled over the plan, Bill couldn't help but insert, "Pretty good cuttin' pony for a guy headed for the glue factory." Then Bill became deathly serious. His smile vanished, and he added, "A life lesson, Brent: never give up on your people or your animals." Bill adjusted his hat, turned, and headed for the house in anticipation of another one of Jennifer's award-winning suppers.

Brent, deep in thought, stayed in place. *Never give up on your people or your animals. There's another one I'll never forget.*

Thunder nudged Brent, reminding him there was still work to be done. Brent turned, put his shoulder under Thunder's neck, stroked his mighty neck, and spoke softly, "Who were you anyway? Where'd you learn all this stuff?"

Thunder whinnied, and a shiver ran through his flanks.

Let's Rodeo

Saturday, 4 October 1997
Cutting competition, Jackson Rodeo, Wyoming

It was a bit after three o'clock in the afternoon in Jackson, Wyoming, on a bright and gorgeous Saturday in early October—the day of the annual rodeo. Brent sat squarely aboard Thunder. They were standing in the middle of the arena as the announcer's voice blasted across the sellout crowd.

"Next for the cutting horse competition is Ron Harris's entry, Thunder—a four-year-old Morgan trained by our own Bill Washakie and ridden by Ron's son Brent. Now, folks, neither Brent nor his mount have ever competed in a rodeo, so let's show them the hospitality we're known for here in cowboy country USA!"

Applause and whistles reverberated off the surrounding structures.

Brent was nervous as a long-tailed cat in a room full of rocking chairs. He could feel Thunder beneath him. He was twitching as if he was plugged into a socket. Brent took a couple of deep breaths as the calf handlers pushed the animals into the holding pen. Brent looked back at Bill and then turned toward the judges, raised his gloved hand, and waited.

The lead judge, on seeing this, keyed the PA system. "Son, you need a moment?"

Brent rapidly nodded his head.

"Well, this is kinda irregular, but this time, we'll allow it."

Bill strode out to Brent and Thunder. Whispers broke out, which crescendoed into hoots and whistles. The ranchers knew Bill for his reputation as a horse trainer, the old cowboys knew him from his rodeo days, and the ladies whistled because he was a genuine Wyoming stud.

Bill stopped in front of Thunder, who had immediately buried his head in Bill's chest. Bill scratched his ears and under his chin. "What's up?"

"Thunder's quaking so bad he feels like a paint shaker, and I'm about to take a crap!"

"That's what you called me out here for?"

"I'm kinda scared, Bill. I've never done this before."

"Look around, Brent. As I told you four months ago, none of these cowboys had done this before the first time. You can relieve yourself later. Right now, you need to rodeo, cowboy. Let's git'er done."

Then Bill leaned close into Thunder and said something Brent couldn't make out: Shoshone words. Bill turned and walked toward the owner seats. The crowd roared, and Bill swept the air with his hat.

Nearly instantly, Thunder's quivering ceased. The little shock waves shooting through his shoulders and flanks stopped. He took an enormous breath and seemed to focus on the far side of the ground where he could see nearly two dozen calves huddled together.

Strangely, with the nervousness now out of Thunder, Brent too was calmer.

Brent leaned over Thunder's left shoulder, his right cheek brushing the left side of Thunder's muscled neck. "Thunder, I don't know what Bill told you. I don't speak Shoshone, but I'm asking you, big fella, make us look good. If I go down, you just do your job. You don't need me anyhow. Do us proud, Thunder. For Dad and Bill, do us proud."

And then Brent remembered something his dad told him during baseball games: "Son, rechannel all that nervous energy and focus on the job at hand." And Brent did just that.

"Mr. Harris, you 'bout ready to go?"

Brent leaned back in the saddle, took a lungful of air, and replied with a thumbs-up and a head nod.

The buzzer sounded, the gate opened, the clock started, and the calves loped into the arena. Thunder had already picked a target deep in the pack. As before, Thunder calmly strode into the center of the group. Brent noticed at once that these were larger calves than they had practiced with and faster to boot.

Thunder shouldered his way toward a fair-sized brindle. The calf seemed to realize something was amiss; he tried to keep himself in the midst of the herd. Brent whispered a running commentary, quiet, reassuring, calming.

When Thunder finally closed the distance to the brindle, the cow bolted to the periphery of the group. Thunder cautiously followed. The cow was now nearly ten yards from the pack and becoming more alarmed by the second. When at last the brindle realized he was cut from the pack, all hell broke loose. He was fast and in full panic.

The cow rapidly changed direction four times, trying to get around the monstrous buckskin. Each time, as if reading his thoughts,

Thunder compressed so his chest was nearly in the dirt, pivoted, and launched himself in front of the escaping calf.

A fifth quick turn of the brindle, Thunder crouched, pivoted, and sprung to cut him off. The calf quickly changed direction again, but not before Thunder, anticipating the next move, quickly pivoted on his rear quarters and sprung to cut off that route also. The calf made three more rapid direction changes, each time being blocked by Thunder's amazing pivots and eye-watering launches.

In over a minute, Thunder had the brindle confined to a small area well away from the rest of the herd. The calf stood and bellowed.

The crowd roared.

"Great job, big fella. Let's go get another one," Brent whispered to Thunder. "But this time, let's pick out an easy one. We're running out of time, big boy."

Brent reined Thunder in and headed toward the group, which, by this time, knew something was awry. Brent and Thunder stuck to the plan, and Thunder thrilled the crowd by his sweeps and tiger-like launches to block the escape routes attempted by the calf.

The second cut took less than a minute. Total time for the entire run was two minutes and twenty-four seconds, just under the two-and-a-half-minute mark.

The buzzer blared. The crowd whistled, hooted, and applauded. Clearly, this was the show they had come to see.

And it was over.

To Brent, it was all one big blur. Four hard months of training, and it was over in a matter of minutes. Brent could hardly remember anything that had happened once the buzzer went off. While the judges tallied the score, Brent and Thunder made for a side gate. They stood just inside the arena. Thunder stood in place, breathing hard and was still totally focused—as if waiting for the next event.

Brent climbed off Thunder and said, "Come on, Thunder. We're done for the day." Brent and Thunder then strode side by side through the exit gate, heading for the stables.

Bill intercepted them just outside the gate. "Well, how do you feel, Brent?"

Bill was caressing Thunder's mane, ears, and neck when Brent responded, "Bill, I can hardly remember a thing."

"You don't need to. You'll find out soon enough how it went. You and Thunder did pretty well. The time shows that. Don't know if you'll get a first, but I'm thinking you'll get on the podium."

"Thanks, Bill. Thanks for everything."

"No need to thank me. You and Thunder did all the hard work. I just watched."

A moment passed between them. Thunder smelled Bill's hair then buried his nose in Bill's armpit.

Brent took a deep breath, looked at Bill, and asked, "When I was out there, about to crap my britches...you said something to Thunder. What was it that calmed him down so?"

Bill smiled and said, "It was Shoshone."

"Okay. What'd you say?"

"I told him that he was a brave heart."

"That's all?"

"No. Then I said, take care of the paleface kid.'"

The PA system shattered the quiet. One of the judges announced the decision of the judge's panel. "Your attention please. We have the scores tallied for young Brent Harris and Thunder. They completed their run in two minutes and twenty-four seconds. The average was seventy-seven points. Very high points for their first performance, but they got special points for bravado, style, horsemanship, and just all-around cow sense. Heck, ladies and gentlemen, they just looked like they knew what they were doing out there. That score will get Brent to a third place. Pretty fine show for a first-time team. Congratulations, Brent and Thunder and their trainer, Bill Washakie!"

The crowd simply exploded—hoots, hollers, whistles, and a round of applause that went on for nearly a minute. Clearly, the crowd saw much of the same performance that the judges did.

Bill smiled then turned and walked toward the reviewing stands and left Brent staring in disbelief. Brent stood and thought for a moment. *It couldn't have been that simple. All that pent-up tension sud-*

denly flowed out of Thunder just because Bill spoke some Shoshone words to him? It had to be something else. But what?

Puzzled and deep in thought, Brent half-turned to continue walking toward the owners' bleachers where his father was seated. There was a hefty snort behind him. Brent turned and came face-to-face with Thunder, his big brown eyes glued on him. Brent had just assumed that Thunder would take off after Bill like a giant puppy dog, but in reality, he'd stayed right there with his rider.

What an incredible day, Brent mused. *A third-place finish in cutting, and this big brute of a horse had decided to stay with me.*

The bond was surely cast.

As it turned out, that was Brent's first and last rodeo. He held no misgivings for ending his competitive riding. He accepted it for what the experience was worth. He was the worthy recipient of several lessons money just couldn't buy. Even when he was scared to death of failing in the arena in front of his father, Bill, and hundreds of spectators, he reached way down deep inside and grunted through the trial and came out a winner, not because of his placement on the podium but because of the personal victory it represented. Additionally, he learned more about animals than he thought possible: their behavior, what motivates them, and how one can communicate with them.

And finally, with Bill's remarkable skills, Brent made a lifelong friend of a monstrous horse that everybody thought was headed for the glue factory. It had been a crazy time, and more were in Brent's future.

At Last—Freedom

June 1998
Etna, Wyoming

High school, by Brent's accounting, was one of those major gates in life that you had to push through but weren't required to enjoy it. And he didn't. He just wasn't academic. While Scott and Kurt pumped out nearly straight As through high school, elevating them to the dean's list, Brent was satisfied, if not elated, with the 2.8 grade point average he earned by the end of his four years in purgatory. In Brent's mind, anything higher than the 2.8 GPA would be an indicator that he had worked too hard. Somehow, he managed to avoid the moniker *Anchormantorium*, although he didn't miss it by much.

A few days short of the graduation ceremony four military recruiters gave individual presentations on the opportunities afforded in the branches of the services. Army, Air Force, Marine, and Navy recruiters each had fifteen minutes to captivate the minds and energize the spirits of the fifty students heading through the archway of formal public schooling and into the real world.

The Marines made a small force level increase that day. Five graduating students signed their papers: four young men and one young woman. Three additional young men hitched up, one each to the Army, Air Force, and Navy. Certainly, there was a sense of commitment and patriotism that moved these young adults, but probably more than that was the dual-edged sword of limited career prospects in Star Valley and, especially with the Navy's pitch, the opportunity for high adventure on the mighty seas—a chance to visit far-off lands.

Brent did not sign papers that day, but he did sit straighter in his seat and stopped doodling on his notebook when the Navy recruiter described life aboard a ship and the vastness of the world's oceans. Most definitely, his interest was piqued, but that was in stark contrast to his obligation to stay and work the ranch as did his brothers.

Still…

Into the Big Blue

July 1998
Manhattan Beach, California

In mid-July 1998, Brent's parents packed up the boys and headed west to California to visit aunts, uncles, and cousins who had somehow escaped the gravitational forces of Wyoming and made their home in Manhattan Beach, California.

Manhattan Beach was a small jewel of a surf town sheltered between Los Angeles and Palos Verdes. It had received recognition in a few lines from the 1963 Beach Boys hit "Surfing USA," and to those lucky souls who lived there, it was Valhalla.

It was the first vacation the Harrises had made in recent memory and the first time any of the boys had seen the big blue. Brent was both bewildered by its immensity and beguiled by its beauty and mysteriousness.

Cloistered in the rugged mountains of Wyoming, the ocean, the surfing, the beach, the volleyball, and the girls were all part of a new world Brent had never even thought about. Brent was seventeen at the time and was just coming to the realization of what girls were all about. He'd had a couple of girlfriends in Wyoming, nothing serious, but he noticed that these California girls were something much different. They seemed all to be tan, slender, athletic, beautiful, and most of them seemed to be blonde. It was a jaw-dropping observation.

The two-week stay introduced Brent to a new dimension where activities abounded all year round.

Kent Layton, a distant cousin Brent had never met before, had become a national champion surfer. He found his niche in surfing at about the same age that Brent began riding horses. Kent had initially competed locally. He did well and was discovered and recruited for Jacobs surf team in Hermosa Beach. Jacobs sponsored Kent in contests all over the world, including big-wave riding in Northern California, Peru, and Hawaii.

Some of those who knew Kent best believed him to be an old seafaring man reincarnated in a young body. He just seemed to know the sea. With just a few pieces of weather information, Kent had the uncanny ability to sense when a storm was on its way, accurately estimate the size of the swell and the direction, determine where the best waves would be found, and figure out the best time to hit the water based on tide cycle.

Kent was two years older than Brent. By Kent's thinking, Brent had two weeks in Manhattan Beach; and when he returned to the mountains of Wyoming, Brent would be a competent, if not accomplished, wave rider.

Kent couldn't have found a better student, and Brent couldn't have had a better instructor. Kent explained the dynamics of surfing and the perils. He was remarkably patient for such a competitive surfer.

While most surfers at the beach were riding short boards, Kent lent Brent a longboard. It didn't turn as quickly, but it was far more stable, faster, and easier to paddle through the breaks. The longboard was one additional tool that Kent employed to smite his fellow competitors many a time: "You can get awesome nose rides!" This was something rarely done on the short boards.

Brent, for whatever reason, took to the sea and was enchanted with surfing from his very first excursion. He was quick to learn the physical demands and surfing basics under the tutelage of Kent, making the experience more fun for both of them.

Everyone wants to excel at a new sport, but Brent had some things going for him that others just didn't. He was strong, focused, determined, exceptionally coordinated, and being from an area six thousand feet higher than sea level, he had incredible stamina. There is one other attribute Brent was gifted with that accelerated training, and Kent recognized it immediately, for it was part of his spiritual structure—Brent embraced the sea. He felt enormously comfortable in the ocean, and as it did Kent, the sea accepted him.

The Harris family spent fourteen days in Manhattan Beach. Brent surfed twelve of those days and not for just a few hours in the morning before the wind blew the waves out. He was in the water when the sun came up and didn't get out until the meatball flag was hoisted on the lifeguard towers signaling the end of surfing for the day. It was a good thing too. Brent had no wetsuit, and at a chilly sixty-one-degree water temperature, plus the windchill factor, there's no telling how close he came to succumbing to hypothermia every day.

The activities weren't over when the flag went up either. Kent introduced Brent to volleyball, sand court style, open-water swimming, and the perfect conclusion for the end of an exciting day at the beach—cruising the strand on bikes—from Redondo Pier to El Segundo on a bike path hugging the beach. Wyoming, for all its natural magnificence and serenity, had nothing to compare it with, and no one would be attacked by a grizzly on the strand.

Twenty-One Miles Across the Sea

Late July 1998
Catalina Island, California

One of the two days Brent didn't surf was spent on a day trip to Catalina Island, twenty-one miles from Long Beach, the point of departure. Brent was awestruck during the ride over on a small passenger ship. He had never seen such an immense body of water. Certainly, Jackson Lake just north of the town of Jackson, Wyoming, was enormous; but by Brent's reckoning, it was a pond. The Pacific Ocean—he'd never seen such vast blueness—filled the horizons.

When the boat landed in Avalon Harbor on the lee side of Catalina, the family's plan was to fall in the mode of tourists and do tourist stuff. They couldn't keep Brent out of the water, though. He'd borrowed a mask, snorkel, and fins; and because Kent volunteered to be his diving buddy, Ron agreed to let him snorkel in Avalon Bay.

The water was sixty-three degrees, and though neither Brent nor Kent wore a wetsuit, the two-degree change was an improvement. Water temperature notwithstanding, Brent was mesmerized by the beauty of a new world below the waterline. The water clarity was nearly thirty feet, which allowed Brent to enjoy the panorama of this exciting world and explore the bottom formations and sea life.

They donned their equipment, entered the water, and cruised northeast from Avalon. Kent gave Brent a "follow me" sign and then dove toward the base of a submerged cliff structure. He pointed out crevices in the cliffs and tunnels bored into rock formations. Then he pointed to the surface. They both ascended. Kent lifted his mask and spat his mouthpiece out. They treaded water for a moment.

Kent explained, "You can pull some nice lobsters out of some of those holes, but you can also piss off some pretty big moray eels. And unlike most other animals, Morays don't release after they get a hold of you—they'll hang on. Sometimes you'll come upon a big ol' lobster just sitting near the opening of his hole. That's the time you need to start looking around. Those are usually guarded by the neighborhood eels."

"Well, how do you tell the difference in the holes so you don't get bit?"

"I leave them alone and order lobster off the menu."

Good advice.

They spent nearly two hours snorkeling and swam as far north as Descanso Bay, a bit less well visited with better sea life. They explored the underwater sights, and then Kent signaled a return to Avalon.

Now heading south, they swam just off the point marking the north end of Avalon Harbor. It was at that time that Brent had the most uncanny feeling he was being followed. He heard whistling and a strange series of clicking for the past several moments, and it seemed to be getting louder. He had no idea what it might be. He looked around and initially saw nothing. He was about to tap Kent's leg when the biggest fish he'd ever seen popped up right beside him.

His initial reaction was to suck in a lungful of seawater but realized at once there was no evil intent in this fish, which he finally realized was no fish at all. It was something he remembered from the color photos of a *National Geographic*. He couldn't name it immediately. His thinking after the fright was a bit jumbled—he wasn't quite right—he'd taken quite a shock. When he regained his composure, he was finally able to properly identify this animal as a dolphin, *or was it a porpoise?* He looked beyond the dolphin and had his second shock of the day. There, not thirty feet away, swimming at different depths but cruising about the same speed, must have been fifteen other dolphins.

The nearest one was within arm's reach. Brent slowly extended his hand to touch it, and in half a dozen powerful thrusts of the dolphin's tail, he and his entire pod had accelerated outside Brent's view.

Brent was amazed and finally touched Kent's leg and pointed up.

Excited, Brent removed his mouthpiece and started to describe what just happened, but he was so excited he got a mouthful of seawater. While he coughed and spat, Kent nodded. "I saw them. A pod of Pacific bottlenose. They're common to this area. There's good fishing here. They're good to have around when you're snorkeling or surfing. They hate sharks. There have been a lot of stories of surfers and swimmers being surrounded by sharks, and the dolphins drive them off. Don't know why they seem so interested in protecting us, but they do."

Kent fitted his snorkel mouthpiece, lowered his head, and continued swimming to the point.

Brent was still trying to grasp what had just happened and realized Kent was ten yards ahead of him. Brent lowered his head and swam a bit faster to catch Kent. Brent was replaying the whole event when he realized the clicking noises had returned and seemed to be getting louder. This time, he spun his head left and aft and had a visual on what he thought was the same dolphin slowly closing the distance. For a time, the dolphin maintained position and simply looked him over.

Brent returned his gaze. He became so entranced with the intensity and the intelligence in the dolphin's eyes Brent couldn't break his eye contact if he wanted to. He was utterly and completely awestruck. There was such an all-consuming depth of curiosity and a powerful sense of kindness that Brent had trouble remembering he was looking into the eyes of a dolphin. Brent had never seen such intelligence and awareness in any other animal—not his horse, not Thunder, not his two very smart Australian sheepdogs—not anything.

He lost track of time, but this contact could not have lasted more than a moment.

And then the event of a lifetime took place. The dolphin swam slightly closer. Brent couldn't resist the invitation. He extended his arm and gently stroked the right flank of this gorgeous beast—from just above the right pectoral fin, down his flank to his fluke. There was neither panic nor annoyance in the dolphin's actions. He seemed to accept the touch. The dolphin took one last look directly into Brent's eyes, accelerated, and rolled left. He was out of sight in seconds.

Brent almost swallowed his mouthpiece.

When Brent looked forward to find Kent, he noticed Kent was making slow strokes on his back, waiting for Brent to catch up. Brent tried to get control of all the adrenaline in his system and tell Kent what had just happened. Kent beat him to it. "I saw. They don't do that very often. That was a big bull. Musta been nine feet long. He was very interested in you for some reason. You're not dragging any fish along, are you?"

"Kent…he looked at me! I mean, he looked into my eyes, and it felt like he was sorting me out. He was clicking at me…er something. I felt like I was getting x-rayed. I've never felt anything like it. I'm still kinda shaken up."

"He was echolocating, kinda like a sonogram, like sonar on ships. You're lucky. It took me years before I finally got friendly enough with a big bull that he actually let me touch him. Never had that same sensation since. I'll never forget the feeling."

"It was so…so…I don't know how to explain it. It was like first contact with a being from another world!"

"Well…it kinda was, wasn't it? I mean, this isn't our world. We're only guests here!"

With that, Kent pushed his mouthpiece back in, rolled over, and headed for Avalon beach.

Brent was quiet for the fifty-minute trip back to Long Beach harbor. He replayed the entire event several times and couldn't seem to come to grips with the uneasiness it produced. *I got to swim at Catalina. I met a big fish. No big deal, right?*

But it was a big deal. And because of it, something was hovering over him.

Ever since the cutting competition, there had been a tugging at the fringes of his conscious thought. Some deep persistent and penetrating stream of awareness had been trying to break into his thoughts, but to date, nothing clear or profound had breached his consciousness. He had been so focused on the cutting competition, graduation from high school, ranch work, the family's visit to Manhattan Beach, and the persistent, youthful pursuit of fun that he had unknowingly pushed this augury deep into his subconscious. The contact with the dolphin had reenergized and sharpened his awareness. It surrounded him, but it did not break through. It was a festering thing. Always there but always just out of reach.

As Brent stared off at the blue horizon and pondered this experience, his mother appeared next to him, leaning on the ship's safety railing as the ship made the final approach to its dock. Looking deep into her son's eyes, she asked, "Brent, you all right, honey? You haven't put two words together the entire trip back to Long Beach. Are you seasick or something?"

"I'm fine, Mom."

"Well, you looked like you just saw a ghost."

"I'm okay. And it wasn't a ghost, Mom. It was something else."

"Well, what?"

"I'm not sure. I'm still trying to figure it out."

Epiphany

Late July 1998 to October 1998,
Manhattan Beach, California; Etna, Wyoming

The families gathered for a final time in the driveway of their cousins' home in Manhattan Beach, packing the big Ford Expedition SUV and having their last goodbyes. The Harrises, with great fanfare and goodwill, were driven to LA International and deposited in front of the Delta terminal. From there, they boarded a Boeing 737. Three hours later, the tires of their jet squeaked onto the runway at Idaho Falls, Idaho—home again. Back to the realities of their world. Back to Bill, Thunder, Dom, Martha and Heather, the crew, and completely displaced from the thing that had been calling Brent for several days now. But what? He was bewildered.

One sunny and completely cloudless day, Brent sat on the top rail of the arena fence line. Thunder pressed against him and gratefully took bunches of alfalfa from his hand. They looked like two best friends leaning on each other and enjoying the gift of life.

Brent appreciated the company and spoke quietly to Thunder, but his mind was elsewhere.

For weeks now, he continued to grapple with his vaporous phantasm and review the events of his adventure. No one should have had as much fun as he did in those fourteen days. Kent taught him to surf, a sport unequaled to anything he had done before or would likely experience again. He swam in the Pacific Ocean and felt completely at home in the water. These adventures he understood and would stand out as some of the most spiritual, wonderful, and memorable events that had ever happened to him. But the contact with the dolphin was something both profoundly moving and wildly confusing at the same time.

It was an awakening for Brent and appeared to be half of a two-event life experience that had a provocative and weighty effect on him. He had no explanation for it, but he was left with a disturbing and powerful calling for the sea. There was no mistaking that. The second part of his awakening was triggered by his involvement in the training of Thunder under the tutelage of Bill Washakie.

Individually, these events would have been very remarkable and memorable experiences. When considered in toto, it was simply perplexing.

An epiphany was upon him. He could feel it about him. And this time, he let it flow, slowly at first but growing stronger each passing moment. This thought, this phantasm, finally materialized like a bolt from the blue. With acute clarity, a spiritual oracle was suddenly cast about him—a clear and powerful intrusion into Brent's awareness.

Was it divine intervention or the sudden internal realization of something very important and critical to Brent's life, his calling in life? The source of the clarion call was not clear to Brent, but the message was unmistakable—Brent was called to the sea, and in some capacity not fully understood at this point, he believed he was destined to work with, train, and help animals.

He saw no overlap, no common ground, and no indelible con-joining path that would allow him to achieve or actualize what he believed to be his destiny, his *calling*. But in this magnificent clear day in early autumn 1998, shortly after graduation at the age of seventeen, he decided to enlist in the Navy.

Maybe, Brent thought, *the Navy would get me back to the sea and, somehow, to my calling.*

Hitching Up

October 1998
Star Valley, Wyoming

It was a tough sell. Jean had a vision of all the family living on and working the ranch happily ever after. Ron would have just been happy to keep the boys in the employment of the ranching enter-prise, or at least keep his sons in the same locale; he was a bit more realistic than Jean.

But Brent sometimes had a streak of stubbornness that eclipsed that of his father. Brent knew what he wanted to do, and no amount of logic, dialogue, or pleading would alter that goal. After weeks of discussion and not a few bursts of tears from Jean, they both con-sented to, if not endorsed, Brent's decision to enlist in the US Navy.

In October 1998, accompanied by Ron, Brent signed the recruiting contract for four years of active-duty service with the United States Navy at the Navy Recruiting Office in Idaho Falls, Idaho. Within a few days, Brent received orders in the mail to report to the basic training facility at Navy Station Great Lakes, Illinois— *boot camp.* Brent believed this was a waypoint, a stepping stone in some grand scheme that would ultimately allow him to reach his calling, whatever that might be.

Boot Camp

October 1998
Basic training facility, boot camp, Navy Station Great Lakes, Illinois

The sting of approaching winter was in the air when Brent reported for duty in October 1998. He was one of seventy-eight young men forming the new boot camp class. The recruits were different in size, shape, color, and of varied backgrounds, some with accents so strong Brent occasionally had to struggle to understand them.

If there was one constant in the mishmash mixture of recruits, it was the shock of their new environment and the persistent grumbling. Not all were so vocal, but those who accepted their new home without fussing were outnumbered by those who did not. The complaining, the whimpering, the bitching were all new to Brent. He'd never seen so many young men whine so much about so little. Sure, the temperatures were a bit robust in late autumn. Certainly, the 0520 reveille and 2200 lights-out call made for a long day for some. No question that the physical training and conditioning routine was hard on those who had spent their previous lives perched in front of a computer monitor, and without argument, the temperature on the exercise field and water temperature in the training tanks weren't the balmy conditions of the waters off Key West. But for Brent, everything at boot camp was easier than life on the ranch. In fact, comparatively speaking, it was a vacation from the chores, long days, and sometimes brutal weather conditions at the Harris Ranch.

Brent excelled in the training program. In the academic, military, and physical syllabi, he consistently scored at the top of his class. The course instructors also noticed he had unwittingly taken on a leadership role within his class of nearly eighty recruits. This was unusual because he was one of the youngest men in the company and had not been formally assigned to any position of leadership by the course instructors for that reason. He had been quiet, unobtrusive, followed directions, and had done well in all graded areas. Perhaps, much like herding animals, the young men in his class saw in him strength and wisdom far beyond his years—a quiet winner, a young man with inner strength. Many gathered around Brent for his guidance, counsel, and for some, to successfully survive boot camp.

His standings in the class and his peculiar unassuming leadership attributes drew the attention of the WARCOM scouts—the snake-eaters from Naval Special Warfare Command. Several Sea, Air, Land (SEAL) and Special Warfare Combatant Craft Crewmen (SWCC) senior chief petty officers routinely scouted, interviewed, and recruited the cream of the crop for WARCOM, the command overseeing both the SEALs and SWCCs. When Brent was directed to meet with two senior enlisted personnel one day, he immediately thought he had hosed something up. After five minutes with two very rough individuals who looked like they had just eaten tuna sandwiches, can and all, Brent was first relieved then excited. He had been courted to join the WARCOM SPECOPs warriors.

The missions, training, and the responsibilities of both the SEAL and the SWCC teams were presented to Brent. He had, of course, heard of the SEALs. Like every other red-blooded American kid, he had seen the 1990 movie *Navy SEALs* staring Charlie Sheen and knew, in broad strokes, of their mission, but the SWCC thing was quite new to him. Where the SEALs' mission is to "conduct, at the tactical level, small-unit maritime military operations often with strategic effects," the mission of the SWCCs was to "support special operations missions, focused on clandestine infiltration and exfiltration of SEALs and other special operations forces; and provide dedicated, rapid mobility and combat support in shallow water areas."

Brent was given several days to consider his options (and his future) before choosing which warfare specialty he preferred: SEALs or SWCCs. After three days of deep consideration and for reasons not immediately clear, he chose the SWCC warfare specialty and signed the papers committing himself to the SWCC community upon graduation from Navy boot camp.

Graduation was anticlimactic following the meeting with the snake-eaters. After that ego-boosting interview with the SEAL and SWCC chief petty officers, anything would be. On a blustery day in late November 1998, Brent graduated from boot camp, was advanced to seaman (E-3), and was handed orders to report to Navy Amphibious Base Coronado, California, for thirteen weeks of Basic Crewman Training (BCT)—the first of several schools that would allow him to earn the prestigious *SWCC* designation.

Brent was given ten days of leave. He traveled back to the ranch to spend time with his family before he reported to COMNAVSPECWARCOM to begin BCT. His family, Bill, Thunder, Dom, Martha, Heather, and the ranch hands were very glad to see him, but there was no special treatment, no quarter, and no breaks—there were fences to mend, barns to clean, and animals to take care of. It was good to be home.

Brent was still torn between a deep commitment to stay with his family and the exhilarating anticipation to begin SWCC training. But by the end of his ten-day leave period, he was ready to head to his new assignment. His parents, his brothers, Bill, Dom, even Thunder looked at him as though they might never see him again, and in truth, that was a possibility, considering the Navy's special forces missions and operating environments. It was tough to go, but the pull of the next adventure was a powerful force.

Special Warfare Combatant Craft

December 1998 to Thursday, 16 September 2001
Special Boat Team TWELVE, Navy Amphibious Base, Coronado, California

Where boot camp was a walk in the park, BCT was a three-month struggle in a man-made hell. Nearly 60 percent of the hand-selected candidates opted out or were released due to mental fatigue, emotional issues, physical injuries, or lack of mettle. It could have been the strenuous physical routines, the frigid winter water temperatures in San Diego, the mental pressure laid on by the instructors, or the enormously high demands for performance in every course that drove much of his class to consider other less-demanding jobs in the

Navy. And to be honest, there were times—wet, shivering, exhausted, hungry, sand-encrusted, and yes, frightened—that even Brent toyed with the idea of DORing (dropping on request). But two powerful forces would not allow him to yield to the concept of quitting. The first was the horror of admitting failure to his father. The second would be tantamount to casting aside his dream, his calling. And although he still couldn't quite grasp what that might be, he couldn't shake the belief that the SWCC assignment was his gateway to it.

Brent figured out early in the program that the instructors could make it very difficult, but they could not make a trainee quit—only the trainee made that decision. For Brent, quitting was not an option. Like every other challenge in his life, he only had to gut through the hard times to be successful. There were no special points for looking cool or getting close to graduating.

It seemed like a lifetime after arriving at Amphibious Base Coronado, much of it a completely fuzzy memory, that Brent Harris, with twenty-two other enlisted personnel, became members of a very small and very special group of warriors.[19] They were designated Special Warfare Combatant Craft Crewmen[20] (SWCC) and assigned to Special Boat Unit TWELVE in Coronado. It was something of a lifetime achievement and a very proud accomplishment for Brent.

The Fork in the Road

Thursday, 16 August 2001
Navy Amphibious Base, Coronado

Brent continued to stare at his at his dress shoes. He had a decision to make, the right decision. Those two experiences in his younger years—his adventure with Thunder and then contact with the dolphin during the Catalina trip—had profoundly changed his life. He'd joined the Navy and was then inducted into the black arts of Navy special warfare at the tender age of seventeen because of his affinity for the sea. Now, three years later, he was wrestling with the reality of leaving his boat team brothers to herd a bunch of big fish around.

Brent thought hard and deeply, *I've come pretty far for a dumb cowboy. I never thought I'd get off the ranch. And now, just when I thought life couldn't get any better, I've got a big decision to make… maybe the biggest of my life. I only get to do this once, so I better make the right decision the first time.*

CHAPTER 5

EXORDIUM

For the animal shall not be measured by man. In a world older and more complete than ours they move finished and complete, gifted with extensions of the senses we have lost or never attained, living by voices we shall never hear. They are not brethren, they are not underlings; they are other nations, caught with ourselves in the net of life and time, fellow prisoners of the splendor and travail of the earth.

—Henry Beston, *The Outermost House*

Leaving the Team

Thursday, 16 August 2001
Naval Amphibious Base, Coronado, California

Thursday arrived, and with it, Brent's meeting with Master Chief Madrigal—the moment Brent had fretted and worried over for the past two days. But at the time of delivering his decision to the master chief, it was neither as painful as he expected nor as gratifying as he'd hoped.

It was later that the impact of the decision set in. It was then that he began to feel thoroughly horrible. Horrible because he sensed he was letting his boat-team brothers down, horrible because he knew he'd miss the action and the camaraderie that can only be experienced in a tight-knit combat team such as a Special Boat Unit, and horrible because despite all the emotional signals, logical arguments, and quiet belief that the Navy Marine Mammal Program may have something to do with his destiny, way down deep, he just wasn't sure it was the right decision.

It had nothing to do with Brent's concern for the risks faced daily by the Special Boat Unit operators. In the two years he'd been assigned to SBU-12 he'd been deployed to WESTPAC[21] twice, totaling fourteen months and on varied detachments for another five months of training and work-up deployments INCONUS.[22] None of it would be considered low risk.

He'd been in Korea working with the South Korean Marines and naval small boat crews, in the Philippines supporting members of the Philippine Armed Forces and in training missions with NAVSOG—the Philippine SEAL teams. In a few cases, the unit got more than they bargained for.

In accordance with the status of forces agreement and under Philippine law, US forces were not allowed to engage in direct combat. SBU-12's personnel were to provide training and support to NAVSOG only and narrowly focused on counterinsurgency and counterterrorism training during sea and riverine interdiction missions in and around Basilan Island, in the Philippine province of Mindanao.

When NAVSOG intelligence discovered that elements of the Philippine terrorist organization Abu Sayyaf were in the area, it was a surprise to no one that several heavy firefights, direct action (DA) engagements, resulted. Brent, on one such lethal exchange, manned the .50-caliber machine gun aboard an RHIB (rigid-hulled inflatable boat). During the engagement, he did not flinch or wilt under heavy fire. He stood with his brothers and poured hundreds of rounds of fire at targets on the beach, wounding and killing an unknown number of Abu Sayyaf terrorists. When the terrorists retreated into the jungle, they left weapons, blood trails, and body parts. Two of the boat-team members and three of the NAVSOG SEALs were wounded.

A highly classified after-action report was submitted, but owing to the sensitivity of the operation and the conditions of the status of forces agreement, no citations were written, no Purple Hearts were awarded. In fact, post-mission debriefs from men wearing sunglasses and Cabela's safari outfits strongly recommended the whole encounter be quickly forgotten—read, *never discussed.*

Brent at first didn't know what to think. He was all of twenty years old, and this was his first combat experience. He was concerned with the fact that he had so little empathy for those he killed, a blight, he thought, on his Christian upbringing. Had the Abu Sayyaf members not been trying to inflict harm upon his brothers and the NAVSOG SEALs, he rationalized, he may have harbored some semblance of guilt. But as it was, he felt little compassion for those dead or wounded on the beach.

It wasn't until days later that one of the boat crew gave him the impact count on the armor plate protecting him on the .50-caliber: twenty-three. Nearly two dozen rounds came within inches of changing his world, maybe ending it.

Huh! Didn't need to know that, Brent thought to himself. *And my parents* really *don't need to know that!*

There was the second realization that disturbed him. At the time of the firefight, he wasn't scared. When the first several rounds lit off, he fell back on hundreds of hours of training, weeks of intense conditioning at the hands of the Navy Special Operations instructors, and endless sessions of combat simulations and scenarios. The action against the Abu Sayyaf force seemed to be in slow motion: things were utterly clear, and his actions completely under control.

There were two powerful forces in conflict: bad guys firing at his team from the beach and good guys, his brothers, laying down fire from the boats. He had several moments of perfect clarity of mind and body, and in that time, he did his job and helped his teammates stay alive.

No, it wasn't fear that pushed him to the NMMP, and he tried to convince himself that he wasn't a quitter. The one unwavering, powerful calling to the mammal program was the unshakable belief that it was his destiny—or the portal to it.

Checking In

Friday, 31 August 2001
Navy Special Clearance Team ONE (NSCT-1), Naval Amphibious Base

The events following that fateful meeting with Master Chief Madrigal happened so fast Brent's head hurt. He had written orders in hand a week later and was to report to Navy Special Clearance Team ONE (NSCT-1) on Friday, 31 August 2001, for further assignment to Foxtrot Platoon, a.k.a. MK 7 mine-hunting dolphins.

This entire ordeal took a short fifteen days following his meeting with Master Chief Madrigal. In Brent's experience, nothing in the Navy happened that fast unless it was something bad. Brent prayed that he had made the right decision.

Brent rolled his truck into a parking place close to the duty office at NSCT-1, aboard Naval Amphibious Base, Coronado. He opened the door, grabbed his training and personnel records, set his white Dixie cover precisely in place, closed the truck door, and headed for the NSCT-1 duty office.

Once in the office, he removed his cover and introduced himself to a sharp, slim first class petty officer sitting at the duty desk. The first class stood, reached across the desk, and offered his hand. "Petty Officer Brent Harris, yep, we heard you were coming, and the command master chief, Master Chief Murphy, he's an explosive ordnance type, wanted to see you first thing." He explained apologetically, "Master Chief Murphy spends a couple of days every month working with the teams at Mobile Unit 3. He knows you'll be assigned to Foxtrot Platoon, but he wants to meet all the personnel checking into units belonging to NCST-1. He's down at Mobile Unit 3 right now. You know where that is, right?"

"Yes, right near SBU-12. I know it well."

"Great. They do some valuable cross-training with Mobile Team THREE. They run the MK 5 sea lions and the MK 6 dolphins and sea lions, but the scuttlebutt is, the master chief has a friend there," the first class said with a sly wink.

Too much info. None of my business, thought Brent, but said, "MK 5 and MK 6? I'm not smart on the terms."

"No worries. You'll get a full brief on the entire Marine Mammal Program after you get settled into Foxtrot Platoon. The master chief will tell you all about it."

"Hope it makes more sense than it does now."

"It will. Don't worry."

"Okay, so I'm headed to see Master Chief Murphy at Mobile Unit 3."

"You got it."

It was a three-minute drive from NSCT-1 to Mobile Unit 3. Ordinarily, he would have walked the distance, but Brent had all his records in his truck, and he didn't want to chance misplacing anything.

Brent climbed into his 1978 Ford F100 pickup and cranked it up. It was not just any pickup. From the exterior, the truck looked original in all respects. But under the hood sat the mighty 1967 Ford Fairlane GTA 390 V8, packing a whopping 440 horsepower. This was the mechanical artwork of Brent's older brother Kurt and the ranch mechanic, Bob Wilson. It had been a working truck on the ranch for years and was given to Brent as a going-away gift when he left for San Diego. To Brent, it was a bit of an heirloom; but to car guys, it was an eye-catching example of rolling Detroit muscle and never failed to turn heads as he cruised through the streets of Coronado.

He parked his pickup in a small parking lot a block away from Mobile Unit 3, grabbed his records, and headed for the security gate on the dock. If he needed any verification that he was headed in the right direction, the bouquet of animal excrement and the sonnet of barking sea lions were the clues. Even upwind, it smelled like an upended outhouse and sounded like free weenie day at a dog show. *This is going to take some getting used to*, Brent said to himself.

A fit and well-tanned young man saw Brent walk down the brow to the security gate. The young man opened the gate and ushered Brent onto the pier. There could not have been more contrast in

the attire. Brent was every bit a poster boy for the Navy in his impec-
cable Navy Tropical White Longs, highly polished black low-quarter
inspection dress shoes, and topped off by his shipshape white Dixie-
cup cover.

The young man at the gate smiled. He seemed quite comfort-
able in khaki shorts, a T-shirt, and flip-flops. "Welcome aboard!
You must be that Bob guy from the boat unit, right? Master Chief
Murphy said to keep a lookout for you."

Brent stepped through the gate and returned the smile and
extended his hand. "It's Brent, and yep, that would be me."

"Welcome aboard. I'm Phil Hamilton, one of the sea lion handlers. Follow me. We'll go find Master Chief Murphy. And don't step
in any sea lion poo. I'm washing it down, but damn, they seem to be
able to crap faster'n I can clean it up."

Brent, eyes on the back of Phil's head, hadn't taken four steps
when—*squish*—he managed to locate the only sea lion guano within
fifty feet.

"Damn!" Brent said aloud as he inspected his shoe.

Phil spun around. "Oh, jeez, Bob. Based on the size of it and
the partially digested fish heads, I'd say that was Gabby's. He's a one-
man shitting machine, and I'm sorry to say, he's mine. But I love him
to death. Sorry about that!"

"My fault. I'll look better next time! You have a hose around
here?"

"Yep. Right down the dock. We'll get that hosed off and then
track down your CMC. Have you met the master chief yet, Bob?"

"It's Brent, and nope, not yet, but when I went to Team ONE,
they told me I could find him here."

"Oh yeah! Well, you have a treat in store. He only visits here a
couple of times a month, but the guys here think the world of him,
and Duffus loves him. Sometimes, when I can't find the master chief,
I just wait a few minutes, and I'll hear him."

What the heck is this guy talking about? Brent had barely completed that thought when a deep baritone voice thundered, "Duffus,
you get over here and get this dam ball off the dock!"

Sure would hate to be Duffus, Brent thought.

"Told ya we'd find him." Phil grinned and pointed.

Twenty yards beyond a storage unit, Brent saw the biggest black man not in an NFL uniform he'd ever seen in his life. Check that, he was the biggest *man* he'd ever seen in his life. And next to him—leaning on him, in fact—was a very large sea lion. *Duffus, I'll bet.*

An XXL T-shirt (still a little snug), boondockers without socks, and a pair of khaki UDT shorts stretched to the limit at the hem, all topped off with a Navy baseball hat adorned with a master chief's insignia was the uniform of the day.

"Master," Phil hollered and walked toward the chief, "this here's the new guy from your Foxtrot Platoon. His name's Bob something."

"It's Petty Officer Brent Harris, Master Chief. Pleasure to meet you, sir!"

The master chief took his unlit cigar from his lips and smiled broadly. He looked like Arnold Schwarzenegger in his prime, not an ounce of fat on him anywhere. He extended his hand. It completely enveloped Brent's, and for just a moment, Brent had visions of his hand in a cast. Despite the calluses and wide girth of the master chief's hand, the shake was firm but gentle.

"Jessie Murphy. Welcome aboard, son. Heard a lot about you from Master Chief Madrigal, a fine man. All good stuff. Thanks for hoofing it down here, but you didn't really need to report in Tropical Whites. Around here, that's considered high risk."

On closer inspection, the master chief spied Brent's offending shoe. "Looks like you already met with Gabby. You can always tell. His crap smells like rotten fish. And this here"—the master chief made a half-turn and pointed to the large sea lion leaning against his right thigh—"is Duffus. This boy is full of tricks, so watch yourself."

The sea lion rocked side to side on his front flippers, and much to Brent's total surprise, his eyes squinted at the corners, and his mouth turned up.

Brent astonished. "Is he actually smiling?"

"Yeah. He thinks he's a ton of fun!"

"And he leans against you?"

"It's a sign of friendship or some such malarkey. It's their way of showing affection. But notice he doesn't look at me. He looks the other way. Not really sure why he does that, but I think it's to be inconspicuous. It would be un-sea-lion-like to lean against somebody and actually look at them too. It just isn't done in their social circle."

A wide grin sprouted on Brent's face, and he just shook his head.

"Well, let's head up to the visitor office, and I'll give you the pitch."

Brent stepped aside and made way for the master chief but then paused for Duffus, who fell in right behind the chief and waddled up the brow.

Brent, for a moment, rubbed the back of his neck and looked around. *I stepped in a big pile of sea lion poo, met the biggest man I'd ever seen in my life, and was just introduced to a big Labrador disguised as a sea lion. This has been the strangest hour of my life. This assignment is going to be the most fun or the worst in my career. Maybe both.*

Brent and Phil followed the master chief and Duffus. Still smiling, Brent asked Phil, "Aren't there rules or something against letting sea lions wander around the pier?"

"Oh, I'm sure there are. Must be dozens of them—Navy regs and federal rules, but Murphy's a bit of a God in the EOD and NMMP communities, and no one that I know of has ever brought that up. But I think it would be a great idea if you mentioned it to him. I'll watch!"

Phil went his own way, and Brent caught up with the master chief and Duffus as they entered a spare office.

Brent noticed a sign tacked to the doorframe, "Visiting VIP Office." The truth was, nobody but the visiting master chief used it, which explained all the EOD and NMMP photos posted about the bulkheads. Brent finally unscrambled the mystery of the CMC at large.

Master Chief Murphy was the command master chief of Naval Clearance Team ONE, and Team ONE was the senior ranking command over four units: the Unmanned Underwater Vehicle Platoon, the Dive Platoons (mine and obstacle clearance teams), the Special Warfare Combatant Craft Platoon, and Brent's new unit—Foxtrot Platoon. It was becoming quite clear that Master Chief Murphy was a hands-on, lead-from-the-front kind of chief. He took the health, safety, welfare, morale, and professional development of the enlisted personnel in his own command, NSCT-1, as well as the four units under NSCT, very seriously and very personally. What Brent did not know at the time but would soon discover was that Murphy made weekly visits to all the units. Although Mobile Unit 3 was of equal stature to, and not within the direct chain of command of NSCT-1, the master chief was well received there also.

Brent was the third one through the doorway just after Duffus, who seemed to think he and the senior-ranking noncommissioned officer shared the office. Duffus sat right beside the door and took a sentry duty pose. Brent made a supreme effort not to laugh in deference to the sea lion, who was taking his post quite seriously.

The master chief slid into his chair carefully. It creaked and gave all the signs of being on the verge of an overstress. "Have a seat, son."

Brent caught sight of an old wooden chair, possibly a remnant of WWII, which fit in perfectly with the rest of the decor.

"'Scuze the furniture. We're way down the food chain as far as budgets go. Most of the funding we get goes into important stuff: our boats, diving gear, equipment for the troops, but mostly things we need to perform the mission and keep our animals healthy, happy, and safe. I don't know how much you understand about the Navy Marine Mammal Program missions or the organization. It can get mighty confusing, especially when you try to sort out the various 'systems,' so let me try to make it simple for you. Explosive Ordnance Group ONE, based right here at the Gator base, is the reporting senior for both Mobile Unit 3 and our command, Navy Special Clearance Team ONE. These two commands are the operational units for all the Navy's mammals. There are other units that train both the sea lions and the dolphins, but Team ONE and Unit THREE are the only *operational* units. Your orders assign you to Foxtrot Platoon, what is also called *mammal platoon*, and that reports to Navy Special Clearance Team ONE. With me so far?"

"Yes, sir!"

"Good, because it's about to get confusing. Foxtrot Platoon operates three systems—all Atlantic bottlenose dolphins. The MK 4 dolphins are specialized in locating, identifying, and marking teth-ered sea mines. The MK 8 dolphins are trained to identify safe cor-ridors for ships to travel through. They come in real handy during amphibious operations. I'm assigning you to the MK 7 system. These are the dolphins specialized in locating, identifying, and marking buried and moored mines on the seafloor. This is a tough job for both the handlers and their dolphins. You'd be amazed at how hard the dolphins work."

"Two questions, Master Chief."

"Go!"

"These are wartime missions. What do we do when we're not at war?"

"Fair question. We train. We train, and we recover practice mines the Air Force bombers and the Navy TACAIR[23] boys drop for training and for their mission certifications. This gives us real-world training and saves the Navy and Air Force millions in reusable, very expensive practice ordnance. Your second question?"

"You mentioned I'd be getting a dolphin. Am I assigned to one yet?"

"Not yet. I have one in mind, but I want to see how you do first. You'll be under training for several months just learning the ropes and the routine. In a couple of weeks, you'll be sent to SPAWAR[24] Systems Center at Pier 159 to get your MK 7 dolphin-handler certifi-cation. Now, Mobile Unit 3 owns both the MK 5 and MK 6 systems and is responsible for the mine recovery and swimmer-defense stuff. What you'll see there is a bunch of working sea lions and dolphins. The MK 5 sea lions do the mine detection and recovery mission. Basically, they mark and help recover anything on the bottom with an acoustic beacon, a *pinger*, that we want to get back. That leaves the sea lions and dolphins in the MK 6 swimmer defense system. They do the force protection mission. Still with me?"

"I think I got it."

"Good. This will all make sense when you get settled in. Let me change the subject a little. The OIC[25] of Foxtrot Platoon, Lieutenant Mike Heinrichs, reported aboard about eighteen months ago after his assignment as the XO of one of the minesweepers. I was EOD[26] and loved the job, but I truly like what we're doing at Team ONE better. You'll find an odd assortment of sailors assigned. Each has a different Navy experience and come from rates and warfare specialties across the board. They have two things in common, though: they're totally dedicated to their job, and they like the animals.

"Maybe it's a bit late in finding this out, but you won't make pay grade very fast here. Advancements are pretty slow. We're kind of tucked away on the periphery of Navy missions. We're not strategic, don't show up on many OPLAN TPFDDs,[27] aren't the tip of the spear, and the only press we get is when some well-meaning but confused animal group goes on a crusade to try and shut us down. You're one of a few special ops guys on board, and I hope you won't be too disappointed, but you won't be able to kill anybody here... unless I say you can."

"I won't be disappointed, Master. Morting bad guys is way overrated."

"That, it is! If I remember right, your personnel jacket seems to indicate you were raised on a horse ranch in Wyoming. You ever do any bronc bustin'?"

Not wanting to put too much personal information out, Brent simply responded, "Some, Master. But we don't break our horses, sir. We train them."

A smile broke out on the master chief's wide face. "Uh-huh! Commander Lear and your old master chief at the boat unit gave you high marks and were clearly cranky with me 'cause they think I stole you away. Said you made E-5 in two years, and you were well on your way to getting skipper certified on the combat RHIBs. They told me you demonstrated"—the chief looked down at his notes—"extraordinary leadership traits and had a natural inclination for taking charge. That true?"

"Ah...I think they were being overly kind, Master Chief. I felt at home with the team out on the water. I just tried to do my job, sir."

"Well, maybe they got the wrong guy, but they also said during the little scuffle around Basilan Island, which will remain forever locked in the annals of things that didn't really happen, you showed some serious courage on the fifty." The chief paused for a moment, awaiting a response from Brent. When he didn't get one, he continued, "So…I've got a question for you, son."

"Yes, sir!"

"Why'd you leave the boat teams and join up with us?"

That was as direct a question as he'd ever been asked, and despite that, Brent was not prepared to answer it. He looked at the overhead and thought for a long moment, trying to carefully shape an answer. Finally, throwing caution to the wind, he went to the fallback position and responded with the truth. "Because I like animals, Master Chief!"

"Brent, your SWCC warfare specialty and boat-handling skills are going to be big juju here. We need a guy who knows the water, knows how to navigate, how to communicate, won't get frazzled when things go to shit, and someone who knows their way around big animals. You think you're the right guy?"

"I'm here, Master Chief, and I'd sure like the chance to find out."

Slowly, the master chief gathered himself and stood; the chair creaked from the sudden unloading. Brent thought he was going to put his head through the overhead.

"You'll do fine here, son! I think you found a home. Now let's head back over to Team ONE and meet Lieutenant Heinrichs." He then turned to his sentinel and hollered, "Duffus, gate!"

Brent stood, grabbed his cover, and asked, "Does he really understand what you're saying?"

The master chief smiled and replied with a wink and a single word, "Watch!"

Duffus grinned his toothy grin then waddled through the hatch and headed down the gangway for the security gate. The master chief and Brent followed.

At the gate, the master chief said softly, "You can't go with us, Duffus. Stay here!"

Brent followed the master chief through the security gate headed for the parking lot and then happened to glace over his shoulder at Duffus. Duffus looked completely befuddled, and if Brent didn't know better, he could have sworn the big sea lion's eyes were streaming with tears.

Foxtrot Platoon

Friday, 31 August 2001
Foxtrot Platoon, Pier 40, Sub Base, Point Loma, California

They took separate cars but arrived at Pier 40 within a minute of each other. This was Brent's second look at his new command, Foxtrot Platoon. He took a closer look this time. He wasn't expecting the Holiday Inn; he was Navy and used to the spartan conditions of most of the Navy's shore facilities. But this, even by Navy standards, was pretty sad.

The master chief led the way to the OIC's office and pounded on the doorframe, which was followed by a loud, "Enter!"

The master chief took four long strides across the deck to Lieutenant Heinrichs as he stood and moved around his desk. They greeted each other with handshakes and a hug. Obviously, they had history together.

"This here, Lieutenant, is Special Warfare Boat Operator Second Class Brent Harris."

"Well, welcome aboard, Brent. Boy, are we going to put you to work."

The welcome-aboard meeting with Lieutenant Heinrichs was short but cram-packed with command history, mission, and organization information, profiles on the team and the animals, and very importantly, their expectations of Brent.

With this information passed, Lieutenant Heinrichs got into the inner workings of the command.

"Most of the men that come to us are pretty surprised with what we do, what we expect, and how much of their time is dedicated to their animals. You were assigned to a combat team, a mighty fine one with a long history of accomplishment and sacrifice. You have just joined a *family*. Our history may not be as colorful or exciting as your old unit's, and we don't get many unit citations or combat ribbons, but this team is every bit as dedicated as Boat Unit TWELVE. And you'll find that it's not just loyalty and dedication to our human teammates. We have a lot of dolphins, and each has their own primary and secondary handler. Most of the handlers, the good ones, are with their animals the great part of the day *every day*, and our workday is pretty long. Again, there are exceptions to this, but our star handlers put in at least a twelve-hour day and then come in once or twice on the weekends just to check on their partners.

"It wasn't but a few months ago"—Lieutenant Heinrichs stood, stretched his back, and walked to the window overlooking the dolphin pens—"that one of our sea lions at the Key West det didn't return to the boat following a dive. His handler refused to leave the area. His team called for another boat to assist in a search, and for the next three days, they looked for his sea lion. Finally, one of the divers came up with the sea lion's harness. It had been torn apart by something pretty big. The handler was devastated. He and his animal had been together for nearly four years." Lieutenant Heinrichs gazed at the panorama deep in thought for a moment.

"Hard to believe we can get so damn close, so emotionally attached to these beasts, but…" Heinrichs returned to his seat.

Brent realized his eyes were rimmed in red. Brent side-glanced at the master chief, who had also recognized the lieutenant's discomfort.

"Well, anyway, there are always risks out there. Even when we try to work as safely as we possibly can and mitigate every risk, there's always something out there we don't expect, something that can bite us. Thing of it is, there is no group, no animal park, no agency, or animal rescue association who cares for their marine mammals as well as we do. The master chief and Captain Dave Greer, our army vet, can give you the details, but these animals have a special diet, get a physical at least every six months, see the vet for any medical issues, and while they're deployed, they see the vet or a tech specialist every day. What's more, they get a complete workup, pre- and postdeployment. Both the dolphins and the sea lions here and at Mobile Unit 3 will outlive their counterparts in the wild by five to ten years, and they'll have a far more productive and happy life than any of their equivalents in the animal theme parks."

"Sir," Brent dreaded the question but had to ask, "what do you do when they get older…you know, kinda too old to work."

"Well, now, that's the best part of the story, ain't it, Master?"

"Yep! Wish I was a dolphin here," Master Chief Murphy agreed.

"They live out their lives as comfortable as a South Carolina senator. Right now, we have an old bull dolphin named Makai that Captain Greer thinks is at least forty-one years old. He's a veteran of Vietnam, and if he wore a uniform, he'd be weighted down with ribbons and medals. He can't hear, has difficulty with his echolocation system, and his eyesight is failing. He's no longer an operational *system*, but that son of a gun still lines up every time we bring the boats around to load the animals. Never saw so much heart, so much spirit in any animal. Anyhow, all his plumbing still works, and he's as horny as a two-year-old German shepherd, so we use him when one of the girls is ready. He's surrounded by people who love him, and by gosh, both dolphins and sea lions think he's Elvis reincarnate. He's a rock star with a reputation that should be in history books. Well, that's it in the *Reader's Digest* form. Any questions?"

"Lots, sir, but I wouldn't know where to start."

"One last thing. I have an open-door policy for immediate safety issues, so if you have any of those, you come right in. Everything else, you go through your leading petty officer or the master chief. He runs the place anyhow. He just lets me think I'm in charge. Ain't that right, Master?"

"We both know better than that, sir!"

"Yeah, right! We have a long day in front of us, and I understand you have the weekend duty, so I better let you go get the duty brief from our watch chief petty officer."

Realizing the meeting had come to an end, Brent stood, grabbed his service jacket and cover, and said, "Aye, aye, sir! Thank you."

On the way to meet the watch chief petty officer, Master Chief Murphy gave a short bio of the man who would pass Brent his next orientation brief.

"Special operations chief,[28] a SEAL, John Sebastian is one of your brethren, a true warrior from the snake-eater clan. Two things—don't ask him where he's been 'cause he won't tell you, and don't call him *Johnnie* 'cause he'll kick your ass. Other than that, you're unlikely to find a finer man or a more professional sailor."

"Sebastian…don't think I recognize the name," Brent returned.

"Doesn't surprise me. It's been awhile since he was on the teams and WARCOM,[29] likes to keep any mention of the DEVGRU[30] boys to a minimum. He was one of their shooters once upon a time, pulled several tours in Iran in the early nineties and was there in that meat grinder at the Battle of Mogadishu[31] in October of '93 as one of four SEALS assigned to *Task Force Ranger* as a sniper. I don't know what he did there. I know it bothers him to talk about it, and I know whatever happened must have been pretty impressive. He's got the Navy Cross, three Purple Hearts, and some combat awards that are as rare as an honest politician. I haven't counted them, but I'll bet you he's got more awards and metals than the CNO,[32] and the CNO's a Navy fighter pilot from the 'Nam era."

"I'd like to meet him, Chief."

"You will soon enough. He'll give you the CDO[33] brief."

The master chief led the way to the duty officer's office and leaned through the open hatch. "John, you've got a new watch stander, a boat guy, Petty Officer Brent Harris. Treat him well. I think we're going to need him."

Chief Sebastian appeared at the door wearing shorts, sneakers, and a NSCT-1 T-shirt.

It would be a monumental understatement to say that SOC Sebastian was a most impressive man. Quiet and unassuming, he had the build of an Olympic swimmer crossed with a mountain lion. Usually, guys who worked out as much as this chief obviously did were a bit more loquacious and a lot more self-absorbed. Not this guy. He was all about business.

"Grab a seat and make yourself to home," he said as he waved to a wood chair and took one of his own next to his desk.

The first part of Chief Sebastian's brief was less about process and procedures and more about philosophy and human-animal relationships; and if Brent didn't know better, he could have sworn that Chief Sebastian was reading from Brent's father's book.

"Petty Officer Harris, ordinarily, a new guy just reporting aboard wouldn't have duty on the weekend, the day after he checked in, but you'll see why I gave you the watch tomorrow. You see, weekends around here really aren't. Almost every handler, trainer, and trainee is going to be here over the weekend, maybe not the entire day of both days, but you'll probably see the entire team here at some point.

"Most commands have hardware assigned that allows them to complete their mission and tasks: boats, ships, aircraft, rolling stock, weapons, and such. What *we* have are living, breathing, thinking organisms. They've come to rely on us, and we on them. You can ignore your RHIBs and Humvees and even your airplanes for weeks at a time, and when you hop in them and fire them up, they work just fine. Not so with our dolphins. And this goes for the sea lions over at Mobile Unit 3 as well. They need the basics in life: food, shelter, security, but they also need attention, contact, reinforcement. Every animal has two handlers, a primary and a secondary. The bond that each of us builds with our animal is not something we take lightly. We don't have other people feed, train, swim, or hang out with our animal. They are our responsibility, ours alone, and we try not to confuse them or cause them to lose confidence. You came from the boat teams, so what I'm about to tell you will make sense. You probably have brothers or sisters."

"Yes, sir, three brothers, all older," Brent replied.

"And what did you call your shipmates on the team?"

"Ah...brothers."

"What's the difference between your family brothers and your team brothers?"

A studied pause hung over the conversation. Having never really thought about it, Brent pondered the question and formed the answer as it materialized. "Well, Chief...we had the same father and mother. I guess we had similar life experiences. Mom and Dad kind of formed our work habits, our home culture, our religious beliefs, and we all had so many of the same adventures. I guess you could say we grew up together, and we're all much alike. We're blood"

"What about your teammates? Are you brothers with them too?"

"Well, we call one another *brother*, and the relationship is much stronger than just a friend. I mean, *love* is maybe not the right word, but if *love* means that you'd give your life for someone else, then yeah,

I guess I love my teammates. Since I don't have a better word than *brother* to describe that bond, I guess *brother* is the right word."

"Now, Brent, you said you'd give your life to save your brother. Why?"

"Because, I guess…I know they'd do the same for me."

"Do you see where I'm going with this?"

A respite in the conversation, a mad cognitive scramble to connect all the dots of the discussion, and then—"Are you saying that these dolphins are like our brothers? Surely, you don't think they'd willingly lay down their life for any of us, do you? Why, they don't even understand their own mortality."

"There has been many a case, a few right here in the early years of this command, where dolphins have saved or rescued their handler and, in some cases, humans they'd never even seen before. And to your point that they're unaware of their fragile existence, they know fear, they know threats, and they understand what causes pain. And yet the bond between them and their handler, in many cases, is every bit as strong as those of your teammates."

This put Brent in a bit of a tailspin. It was a complex and confusing discussion. He reflected back on Thunder, Domino, his little pinto, the two Australian shepherds, Martha and Heather, and all the other animals he became close with. *I reckon it's possible that we had a bond as strong as that*, Brent considered. *But it was never tested. Thank goodness we never had a reason to test it. But I know there was a strong sense of loyalty and something much deeper than friendship with Domino and Thunder.* This logic train left Brent in deep thought.

He was shaken out of his reverie by Chief Sebastian. "Brent, you still with me?"

"Yes, sir. I was just thinking."

"A word of caution. Not everyone shares my opinion on this. Most of the team, I think, is onboard with the notion, but at least one of our guys hasn't quite figured out his responsibility unfortunately. For the most part, though, you are in good company. Now, let me switch to the watch procedures."

For most of an hour, Chief Sebastian gave a detailed brief on the contact points, responsibilities, duties, and procedures of the watch.

Not surprisingly, they were much like the watch-standing duties at the boat unit. But all the while, Brent had some difficulty channeling his attention to the brief. He was pulled back to the concept of a human-animal bond stronger than the fear of death. It was baffling…and intriguing.

Marine Mammals—The Basics

Saturday, 1 September 2001
Foxtrot Platoon, Pier 40, Sub Base, Point Loma, California

Brent arrived a few minutes before 0600 for the turnover brief from the offgoing duty officer, BM2[34] Dan Dunaway. Dan had been with NMMP for over three years and was one of the few handlers who had pulled a tour at Mobile Unit 3. There he had trained and handled both sea lions and dolphins.

Brent received a detailed brief on the previous day's events and a heads-up on what was planned for the weekend. Brent felt he had jumped off the deep end. There was an amazing amount of activity. Clearly, this was not your weekend day at a typical Navy command.

Brent met with nearly all the handlers, save one, and most of the animals and filled his pocket notebook with names, procedures, schedules, responsibilities, combination numbers, phone numbers, and myriad of data that boggled the mind. When he could, he followed the handlers through their chores, and he watched with great interest at the interaction between the handler and the animal. He had a ton of questions, and when he thought he wasn't interrupting, he asked them. His interrogatives came like the staccato of a machine gun, but each of the handlers seemed most willing to answer the questions and show off their animals. Brent was fascinated.

While most of the dolphins eyed the newcomer with some skepticism, many came right up to the side of their pens to assess Brent. Unfamiliar with the procedures here but very familiar with horse protocol, he was reluctant to approach any of the animals until his handler gave him the okay.

While touring the pens, Brent found a handler in the water with a big bottlenose. Being in the pen with a mammal was against all the rules, and if someone wanted to make a big stink about it, they could; but generally, it was ignored.

The handler introduced himself as EN3[35] Anthony "Tony" Petri. Anthony had come from the black shoe Navy, the surface warfare side, and had been with Team ONE for a year and a half. The newness, the prestige, the pride, and satisfaction was very evident as Tony spoke.

His dolphin was a nine-year-old bull by the name of Zeus. Tony wore a T-shirt, khaki shorts, and a mask—no fins, no snorkel. When Brent asked Tony what he thought about his job, he swam to the side of the pen, pushed his mask up, laid his elbows on the bulkhead, and grinned a wide grin. "I really don't know where to start. Zeus and I have been together for over a year, and I'm still learning more about him and other dolphins every day. My job is to work with and train Zeus, but the more I work with him, the more I realize that sometimes I'm the one getting trained. He's a mystery, so patient, and gentle. It's hard to believe these guys can do the tough job they do.

"I'm always surprised by just how much capacity he has to learn new things. You'll get a rundown on the behavior and bio info on each of the animals when you start the training syllabus, but I can nutshell the dolphin's profile by saying, think of a Russell terrier, probably the smartest dog out there, then make him twenty times bigger, reshape him like a torpedo, replace his furry coat with neoprene, and make him three times as smart, and you've got yourself a dolphin."

No sooner had Tony completed that thought than Brent watched in amazement as Tony seemed to be pushed away from the dock even while grabbing for the side planking. Looking deeper into the water, Brent now saw that Zeus had wedged himself in between Tony and the edge of the planking and was easing him away from Brent.

Brent watched all this then asked, "Looks like he's trying to get your attention."

"Hey, no problem. He does that all the time. He's a little jealous with you around, so he wanted to grab ass. For a big guy, he's really quite gentle and nurturing. It's part of the dolphin characteristics. He would never hurt me, but he wanted my attention."

"Amazing!" was Brent's only comment.

"Yeah. He can be a handful, but he's a hard worker and has a wonderful sense of humor."

"I can see that. But how do you get to know them? I mean, I met a few of the sea lions over at Mobile THREE yesterday. They're not shy at all, but the dolphins are a different story. I've watched a few for hours, and they'll occasionally cruise by me and take a look, but they don't seem to be that friendly."

"Has anyone explained how to call them?"

"Huh? Nope."

"Okay, just lie down beside their pen and pat the water with an open hand. You may have to do that for a few minutes, but eventually they'll come over and size you up. If you don't appear to be a threat after a few passes, they'll swim over to you. Try it with Zeus. He'll respond pretty quickly. He's not shy, and he hasn't quite figured you out yet. He'll be interested."

"I'm game." Brent lay down along the edge of the pen, extended his hand, palm down, and began to pat the water. "Like this?"

"Yeah, that's it."

Zeus had been watching the encounter all along, and after less than a minute, he cautiously glided toward Brent's extended arm. He cruised right past him and, at his closest point of approach, looked deeply into his eyes then continued in a large circle. He dove, reversed course, and surfaced very near Brent; but this time, he came to a complete stop and blew air. After a moment, he approached Brent and emitted a high-pitched whistle. Again, the eye contact with the dolphin was unnerving and very powerful. So intense was Zeus's stare that Brent, for a moment, had the strangest sensation that he was being x-rayed. It was much like Brent's first contact with the dolphin off Catalina Island years before. It wasn't just eye contact; it was something akin to interrogation. *These animals seem to see right into your soul*, Brent thought.

When Zeus was within arm's reach, Tony said almost in a whisper, "Now slowly rotate your hand, palm up, and keep it a few inches off the water."

This was new. Not knowing what to expect, Brent did as he was told. Nothing happened for a long moment. Brent used this opportunity to look at Zeus, and what he saw warmed his heart. He was utterly and completely beautiful. Brent never in a million years would have thought that a big animal could be so exquisite, so completely lovely to look upon. From his rostrum to his pectoral fins and down his flank, he was a pinnacle of engineering achievement and a magnificently gorgeous creature.

Brent thought back on the graceful lines of his pinto Domino and how sleek and lovely she was, and the massive flanks and bulging withers of the big brute Thunder. He was absolutely handsome. And here, Brent was eye to eye with one of nature's most elegant and strikingly beautiful animals. Brent, for just a moment, was enraptured.

Zeus continued to look at Brent's face and stare deep into his eyes. He whistled again. Then, with an imperceptible sway of his massive fluke, closed the distance. In an act that would forever live in Brent's memory, he delicately laid his rostrum in Brent's palm. Unwillingly, Brent gasped. "Oh my gosh! What's he doing?"

"He's telling you he trusts you. This is a form of greeting for dolphins. He doesn't do this for many people. You should feel honored."

"I feel something, but I don't know that *honored* is the right word. He kind of took my breath away."

"Yeah, he's inquisitive and seems to be a pretty fair judge of people."

Brent spent nearly an hour with Tony and Zeus. Brent was full of questions about Tony's dolphin, Tony's background, the command, and what he could expect in the next four years. But most of the time was spent admiring and getting to know Zeus. By the time Brent left, he was able to stroke Zeus's flank, hold his pectoral fin, and gently pet his melon. Zeus clearly enjoyed the contact.

Brent stood. "Thanks for all the gouge, Tony. Learned a lot and had a big thrill with Zeus."

"I think he did too, and I can tell he really likes being around you. He's never warmed up to anybody that fast. Including me."

"He's something special, no question there."

Brent turned to go, then paused and turned back. "Tony, there's a big dolphin in one of the pens toward the end of the quay. So far, no one's been down to visit him. What's the story?"

Tony hoisted himself out of the water and sat on the edge of the pen. Zeus swam under his legs in an effort to induce him back in the water.

"Sad story really. The handler is a guy from New York. Big guy by the name of Pete Schultz. I don't know what he's doing here, nobody does. He doesn't really fit in. Doesn't seem to like his job much and isn't really friendly. Word is, he was rolled early from his last assignment. He was assigned to one of the cruisers at Thirty-Second Street. Big troublemaker. Got in a couple of scuffles, and the skipper of the ship took him to mast. He accepted a transfer in lieu of administrative disciplinary action."

"Why did our skipper agree to take him? I thought they had a pretty tight screening process here."

"Yeah, well, that's another story. They tried to get him orders to some other ships. All the ship skippers knew about him, and no one wanted him. We heard our OIC, Lieutenant Heinrichs, asked all the right questions and got all the wrong answers. They said he was a good guy, worked well with ship's company, and had all the makin's for a good petty officer. Couldn't have been further from the truth. We were down three handlers, so the lieutenant bought the BS, and now he's our problem."

Brent didn't have a comeback. He took his hat off, looked down at his sneakers, and rubbed the back of his neck. "So, what's the story on that dolphin, and who takes care of him?"

"The second question is easier to answer than the first. He has a secondary handler, but we're still down a few people, so we all pitch in. I'll be headed to his pen as soon as I finish with Zeus. And the answer to the second question turns into a pretty sad story, but with a happy ending...kind of."

Brent took a knee and stroked Zeus's flank and around his dorsal fin. He studied Tony carefully, urging him on.

"Several years ago, two little kids found a baby dolphin stranded on the beach in Florida. The state guys also found an adult cow on the beach nearby. She had been lactating. She was gutted by something big. They put two and two together and figured the dead dolphin was the little guy's mom and decided not to try to release the baby back in the wild. He never would have made it. Well, they took him to one of the marine mammal rescue groups. I think it was Gulf World in Panama City, Florida. They stabilized him but then realized the little guy was going to need a whole buttload of medical treatment and therapy. He was really having some emotional problems. Then some really smart vet there remembered us and contacted SPAWAR Systems Center, Pacific, here in San Diego—you know, just to get the ball rolling.

"So there was some finagling I'm not smart on, and the National Marine Fisheries Service[36] got involved. Pretty soon, a couple of our Army vets and two civilian biotechs went out there to determine the best recovery and rehab plan with the marine biology guys at Gulf World, Florida. Seeing as how it was going to take months of rehab, both medical teams figured the Navy was best suited over the long haul. I'm pretty sure the fact that our Marine Mammal Program has the best therapy and rehab program of any marine mammal organization in the world entered into the picture.

"The recommendations of the medical guys were forwarded to the fisheries group at US Fish and Wildlife. They made the call that the dolphin should come to us, and before you knew it, VR-57[37] at NAS North Island[38] spun up a high-priority flight into Tyndall Air Force Base, just a stone's throw from Panama City. I know Doc Greer made the trip, and I think Master Chief Murphy led the team. Anyhow, they brought him back safe, but not so sound. He's had some real stress issues.

"Just like all new dolphins, he first went to Pier 302. That's where they do a complete physical eval, psych assessment, and provide medical treatment. Well, they gave him a surrogate mom, Emily. She's a feisty and, some might say, overly protective mother, typical of Atlantic bottlenose dolphins, but you'll never find a sweeter, more attentive mother. And boy, did she dote on that little dolphin. Only a few of our handlers could even get close to the little guy. She let Kahuna, Master Chief Murphy, and a couple of Pier 302 biotechs handle the baby, but she got real pushy when someone got in the water she didn't like or didn't know.

"Anyway, he spent months with Emily and many more in rehab getting socialized with older dolphins and some of our veteran system dolphins. When he as about four, he went to Pier 159, also at Point Loma, and started his fleet training. He was fleet certified as a Mark 7 dolphin and was sent to us about six months ago. Word was, he barely passed his first fleet certification, and he's not doing all that hot here, what with his emotional problems and all. And that idiot Pete ain't helping things either.

"We heard that Pete was ordered over to the Pier 302 to take a look at his new dolphin, but something must have happened because Emily went nuts. She came out of the water and tried to bite him. The same day, he was standing on the edge of the pen, and Emily walloped him with her fluke and spun him like a top. Bushwhacked him good. Wish I was there to see it. He sure had it coming. Anyhow, Emily hates his guts, and he's not doing the youngster much good here."

"Why don't they assign a different handler?"

"Master Chief Murphy is working on that. Pete's a handler in name only. Until the master chief does assign someone else, we all pitch in to work with and socialize Alika."

"Wait a minute. You just said Alika? That's his name?"

"Yeah. It means 'defender' or 'guardian' in Hawaiian. Little Kahuna named him. You met Kahuna yet?"

"Nope. Not yet."

"He'll be around today. He's a Samoan guy. He's the leading chief petty officer for Foxtrot Platoon. Good man. He takes real good care of the animals and the troops. Anyway, Kahuna thinks Pete's been screwing with the baby, though by his size, he doesn't look like a baby anymore. He's bigger than his mom. Master Chief Murphy— and there may be nothing to this—is kinda concerned that Kahuna may just kick the crap out of Pete if he catches him messing with Alika."

"Humm, I heard Pete's a pretty big guy. Maybe that's not going to happen."

"You haven't seen Little Kahuna yet!"

Brent left Tony and Zeus and walked to the duty office pondering the vast abyss between what he now knew about dolphins and what he needed to know. He was mesmerized by Zeus and envied the relationship between him and Tony. The amount of information that Tony had shared with him was stifling. He felt like he just ate the encyclopedia on dolphins. His head hurt. He knew they were complex animals, but he now had a new and reenergized appreciation for them and, in truth, for the Foxtrot Platoon.

This may have been the right decision, after all.

CHAPTER 6

THE PLAN OF THE DAY

*Until we recognize animals as living beings with emotions and feelings
we will not fully understand their presence and purpose on earth.*

—Anthony Douglas Williams, *Inside the Divine Pattern*

A Day in the Life of a Navy Dolphin Handler

Monday, 3 September 2001
Foxtrot Platoon, Pier 40, Sub Base, Point Loma, California

Brent arrived at Foxtrot on Monday, 3 September, fresh and invigorated. It would have been considered by any warm-blooded, unwed American twenty-year-old as a weekend void of all and any form of excitement—one fit for a reclusive monk in the extreme. But for Brent, it was forty-eight hours of cerebral enrichment, a weekend of enchanting discovery.

Brent had been invited, almost shanghaied, to go booming with his two roommates, brothers from SBU-12, but Brent deferred instead to studying the manuals, training, and handling procedures and operational tactics, techniques, and procedures of the MK 7 system. Interestingly, he was never academic during his school years.

He struggled in high school just to make Bs, but studying the manuals and handbooks on the dolphins was not like schoolwork at all. He was fascinated in the protocol of building strong bonds between these marine mammals and their human counterparts. Further, he was intrigued with the process of harnessing the biological talents and physical capabilities of a dolphin in order to perform underwater tasks man could not do by himself or, for that matter, with any form of advanced equipment, machinery, or technology. The truth was that dolphins and sea lions, with the right training, were decades ahead of what might, on the technological horizon, replace them. And again, with proper handling, training, and bonding, these Navy marine mammals were quite satisfied to work with their human handlers and trainers. It was this concept, and now accepted science, that utterly fascinated Brent.

Normal reporting time for the Foxtrot Platoon staff was 0630. Brent arrived a bit before 0600 toting a parachute bag full of equipment and boat gear he figured would come in handy on his new job. He changed into his board trunks and T-shirt and then spent nearly ten minutes stuffing the rest of his gear into his personal locker. When it was apparent there was a conflict between volume of personal gear and cube size of his locker, he resorted to putting his back against the door and compressing his stuff just to get the door latched. Anybody who happened to unlatch the door without a warning could be seriously hurt.

Brent left the locker room and began his stretching routine on the dock. He couldn't help but survey the dolphin pens and occasionally spotted big gray and white heads popping above the water line to take a peek at the new guy.

The rest of the team trickled in just before 0630. The staff assembled in the parking lot, each person going through the pangs of their own stretching routine. For the next hour, they were on their own. Some headed to the gym to lift weights, many jogged, but Brent and a dozen others chose to hit the pool. A few jogging minutes from Foxtrot Platoon was an Olympic-sized pool that was kept at a stimulating seventy-two degrees, much cooler than most community pools. For nearly an hour, Brent swam laps using each of four techniques he'd learned in SWCC training. He practiced his kick turns and worked on holding his breath. He was off his three-minute target by twenty seconds. This was a long way from the world's record of twenty-two minutes, but most male adults had difficulty even making it to the one-minute mark. Clearly, this was something he had to work on.

Brent jogged back to the unit, took a quick shower, then eyed his locker with some anxiety. He did not want to open the locker door again, then remembered he'd set a pair of shorts, his deck shoes, and a Navy blue T-shirt above his locker. That was thinking ahead.

By the time he'd dried and changed, personnel were falling out for quarters in a large enclosed area near the platoon. At 0745 each day on the dot, Chief Petty Officer Park, one of the senior enlisted leaders, called the command to attention. Dressed as they were in a broad assortment of shorts, sneakers, and T-shirts, the spectacle looked more like a *Gilligan's Island* set than a US Navy command; but to Brent's satisfaction, each man wore an appropriate regulation Navy cover and assembled in laser-straight lines and columns assuming a position of attention that would make any marine drill instructor proud.

As Lieutenant Heinrichs approached the formation, Chief Park executed a quarter-facing maneuver and rendered a crisp salute. "All personnel present and accounted for, sir."

"Very well, Chief. I got it," Lieutenant Heinrichs returned.

As the chief posted behind the OIC, Lieutenant Heinrichs boomed, "At ease, Foxtrot Platoon."

For the next five minutes, the OIC reviewed the high points of the plan of the day. He injected additional information not covered in the POD but which would undoubtable be of interest to his men. Lieutenant Heinrichs always added a bit of world news near the conclusion of quarters. This kept his people alert to the fact that they were in the business of defending their country. It wasn't day care for big fish. They had a job to do in support of frontline forces. If things were going to go high and right, Explosive Ordnance Disposal and those commands and units under it would be among the first to deploy to any part of the world that had a coastline.

"Last thing, we have a new shipmate aboard. Chief Park, would you do the honors?"

"I'll be glad to, sir," the chief replied and stepped forward. "Foxtrot Platoon, I'd like to introduce Special Boat Operator Second Class Brent Harris from Special Boat Unit TWELVE. Petty Officer Harris, would you join me front and center?"

"Yes, Chief!" a surprised Brent replied. He took a single step to the rear leading with his left foot, executed a left-facing maneuver, and smartly marched to join Chief Park at the head of the formation.

"Petty Officer Harris," the chief began, "is a cowboy from Wyoming. He knows three things: small-boat handling, breaking broncos, and that this is a better place than the one he left. Please tell us a little bit about yourself, Petty Officer Harris"

Brent, not used to speaking before an audience, cleared his voice and started off, "Well, Chief…"

And with that, the relative quiet of the morning was shattered by scores of booming voices, in unison roaring, "Shut the hell up!"

I'm home, thought Brent, beaming.

Quarters ended, and everyone seemed to know exactly where to go and what to do—everyone, that is, except Brent. He stood in place for a moment and looked around, thinking a light from above would point him to his next task. And in a way, it did.

Master Chief Murphy, all 270 pounds of muscle and goodwill was headed toward him wearing his customary grin forming around a cigar. Brent turned to greet him, "Good morning, Master Chief."

"Top of the morning, Brent. If you've got nothing on your schedule, and I expect you don't since I didn't put anything on it yet, EN3 Tony Petri specifically asked me if he could do your indoctrination."

"That would be great, CMC. I spent some time with him and Zeus on Saturday. Great team. Learned a lot!"

"Yep. They're quite something to watch, and you're about to learn a lot more. So, head on down to Zeus's pen. Tony should be there soon."

"On my way, Master Chief."

Brent turned and made a beeline for Zeus's pen, taking in the sights, sounds, and smells as he walked. And what smells! Lordy, he couldn't really put his finger on it, but he identified some of the primary ingredients in the low-tide dock brew: dead fish, drying crustaceans, creosote, and feces—not just from the dolphins but also from the local seals and sea lions that seem to enjoy their time spent swimming with the Navy dolphins.

Does anyone get used to this smell? Brent thought to himself.

Tony was already at Zeus's pen when Brent arrived. A hundred feet away, Brent had a visual on Zeus's gorgeous head extending out of the water watching the morning rituals. Tony glanced up at Brent, waved, and said, "Morning!"

"And good morning to you. How's Zeus?

"Come on down and see for yourself."

Brent stepped to the edge of the dockwork and immediately lay on the deck beside Zeus's pen. This time, there were no introductions and no delay. Zeus greeted him as if he were a longtime friend, bringing his head within easy reach of Brent's extended hand. He stroked his melon and down his flanks and spoke softly. The jury was still out on whether or not all dolphins could hear in the frequency range of an average human adult male's voice spectrum, but this dolphin clearly enjoyed the attention. And as Brent watched Zeus, it appeared that he was on the teetering edge of a large smile.

"Big day for you, Brent. I'll take you over to watch the handlers complete the body inspections and load the boats for this morning's training. I also told Dale you could give him a hand later in the morning."

"That's good with me, but who's Dale, and what did you volunteer me for?"

"Ah, that's a surprise. But I promise you, you're not going to forget it!"

"Thanks a bunch. Can't wait."

"We'll head down to the holding pens just down the pier. The girls are in the west pens, and the boys are on the east."

"They're separated? Why?" inquired Brent.

"We never let them mingle at the fleet level, except when they're training or doing an operation. We try to keep any hanky-panky to a minimum. The young males are pretty easy to stimulate, and we need the animals to be focused on their job. Female dolphins are pregnant for eleven months, and then they nurse for nearly two years. If one of our girls gets knocked up, she'll be off the team for nearly two and a half years."

"Ahhh. Got it!" Brent replied. "But you do have babies here, right?"

"Yea, but they're planned pregnancies, and only when we need more dolphins. Let's go watch them load up."

A last stroke down Zeus's flank, and Brent stood and followed Tony down the brow. Brent looked back just in time to see Zeus come completely out of the water, make a turn at the apex, and reenter the water rostrum first with hardly a splash. *Wow! Very cool!*

Tony and Brent took a short walk down the brow to the holding pens. Here, there were several very large pens and quite a number of adult dolphins. Brent noticed several handlers on their hands and knees or lying on the side of the pens, hands and arms in the water. What caught Brent off guard was that next to the dock, adjacent to each of the handlers, was a very large dolphin. And whatever the handlers were doing seemed to be just okay with them. Nowhere was there any appearance of frantic activity or complaining. To the dolphins and handlers, this was business as usual.

Tony explained, "The handlers are checking their animal before they load up in the boats. They'll look over the dolphin's entire body for lesions, cuts, bruises, parasites, basically anything out of the ordinary. They'll look in their eyes, check their rostrum, blowhole, and even—and this is going to sound funny—their breath. If it's sour or doesn't smell right, it might require a visit to one of the medical techs. If there's anything unusual or obviously wrong, we'll get a second opinion, usually from a tech rep. Tech reps are also called biotechs. They're subject-matter experts, very experienced professional marine mammal trainers. They're usually civil servants and civilian contract trainers assigned to Foxtrot Platoon, and often they're ex-Navy handlers. These guys bring a world of knowledge and experience to the team. We couldn't do the job without them.

"If we suspect one of the dolphins is sick, we'll pull the animal off-line and notify the biotechs and the vets pronto. It's unusual for these guys to become injured or ill, but they're working animals, and it happens sometimes. When it does, there are no dolphins in the world that get quicker or better medical treatment. In fact, I think they get better medical attention than we do sometimes."

Tony paused, looked at Brent, and waited for a comment or question. Nothing. Brent was glued to the scene before him, completely engrossed as he scanned the scene. *Amazing! Just amazing!*

"When they complete the checks, the handler will *ask* their dolphin to put their harness on. This is the one piece of equipment they wear so we can keep track of them."

"What do you mean you *ask* them to put it on?"

"First, they're too damn big to force them to put it on. They don't do anything they don't want to. And second, this is a team event. It takes complete and total cooperation from both partners. We never stress them. If they're having a bad day, they're not up to it, things are just not going right—we back off and come back in a few hours or the next day. If it continues, we may have a problem, and then we'll bring in the biotechs to troubleshoot. But so far, I only know of only one dolphin who's got *issues*."

"Issues? What do you mean?"

"I mean, this guy can get flaky, undependable, moody, depressed. And honestly, I think it's more the fault of the handler than it is the animal."

"Is this the dolphin you told me about on Saturday… *Alika* 'er something."

"The very one."

"And you said the master chief was working on getting another primary handler for him, right?"

"They are, but they may have to send Alika back to get retrained and recertified as an MK 7 dolphin. The fleet certify them at Pier 159. But eventually—and the sooner, the better—they're also going to have to find a new handler. We talked about this. Pete Schultz, he's a boatswain's mate third class and is supposed to be Alika's handler. He shouldn't even be here. For the most part, he just ignores Alika. But Pete's got it in for another dolphin, or so I hear, Kona. That's Rick Turner's dolphin. Kona's a little bit slow. Not stupid, mind you. He's a hard worker, very dedicated. You can't help but love the boy. He knows his stuff, but he doesn't learn as fast as most of our dolphins.

"Well, Kona has this boat bumper. It's his toy, and he just loves the dickens out of it. He'll drag that thing around, toss in in the air, and drag it down to the bottom of his pen and let it go. Of course, the thing takes off like a missile shot into the air, and that crazy dolphin will rush to the surface and try to catch it as it comes down. And you won't believe it until you see it, but that darn dolphin can toss that bumper with impressive accuracy. I've watched Kona and Rick play catch with it. They have to be careful because it must weigh five or six pounds. It is the funniest darn thing to watch.

"A couple of weeks ago, Pete, for whatever reason, took the bumper away from Kona. Kona was visibly depressed until Rick found his bumper and gave it back to Kona. When Pete found out Kona had his bumper back—and again, this is secondhand info—Pete flipped. He threatened Rick and then tried to take Kona's bumper away from him again. This time, when Pete got near Kona's pen, Kona splashed him with his fluke. Darn near knocked Pete off the dock, I heard. Even now, if Kona sees Pete walk down the quay, he'll soak him. Anyhow, Kona has his bumper back, and when he isn't out in the field or on an op, he'll play with it all day. Funny as all hell. We'll go watch him if he doesn't go out this morning. But back to Pete. He needs his ass kicked. And he needs to be replaced and soon. Alika's a good dolphin. He needs someone he can trust. He needs a friend. Anyway, this is all out of my pay grade. I've got enough stuff going on just keeping up with Zeus."

Brent couldn't help but flashback to his days working with Thunder. Clear as crystal in his mind's eye, Brent could see Bill Washakie smile at the sight of the big brute Thunder on that very first day when he said, "I think he wants to be a good horse, but he's been mistreated. He just doesn't seem to trust us. Not yet anyway. We need to change that." The comment seemed to fit perfectly with this situation four years after it was spoken.

Tony continued a running commentary of the activity and interaction between the dolphins and the handlers as they walked along the quay.

Brent noticed that several 7-Meter RHIBs[39] were lashed to the dock.

"They're about to start loading the dolphins," Tony said. "This is always interesting."

Brent quickly looked about for cranes or something in which to lift five-hundred-pound dolphins from the water to the boat deck. About that time, one of the handlers made a gesture, and a beautiful glimmering gray dolphin leapt from the water and slid gracefully into the port side of the boat. That was followed in short order by a second dolphin in a second boat.

"They'll normally only load two or three boats at a time. We've always got some work-arounds: equipment constraints, dive stations, and mine-field deconfliction coordination. It's a fact of life, but we manage to get the job done."

Tony glanced at Brent. Brent was locked on to the scene before him and looked as though somebody had just performed a dazzling magic trick.

After several more moments, helms were manned, lines were tossed, and the boats laden with their precious cargo, headed away from the dock southwest toward the mouth of the San Diego Bay.

"Show's over, Brent." Tony turned and headed down another quay. Brent joined him.

"Now," Tony said with a sly smile, "it's time to earn your keep."

"After that show, I'm ready to do anything. I've never seen anything like it. They were actually hopping into the boats as if they were excited to be going."

"They are! This is their job, and well—this is going to sound crazy—they look forward to the adventure and the work and just to be with their handler. How's that go? Show me a man who loves his job, and I'll show you a man who will never work a day in his life. It goes for dolphins too!"

Tony's Fish House

Monday, 3 September 2001
Foxtrot Platoon, Pier 40, Sub Base, Point Loma, California

Brent wasn't sure where Tony was leading him, but he was enjoying the tour. *The fish house. We're headed to the fish house,* Brent finally realized. *Well, nothing can be as bad as the stink coming from our barn in late August.*

But Brent's surprise only grew the closer they came to the fish house. By the very sound of it, he expected the *fish house* to be a scene out of the *Texas Chain Saw Massacre* movie—blood, guts, and fish scales coating the bulkheads and deck and reeking of rotting sea creatures. What he saw instead was a near-state-of-the-art kitchen with stainless steel fixtures, giant sinks, large preparation tables, and a big rack with clean bins and buckets.

"Dale, come meet your new helper," Tony yelled. Dale peeked out the hatch, saw Tony and the new guy, strolled toward them, and extended his hand. Without thinking, Brent gripped Tony's gloved hand. Fish scales and gooey things were now squished across Brent's right hand. Tony and Dale broke out in a gut-buster laugh, but all Brent could do was try to shake some of the goo onto the deck.

"Damn, that trick hasn't worked since forever." Dale laughed.

"You can wash off at the sink, Brent, but you, being a snake-eater and all, I figured you'd just lick it off," Tony said.

"Brent, this guy with the sick sense of humor is OS-3[40] Dale Thompson. Been with the team for a couple of years and knows his way around our animals. He's the primary for Brutus and stands in occasionally with Alika, but we all kinda do that."

Brent was wiping off the last remnants of the fish slime on what had been his fresh PT shorts, but looked up in time to say, "Howdy, Dale. A pleasure!"

"Word is, Brent was a horse trainer and a rodeo cowboy, so he has a bit of a head start on your basic new guy. He's all yours for the rest of the morning. Have fun, Brent!" Tony finished.

Tony headed back toward Zeus's pen, leaving Dale to brief Brent on the morning task of preparing the food packages for the dolphins.

Brent did a quick survey of the area. "So…what can I do?"

"Well, come on in and let me give you the grand tour, and then you can help me pack the meals for the dolphins."

As they entered the fish house, Dale began, "Everyone thinks we gut and clean fish here, but it's quite the opposite. We start with market-quality fish. I mean good stuff: mackerel, herring, squid, and capelin. We'll wash them then inspect each and every fish. I'll look at the gill plates—they should be pink or red. I check the general condition of the body and ensure there's no damage, lesions, and no signs of infection or parasites. We don't touch these fish with a knife. They're fed whole to the animals. If you look up at the white-board"—Dale pointed to the large whiteboard affixed to one side of the bulkhead—"each of our animals is listed on the board, and each has a specific diet. The board lists the dolphin's names, handler, weight, diet, and other information. This lists what kind and how much fish will be packaged for each dolphin. Each of our animals has his own bucket with his name printed on it. After we inspect the fish, we'll fill their buckets with the type and amount of food listed on the board."

"So we don't actually have to gut the fish or get all goo'd out?"

"Nope. It's a pretty clean operation actually. But we're not done when we have all the meals packaged. Then we have to clean the entire fish house. If the med techs find so much as a scale in the sinks, the drainboards, prep tables, or the decks, we have to clean the entire place again."

"I take it they're pretty serious about the conditions of the fish house," Brent said.

"Very!"

"Well, I'm ready to get started," Brent said.

And he did. For the next two hours, Dale and Brent inspected and packaged fish for each of the dolphins. During that time, Dale gave an interesting monologue on the command, the animals, the mission, the routine, and what Brent could expect in the next several days.

"I'll bet you're already on the schedule for handler training with the SPAWAR trainers at Pier 159. Learn as much as you can before you start the class. There's a lot in the syllabus, and they don't dilly-dally. But it'll be the best six-week school you'll ever go to.

"Can hardly wait. Tony mentioned you were the secondary handler for Alika. Any chance of seeing him today?"

"Yeah. A big one. I was headed down there as soon as we clean the place up."

Fifteen minutes later, Dale and Brent had the place sparkling. "It looks good. Let's go see my boy."

Meeting Alika

Monday, 3 September 2001
Foxtrot Platoon, Pier 40, Sub Base, Point Loma, California

As they made their way to Alika's pen, Dale pointed out and named each of the dolphins. Nearly one hundred feet away, a tall, heavy-set man in PT shorts and a dirty T-shirt left Alika's pen and headed toward Dale and Brent. The quay was fairly narrow, but four men could comfortably walk abreast. As they neared the oncoming person, Brent noticed the guy walking in the opposite direction remained in the center of the quay. Dale moved in front of Brent to give him more room, but as they passed, the stranger bumped Brent's shoulder and, without so much of an apology, continued down the quay.

"Excuse me," Brent let out.

Dale looked over his shoulder to ensure they were out of ear-shot. "You've just met Pete, Alika's primary," Dale explained. "He doesn't get any nicer. Just give him room and don't expect much. He's like that with about everybody but the master chief and our leading chief, Little Kahuna."

"I've already heard about Pete, and I have no intention of getting cross-threaded with him."

"Good. The problem now is, if he's spent any time with Alika today, he'll be tough to console."

"What's the problem with Pete? What does he do with Alika?"

"Nothing. And that's the problem. I can't say he actually mistreats him, but he sure doesn't do anything good for him. Alika is… well, neglected. Pete'll tell you it's the dolphin's fault. He claims he wasn't trained right, and they fudged on the certification the first time. But everybody that was here when Alika came to us knows he was a good boy. A little young, and he had some issues—we think because of the loss of his mother. But Alika was a good dolphin when we got him."

They arrived at Alika's pen. "I was afraid of that."

Brent looked around and realized that a big gray dolphin was up against the far side of the pen looking tentatively at Dale and Brent.

"Damn!" Dale exclaimed. "I'll see if I can get him over here." With that, Dale took off his sneakers, sat on the edge of the pen, and extended his legs into the water. "If he doesn't come to us in the next few minutes, we'll leave and come back later. But I think, after Pete was here, he's probably craving for some attention."

For the next five minutes, Dale slapped the water and spoke in a sotto voce. Then he paused and watched. No movement in the big shape on the other side of the pen was noted.

"Ah, boy, he's pretty upset. Brent, would you grab a bucket of fish and see if you can find the volleyball I keep in the fish house? That usually cheers him up."

A few moments later, Brent returned with the bucket and the ball and set them on the edge of the dock. Dale tossed the volleyball into the water toward Alika, grabbed a couple of big mackerel, and showed Alika the offering. Initially, there seemed to be no response; but at Dale's urging, Alika slowly cruised toward him. Alika pushed the ball out of the way and nudged up against Dale's leg. He then opened his mouth, showing all eighty-eight bright white teeth and gently pulled a mackerel from Dale's hand. Alika was offered and took a second and a third, then seemed to finally become aware of Brent's presence sitting next to Dale with his legs in the water.

"Extend your hand, Brent, but don't splash. Just see if he'll come to you."

Brent slowly reached out and, using the same calming tone he used on his horses, spoke to Alika. A minute ticked by, then… slowly…cautiously…Alika gave a miniscule twitch of his massive fluke and glided toward Brent but hovered just outside Brent's reach. Brent had lowered his right arm so most of the lower portion was submerged. Alika ran a short click train then paused.

"Patience, Brent. He's still upset, and he's trying to size you up. The fact that Pete just pissed in his punch bowl bummed the poor guy out pretty well. I'll be surprised if he wants to meet any more humans today. By the way, he just pinged your arm. Kinda like running a sonogram on you."

Brent continued to whisper calm words to Alika. It was another minute before Alika closed the remaining distance and actually slid his rostrum into Brent's hand. Another click train and a series of whistles ensued. Then there was the now familiar rush of excitement as Alika looked up at Brent.

And there it was—contact. Deep, probing eye-to-eye contact. It made Brent's heart rush.

"You notice all the loose skin on Alika?"

"Yeah. What is that?" Brent questioned.

"It's dead cells shedding from his skin. Dolphins constantly shed and replace skin cells, especially when they're sedentary for a while. These cells build up, and they shed them. It's called *sloughing*. It's one of the reasons they're so fast in the water. They're constantly replacing old epidermis with new, smooth, low-drag skin that improves laminar flow of the water molecules."

Dale took a close look at Alika. "It's pretty obvious that Pete never had much physical contact with Alika. His skin is sloughing off. Pete's completely ignored Alika—again! You could be a big hit with Alika if you just started rubbing all over his body and helped him shed this stuff."

"Heck, yeah. Be glad to." Brent repositioned himself so he was lying alongside the edge of Alika's pen and slowly rubbed down his flanks.

Initially, Alika seemed to enjoy the contact; then suddenly he dove and flapped his fluke, drenching both Brent and Tony.

"Hey! What just happened?"

"Well, that was interesting!" Dale exclaimed.

"What'd I do? He was right here, I was rubbing him, and then he dove. Did I scare him or something?"

"Quite the opposite. I've never seen him react like that with anyone. And he was pretty upset to begin with. Something in your touch, in the click return, or your voice. I dunno. It's weird. These animals are so complex. Maybe he just wasn't quite ready for all the attention from a complete stranger. Try that again in the next couple of days. He likes you. I think he'll do better next time you see him. We better go. Pete might come back, and as cantankerous as he is, I don't want to be here when he does."

As Dale and Brent stood, Alika looked slightly alarmed and produced a whistle.

"Alika, we'll be back, partner. Hang tough," Dale said, trying to reassure Alika.

As they walked away, Brent looked over his shoulder and into Alika's big sparkling eyes. *He really is troubled, poor guy*, Brent thought to himself.

Dale led the way back toward the fish house.

"So, you just met our problem child. But is it the child or the handler that's the problem?"

"Couldn't tell you, Dale, but that was one magnificent animal. What a boy."

"Yeah. He's something," Dale agreed. "I'll come back and check on him later, but we gotta go. We've still got a lot to do."

"Do you think it would be okay if I visit him occasionally?"

"It'd be a great idea. I'm sure Alika would like it. We need to get that skin off anyway since Pete doesn't seem to be interested in taking care of him." Then Dale added, "But I'd be real careful of Pete. He's a dick, and for reasons I don't get, he doesn't like people around Alika. I work with Alika because I'm the secondary handler, but Pete can get testy. Just give him plenty of room."

"I'll keep my sensors up. Thanks for letting me meet Alika. He's a very cool dolphin."

"That, he is. Let's get moving."

The rest of the day was a cram-packed tour of the Foxtrot Platoon facility: the boats, equipment, offices, and a visit to all the pens. Dale knew the history, the disposition, and character of all the dolphins and introduced Brent to most of the handlers.

Brent began to realize there was a common denominator among the handlers. They were young, all under thirty, in good shape, gregarious, and seemed to be fully committed. Without question, these people truly enjoyed what they were doing and seemed totally in tune with their animals. And if Brent could draw any conclusions from the observations he'd made of the dolphins in the last couple of days, it would have been that they weren't a bunch of mindless fish. They had personalities and seemed to be alert to all that was going on and interested in everything that took place within their little world. Surprising to Brent, they spent considerable time with their head out of the water—watching.

Also, a bit of a surprise was that there were occasional whistles, properly termed *signature whistles*, but Brent noticed that not all the whistles emanated from the dolphins. Sometimes he'd hear a whistle followed by a return whistle that was from one of the handlers.

Dale and Brent worked their way to one of the RHIBs tied to the dock. "I'll take you over to Pier 302 to meet the Army vets and med team at the vet lab near SPAWAR. That's what we call Space and Naval Warfare Systems command, SPAWAR for short. We'll go meet the docs and see what they have going on. I need to pick up some supplies anyway, and it's just a five-minute boat ride."

While Dale prepared the launch, Brent just stood in place and watched the activity. *I know nothing. These animals are complicated beyond my wildest imagination. But what a day. No wonder all these guys seem so up. What a great adventure!*

Brent shook himself out of his reverie and jogged down the dock to catch Dale. While Dale fired up the outboard, Brent tossed lines and pulled the bumpers up. In under a minute, they were cruising toward Pier 302, the wind tossing their hair, the sun warming their backs, and the salty air filling their lungs. *No one should have this much fun and get paid for it.* Brent beamed.

That first full week at Foxtrot was a learning experience second to none. The normal workday encompassed ten to twelve hours. Work hours varied according to tasks and training schedules, but seldom did the team work nights. The Army vets and medical techs occasionally stayed late and, when called on if they had a sick or injured dolphin, spent the night with the dolphin in the medical facility. When Brent realized the medical team worked well into the evening, he became a regular groupie and was soon invited to assist in simple medical procedures, physicals, and body checks.

High Cover

Monday, 10 September 1999
Foxtrot Platoon, Pier 40, Sub Base, Point Loma, California

"Yo, Master Chief!"

"Kahuna, come on in and close the door," Master Chief Murphy mumbled through his unlit cigar as he sat comfortably in his well-worn Navy-issued chair.

Chief Petty Officer Engineman Malakai Olopoto, known to his friends as *Kahuna* and to his few enemies also as Kahuna, was a Samoan and hailed from Hawaii. He stood five foot eight barefooted, but what he lacked in altitude, he more than made up for in corded girth. He looked like a cement truck suspended by giant sequoia tree trunks.

A beach volleyball player with national ranking, Kahuna had hands the size of tennis rackets. People who saw him in action swore he could hit against the tallest beach volleyball players. He could jump at the same time as the blockers, and as the blocker peaked and headed downward, Kahuna would still be climbing. To add insult to injury, he could take his eye off the ball for a split second, target a specific unguarded area on the court, and let loose a cannon shot that defenders didn't even want to block if they could.

Among his many talents, Kahuna was a mainstay in the command, well-liked and respected as a professional. He was also Foxtrot's leading chief petty officer. One of the most knowledgeable handlers in the command, he was a natural with the dolphins: kind, patient, empathetic, and very protective of his charges.

It wasn't through any academic research or book learning that he came by his gifts. Much through his observation and insight of the characteristics of the bottlenose dolphin during a stint with the bio-techs and engineers at Pier 159, Kahuna was able to understand and clarify the operational parameters for the Navy dolphins' capabilities and capacities for mine detection, marking, recovery, and sea-lane clearance. He further assisted in formally defining the true capabilities and limitations of the MK 7 dolphins. If there were such a thing as a dolphin whisperer, Kahuna would be him.

Kahuna was on his third set of orders to Navy Special Clearance Team ONE, or a component of Team ONE. When he was approaching the end of his second tour at Team ONE, the detailers attempted to cut him a set of orders back to the fleet. His response was simple enough. If they didn't write him a set of orders to extend him at Foxtrot Platoon, he'd hand in his papers.

He had twenty-two years in the Navy, having joined when he was seventeen. If the big marine theme parks knew he was loose and on the free market, they'd hire him in a New York second at three times the salary. But Kahuna liked where he was and loved what he was doing.

The orders hoopla was elevated to the lofty heights of the Chief of Naval Personnel, Vice Admiral Daniel Oliver. It was a test of wills—Navy policy versus a practical compromise benefiting both the Navy and the individual. Many of the inner circle thought the idea made so much sense it had no chance of being successful.

In a counter to the logical solution, the detailers quoted the book and detailing *procedures* manual. The reporting senior in Navy Special Clearance Team ONE's chain of command put forth an immaculate and iron-clad argument: if Chief Petty Officer Malakai Olopoto did not receive orders to Foxtrot Platoon, he would leave the Navy, and with him would go a treasure trove of experience, competency, and operational innovation concerning mine counter-measures warfare and all the system dolphins.

The Chief of Naval Personnel thoughtfully listened to both positions and then ruled in favor of Chief Olopoto. Rational minds prevailed in the face of *procedures* and *directives*. Score one for the Navy.

"Wassup, Master Chief?"

The master chief leaned back in his chair at an impossible angle, testing the structural limits of the equipment. He placed his size thirteens on his desk, wrapped a large rubber band around his wrist, and pulled the ever-present cigar stub out of his mouth. "I've got a mission for you, Kahuna. We've got a troubled dolphin over at your place, Foxtrot Platoon. His name is Alika. Problem is the med biotechs don't know if he's having emotional issues based on his experience from the loss of his mother or the problem is his handler, BM3 Pete Schultz."

"I know. Been watching Alika. Good dolphin. Pete is not good, not good for Alika and not good for Foxtrot."

"Well, we may have a savior. Our new guy Brent Harris seems to be picking this business up pretty quickly. He spends an awful lot of time here, and he seems to be hooked on the job. Dale told me Brent asked to visit Alika when he had the time, and by all accounts, Alika is responding to him. Quite a surprise, considering Alika doesn't respond to anyone but Dale and you. So here's what I'd like you to do…"

For the next five minutes, Master Chief Murphy laid the job out. There was a bit of ambiguity and some gray areas Kahuna wanted clarified.

"So I'm supposed to help Brent with Alika, keep an eye on both of them. And if Pete hassles Brent, I'm supposed to ensure Brent doesn't get hurt"—and this was the gray area—"but I can't come down on Pete?"

"Right. I don't want anything broken on Pete, even though he deserves it. I just want to be sure Brent has some…some…*high cover*. We're working on getting Pete out of here, but there's a delay. There's been a Navy Investigative Service investigation on Pete for a few weeks—dealing drugs, they think. We weren't supposed to do anything that might tip him off. NIS was concerned he might hiyucca out of here if he caught wind of it. But that is *close-hold*, Kahuna."

"I see now. I can do this, Master Chief, but are you sure I can't tenderize him a little?"

"Kahuna, there is nothing I would enjoy more than to watch you dismantle Pete, but we're pros and above all that. And besides, NIS wants a complete, intact body to arrest when the time comes."

The rubber band finally snapped and flew in the air. The master chief tracked the errant rubber band for a second then shifted his attention back to his soggy cigar. "Think you can handle the job, Kahuna?"

Kahuna smiled.

The Day America Stood Still

Tuesday, 11 September 2001
Foxtrot Platoon, Pier 40, Sub Base, Point Loma, California

The day following the discussion between Master Chief Murphy and Chief Olopoto, an event twenty-eight hundred miles away took place that would change the world and in a more draconian way, fundamentally change the lives, the peace of mind, and the very spirit of all Americans.

It was a few minutes before 0600 on Tuesday, 11 September 2001. Brent had just stepped through the security gate at the top of the Foxtrot Platoon brow leading down to the dolphin pens when he noticed Petty Officer 3rd Class Phil Hamilton step out of the watch office and yell, "Brent, before you go anywhere, please come and see me. It's important."

Brent shot him a thumbs-up then shouldered his backpack and began to jog toward the office. Brent stepped through the hatch. "What's up, Phil?"

He'd barely got the question out when Phil, with a grave look on his face, one that replaced the usual jovial persona that was Phil, said with obvious tension, "We just received a phone call from Group

One's duty office about a flash message from CNO." Phil paused to gather his thoughts and calm himself. He took a deep breath. "We got hit in New York. Both the World Trade Centers are on fire."

Brent's jaw dropped. His head spun, and he leaned forward on the desk, trying to make sense of what Phil had just reported. "We got hit? How? Who hit us?"

"FBI is on scene. National Security Agency is still trying to put the data together."

Phil took another deep breath. "Terrorists, they think. They hijacked two or maybe three airliners on the East Coast and flew them into the both World Trade Center buildings in New York. It's bad, Brent. It's being televised. That's all we know now."

Brent, head spinning, looked out the door at the beginnings of another magnificent day in San Diego. *How can that be? We're not at war with anyone. Why would anybody want to kill innocent people?* And then the answer hit him. *Islamic terrorists. Who else?*

Phil added, "Their ratcheting up security all over the base and probably at every base across the country. I have no idea how this will affect us here at Foxtrot, but I'll bet they'll task the Mark 6 force protection animals to patrol the bay. And I'm sure that later today, Lieutenant Heinrichs will call a huddle and let us know what's happening. Until then, just keep your head on a swivel and put the word out."

Brent was physically rocked. His head went down, and for a moment, he studied the deck. "Okay, Phil. Rough way to start the day."

"That's an understatement."

The personnel in Foxtrot continued to arrive, and every one of them seemed to have caught up on the news. Most of the team was gathered in the training room, huddled around a small TV hung from the overhead. Fox News and all the major news agencies broadcast live feed and often switched to the recorded video of the airliners crashing into the buildings and the reaction of people on the street. Suddenly, at 6:40 a.m., the image on the TV switched to a new reporter.

"I interrupt our reporters on site in New York City to bring you breaking news just in. We've just learned a few minutes ago, that would be 9:36 a.m. Eastern Time, that American Airlines Flight 77 crashed into the western facade of the Pentagon. Fire trucks, ambulances, and police are rushing to the scene. Deaths and injuries are not known at this time. We will bring you updated information as it is released. Now back to our live correspondents on scene in New York."

There were over thirty-five people in the training room, and for nearly a minute, no one uttered a sound. Then a slow crescendo of voices from the gathering expressed a range of emotions: disbelief, bewilderment, grief, confusion, and anger. There was a lot of anger.

Lieutenant Heinrichs mustered the troops later that morning. Despite the catastrophe that had befallen the nation, the lieutenant was calm, collected, and focused.

Chief Park had assembled the men in the training room, called them to attention, then reported to Lieutenant Heinrichs, "Foxtrot Platoon, present and accounted for, sir!"

"Thanks, Chief. At ease, men. You've all heard about the terrorist strikes on the two World Trade Center buildings in New York and the Pentagon. I just learned that at 0707 East Coast time, another airliner, United Airlines Flight 93, crashed into a field in Summerset County, Pennsylvania. There were no survivors. Initial reports indicate that this plane was also hijacked by terrorists. The target was unknown at this time, but authorities believe the passengers and crew knew about the other airliners and mounted a brave attack on the terrorists, who then crashed the airplane short of their intended target.

"Now, I don't need to tell you the first news reports are usually wrong, and we'll have the usual pundits speculating, hypothesizing, and weaving stories out of thin air, but don't believe anything until it's confirmed through DoD. We have suffered a great blow today, probably the worst since the Japanese sneak attack on Pearl Harbor sixty years ago. In the next several days, we'll get the full account. Now, what I'd like you all to do is go about your normal routine. Take care of your animals, your teammates, and your family. Our lives and our nation will never be the same, but we will weather the storm. We'll get through this, and we'll be better when we do. Chief Park, please take charge and get them back to work."

"Aye, aye, sir!"

Standing Ground

Friday, 12 October 2001
Foxtrot Platoon, Pier 40, Sub Base, Point Loma, California

It was late in the afternoon on Friday, October 12, slightly more than five weeks after the 9/11 terrorist attacks. There was a certain degree of normalcy returning to Foxtrot, at least in regard to getting the job done and taking care of the animals. That is not to suggest, however, that anyone had forgotten for a second that America suffered a barbaric and cowardly attack at the hands of Islamic terrorists. While each and every one of the Foxtrot team was itching for payback, each was quietly confident that America would not go lightly into the night. Retribution and justice would rain down from the heavens.

Brent had spent six weeks with Foxtrot Platoon, and each day, it felt like he was drinking from a fire hose. There was so much to learn, and Brent, typically wanting to know everything *now*, assimilated as much information as his noddle could accept. He was a stranger in a strange land but becoming more comfortable and at ease each day.

It was nearly 6:00 p.m. Usually, by this time of day, most of the team had secured. Brent had just left the medical hut, and since there wasn't much going on, he decided to head home. But first, he wanted to spend some time with Alika.

He was cautiously jubilant with the progress he'd made with the big bottlenose. Dale was highly impressed as well, and that was a good sign.

Adapting the trick of some of the other handlers, Brent whistled as he approached Alika's pen; and more often than not, Alika would respond by popping his head up and releasing a series of whistles of his own. Brent had not a clue as to what Alika might be saying, but just getting him to recognize Brent's whistle and getting a response was still a breakthrough by any measure.

Brent lay himself on the edge of the pen, and Alika glided toward him. Brent looked around to ensure no one was near. He didn't want his purrings to this big dolphin to be overheard. Of course, Alika had no way of understanding what was being said, but he truly enjoyed all the physical contact and the inflection of Brent's voice.

Brent had been with Alika for just a few moments when three things happened almost at once: the dock creaked, Alika dove for the bottom of his pen, and a large shadow hovered over Brent. Brent rolled slightly and looked over his shoulder.

"Hey, you little shit, whatayou doin' with my dolphin, huh?"

Pete Schultz, perfect!

Brent calmly got up and brushed his hands off on his trunks. "Just visiting. No harm done."

"I know who you are. You're the dipshit cowboy from the boat team. Well, you may have been a big deal there, but here, you're just a little turd."

So far, Brent was just taking it all in. This guy was about to come unglued, and Brent saw the telltale signs.

"I sure didn't mean to cause a commotion. I had permission to visit Alika, but he's your dolphin, and if you don't want me to, I sure won't."

"Just keep away. He's a one-man dolphin, and you're not that man. So just stay away from him. Next time I see you anywhere near his pen, you're going to get hurt. Got it, cowboy?"

Brent squinted into the sun, realizing that Pete was a head taller than him. He also took into account that despite the height and the mass, Pete had very little muscle. He had a paunch, flabby arms, and though at one time he may have had a big set of shoulders, now they seemed to have become a victim of gravity.

"Yep. That's pretty clear to me. No issues."

Brent turned to leave and glimpsed the shadow of Pete's fist in line with the shadow of Brent's head. There was no time to think about it. Brent snapped his head forward and spun to his right. The action was completely involuntary, but it saved him from most of the impact to the back of his head from Pete's massive fist.

Pete had made a mistake, though. He had put all his force into the swing, but the missed contact threw him off balance for a moment. When he regained his balance, he turned to Brent, and a strange sensation came over him—a first, in fact: Pete was confused.

Standing in an odd posture was this cowboy horse turd with his open hands up and covering both sides of his face, weight on his rear leg. But what was disconcerting to Pete was this kid didn't look scared. In fact, if he was reading this right, he had a hint of a smile on his face.

This just wasn't right. Usually by now, his target, always somebody much smaller than himself and usually caught by surprise, was either quivering or running. But this guy was standing his ground. This should have been a warning to Pete, but instead, he became incensed, and that made him do a foolish thing. He rushed Brent and threw a second powerful roundhouse.

Brent knew this was coming probably before Pete realized what he was going to do. Brent stepped in with his left foot, ducked under Pete's fist, and rocketed his right knee into Pete's solar plexus. Pete folded like a cheap jackknife and crumbled headfirst on to the dock. Brent finished with a powerful right elbow jab at the top of Pete's right shoulder blade. A loud pop and one large grunt was all that came from Pete for several seconds. He had the wind completely knocked out of him, and there was something very, very wrong with the angle of his right shoulder: Pete couldn't move it, and he couldn't feel it. But this was secondary to his near-panicked state—he couldn't get any air into his lungs.

Brent, for a second, stood over Pete, vigilant for any residual signs of fight. When he realized Pete was down for the count and gasping for air, he rolled him to his right side and then laid him on his back.

Pete had all the facial expression of a landed grouper. It took a few more seconds and a couple of additional massive contractions of his diaphragm, but Pete finally inhaled several large lungfuls of air.

Brent was still cautious and remained out of reach. "You okay?"

Between gulps of air, Pete replied shakily, "You asshole. You tried to kill me"—gasp—"I'm putting you on report. You're going to get kicked out of the Navy. Your career is over, cowboy! No more dolphins for you. You can go back to shoveling horse crap," he cried.

Pete rolled to his side then finally made it to his knees. In between gasps, he whispered to no one in particular, "Little asshole!"

Brent stayed with him until he was sure he wouldn't roll into the water and drown.

Brent turned and walked toward the locker room but stopped to ensure Pete was recovering. It was at that moment that Brent saw a curious thing. An image, upsun. He couldn't be sure, but it looked at first glance like a gear locker on the dock—big and square. But then it turned and walked up the brow toward the security gate.

Uniform Code of Military Justice

Monday, 15 October 2001
Foxtrot Platoon, Pier 40, Sub Base, Point Loma, California

Monday opened up to a bright and beautiful morning. Brent had arrived about 0530 to help Dale with fish-house duties inspecting and packaging the meals, but first, he wanted to swing by and see Alika—Pete's warning days earlier dissipated like smoke rings in the breeze. After a short visit, Brent hustled down to the fish house.

He'd come in for several hours on Saturday and Sunday and couldn't shrug the feeling that something had changed. Suddenly everyone seemed to know his name. The team members were always courteous, but at this point, they seemed to be downright friendly. It was a complete mystery as to the source of the change.

It was right after PT, as Brent was heading for the locker room, that the duty officer, Second Class Boatswain's Mate Casey, intercepted him. "Hey, Brent, Lieutenant Heinrichs and the master chief would like you to join them at the OIC's office as soon as you can shower and change. PT gear is fine."

"I'll be right up." And as an afterthought, he asked, "Casey, you know what this is all about?"

"Nope. I'm sure you'll hear all about it when you see them. And by the way, nice job!"

"Nice job? Ah…what do you mean?"

The question went unanswered; Petty Officer Casey was already in a jog heading back to the duty office.

Nice job? What the hell's going on here?

Twelve minutes later, Brent, hair wet and wearing a damp T-shirt, was pounding the pine on Lieutenant Heinrichs's doorframe.

"Enter!"

Brent opened the door and stepped into the OIC's small office. Three people were already seated. Brent, the fourth, pretty much filled the office to capacity. "You wanted to see me, sir?"

"Sure do, Brent. Grab a chair."

Brent took the only remaining chair. Sitting straight as a drive-shaft and holding his baseball hat, he listened. He figured the OIC and the CMC would be at this gathering, but the third person, Chief Petty Officer Olopoto (Kahuna), was a wild card.

"No doubt you're wondering why you're here, Brent," the OIC remarked.

"Yes, sir. I am."

"I have on my desk a report chit on you written by Petty Officer Peter Schultz. Do you know anything about this?"

Brent paused and focused. "Yes, sir, I think I do. Pete and I had a bit of a…an altercation Friday afternoon."

"An altercation? That's putting it gently. The medical report from Balboa Naval Hospital indicates that he had bruised sternum and a dislocated shoulder. The report chit, and I site the Uniform Code of Military Justice Article 128—Assault, and it reads, 'Any person subject to this chapter who commits an assault and intentionally inflicts grievous bodily harm with or without a weapon is guilty of aggravated assault and shall be punished as a court-martial may direct.'"

Lieutenant Heinrichs looked up from the report, his eyes fixed squarely on Brent.

"Sir, I'm guilty as charged. I wish this hadn't happened and—"

Both hands came up. "Brent, we all know this report chit is bogus, but we have to go through the drill. Kahuna, lucky for you, just happened to see the whole thing and brought out one very important fact that was somehow left out of the report—it was self-defense. Pete threw the first punch. That right?"

"Yes, sir, but if I was thinking, I probably could have figured out a way to avoid a confrontation. I'm really sorry this happened. I wish I could do it over again. It would come out differently."

In his best conspiratorial tone, Lieutenant Heinrichs leaned forward and, just above a whisper, said, "We don't. Petty Officer Schultz has been a jellyfish in my knickers since he got here, so this report chit isn't going anywhere, and Schultz has bigger problems. What I'm about to tell you is very sensitive. Not a word of it gets out."

Brent nodded.

"Sometime this afternoon, Master Chief Murphy and Kahuna will escort Pete to the locker room so he can pack his crap. Then they'll walk him to the security gate where two Navy Investigative Service agents will take him into custody."

"Is this just because of a fight?"

"No, it's because he's been under investigation for over a month now, and NIS has all the evidence they need to take him into custody. The charge—again, this doesn't leave this room—is UCMJ, Article 127, possession and distribution of drugs. If this sticks, and I believe it will, Petty Officer Schultz is going to spend some time making little rocks out of big rocks. There's a good side to this for you. Master Chief, you want to fill him in?"

Master Chief Murphy added, "Brent, we know Pete has neglected his dolphin. Alika has some emotional issues that were only compounded because he didn't have a good, caring handler. We were warned against reassigning anyone to Alika for fear of tipping Pete off before NIS could complete their investigation. The fight was the tipping point for NIS. With Kahuna's testimony, they have everything they need to take him off our hands. So how is this good for you?"

Brent looked expectantly at the CMC.

"We'd like to assign you as Alika's handler."

Brent felt as if he'd just won the lotto.

"You're new to the command and the job—okay. But Kahuna, Tony, Dale, and the med team all believe what you lack in experience is more than compensated by some innate gift you seem to have in working with our mammals. 'An uncanny ability to communicate with and care for the dolphins,' I think is how Doc Hamilton described it."

"Good grief, Master Chief, I don't know what to say."

"Don't say a thing. You're being thrown in the deep end, and in a few weeks, you're probably going to be wishing you were back at the boat team."

"I don't think so, Master Chief. I think this is where I belong. It just feels right."

"We've come to the same conclusion," Lieutenant Heinrichs added.

"And there's one more piece of good news," the master chief explained. "We're sending Alika back to Pier 159 for fleet recertification, and you're going with him. This is a very unusual opportunity. Normally, the Pier 159 boys do the socialization, the task-specific training, and certification, and our handlers receive the animals after they're fleet certified. But this time, our handler—that would be you, Brent—will be going through every bit of training and certification with your own dolphin. That would be Alika. This promises to have very positive rewards."

"I...I...ah, just don't know what to say, sir. This is all so sudden. I came in here thinking I hosed something away. Now I find out Alika doesn't have to put up with Pete, I get my own dolphin, and I get to go to school with him. What a great day! Thank you, sir!"

"Don't thank us too soon. There're a thousand things out there that could blow this plan," Lieutenant Heinrichs offered. "You'll be reporting to Pier 159 with Alika on Monday, the twenty-fifth of October. Until then, I want you to join up with Kahuna and learn everything you can. Kahuna's the best. The more you learn from him, the better prepared you'll be for Pier 159. You only have about two weeks to get spun up, so make it count. Questions?"

"I don't know where to start, sir."

"You start right here, right now," Master Chief Murphy injected.

Perp Walk

Monday, 15 October 2001
Foxtrot Platoon, Pier 40, Sub Base, Point Loma, California

Not three hours following the discussion with the OIC, two men in dark suits stood stiffly and quietly at the top of the brow near the security gate. Master Chief Murphy and Chief Kahuna Olopoto escorted PO Schultz to the locker room where he packed his few belongings into a seabag. As they exited the locker room, it was evident that word had spread like a rash—Schultz was being taken into custody by NIS.

Handlers, vets, and admin personnel were quick to line the docks and brows. Officially, the charge was violation of UCMJ Article 127, possession and distribution of drugs. But there was another charge for which Pete was guilty. Although not covered by the UCMJ, Pete was guilty of the crime of not being a team player and, as a sub-component to that, of being a general ass. In a command as tight as Foxtrot, this second charge was nearly as serious as his drug charge.

He had made no friends during his assignment at Foxtrot, but he had made several enemies, several of which weren't even human.

As Pete made his perp walk up the gangplank, everyone sensed the significance of the event. One of the dolphins, Kona, who had had his favorite toy, a simple boat bumper, taken from him by Pete, lay in ambush. As Pete, the master chief, and Kahuna approached Kona's pen, Kona surfaced with his bumper in his mouth. Master Chief Murphy and Kahuna at once realized a reprisal was about to be levied and backed away. Pete, head down and totally unaware, continued walking into the free-fire zone. Kona reared his head back and, biting into the line attached to the bumper, snapped his head forward, releasing the bumper.

It was a short time of flight. At the last second, Pete saw it coming, but it was too late to take evasive action. The bumper gave a glancing blow to Pete's right shoulder and neck, knocking him off-balance. The force of the impact caused him to stagger forward. Complicating matters, Pete's seabag tumbled forward in direct line of Pete's movement, tangling his feet. The impact of the bumper and the collision with his seabag caused him to go down face-first on the dock.

Luck was not with Pete that day. Pier 40, being one of the favorite hangouts of feral sea lions, was often the preferred dumping ground for their processed seafood. Pete landed chest down in a rather large pile of sea lion poop. He staggered to his feet, looked down, and didn't even attempt to scrape it from his shirt.

A large roar, cat whistles, and applause reverberated off the surrounding structures. Even the two men in dark suits at the top of the brow let a small smile creep across their faces.

It was a bad day for Pete but appropriate retribution.

CHAPTER 7

PREP SCHOOL

The nai'a (dolphins) are members of the family of Oiwi, people of the bones of our ancestors of these lands. The nai'a are esteemed, beloved family to us, and the relationship between they and our original people perhaps needs to be fully discovered, like the relationship of the stars to the lands in our Pacific and in our Hawaii. They are highly placed–the nai'a are highly placed in a pantheon that only some of us may understand at this time. Perhaps this hierarchy of spirit is the reason that human beings of all racial backgrounds may be able to tell about our brothers and sisters, the nai'a.

—Mikahala Roy (Kona and Ōiwi)

Cram Session

Tuesday, 16 October 2001
Foxtrot Platoon, Pier 40, Sub Base, Point Loma, California

Both Kahuna and Brent took Master Chief Murphy's words quite literally: "You start right here, right now."

At the crack of jack the next day, Tuesday, Brent met Kahuna at the loading pens. Brent had already checked out a seven-meter RHIB and had positioned Alika in the pen near the boat when Kahuna arrived. As he came down the brow, Kahuna yelled, "You ready, little brother?"

"Yep, and we're rarin to go," Brent returned.

Alika saw Kahuna as he approached the boat and whistled. Kahuna let out one of his own. Brent was surprised with the return, but maybe he shouldn't have been. Alika squealed and nodded his head rapidly up and down. Brent had never seen this response before. It was anyone's guess what it meant, but Kahuna seemed to be taking the greeting all in stride as if this was something that happened every day. And maybe it did, but it was wonderful to watch. Brent was indeed "rarin to go," but he had a surprise in store—this first day would be a very short training day. Kahuna, as a matter of habit, did a quick inventory of boat equipment and checked out the gear: radio, fuel, life vests, flare gun, anchor and line, fish bucket, and beaching tray. Alika watched Kahuna and Brent with great interest. He seemed to know something was up.

"You ever beach him?" Kahuna inquired.

"No! I've never beached anything."

"Well, today we'll get you started, but we're going to do this in increments. And before we do anything, you need to know something about beaching. Beaching is a really big deal in the community of dolphins, and so it should be to us also. This act acknowledges that they have given up the right of self-determination. It is a first and major step in showing trust in a human and a significant building block in establishing the bond between the handler and his dolphin. Remember that! Now, I know you've seen the handlers beach their dolphin before, but I'm going to go over it so you learn it right. Some of our handlers have their own procedures. Sometimes they take shortcuts. We're not going to do that. First, we'll make sure we have the beaching tray in place and secured on the port side in-line with the cutout area in the gunnel.

"If you look, you'll see that this cutout area lowers the gunnel to about eighteen inches above the deck on the port side near the stern of the RHIB. It's aligned with the beaching tray, and it makes the dolphin's entry and exit much easier."

Kahuna inspected the beaching tray and the area around it.

"Go ahead and let Alika out of the pen, and we'll bring him over to the boat. He's going to swim a big circle around us. That's normal. He's just doing a recce-run to see what's going on."

Brent hopped out of the RHIB, walked over to the pen, and opened the gate, allowing Alika to exit the pen. Sure enough, Alika accelerated and swam a large oval pattern next to the boat, pinging as he swam. He then glided to a stop at the stern of the RHIB and looked up at Brent, who had come back aboard the boat.

"Good. Now we'll get your dolphin on the port side of the boat just forward of the transom. This is called the *hand station*. Pretty much where he is now. Go ahead and get on your knees at the aft edge of the tray."

Brent did as he was directed.

"Extend your arm down to the water so you can reach him." Kahuna handed Brent a fat herring. "Take this and hold it out for him."

Brent turned toward Alika and extended the offering. Alika took it gently, gobbled it up, then studied Brent expectantly. To Brent, who had studied the process but had never actually done it before, this was pretty exciting stuff. He could hardly wait for the next step.

"Okay, we've got Alika here. Now what?"

"Now nothing. That's all we're doing today. Close up the mat. The name of the game is incremental successes. We want Alika to get comfortable with one task at a time, and we want him to stay excited to want to learn more. Tomorrow, you'll beach him."

Brent glanced at Alika. He seemed to have the same question on his mind as Brent—*Is that it?*

Day two began much as the previous day. The RHIB was tied up to the dock, and Brent had already checked all the gear as well as the boat systems. Alika was in open water near the RHIB and was paying close attention to Brent's activities. Kahuna called out as he walked toward the boat, "You two ready to go, little brother?" At the sound of his voice, Alika released his whistle and followed it up with several click trains, and as before, a rapid nodding of his head. As stoic as Kahuna was, he couldn't keep a big grin from forming. He returned Alika's whistle.

It was at that moment that it finally occurred to Brent that "little brother" may be Kahuna's greeting to Alika and not him. *No matter. We're a team now*, thought Brent.

"Good to go, Kahuna, and Alika is about as excited as I've ever seen him."

Standing on the dock to get full visibility of Brent and Alika, Kahuna said, "That's why we quit so early yesterday. We want him excited to go for a ride and stay focused on learning the tasks. We won't disappoint him today. He'll be hungry to learn. Now let's crank up the engines and get the big guy in the boat. Show me your stuff, Brent."

Brent started the left outboard and then the right. The engines were always started before the dolphin came aboard. This reinforced in the dolphin two important points: that they only beach in craft when the engines were running, and once running and beached, they were going someplace.

Without another word from Kahuna, Brent moved to the edge of the beaching tray, knelt, and called Alika. Alika glided to the hand station and was rewarded with a big fat herring. He scarfed it up. As soon as Alika had it down the hatch, Brent extended his hand, palm up, and lightly touched the water.

The next step was unrehearsed and certainly not *procedure*. Brent suddenly had a question for Kahuna and made the mistake of standing to turn toward Kahuna. At the same time, having done this many times before, the big dolphin smoothly launched himself over the gunnel onto the tray—exactly where Brent was standing. Nearly 500 pounds collided with Brent's 170-pound frame and in testimony to the persistency of Newton's laws, Brent was inelegantly taken to the deck. Brent lay for a moment flat on his back, staring at the deep azure sky and wondering as to the reason he was in that reclined position.

He rotated his head to the left and came eye to eye with Alika. His perennial grin seemed more pronounced as if to say, *Gee, wasn't that fun!*

"That's a stout dolphin," Kahuna commented in good spirit. "You're going to have to learn to get out of the way or at least not take your eye off him!"

Brent picked himself up, all smiles but embarrassed. "I guess I'm going to have to. I didn't even see him jump."

"If that's the first time you've ever been hit by a dolphin, stand by. There's a lot more where that came from."

Brent folded up the outboard panels of the tray and secured the triangular panel at the rear of the tray while Kahuna cast lines and came aboard the RHIB. Kahuna tossed his dry bag forward, positioned himself behind the steering console, and made a visual sweep around the boat. Brent placed a plastic bucket upside down just forward of Alika. He sat on the bucket just as he had seen other handlers do. From this position, the handlers could monitor and maintain physical contact with their dolphin. It's not a comfortable position for the handler, and that was the point. If they hit heavy seas, the handler will share the discomfort with his animal. When it got too rough for the handler, it was too rough for the dolphin, and the coxswain would then head for calmer waters, adjust speed, or change tack.

While the engines warmed up, Kahuna checked on Brent and Alika a final time. Satisfied that everything was shipshape, Kahuna slipped the engines into gear and pointed the boat seaward, heading into the San Diego Bay.

A mile from the pier, Kahuna cut the engines and turned to Brent. "Okay, shipmate, let's get that boy in the water."

Brent unfolded the two side sections of the beaching tray and laid them on the deck. "Let's go for a swim, boy." With amazingly little effort, Brent carefully eased Alika backward over the pontoon gunnel and into the water.

For the next three hours, Kahuna patiently taught Brent about the *stimulus discriminators* (SDs): specific whistles, hand commands, and other visual stimuli. SDs were the fundamental communication methods handlers used to direct their animals to perform all basic tasks inherent in their mission. The SDs were also standardized for all NMMP dolphins and included signals for jumping, boat following, beaching, vocalizing, exhaling, rolling over, fluke presentation, and many others. In this way, different handlers could work with any of the NMMP dolphins.

Interspersed with several beaches and launches, Alika was also treated to free-time swims, jumps, wake riding, and other dolphin games.

By the end of the period, Brent had the beaching and launching process down pat. And as tedious as it might seem to a human being, not once did Alika seem distracted or unfocussed. It could have been the juicy herring he received each time he beached, but it could also have been the activity, the chance to perform a task with a human he apparently very much liked.

Dolphins can be amused for hours on end with the simplest of toys, tricks, and challenges. Even adorning themselves with pieces of seaweed can bring endless hours of joy and amusement. Alika was no different. Everything was an adventure, new and mystifying, and only made more interesting by the fact he was working with *his* humans.

When Kahuna was satisfied that Brent understood and had mastered the SDs for the basic tasks, he suggested that Brent toss the bait bucket lid. This was new to Brent, but apparently not to Alika. Brent flicked the lid like one would toss a frisbee. Alika dashed off to recover and return it to Brent's outstretched hand. Like a big gray-and-white Labrador retriever, Alika retrieved everything Brent tossed. Alika, unlike Brent, seemed not to tire from the exercise, and Alika was doing all the work.

When Kahuna was satisfied with the day's progress, he said, "Good job. That's enough for today. Get your boy in the boat. We're heading in before it gets dark and he gets bored. Tomorrow you two are going to learn to transfer from this RHIB to the control boat. It's not a tough lesson, but it is one of those building blocks you two need to have down perfectly when you go to Pier 159."

This time, Brent beached his dolphin without the humiliation of getting knocked on his keister. Even Brent had a learning curve.

Kahuna expertly landed the RHIB near the loading dock at Foxtrot. Brent hopped out of the boat with the painter lines and quickly secured the RHIB to the dock.

"Go ahead and unload Alika. We'll let him explore a while, and I'll brief you on what we're going to be working on before you two head to Pier 159."

"Great!" exclaimed Brent then moved to ease Alika out of the boat. As soon as Alika hit water, he took off, eager to see what had changed on the block in the several hours since they departed.

Kahuna took a comfortable position on the starboard sponson; Brent sat on the overturned bucket and waited with interest.

"Now, none of what I'm going to describe to you is hard," Kahuna began. "Alika's already done everything he'll be tested on at Pier 159 before. Remember, he's already been certified once, but the higher-ups had some concerns that he wasn't up to fleet standards for an MK 7 dolphin. He's young, and from what I know of him and what I've seen of him in the last couple of days, he's sharp, can focus well, is interested in the job, and has confidence in you, and that's big voodoo. I'm thinking all his problems were because of his old handler. Now he has a new one—you. Together, you two have all the stuff needed to be a first-rate team. Maybe one of the best."

"Thanks, Kahuna. Coming from you, that really means something."

"Don't get too far down the road just yet. You still have to complete the handler's course, and Alika has to do well in the fleet recertification tests. We had to pull some strings for you and Alika. Normally, a new handler would only attend the course. He wouldn't have his animal with him in the certification program. Considering we're shorthanded and Lieutenant Heinrichs is confident in you, the biotechs have agreed to let you work with them and Alika in the morning and attend classes in the afternoon. So don't hose it up!

"The people at Pier 159 work under the Biosciences Division of Space and Naval Warfare Command Systems Center. They're civilians, and many are ex-Navy marine mammal handlers, probably the best biotechs and engineers in the world. This time, they'll be looking harder at Alika. They don't like getting one of their animals back after they've been certified, and they know Alika's had some issues. So Alika doesn't just have to pass—he has to impress them and pass. Same as you!

"That's why we're going to be working pretty hard for the next week and a half. We're going to be practicing everything the biotechs and engineers are going to be throwing at you: beaching and exiting, the hand signals, and all the tasks an MK 7 dolphin is responsible for in his mission. You two nailed the simple tasks today. Transferring from the seven-meter RHIB to the eighteen-foot RHIB—that comes tomorrow. Watching Alika today, he shouldn't have any problems. Then comes some more challenging tasks—and it's a one-dolphin show—he'll need to detect practice mines.

"Alika will not only have to locate targets. He'll have to discriminate between big hunks of metal we place on the seafloor as decoys and the actual practice mines. Occasionally, the young dolphins will give you false hits. We need to explain the difference between a valid find and a decoy. No food, no strokes for a bad hit, but lots of both for a good one."

As Kahuna laid out the syllabus to Brent, Alika explored around the pens and socialized with both the MK 7 dolphins and the local sea lions that frequent the dolphin pens. The sea lions came for the occasional food scraps but also for the social experience of being with dolphins. They all seem to get along; they are both easily entertained and quite sociable.

"Once the dolphin has detected a target and determined that it's a mine," Kahuna continued, "he'll come back to the control boat and notify his handler by tapping one of two small disks tied to the port side of the control boat. The disk is called a malipuladium. And no, it is not a test question. The handler will then decide whether it's a good hit or not. If he believes it's good, he'll give the dolphin a marker. The dolphin will return to the mine and lay the marker near the mine and return to the boat. Notice I said *near* the mine. They are never allowed to touch the mine—practice or real mines. It's unlikely, but it could detonate the mine. We don't want them touching any mines with anything.

"There's a third boat in the package—the dive boat. There are usually two divers in the dive boat, and they'll follow the control boat but are not supposed to interfere with the dolphin's tasks. When the dolphin puts the marker in place, the coxswain or the handler of the control boat will ask the divers to check the placement of the marker. The divers will then swim to the location of the marker and determine if it's a mine or a hunk of metal and then assess the marker placement. Finally, they'll have to make some more decisions: defuse it, bring it to the surface, or if it's a real-world operation and once the animal is out of the water—blow it in place.

"You can see that there are quite a few moving parts in this operation, and everybody needs to pull as a team. It's a dangerous game in the real world, and no one can afford to make a mistake. Lives are on the line."

Brent seemed somewhat surprised. "Nobody's explained the mission like that. I mean, I knew what we did. It was just never clear to me how we did it. Thanks for the explanation. I didn't know it was so complicated."

"Well, that's just the top layer. We haven't even begun to talk about tactics, techniques, and procedures yet. That'll come, though. For now, and for the next several days, we're going to work on the basic building blocks. There's lots to learn, but with Alika's interest and focus, and your ability to work with him, you two will be good to go when the class starts."

"Thanks a ton, Kahuna. I'm feeling better about this."

"Good. Now get your boy into the pen with the rest of the dolphins."

Brent collected his dolphin and, with an appropriate reward of fresh herring, escorted him to his pen.

Kahuna had departed by the time Brent finished the cleanup of the boat. It may have been the several references Kahuna had made to *real-world* scenarios that got Brent thinking. He was becoming more concerned with the growing instability in Iraq and wondering about all the permutations of the terrorist attack on the Pentagon and Twin Towers. The reality of another flare-up in the Mideast was beginning to seem more likely, but he was having difficulty imagining Alika and him going into harm's way without a contingent of heavily armed and very dangerous brothers protecting them.

Sometimes, Brent mused, *it's better not to think about all the things that can happen, especially when you can't do anything about them.*

Training Progress

Thursday, 25 October 2001
Foxtrot Platoon, Pier 40, Sub Base, Point Loma, California

Approaching the finish of his morning PT run, Brent huffed and puffed like an old steam engine pulling freight. *I gotta get back into shape. If the brothers at the boat unit saw me now, they'd laugh me off the dock.*

It was painful, but in the last two hundred yards of the run, Brent uncorked, passing many of his teammates. Clearly, his physical conditioning time was being encroached upon by time spent at his new job. It seemed that learning the ropes and taking care of Alika was leaving little time for much else. Between fish-house duty, watches, and working with Alika under the tutelage of Kahuna, and volunteer time with the med team, there just wasn't enough time in the day to get everything done.

Brent and Alika had been under the guiding hand of Kahuna for nine days. Brent was satisfied, in fact amazed, at the progress so far. Kahuna had taken a Wyoming cowboy, a onetime special boat driver, and reprogrammed him to become an acceptable fledgling dolphin handler.

In truth, Brent was more impressed with Alika's progress than his own. Alika had made a miraculous rebound. Brent gave credit for the overhaul to Kahuna. His magic touch, patience, and encouragement turned a nearly despondent (verging on becoming a dolphin recluse) into a confident, convivial, energized, and at times utterly jubilant dolphin. The change was astounding. Kahuna's mien reminded Brent of the easy, calm, and reassuring demeanor of Bill Washakie. And it didn't get much better than that.

Brent reflected on that wild beast Thunder and how, in the course of a few months, Bill had cast him into a prize-winning cutting pony, probably the most dependable and steady workhorse on the ranch, and unquestionably the most sought-after stud in Star Valley.

Yes, their training approaches seemed very similar in nature, and the common denominator was kindness, understanding, and the tactile, no-pressure approach they took in training their animals.

I have a lot to learn, Brent reflected. *Maybe not so much about treating the animals with respect and kindness—I learned that from Dad—but I have a long way to go to develop that incredible special communication skill that builds confidence and motivates the dolphins.*

Then one of the key secrets to training dolphins came rushing back to Brent when Kahuna said, "Dolphins are pretty easy to motivate. Unlike some people, they want to work."

War Drums—SITREP-CENTCOM

Thursday, 25 October 2001
Foxtrot Platoon, Pier 40, Sub Base, Point Loma, California

Brent was nudged out of his reverie by the flow of personnel forming for morning quarters. He headed for the formation and took position toward the front ranks. Just in time too. Chief Park appeared and called the formation to attention, put the unit at ease, went through the formalities of quarters, and reviewed the Plan of the Day. When Lieutenant Heinrich approached the formation, Chief Park called the unit to attention, turned to Lieutenant Heinrich, saluted, and reported, "All personnel present and accounted for, sir."

"Very well. Thank you, Chief."

"Foxtrot Platoon, at ease! Good morning, team. I wanted to update you all on some of the developments in the Mideast. While I don't think there's anything for us to get all spun up about, we do need to keep all our sensors up. I just attended a brief at Navy Special Clearance Team ONE. The security situation in Iraq continues to degrade. One of the items the intel officer covered was the situation report in and around Iraq. It should be a surprise to no one that the diplomatic and military conditions there are pretty poor and seem to be getting worse every day.

"Here we are ten years after the end of Desert Storm, a war in which a coalition of thirty-four nations joined in battle to defeat Saddam Hussein and his army. And after years of international political, military, and economic sanctions, Hussein continues to ignore UN directives, defy established no-fly zones, and bar the weapons inspectors from entering Iraq. Even after his monumental defeat, he's continued to terrorize, brutalize, and yep, murder his own people by the thousands.

"You'll remember in December 1998, President Clinton ordered air strikes against several Iraqi military target sets. This op Desert Fox went on for four days, but listening to the intel weenies and planners, it did little to change Hussein's position on letting weapons inspectors back in. There is talk that the only way to be absolutely sure that Saddam Hussein ends his WMD program is to go to war again. A horrible thought. The SITREP this morning brought a lot of sobriety to the situation.

"Those old enough to remember Desert Storm may recall the monumental ruse the Navy and Marines executed in the first days of the war. In a stroke of genius right out of the teachings of Carl von Clausewitz,[41] operational planners devised a component plan within Operation Desert Sabre to create a feint to land a Marine Expeditionary Battalion on Kuwait's Failaka Island on February 23 and a second amphibious assault feint at Ash Shuaybah on the twenty-fifth, two days later.

"These and other amphibious assault feints from 29 January to 26 February were successful in tying down nearly eighty thousand Iraqi troops that would otherwise have joined the main defensive action against the coalition forces and would, no doubt, have caused some serious problems with the left hook strategy. What many of you are probably thinking is interesting stuff, but what does this have to do with us? Well, guess who goes onto the beaches before the Marines? Guess who clears the way for the gators and all the support ships? Guess who clears all the mines for an amphibious assault force? If you said Special Clearance Team ONE, you earned yourself a cigar.

"Mobile Unit 3, the Mine Counter Measures group, Unmanned Underwater Vehicle Platoon, dive platoons, the SWCC platoons, and yep, Foxtrot Platoon would clear any minefields and obstacles *before* the Marines went ashore. We are now in the operations plans for this major regional contingency, and we're in the Time Phased Force Deployment Data right near the top of the list to go. Now, gents, let me bring you up to speed on a more recent event...the 9/11 attack. Here's what we now know. We know that the assault was a series of four coordinated attacks by al-Qaeda terrorists. About three thousand people were killed. The number of injured is difficult to determine, but it was also the deadliest single incident for law-enforcement officers and firefighters in our history. We lost 72 policemen and 343[42] EMT personnel—our nation's best.

"What are we doing about the attacks? Well, as you might guess, there are a number of ongoing investigations taking place by the FBI, CIA, NSC, and a host of other alphabet-soup agencies. We know that there were nineteen terrorist hijackers. They were primarily from Saudi Arabia, but a few were from other Muslim nations as well. Based on best intelligence estimates—and, as I understand it, irrefutable evidence—all fingers are pointing to Osama bin Laden as the mastermind and the man who funded the operation.

"The 9/11 acts were a pretty tough wake-up call for most Americans, but this is hardly the first time Islamic terrorists have attacked Americans on our home turf, and I dare say it won't be the last. In fact, I've been doing some research on my own, and I was very surprised to realize that terrorist attacks on Americans by Islamic radicals go back as far as 1972. Then, ten members of a mosque in New York called in a false alarm then ambushed the police officers who responded. Since 1972 and up to September 11, Islamic terrorists have killed at least forty-five people on American soil. When you include attacks on Americans abroad, the number increases substantially. The point I'm making is, attacks on Americans by Islamic terrorists did not begin on 9/11. They've been taking their toll on our people for nearly thirty years, and while the recent attacks on the Pentagon and the World Trade Centers were a great coup for the terrorists, it isn't going to end there. In fact, my bet is that this will just embolden them.

"President Bush has demanded that the Afghan government turn over bin Laden to us. The Taliban-led government declined the extradition order. In response to that and to dismantle al-Qaeda, the terrorist organization behind 911, Operation Enduring Freedom, a joint operation with Great Britain, began about three weeks ago on 7 October 2001.

"What does this have to do with our focus on Iraq and Saddam Hussein? We don't know yet. There doesn't seem to be much hard evidence yet that Saddam supported al-Qaeda in the 9/11 attacks. There seems to be some serious ideological differences between bin Laden and Saddam. That said, Saddam would take great satisfaction in any event that would damage our nation or hurt our people. So, at this point, it doesn't look like we can pin any involvement of the 9/11 attack on Saddam.

"Now, do I think we're going to war? Not tomorrow. Not the next day. But our intel experts and the planners are looking very nervous, and that makes me nervous. It's all up to our leadership and Saddam Hussein at this point. If the UN, the US, and our coalition partners are successful in convincing Saddam we mean business, we may be successful in restarting the weapons inspections. If they aren't, I think the smart money is on a second war with Iraq.

"I brief you all on this because you need to know what's out there, what's going on. We all have a part to play if this thing blows up. Some of our forces carry M16s, some fly jets off carriers, and others operate the command, control, communication suites. Our contribution to the effort will be our mammals. If it comes down to it, our dolphins and the sea lions will save lives—thousands of them—and contribute mightily to the campaign. Just be thinking about that the next time you take your animal out."

The men in the platoon were utterly silent, fixed in place by the realities should the balloon go up.

"That is all, Foxtrot Platoon. Ten-hut!" He turned to face the chief. "Chief Park, take charge and carry out the Plan of the Day."

"Aye, aye, sir!"

And Lieutenant Heinrichs left the podium.

"Foxtrot Platoon, dismissed!" Chief Park barked.

There was some playful bantering following this address, but one could sense the tension in the atmosphere. Every member of the platoon was thinking deeply about the possibility of war in a far-off place. As they made their way back to the docks and workspaces, they thought quietly about their families, their job, and their animals.

Brent was no different. He was transfixed on the news from Lieutenant Heinrichs. Well before his time in the service, he knew about Desert Storm, and he was alert to the escalating tensions in the Mideast, but until this morning, he had not extended the logic line to the final conclusion—the United States could go to war with the madman Saddam Hussein.

Brent pondered the obvious question: *Surely, he wouldn't do that twice...would he?*

Overview of the Persian Gulf War

Thursday, 25 October 2001
Foxtrot Platoon, Pier 40, Sub Base, Point Loma, California

To answer that question, one only had to reach back in history and consider the decisions and actions of Saddam Hussein and his staff—those who precipitated in the Persian Gulf War.

In the wee hours of 17 January 1991, the dogs of hell were unleashed in the skies over Iraq. A coalition of thirty-four nations joined forces—the largest coalition since WWII. This force engaged in military operations under Operation Desert Storm (17 January–28 February 1991). Led by the United States, coalition air forces pounded strategic targets throughout the country concentrating on Iraqi defense networks to include tactical aircraft, command and control headquarters, and upper-tier military leadership—Saddam Hussein, in particular.

It was a masterfully planned, synchronized, and executed tsunami of air power. Tomahawk cruise missiles launched from warships in the Persian Gulf in conjunction with F-117A Nighthawk stealth aircraft struck at the heart of Baghdad. F-4G Wild Weasels fired scores of HARM antiradiation missiles in support of the Suppression of Enemy Air Defense (SEAD) mission, allowing F-15s, F-16s and carrier-based F-14s, A-7s, and FA-18s to provide both strike and air-superiority missions.

For thirty-eight days, coalition strike and fighter aircraft, close air-support fixed-wing aircraft, attack helicopters, and the aging B-52 long-range bombers pounded primary targets on the Joint Integrated Prioritized Target List (JIPTL). Much of the Iraqi Air Force defected to other countries. Those who chose to stay and fight were annihilated. By mid-February, coalition tactical aircraft were returning with unexpended weapons on board—aircrews were running out of targets.

On 24 February 1991, with air supremacy established, Iraqi communication, command, and control (C3) networks largely destroyed, and Iraqi military leadership huddled in bunkers, Operation Desert Sabre began.

To further confuse and confound the enemy, two events convinced the Iraqi ground commanders that the main thrust would come from the south. The four-day battle of Wadi Al-Batin—a masterpiece of military dupery—and the massive ground push into Kuwait proved to be very successful feints for the main mechanized thrusts into Iraq.

Coalition forces crossed into Kuwait, but in most regions, they were met with little resistance; Iraqi troops surrendered in droves. The liberation of Kuwait was a necessary component to the campaign plan, but the real threat to Iraqi forces came from a different direction.

While Iraqi ground commanders concentrated on the battle for Kuwait, the main coalition force rapidly moved up from positions in Northern Saudi Arabia, well to the west of where Iraqi leadership expected the main thrust. There were 150,000 troops and 1,500 front-line tanks and hundreds of support vehicles that flowed north into Iraq then pivoted to the east—General Schwarzkopf's *Left Hook*[43]— to cut off and obliterate Iraqi's main ground forces. Although initial contact with the Iraqi forces was fierce, the onslaught of mechanized armor, thousands of well-trained and equipped ground troops, close air-support aircraft, and fast strikers caused Hussein's frontline troops to break and run, leaving much of their equipment in place.

Coalition air and ground forces continued to engage retreating Iraqi soldiers as they fled north along the Highway of Death, heading back to Baghdad. In the course of four days, Operation Desert Sabre nearly eradicated the Iraqi army.

On 28 February, one hundred hours after the commencement of Operation Desert Sabre, President Bush declared Kuwait liberated and issued a cease-fire order. The Persian Gulf War would go down in the history books and consecrated in military doctrine as one of the most successful and decisive battles in the history of modern warfare.

The loss to the United States in terms of lives, equipment, and dollars were expected to be much higher, but victory came at no small cost: 145 US service personnel killed in direct action, 4 tanks, 9 infantry fighting vehicles, and 51 helicopters and aircraft were destroyed at a monetary cost of $61 billion.

It was a war of many firsts: first use of Patriot missile systems in combat, the first time enemy forces surrendered to a UAV, first use of the F-117 in combat, first combat firing of TLAMs from USN ships, first use of GPS in combat, and the first time women flew combat missions in Navy strike fighters. It was also deemed the first war of the twenty-first century, but it was noted that only one side was fighting it. Iraq, mired in a combined air, land, sea, and cyber battle continued to exercise warfare doctrine based on twentieth-century strategies, tactics, techniques, technology, hardware, and training. They were still fighting the Iraq-Iran War.

The United States and coalition nations executed a near-flawless military campaign that, in one hundred hours of land combat, annihilated the fourth largest military force in the world. It has been noted by many historians, strategists, and military leaders that the termination of one war simply sets in place the playing pieces and conditions for the next. On 28 February 1991, when President Bush ordered the cease-fire, he also allowed Saddam Hussein to live—there would be no regime change. Although there remain some salient arguments supporting that decision, it would also portend that terrorist support from Iraq, WMD development, and atrocities against Saddam's own people would continue.

For years following the end of the Persian Gulf War, Hussein continued to deny access to UN weapons inspectors, violate no-fly zones, refuse to turn over WMDs, brutalize and murder Shi'ites in the south and Kurds in the north. Ultimately, Hussein's belligerence, brutality, and continued support to terrorist organizations around the world would ignite a second Iraq war.

Units within the Navy Marine Mammal Program had little operational tasking during the first Persian Gulf War. That would change during Operation Iraqi Freedom. Coalition forces, especially those operating within strategic littoral areas along the eastern side of Iraq, were dependent on safe, mine-free waters in which to operate. EOD Group ONE would have major play during the Second Persian Gulf War—OIF.

Safe for Solo

Saturday, 27 October 2001
Foxtrot Platoon, Pier 40, Sub Base, Point Loma, California

It was suddenly Saturday, the twenty-seventh day of October, an exquisite autumn day. Kahuna and Brent drifted with a slight current seven miles southwest of San Diego Bay. A light wind brushed the blue Pacific and rippled the water; the RHIB rocked lazily under a warm autumn sun.

Kahuna and Brent sat on sponsons on opposite sides of the seven-meter RHIB as Alika explored the perimeter of the boat and occasionally leapt out of the water.

Where has the time gone? This is our last training day. I know we've made some headway, but we still have so much to learn. Alika and I report to Pier 159 for fleet recertification in two days. Seems like we should be doing something, Brent thought.

Brent was prepared for a long day that would test both Alika and him to ensure they had everything nailed down.

The last two weeks of training and preparation had been a tightly packed learning experience for both of them. This day was their last day to train, but it seemed to be turning into a day of free play and reflection. Perhaps this was Kahuna's gift in recognition of their hard work and progress.

They watched in serene silence as Alika played and breached and swam in large circles around the boat. Occasionally, Brent would toss the bait bucket lid for Alika to retrieve. He never seemed to tire from this sport. Clearly, he was enjoying his outing, oblivious to the upcoming training starting on Monday—the tranquil bliss of the uninformed.

Except for the lapping of the light waves against the sponsons and the occasional splash made by Alika, all was quiet. In the last two weeks, Brent worked closely with Kahuna and was quick to realize that if there wasn't something important to say, Kahuna did not speak. He was not a conversationalist. Many people would have been uncomfortable around a person so reticent, but Brent had grown accustomed to the reserved persona of the man and appreciated it. When Kahuna did speak, Brent's receivers went on high gain.

From out of the blue, Kahuna said, "You are new to these mammals. I can tell, though, you have strong connections with animals. That will help you in understanding and training and working with our dolphins. They are complicated animals—very spiritual. I've worked this program twelve years. I learn something new about them every day. I've had dogs. Good ones. They were good friends. Loyal, protective, smart. Dolphins are like good dogs, but they are much more.

"I read a Navy message a couple of years ago. A little boy was blown out to sea on his surf mat. He was in a protected cove in Diego Garcia. Diego Garcia has many sharks. The cove was ringed by a long shark net. It was good for swimming, but the wind was strong that day and pushed the boy beyond the swimming area. Luckily, the lifeguard saw the little boy drifting across the shark net and into deepwater. He called for a rescue boat to go after the little boy, but he also called the control tower, hoping they had an airplane available to keep the boy in sight.

"There was a Navy P-3 returning from a mission. They were vectored to the little boy and held position over him while the rescue boat came. One of the crewmen realized that the boy was surrounded by large fish. There had been many shark attacks around the island, and he thought these were big sharks circling the boy. The rescue team speeded to the boy with the help from the P-3 crew. The men in the boat pulled the boy from the water and headed for home. One of the hands on the rescue boat asked the little boy if he saw any sharks. The little boy said that he had…many. And then he said that the dolphins came and scared them all away."

Kahuna paused and stared at Alika still frolicking in the brilliant blue water. Brent, elbows on his knees, stared intently at Kahuna, silently urging him to continue.

"My people have many stories of these great animals saving people. Many believe they are our brothers and sisters. I'm not sure. But I believe they have powerful spirits and are filled with great goodness."

Brent noodled over all that Kahuna had just said. Nothing was in contradiction to the beliefs Brent had been forming in the last several weeks. If anything, Kahuna's reflections had only solidified Brent's beliefs. *Dolphins, especially Alika, are pretty amazing animals.*

Brent's serenity was interrupted. "Get your boy aboard, Brent. We're heading in."

"What? I thought we were going to do some final training today. There's still a lot I don't know."

"You know enough. You will do well." And then he added, "Trust your partner. He will keep you right. He's smart, motivated, and he's done this before. He just needed someone he could count on, someone he could trust, and now…he has you."

Kahuna continued, "Brent, just remember, believe in your animal. Watch his head. Make sure he's looking at you when you give him commands. There is a time for work and a time for play. Don't get them confused, or he'll get equally confused. Alika knows his job. Don't sweat the small stuff. Focus on strong fundamentals. Remember, we can fix anything as long as we have a dolphin and a bucket of fish. But if he's not with you, if he's not focused on the job, you have nothing.

"Alika is your sensor. Together, you and he are a system. You get in a minefield without your sensor, you're in a bad spot and not helping anyone. Rewards are an interesting motivator, but it's better to not reward him if you're uncertain about his accuracy or with the precision of his marking job. If you feed one wrong behavior, if you reward him for a bad marking, you will raise doubt in his mind about what you're doing out there. If you do that, you've just ensured that it's going to happen again."

There was a moment's pause, long enough for Brent to file away each word and long enough for Brent to wonder what triggered this epiphany. This was more monologue and more philosophy and guidance than Brent had gotten out of Kahuna in the last two weeks. It was sage counsel, and Brent put it in a place of his memory reserved for important things.

Brent looked at Kahuna, wanting more, but turned to where Alika was swimming and, just in time, saw his dolphin launch himself out of the water and finish with a beautiful reentry. Brent whistled, and Alika responded with one large high-speed circle around the boat and ending with a fairly impressive stop at the gunnel. Alika's head came out of the water and looked straight at Brent, as if to ask, *What's up?*

Moving to the hand station at the edge of the beaching tray, Brent extended his hand just above the water. Alika glided over and gently laid his rostrum in Brent's hand. Brent then moved forward on the tray, slapped the tray, and said, "Get in the boat, Alika. We're going in."

With a powerful thrust of his fluke, Alika made a perfect jump into the beaching tray. Brent then brought the edges of the tray together to form a long triangle and closed the aft section of the tray, securing Alika within the tray. While Kahuna slipped the engines into gear, Brent sat on the upturned bucket and whispered to his dolphin, "I know you're ready, Alika. I sure hope I am."

CHAPTER 8

FLEET RECERT

The only animal to have a more folded cortex than man is the dolphin. The theory most commonly accepted is that this larger brain evolved to support more complex cognitive abilities. They can remember events and learn concepts, changing their behavior as a result of previous experience. They can communicate with each other during cooperative behaviors, manage relationships in their pods and raise their young. They can understand not only symbolic (sign) language words but can interpret the syntax (word) order of language. This understanding of syntax is highly indicative of intelligence. Signature whistles produced by dolphins serve to offer some evidence that dolphins have a self-awareness, or the capacity to have a concept of "self" and to know that one exists as an individual being.

—Kevin Green, "Are **Dolphins** Intellectually
Superior to Us Humans?"

Marine Mammal Systems Operator and Maintenance Course

Monday, 29 October 2001
Foxtrot Platoon, Pier 40, Sub Base, Point Loma, California

Bright and early Monday morning, 29 October 2001, Brent loaded Alika into a seven-meter RHIB for the trip to Pier 159. Kahuna assisted in the load and then planted his fanny on the upturned bucket within easy reach of Alika. With his forearm resting across Alika's melon, Kahuna said, "Good to go. Take us out, Brent."

"Roger!"

Brent slipped the painter lines, climbed behind the helm, and eased the RHIB into open water headed for Pier 159. "Coming up," Brent hollered over the sound of the twin outboards as the seven-meter RHIB came up on plane and shot across the waters of San Diego Bay.

It was a short trip, perhaps too short. Kahuna seemed to relish every second of his time as he gazed off in euphoric bliss at the San Diego Bay panorama—the bright cerulean sky, the city skyline, the salt air, and the contact with the big dolphin next to him. *How could things ever get better?*

As they approached Pier 159, Brent could make out two individuals standing on the dock, apparently there to receive them. Kahuna joined Brent at the helm. "The guy on the left is Mark Cory, old Navy mammal trainer. Been around forever. Worked all the systems—dolphins and sea lions. He'll be running the school. Pretty smart old man. Listen to everything he tells you. You'll come back to us a lot smarter."

"I'll do my best, Kahuna."

Unknown to Brent at this time was that Mark was a biotech and a subject-matter expert (SMEs) of some fame and distinction within the community of marine mammals. The good news was that Mark was assigned to Brent and Alika as their biotech and trainer for the next five weeks.

The closer Brent got to the pier, the better acquainted he became with the lay of the land. The Navy never tries to impress anyone with architectural design or tall buildings. The Navy has to budget for warfighting systems, manpower, training, support equipment, and facilities. With little to spend on niceties, the Navy is very constrained to form, fit, and function contributing to the operational mission.

As Brent closed on Pier 159, he became increasingly impressed with the layout of Pier 159. It looked like a typical Navy facility, but there was order and logic to its footprint. It encompassed about two acres and consisted of numerous boat docks, mammal pens, several shacks, and a handful of single-story buildings. There were a number of thirty-by-thirty-foot dolphin pens separated by removable gates, allowing migration, grouping, and easy access to open water and the workboats.

The facility belonged to Space and Naval Warfare Command (SPAWAR) Systems Center (SSC), Biological Sciences Division, but it was run and operated by a staff of about forty civilian engineers, biotechnicians, scientists, and veterinarians. Some of these were very experienced ex-Navy mammal handlers and trainers—it wasn't their first square dance. These were the first-string team and some of the leading subject-matter experts in the field of marine mammals *worldwide*.

As they closed on the dock, Brent reversed the engines and swung the helm so the props were pointing toward the dock. A quick thump on both throttles followed by engine shutdown set the RHIB up for a precision landing against the dock.

"Mark, 'sup? Long time, bro!" Kahuna said as he tossed the painter lines to Mark.

"Too long, Kahuna. How's your dolphin been keeping you?" Mark returned.

Instantaneous recognition of Mark's voice was apparent. Alika whistled and cycled his big fluke up and down.

"He's like a kid. Never a moment without needing some attention."

Kahuna stepped off the boat as Mark turned to greet him. With big smiles on both of their faces, they clasped hands and bumped shoulders. It was a greeting common within the SOF forces, but Brent was a bit surprised to see the ritual here in marine mammal land. *Kahuna and Mark have history together*, Brent realized.

While Mark assisted in securing the boat, Kahuna made the introductions. "Brent, this is Mark Cory, senior biotech at 159. The gent tying the boat up is Craig Holden."

Brent nodded to Craig and shook Mark's hand.

"Mark, this is our cowboy from Wyoming, Brent Harris. He just came aboard a few weeks ago. Got him from Boat Unit TWELVE. He's working hard to learn about our animals, but he keeps trying to throw a saddle on 'em. So far, they're not liking it much. I dunno. I don't think there's much hope for him as a dolphin handler. Do what you can. If you can't train him, no issues. We can always use a permanent fish-house guy"

"I'm sure we can break him off his bad habits!" Mark grinned widely.

"And this big boy in the boat is Alika," Kahuna continued, "our problem child. Now he's Brent's problem. We teamed them up a couple of weeks ago."

"I remember Alika. I was here when he first arrived. Little dude and afraid of everything. When he got over his fear and anxiety, he was a good boy and a fast learner. Emily, his surrogate mother, carried him through a pretty tough time and just may have saved his life."

"I remember," Kahuna responded. "Emily still here?"

"She is and doing well. Best mom on the whole West Coast. And, Brent, I'll take you and Alika over to see her later. It'll be an exciting reunion."

A big grin grew on Brent's face. "Wow, yeah! I'd really like that. Thank you."

"No problem. Now, let's get this brute out of the boat."

Brent took a knee and laid the sides of the beaching tray down. "Let's go swimming, big boy," Brent whispered to Alika. He then gently eased Alika off the tray and into the water. Mark, already on his knees near the edge of the dock, stretched his arm out to Alika, who glided directly to him—head up, eyes on, clearly excited.

"Dang, he got big. He's a handsome devil. Looks like you guys have taken good care of him. Sure seems happy!"

Mark continued to mutter to Alika in unrecognizable syllables and rubbed him from his rostrum to his fluke. The big dolphin's permasmile became exaggerated. Alika ate it up. If he had been given rear feet instead of a fluke, he would have been hopping around like a puppy.

"He is now," Kahuna returned. "He was a pretty sad and miserable boy under his old handler. He's gone now. Brent has been taking pretty good care of him."

"Yeah, the news got out. We heard NIS took Pete away. No loss there. Things like that should never happen."

"No. But I think this story has a happy ending."

Mark gave Alika a lingering last stroke down his flank then stood. "Brent, Craig will put Alika in with the boys, and I'll run you up to the classroom. You can grab a cup of our world-famous coffee, which some believe is spiked with giraffe piss. Then we'll get you registered."

"That's good with me, but you sure you don't want me to help Craig move Alika?"

"Naw," Mark reassured him. "Been doing this awhile. We're pretty good at it."

"Okay." A slight note of disappointment registered in Brent's voice.

Brent returned to the RHIB and retrieved his dry bag—a small waterproof backpack that contained all the essentials needed by a special boat driver. It went pretty much everywhere he went.

As Mark and Brent walked up the brow headed for the classroom, Brent looked over his shoulder at Alika and whistled. Without any hesitation, Alika returned Brent's whistle, one that Brent would recognize anywhere.

Introductions and Coursework

Monday, 29 October 2001
Pier 159, Sub Base, Point Loma, California

With Mark's help, Brent completed a short survey form for the class and grabbed a cup of coffee. He sipped it cautiously. *Jesso, he wasn't kidding.* As described, the coffee tasted like something that may have come out of the south end of a northbound giraffe. Brent did not complain. He'd had worse, but it was always mystifying how the Navy could take store-bought coffee and turn it into something almost unrecognizable and nearly undrinkable.

Brent lugged his coffee and dry bag to a seat near the rear of the classroom. A syllabus outline, course guide, a notebook, a stack of reading material, a name tent, and a pencil had already been laid out at each seating area.

Brent set his bag on the floor, his cup on the desk, and his fanny in the chair. He scanned the syllabus outline. It was three pages of small type and covered all five weeks of the course. He wasn't so much surprised that most of the course was taught in the classroom; what caught his attention was the amazing scope of the classes: Biology, Animal Husbandry, the Basics of Learning, Ten Rules to Good Training, three levels of training animals—Dolphin Sonar, Animal Interaction, Combat Swimming Tactics, Pools, Pumps and Support Equipment, Animal Transports, Shipboard Forward Deployment, Media Training, Medical Care for Mammals. And there was nearly a week dedicated to small-boat handling, maintenance, navigation, and communication. That was the only area Brent felt comfortable with—he could probably teach that class. The rest of the course content was remotely familiar. Kahuna's teachings, by other names and titles, seemed to brush on most of the subjects in the course. Brent relaxed a little. *Maybe I am ready for this!*

Brent was reluctantly sipping the giraffe piss when—

"Good morning, gents," Mark Cory greeted that class as he walked toward the head of the classroom.

"Good morning, sir," came the unanimous response from fourteen Navy petty officers and two enlisted Marines.

Mark, as a retired Navy senior chief, did not rate the "sir," but a glimmering career as one of the pioneers in training and operations of marine mammal systems ensured the "sir" was not misplaced. Mark stood to one side of the podium, scanned the faces, gave Brent the slightest nod of recognition, and then began.

"My name is Mark Cory. I'm the senior Navy biotech here at Pier 159. We have your little bodies for five weeks. Where your brain chooses to go is your decision, but know ye this—you can flunk out of this course. You're not here to enjoy the Southern California surf, nightlife, chase the beach hotties, or make geedunk runs to Mexico. You're here to make yourself one-half of an operational team that will save lives when, *if*, we go to war.

"Our job, even in peacetime, has risks. If we go operational, the risks and the hazards skyrocket. The more you know, the more you take away from this class, the more you draw from the experiences of the old-timers—those that have been *there*—the less the risk to you and your partner, and for that matter, to the combat teams that follow you in. Now, if you flunk out, if you begin to reevaluate your decision to join the Navy Marine Mammal Program, if, for any reason, you decide you're not cut out for this, we need to know soon.

"If you'll open your course notebook, you'll notice we have quite a varied course structure and quite a demanding schedule. You'll need to listen, think, take notes, and study the course material. You'll have quizzes several times a week and a final at the end of the course. What'll be a little different in this class is that Petty Officer Brent Harris, seated at the rear—Brent, hold up your hand—will be working with his animal, Alika, a big Atlantic MK 7 bottlenose, in the morning and attending the lectures and discussions in the afternoons. Alika will be recertified, and Brent will get his handler qualification, if he passes. Unless you have any questions, I'll turn this over to Mr. Josh Reinhardt. Josh…"

"Thanks, Mark! Gentlemen," Josh—another highly acclaimed SSC trainer whose list of accomplishments, citations, and bone fides read like a course syllabus for a marine biologist—said, "I'd like to start off with short introductions from each of you. Please also give us an explanation of why you joined the mammal program. We'll start with"—Josh squinted at the name tent of a young Marine in the first row—"Sergeant Miller. You're up, Sergeant!"

Sergeant Miller stood, glanced around the classroom, and in a voice that came from way down below, a voice that only Marines can summon, spoke, "Good morning, Mr. Reinhardt, gentlemen. I'm Sergeant Miller…"

The Reunion

Monday, 29 October 2001
Pier 159, Sub Base, Point Loma, California

The rest of the morning was devoted to the course introductions, rules and regulations, and animal husbandry. They had an hour break for lunch, and using that time, Brent made a beeline to Mark's office and politely knocked on the door.

Mark opened the door and smiled knowingly. "Hey, Brent. I'll bet you want to take Alika to see Emily."

"Yes, sir. Been thinking about it all morning."

Mark reached around the doorframe and pulled a well-used NMMP baseball hat off a peg. "Well, let's do this."

Mark led the way. Brent kept his scan going on the distant pens. He picked Alika out of several dolphins in the pen and whistled. Alika almost came out of the water. He twirled on his tail, spy-hopped,[44] and when he finally caught sight of Brent and Mark, whistled several times. As soon as Brent got near the pen, he got down on his knees and began stroking Alika. Alika rolled on his back, enticing Brent to rub his tummy.

"Brent, help me pull this gate, and we'll get Alika into open water. Then we'll herd him over to Emily's pen."

In a few seconds, they had Alika out of the pen and next to the dock. They closed the gate then headed for Emily. Mark and Brent walked, and Alika followed as if in *heel* position.

"Emily shares a big pen with the girls, some of which are pregnant. She's been around for a long time and has this place figured out. I'll enjoy watching this reunion."

"No doubt about it," Brent interjected. "This is going to be something to watch."

"You may already know this. We have a dolphin-breeding program. We breed only what we need to fill the ranks. Occasionally, when we're lucky and when we think we can do some good, we'll take a stranded or injured wild dolphin. We'll design a specific rehab program, provide medical treatment and therapy, and when they're ready, we'll begin training them as one of the systems. Alika is one of those fortunate dolphins we were able to adopt into the program, and we haven't been disappointed. To help socialize the young dolphins—teach them to be dolphins, if you will—we have a few surrogate mothers. Again, Alika really lucked out. His adopted mom, Emily, is a bit of an icon around here. She's one of the best we have, maybe the best we ever had. You just couldn't find a better mother."

Brent took all this in and reflected on just how incredibly lucky Alika was, and also how lucky he was to be teamed up with such a magnificent dolphin.

There were occasional signature whistles in the air, but Alika, for the most part, ignored them. He did transmit a few click trains just to get oriented. When it appeared he got his bearings, he suddenly took lead and dashed off on a direct line to Emily's pen. By the time Mark and Brent arrived, Alika had his head out of the water and was whistling furiously. Almost at once, a beautiful female dolphin elevated her broad gray head above water and returned the whistles. She was stately and very elegant.

"Well, that didn't take long," Mark intoned. "Looks like they remember each other. Not surprising. Help me pull this gate, and we'll get them together."

Mark and Brent hardly had the barrier out of the way when Alika burst into Emily's pen. They immediately joined and rubbed up against each other. Emily swam slowly away, looking over her left pectoral fin in encouragement. Alika quickly joined her and fell into position about a third of a length behind her. She circled the pen while Alika moved to her other side and slightly stepped down but was always in gentle contact with her, sometimes side by side and at other times directly underneath her. On one occasion, they circled the entire pen while Alika was tucked in close underneath her, his head just under her belly.

There were no conversations between the two dolphins, but there didn't need to be. The affectionate and persistent touching attested to the warmth, tenderness, and endearment shared between them.

"When it comes to reunions," Mark began, "dolphins have it all over humans."

"What do you mean?"

"Think back to when you and Kahuna came in this morning. I hadn't seen him in over a year. We're very good friends—in some ways, maybe best friends—and all we did was shake hands. Contrast that with these two. Sure, Emily raised him, and as you can see, they just can't get enough of each other. This could go on all day." Mark took a knee and continued to revel in the tenderness of the reunion. "The bond between mother and youngster is incredible. A solo dolphin is not really a dolphin at all. A true dolphin is just one of many parts of the pod, of the society.

"The nexus between a dolphin and its pod is something to behold. It's mysterious and complex. Without getting too deep into the neurology, many marine biologists believe the dolphins' limbic system—that's the very complex system of nerves and networks in the brain—involves a number of areas around the perimeter of the brain cortex. This area has much to do with their instincts and moods. What is pertinent is that it seems to control their basic emotions. Those are very similar to ours and include fear, pleasure, and anger. It also has a big influence on hunger, sex, dominance, and—here's the kicker—care of their offspring.

"To suggest that cetaceans, dolphins, have a much closer relationship to their society, their pod, than do humans in our society is a titanic understatement. Dolphins have a metric of connectivity with the *whole* that would explain many aberrations of what we humans would consider as *abnormal behavior*. They've been observed banding together to defend themselves against big predators: great whites, tigers, even orcas. Even when many of them can escape with no risk, they'll generally circle the wagons and fight, often at great cost to their number. And amazingly, similar to our SEAL brethren, they generally will leave none of their pod behind, even the wounded dolphins. That would be considered abnormal behavior in the civilian sector where usually *flight* wins over *fight*."

Mark, clearly in deep thought, continued, "I've read studies that seem to indicate that even when only one or two dolphins or whales are sick or disoriented, so tight, so driven are they to maintain integrity of the *whole* that all the animals become stranded rather than detach themselves from the pod. This would also hold water in the case of those occurrences when dolphins get encircled in fishing nets.

"We know how athletic they are. We've seen them do magnificent aerial leaps and acrobatics, but when the pod is encircled, oftentimes the whole pod will remain intact at great peril rather than jump the net and survive. There is a power of connectivity, of communal attachment, and of being part of the *pod* that we humans just don't get."

Brent stared at Mark and savored every word. Mark seemed to be fully entranced with the water ballet, the unrestrained affection between Alika and Emily. There was no suggestion of sexual attraction. What they shared could only be considered *true love* by humans who had the pleasure of observing the interaction.

"I had the opportunity to visit the Pentagon several years ago," Mark said. "If you get a chance to visit, do it. But if you get offered orders there, do anything to get out of them. For me, the most interesting and emotional part of the tour was the *Medal of Honor* room in the 'A' corridor. It listed all the MOH awardees of all America's wars. Each awardee had a plaque on the bulkhead. On it was engraved a summary of their actions that had earned them the medal. There were over three thousand medals awarded. It took a while, but I read a lot of the citations. I wanted to understand what made these men tick, what made them lay their life on the line, sometimes knowing full well they were giving it all up. And you know what I figured out?"

"No idea, Mark."

"According to the citations I read, of all the medal winners, guess how many risked or sacrificed their lives for their nation?"

Brent pondered that question for what seemed like moments. It was puzzling but captivating.

While deep in thought, Mark said, "You're going to be late for class. Let's get this big boy back to his own pen. Right now, they're enamored with each other, but I don't want to take the chance that this reunion turns into a love fest. A young male dolphin can put a two-peckered owl to shame."

Brent helped Mark with the barrier and, after several attempts, finally got Alika over to the opening and separated from Emily, much to his disapproval.

With the gate replaced and Alika reluctantly in tow, Brent said, "Okay, I give. How many?"

Mark looked at Brent as they strode toward the classroom. "Not a one! If the summaries are accurate, every single one of the medal summaries that I read described a warrior who risked his life not for flag or country but for his fellow warrior. They were trying to save their buddies, their teammates. These guys were gallant, brave, and loyal to a fault and risked everything for their buddies. And that"— Mark turned, his eyes squinted as a smile formed—"is about as close to becoming a dolphin as we humans will ever come."

Midcourse Progress

Wednesday, 14 November 2001
Pier 159, Sub Base, Point Loma, California

Interspersed among the battery of classes, lectures, quizzes, and admin duties, the course schedule also laid out practical, hands-on training with many of the mammals, both dolphins and sea lions. Brent's schedule had been further modified, however. Considering the extenuating circumstances at Foxtrot Platoon—the paucity of handlers, a growing demand for MK 7 services, and the fact that Alika seemed to be a full-up round—Mark adjusted Brent's schedule to allow him to work with Alika from 0600 to 1200 then attend classes into the afternoon. It would, of course, mean that Brent had to do double duty to stay up with the rest of the class in all the academics, but Mark believed Brent could pull it off.

Practical, hands-on training started early for Brent and Alika. Brent was usually at Pier 159 by 0600, positioning the seven-meter RHIB by Alika's pen and checking out the systems. Mark arrived shortly after and would act as backup when Brent loaded Alika. They were usually cranked up and heading out to the training areas by the time the sun peeked over the hills east of San Diego.

In the first two weeks of the course, Mark went through the basics of single boat, dolphin handling, focusing on general safety and operating procedures. This was more of a review and opportunity to refine what Brent and Alika already knew after having spent considerable time with Kahuna. Still, there was no such thing as learning too much.

During the first half of the course, things were progressing quite well. Alika plowed through the learning objectives—after all, he'd done all the assigned MK 7 tasks before. Brent, on the other hand, was working like a rented mule: practical training in the morning with Alika and Mark and classroom work, lectures, quizzes, and field assignments in the afternoon. In the evening, Brent studied the reading assignments he'd missed during the morning classes and prepared for the quizzes. He was keeping his breathing ports above water level but just barely.

The weekends were void of classes, but Brent still spent much of each day working and frolicking with Alika. When he could, and with Mark's permission, he let Alika and Emily play together. There was so much attraction and, in a cetacean sort of way, love between the two. Brent was entranced by the affection and the tenderness they always exhibited toward each other.

In truth, there were few things Brent would rather be doing. He was without a girlfriend at the time and had no likely prospects in sight. His pick-'em-up was in tip-top mechanical condition, and he had lost interest in hitting the beach and drinking with his Special Boat Team buddies. He'd learned firsthand that nothing good ever came after midnight and a six-pack. In the last several months, Brent's life priorities seemed to have become completely reordered—for the better.

He took pride in what, as a team, Alika and he had accomplished together. They were approaching the halfway mark of the course, and by all reports from the trainers and biotechs, Alika was setting new benchmarks in performance. Alika was attentive, quick to learn, seemed to enjoy his job, and was always ready to go to work. But what really sealed the deal for the Pier 159 folks—he was just a likable dolphin. Only a drunk homecoming queen could have been more popular.

In weeks two and three of MK 7 recertification, the handlers introduced building-block tasks to Brent and Alika. As a new learning objective was introduced, it was practiced, perfected, and then included in the established set of tasks. In this way, a chain of individual learned fundamentals were built one upon another and became a compilation of linked tasks, each reinforcing the other. By the end of the course, these building blocks would form a complete and, oftentimes, complex procedure associated with boat operations, mine location, assessment, identification, and marking.

As time went on, the tasks became increasingly more complicated for Alika, but Brent became quite adept at keeping the tasks focused and well defined. To ensure Alika understood his successes and to keep him interested, Brent was quick to lavish Alika with praise and rewards, but there was a fine line to walk. Mark liked to summarize the rule with a short adage, "There's a time for work and a time for play. Know the difference and make sure your dolphin knows the difference."

Rarely did Alika falter, but in those few cases when he did, preserving the high canons of Pier 159's *operant behavior*[45] protocols, there was never any punishment, simply a lack of reward. But to Alika, who craved positive reinforcement, a lack of reward was punishment enough.

So much of Mark's guidance sounded as though it was a sermon from Kahuna that Brent suspected there must be a little-known bible on the psychology of dolphins that Brent had not yet discovered. But it was always good to have the big lessons reinforced. Mark often reminded Brent to ask himself, "What am I rewarding Alika for—acting like a dolphin?" Mark explained, "You don't need to reward him for that. It's okay to act like a dolphin, but it's not something you would reward him for. Sometimes it's better not to feed your dolphin than it is to reward him for doing nothing. Reinforce the activities and tasks Alika does correctly, but don't reward him for things that are already in his nature or for those things he may have fumbled."

Brent had learned that if Alika botched a task, he should always give him an opportunity to do it again, to correct his mistakes. And when he did it right, especially something difficult, then lay it on him and let him know he had done well.

At the midpoint of the course, Brent and Alika practiced boat transfers. Transfers from the transport boat, the seven-meter RHIB, to the smaller control boat: an eighteen-foot RHIB. The dolphins did not actually come aboard the control boat. There was no beaching tray, and without it, the dolphin could be injured. Instead, the dolphin was trained to come to a position on the port side of the control boat near the midsection of the sponson: the hand station. That is where the handler and the dolphin joined to communicate. When stopped, Alika would maintain position in the vicinity of the *hand station*; when underway, he would swim in the stern wake on the port side of the control boat: the *following position*.

Boat transfers were considered a primary gateway task and fundamental to all Navy dolphins. Although new to Brent, Alika had some level of proficiency in this. Brent's first introduction to this took place on Thursday, 15 November 2001.

Joining Mark's crew in the seven-meter RHIB was an ex-Navy first class petty officer gunner's mate (GM1), Sean Sullivan. They were escorted by a control boat, helmed by Tommy Morison, a retired Navy chief boatswain's mate. Mark enjoyed working with these two watermen. He'd known them for quite some time, and that familiarity only reinforced their reputations as rock-solid team members. Their level of knowledge of the mammals, the sea, and small boats was impressive, but what appealed most to Mark was their ability to stay cool and think calmly in critical situations.

Mark conned the seven-meter RHIB into the practice area six miles southwest of San Diego Bay. Alika was snug in his tray, and Brent sat beside him on an upturned plastic bucket. Once established in the working area, the seven-meter RHIB carrying Alika, Brent, and Sean was secured, starboard to starboard, with the eighteen-foot RHIB. The smaller boat, the control boat, was used to guide the dolphin into the training area. Because it was smaller, quieter, and had a reduced acoustical signature, it was the preferred vessel once they neared the training or operating area.

When the two boats were lashed together, it was the handler's job to lay out the panels of the beaching tray on the transfer boat, ease his mammal backward over the port gunnel and into the water, then quickly cross over to the smaller control boat to receive his dolphin at the hand station.

The results of Brent's first try at this relatively simple process were hilarious to the crews, capital fun for Alika, and not a little embarrassing to Brent.

The two boats maneuvered to align the sponsons starboard to starboard. As soon as the boats were secured, Brent opened the tray and, gently pushing on Alika's rostrum, eased him over the gunnel and into the water, fluke first. While Alika swam under the two boats, Brent quickly crossed over the gunnels to get into position to meet his dolphin on the port side of the smaller boat. This is where it fell apart.

Trying to make a good impression and be quick, Brent lost sight of the fact that the tray, the gunnels, and the decks were soaked and extremely slick. He made a good run from the transport boat but carried a bit too much speed crossing over the gunnels. His effort to stop prior to the control boat's port sponson was in vain. A slip became a trip, which led to a stumble, and that sealed his fate.

Without so much as a hint of deceleration, Brent tumbled onto the sponson, which catapulted him over the gunnel and into the water. This one-man circus act happened about the same time that Alika surfaced at the hand station. Brent missed Alika by a matter of inches. When Brent surfaced, Alika was so excited to have his partner in the water with him Alika lifted his rostrum and placed it on Brent's shoulder—a dolphin's universal act of appreciation, gratitude, and in this case, *affection*.

An enormous roar of laughter broke out among Mark and the crew. When things settled down, Brent, now dripping wet and mightily embarrassed, climbed back aboard and called Alika back to the hand station. A reward was in order. Brent offered Alika several anchovies. "At least you did it right, Alika!" Brent whispered.

They practiced boat transfer for nearly an hour interspersed with a few play breaks for Alika. Each time they practiced, the procedure became smoother, and Brent managed to stay in the boat.

"Boat transfer is a key task to the next building block task—*boat following*." Mark explained to Brent, "The objective is to get the dolphin into the water so he can become familiar with the terrain and then move to a specific location within a search quadrant where he can begin his recce. At the same time, he'll be conserving energy while underway.

"As soon as you have Alika in the water, guide him to the hand station. You'll have good visual contact there. He can see you and everything he needs to on the boat. Tommy will accelerate to about ten knots and head for the search area. We want Alika to stay on the port side and maneuver in the stern wake. He'll pretty much surf beside the boat. This will keep him in the right place to watch you and, at the same time, reduce his swimming effort. Any questions?"

"Ah…not yet."

"Let's do it!"

Brent called Alika to the port side of the RHIB, the following position. He then swiveled around and gave a thumbs-up to Tommy, who gradually eased power on. As soon as he realized the boat was moving, Alika put his head down, trimmed himself for swimming, and moved into the forward edge of the stern wake. Obviously, he'd done this before. Brent couldn't help but smile. The capacity of his dolphin to learn and retain so much was simply amazing.

Tommy stopped and started the boat several times to reinforce the process. He also made small and large arcs in the water, starboard and port turns, and adjusted boat speed to determine the best swimming speed for Alika. This went on for some time. To keep the interest level up, Alika was rewarded with a few herring and some playtime.

The tasks became more complex and challenging for both Brent and Alika the following week. With beaching, exiting, boat transfer, and boat following now a solid part of Alika's skill set, Mark introduced the meat of an MK 7 dolphin's job: locating targets, discriminating, confirming, and marking bottom mines.

At the beginning of the fourth week Mark, Sean, Brent, and Alika manned the transfer boat and headed to the working area in company with the control boat driven by Tommy. But this time, there was a third boat in the package, the dive boat, a Boston Whaler. Navy Diver Chief Petty Officer (NDC) "Big" Ben Skylar came aboard as the dive supervisor. He was a big guy well-known in the trade and a man who probably had more sea time than Captain Ahab. The rest of the crew included a coxswain, Colin Lang, and two Navy divers: Dave Buss and Malcom Giannetti, both experienced ex-Navy divers.

Their job was to assess the accuracy of the marking job done by Alika. They determined if the marker was set within the proximity standards and that the target that Alika marked was an actual practice mine and not some hunk of bottom junk that produced a similar metallic return.

Mark led the boat package to a specified area just southwest of the San Diego Harbor mouth using GPS. Mark cut the engines, and Tommy swung the eighteen-foot RHIB around so the starboard side of the transport boat and the control boat could be lashed together. Brent laid out the beaching tray and eased Alika into the water. Like a pro, Alika swam under the two boats to the port side of the control boat and met Brent at the hand station.

Mark came aboard the control boat and left Sean to follow in the transfer boat several hundred yards behind. Ordinarily, the transfer boat would stay out of the search area to minimize the distractions and the magnetic interference.

Tommy fired up the control boat engines and turned to a new course. Alika positioned himself on the port side and swam using the wake of the boat to help propel him forward. The dive boat took a trail position two hundred yards to stern.

A few minutes into the transit, Tommy, monitoring several sophisticated navigation and mapping systems, eased the engines to idle and nodded to Mark.

Mark turned to Brent. "We're in the training area, Brent, and within a hundred yards of a practice mine; send Alika out, and let's see what he can do."

"Roger!"

Brent kneeled, leaned over the sponson, and looked at Alika with some intensity. Alika was clearly amped up—head held high, clear, sparkling eyes focused on Brent. He was ready to go to work. "Make me proud, big boy," Brent said, then gently held Alika's rostrum and pushed down, the signal for Alika to search.

Alika instantly jetted away, made a large orbit around the control boat, pinging during the circuit. Suddenly Alika straightened his course and set a beeline track southwest. He swam straight for sixty yards then dove. As soon as he did, Brent hit the stopwatch function of his watch and began to time Alika's dive.

Mark smiled. "Gezzo, I think he's already got a return off the mine. At least he's heading in the right direction."

Brent couldn't help but grin. "Shit hot! He's a firecracker."

"He is that!"

Mark turned to look at the divers in the dive boat drifting about one hundred meters away. They had placed the target mine and had the best idea of where it lay. Thumbs-up from both the divers confirmed what Mark had already concluded: Alika was on the right course.

A few minutes later, Alika breached the surface and raced back to the control boat.

On the port sponson, two eight-inch disks termed *manipulandum* were suspended by paracord. The disks were set about six feet from each other, within easy reach of Alika. The forward disk, the one on the left as viewed by a dolphin, indicated that the dolphin had located and identified a target he believed to be a mine. The aft disk, the one on the right, indicated that he had not found a mine.

Alika came to the port side of the boat and anxiously tapped the forward disk with his rostrum.

"Alika thinks he found it," Brent reported.

"He probably did. He was in the right area, but let's ask him to confirm."

Brent saw the wisdom of this and leaned back over the rail. "You probably got it right, Alika, but double-check this." He pushed down on Alika's rostrum once again, and Alika took off. This time, however, Alika went directly on course without swimming a circle.

As soon as Alika dove, Brent started timing. Less than two minutes later, Alika made a spectacular jump out of the water and sped to the port side of the boat. Without any hesitation, he again tapped the forward disk, confirming what he had found, head up and looking intensely. Brent could almost read his mind, *It's there, just like I told you. Now let's get this done!*

Brent twisted toward Mark, who said, "Okay. Give him the marker."

Brent stretched forward toward the bow and retrieved a red marker. It was made of plastic and shaped like a large horseshoe about eighteen inches in length and width and weighed about seven pounds. It included three basic components: a base plate that acted as an anchor, a floating section that would rise to the surface when activated, and a line connecting the two.

"Standby, divers," Mark transmitted over the VHF radio to apprise the divers that they were preparing to mark the target.

Brent lifted the marker over the gunnel and down to the water. Without a moment's hesitation, Alika accepted it and allowed Brent to slide it over his rostrum. Alika dove, Brent started his stopwatch, and Mark transmitted to the dive boat, "Marker's away!"

It was just slightly over a minute that Alika reappeared on the surface, jovial and triumphant. About the same time, the floatation section reached the surface. Mark made another transmission to the divers, "Marker's on the surface."

Alika swam up to the boat near Brent. Brent reached down and stroked his big melon. "Let's see how you did, Alika."

The dive boat cruised to the floating marker. Both divers had already geared up. They fitted their masks, cleared their regulators, rolled into the water, and dove down, following the marker line.

Brent was tense as he awaited the assessment of the divers. Alika, not a care in the world, waited at the hand station next to Brent and pinging occasionally, apparently tracking the two divers. A few minutes later, the divers came to the surface lugging the anchor section of the marker with them and swam to the dive boat. As the divers climbed back onto the dive boat, Brent waited impatiently. One of the divers extended his arm, thumb pointing up. Big Ben gave the report on the radio, "Good mark. He found the target mine, and the marker was placed well within limits. Give that big guy a fish!"

In response, Brent reached into the fish bucket and awarded Alika half a dozen anchovies. "You did good, Alika!" Then he reached down and, with both hands, held Alika's head and kissed him vigorously on the melon.

This act of affection was not something the handlers did as a matter of practice, but Brent didn't care. This was the first time Alika and Brent had marked a mine as a team, and Brent was jubilant. Alika didn't know what to think, but he must have felt that it was an okay thing because he did a very impressive tail dance that lasted about ten seconds.

The excitement of the accomplishment was shared by everybody in the boat, but to Brent, it was a spectacular achievement, the kind long and happy memories are made of. He could not have been prouder of his boy.

They pushed the clock knowing that Brent was scheduled to be in class by noon. At 11:15 a.m., Mark announced on the radio, "All right, team, we need to get Brent back to the pier. He's got class. Sean, I'll transfer to the seven-meter. We'll get Brent and Alika aboard and head home. Great job, guys!"

Sean fired up the engines. Mark and Brent came aboard and beached Alika. Sean put the engines in gear and swung the boat to a course of 030 degrees heading for the entrance to the bay. It was just a few minutes shy of noon when they arrived at the pier. Brent sprinted to class while Mark and Sean took care of Alika and the RHIB.

Brent was on his second hour of the afternoon class session, and he caught himself again drifting back to the morning's training session. *What an exciting day. The results were great. No miscues, no missed practice mines, terrific marker placement, and Alika was never sidetracked. He worked like one of the old guys, one of the indomitable dolphins that had been around the block a time or two.* Brent beamed. He couldn't have been more pleased.

Trials and Tribulations

Wednesday, 21 November 2001
Pier 159, Sub Base, Point Loma

Mark, Brent, and Alika continued refining the procedures and honing the techniques of mine detection and marker placement each day. Brent had nothing to judge Alika's performance against. He'd never seen Navy dolphins in action, but Mark, who had, assured Brent that Alika was performing well above his experience level and far better than he had expected, considering his ghosts and previous history. That was about to change.

On Wednesday, 21 November, Alika stumbled and stumbled badly.

As they had in the previous several practice sessions, Mark and Brent transferred to Tommy's control boat; Alika took his standard boat-following position. Sean, in the seven-meter RHIB, drifted in the gentle water two thousand meters from the control boat. Colin drove the dive boat, which was manned by Big Ben and both divers, Dave and Malcom.

The first three practice detection and marking events went smoothly, so smoothly in fact that Mark was slightly concerned that the team might lose focus, lose their edge. These were the times when Mr. Murphy often made a violent entrance and transformed a perfect day into a complete catastrophe.

Tommy headed for the fourth practice area of the morning. He scanned the GPS, cut power, and pointed forward, "This should be the place. The divers set a single calibration target mine within two hundred yards of this location."

"Okay, Brent, launch him," Mark said.

Now second nature, Brent sent Alika on a search mission with a gentle push on his rostrum. Alika swam his typical large search pattern, but this time, instead of accelerating on a straight-line course toward the ping returns, he slowed, sent out a long string of clicks, raised his head, and looked back at Brent. Then he returned to the hand station and stared at Brent apprehensively.

"What's going on?" Brent questioned as he leaned over the gunnel to stroke Alika's melon.

"Don't know," Mark returned. "He's upset. Something's bothering him. Did he look okay to you this morning?"

"Yeah. Fine. Ate all his chow. He was raring to get out on the water. He acted…normal!"

"Hmm. Send him out again. Let's see what happens."

With that, Brent pushed down on Alika's rostrum, but this time, Alika brought his head back to the surface and, for a moment, stared at Brent. There were a few seconds of complete confusion. *What is going on with him?* Brent fretted.

Suddenly Alika took off on a straight line toward his initial ping returns and then dove. Brent hit his stopwatch. Everyone was stunned when, in less than a minute, Alika breached the surface and sped toward Brent. With hardly a pause, Alika tapped the rear disk: *no mine.* He moved toward Brent and cycled his massive fluke in order to elevate himself and lean on the upper side of the gunnel as if to climb back in the control boat—a big *no-no.* Clearly, Alika was very agitated.

"Don't let him come in the boat, Brent. We've got to figure this out. Something's bothering him."

Brent spoke quietly to Alika and caressed his melon and down his flank while Mark pondered the problem.

"Okay…we know there's a practice mine here. Alika's telling us there isn't. I want you to send him out one more time. If he has trouble again, we're done for the day. But I'd like to figure this out now, so we can resolve it and end with a successful mission. If we quit now, it'll weaken his confidence."

"Okay." Then to Alika, Brent said, "Cowboy up, Alika. Show us some cool stuff." He eased Alika's rostrum into the water, and he was gone. Brent hit his stopwatch.

Brent was still on his knees positioned above the hand station. Mark leaned against the helm amidships. The divers geared up and watched from the dive boat one hundred yards away. Three minutes later, Alika appeared at the port side of the control boat and vigorously tapped the forward disk: *a mine.*

Mark thought for a moment and then said, "Looks like he's over whatever it was that was bothering him. Ask him to confirm."

Brent pressed down lightly on Alika's rostrum, directing him to confirm the hit. But this time, Alika backed away from the boat and chuffed—he slapped the water with his fluke. In dolphin speak, this signaled agitation or frustration. Both Mark and Brent were growing increasingly concerned by Alika's conduct.

"Uhm. Maybe this isn't fixed," Mark commented. "He's either very sure he has a positive hit on a mine and he's exhibiting his frustration that we don't believe him or…there's something else bothering him."

"I've never seen him do that," Brent cut in.

"It happens. It's characteristic of some of the very experienced old-timers who have a tendency to question their handler's situation awareness. It's a dolphin's version of a pissing contest. We can't back down on this, Brent. Call him over and send him down. We need to assert authority here."

Brent did just that. He leaned over the gunnel and slapped the water. Alika glided to him. Brent then gingerly but firmly pushed Alika's rostrum down. And then Alika did a strange thing. He eased away from the boat and looked deeply into Brent's eyes, his perennial smile fading. Brent sensed a certain defiance…or was it something else? The staring contest lasted no more than ten seconds, and in the end, Alika headed toward the contact and dove.

Brent started his stopwatch, rocked back on the balls of his feet, and turned toward Mark. "What the hell was that all about?"

"Interesting. What you've just seen is a dolphin having a tiff with his handler. But why? No doubt he correctly ID'd the mine, but we have to reinforce the leadership relationship. He's a smart boy. This isn't like him."

Brent looked on the horizon, then at his watch: two minutes and twenty seconds. "Maybe he's not challenging us. Maybe it's something else."

"Maybe. We'll see in a moment."

Brent continued to scan the horizon in the direction Alika dove. "We had a horse like that, Thunder. Big guy. Pretty wild. Very smart. Defiant as hell. But as soon as he figured out his role on the ranch and his relationship to his trainers, he was a star. Turned into quite a champion cutting pony too."

"Yeah, there's probably a lot of similarity between Alika and your horse. We just need to be sure he understands that he's the worker in the system. If we let him get away with what he just did, he'll want to be driving the boat next."

Mark was checking the dive time when he heard Brent excitedly say, "Here he comes, and he's got some heat on him."

Brent was still kneeling, positioned above the hand station.

"I don't think he's going to slow down," Mark cautioned.

Alika was breaching, doing nearly fifteen knots and still on a collision course with the RHIB. At ten meters from the boat, Alika still had a head of steam. With no beaching tray and a variety of equipment in the forward area, Alika could get severely injured if he came aboard. Alika outweighed Brent by nearly four hundred pounds and was moving about ten knots when he made a final breach.

"GET OUT OF THE WAY, BRENT!"

But Brent didn't get out of the way. He didn't have time. Alika made a jump for the safety of the boat but collided with Brent. Brent tried to wrap his arms around him to keep him out of the boat. Just when things were getting ugly, Mark came to Brent's aid and, together, managed to push Alika back into the water.

It was a Pyrrhic victory. Brent was successful in keeping his big dolphin out of the boat but at great cost. Brent took the blow square in the chest. The impact completely knocked that air out of Brent, nearly pushed him over the other side of the boat, and may have bruised some ribs.

At the instant of impact, Brent looked like a surprised hood ornament. It was remarkable that he had managed to keep Alika, a five-hundred-pound torpedo, from coming aboard.

While Brent tried to jump-start his breathing again, Alika hit the *mine* disk. Then he did something out of character. He made a fast, short radius circle around the boat, pinging the entire time as though he was searching for something. Satisfied there was nothing out there, he returned to the hand station.

Brent finally got his diaphragm working again and immediately went to Alika.

Had it been a different setting and under different circumstances, the antics would have rivaled a Keystone Cops episode. Mark had the indelible vision of Brent taking the entire impact of a mature male dolphin in the chest at ten knots. He thought Brent was very lucky to still be in the boat. Brent's look of surprise would forever be seared into Mark's memory.

"What in the hell just happened?" Brent intoned, bent over with his hands on his knees, still trying to gather his breath."

Mark didn't answer, but a thought came to him. He grabbed the radio. "Big Ben, you up?"

"Gotchya five square, Mark. What's up?"

"Did you see what just happened?"

"Hell yeah! That looked like it hurt. How's the kid?"

"Still trying to catch his breath."

"And Alika?"

"He seems pretty anxious. Listen, have Dave and Malcolm check out the area around the mine, will ya?"

"Roger! Dave and Malcolm are splashing now."

By the time Big Ben lifted the transmit button, Dave and Malcom were in the water and headed for the mine.

Mark studied Brent. "You okay, shipmate? That was an impressive hit."

"Yeah. Alika's head is a lot harder than you'd think. I'm kind of concerned about this. Alika's been a rock star. What's going on?"

"I think I know. But I think we'll find out for sure in a second."

Five minutes later, Dave and Malcom returned to the dive boat and climbed in. Dave grabbed the radio and hit the transmit key. "We saw a small blue shark, maybe six or seven feet long. He was cruising around the mine. He hauled ass as soon as he saw us. Maybe that's what was bothering Alika."

"I'll bet you a case of beer that's it. Okay, here's the plan. I don't want to end the session like this. We've got to get Alika back on the horse. Let's set a course for target run number 0002 in Echo Field. It's on the way home. Any questions?"

"Negative. We'll be in trail."

Then to Sean in the transfer boat, Mark said, "Sean, we're changing locations. Set a course to the Echo Field."

"Roger!"

Then to Brent, he asked, "How's your boy doing?"

Brent looked into Alika's eyes and leaned over the sponson to stroke his flank. "He's fine now. Like nothing happened." Brent continued, "If it was a shark, why didn't he just haul ass?"

"Good question. Maybe 'cause you're here. Don't know if he came back to protect you or to be protected by you. Either way, I'm kind of surprised he didn't bug-out back to home."

Brent leaned closer to Alika. "Is that why you're acting so weird, Alika? A little shark?"

Alika whistled, and Brent whistled back.

It was a ten-minute ride to the next practice area. Alika cruised in a tight formation alongside the control boat, emitting click streams often.

The final search-and-mark process in the Echo Field was near letter perfect. The diver's report came back: great search grid, no hesitation, no confusion with the decoy target, no distractions or delays, and excellent marker placement. It was a good way to end the day, for things could have gone either way after Alika's shark encounter.

With Alika secured in his tray back aboard the seven-meter transport RHIB, Sean brought the RHIB to a course direct to Pier 159. Brent silently released a long sigh of relief. Mark sat down next to Brent and within easy reach of Alika. He gently put a hand on each side of his jaw and said, "What's got into you, ya big dummy?"

He then rolled back against the sponson and said quite seriously, "Brent, there's no fault here, but what we saw was not a good thing. We've got to talk about this."

Brent looked back at Alika, who seemed all consumed by the touch of Brent's hand across his flank. Brent simply nodded in agreement.

The Council

Evening of Wednesday, 21 November 2001
Pier 159, Sub Base, Point Loma

That evening, well after class had secured for the day, Mark called the school's three most experienced biotechs for an emergency meeting. He laid out the situation, carefully addressed the knowns and the assumptions, and then asked for their inputs and recommendations.

Each of the experts knew of Alika's background, the loss of his mother, and the issues springing from his previous handler. Mark updated them on both Brent's and Alika's progress, stressing the points of their bonding, the precision of Alika's procedures, and his focused concentration to the tasks. Clearly, he had all the hallmarks of becoming one of the most gifted MK 7 dolphins at Foxtrot.

Mark countered his own praise by describing Alika's sudden panic earlier that day and the dangerous beaching attempt after sighting a shark swimming in the training area. Mark explained that while they couldn't positively connect Alika's unusual behavior with the presence of a little blue shark, it was the only logical explanation for his sudden breach of procedures.

"Did he really try to get on the control boat?" one of the members asked.

"He sure tried! If Brent hadn't caught him, he would have been in the boat fer sure," Mark returned and continued.

"Let's get down to the salient points. Does he beach up?"

"Yep," was the chorused response.

"Does he find targets?"

"Yeah."

"Does he mark in spec?"

"Hell yeah. He does good marks," they said almost in unison.

"Since Brent took him, Alika hasn't refused to beach once, and he doesn't bolt. He knows where to go and what to do."

"What happened when you took him to Echo?" one of the biotechs asked.

"He was fine, a champ. We pushed him in. He went to work, found the target, and made a perfect mark. When we were done, Brent beached him up and brought him home like nothing ever happened, like no big deal. This one event—well, it's just one data point—but Alika has a take-home lesson: he didn't get bit by the shark, and he properly marked the mine. And those are some very important lessons for him. If this becomes a pattern of behavior, we'll have to address that when and if it happens again. Other than that, he's an impressive boy. I'm all for proceeding on course, but I ask for your input."

In the end, they all agreed, Alika was too good a dolphin and far too young to be relegated to retirement. The fact was that all the animals, humans included, had bad days; and while the likely cause of this incident, if indeed it was the presence of a shark, was probably not a controllable condition, the team believed it could be mitigated. Bottom line, Alika would continue with the recertification process, and Brent would remain his handler.

Pins and Needles

Fri, 23 November 2001
SSC, Pier 159, Sub Base, Point Loma, California

When Mark walked down the brow to the RHIB early the following morning, he saw that Brent had already loaded Alika aboard
and was preflighting some of the systems. "Morning, Brent."

Brent turned toward Mark. "Good morning, Mark. We're about
ready to go, and Alika's all spun up to get to work."

Mark threw his gear in the boat. "Well, let's talk about that."

The bottom just dropped out of Brent's elevator. "Yes, sir!"

Now closer, Mark could see the strain on Brent's face and the
large dark rings under his eyes. "You getting any sleep?"

"Sure! I'm good to go."

Mark didn't respond, but he knew better.

"Well, this might put your mind to rest. As you know, I pulled
together some of the old, experienced biotechs last evening."

"Yes, sir."

"We were all in agreement. Alika's conduct yesterday fell way
below standards of performance and a mile short of our expectations, but the good news is, he'll continue with the training and the
certification."

Brent suddenly looked as though a car had been lifted off his
chest. He took a large lungful of air and straightened his posture.
"Thank you, sir."

"Don't thank me. We still have a knee knocker in our way. How
big is this shark thing? Is it going to happen again? I don't know the
answers to these questions, but it might bite us on the ass if we don't
face the problem."

Mark wasn't through. "Not so surprisingly, Alika seems to have a
sort of fan club at the waterfront. Our guys have been very impressed
with his progress, as they should be. Alika's an extraordinary boy.
That said, it's pretty clear he has a problem with sharks and maybe
other top-tier predators. This is a problem that may affect his performance and his reliability. Placed in the same kind of environment,

he may get flaky on us. He could easily jeopardize a mission. And if he does that, he could put several hundred lives at risk. We're going to have figure out a way to fix this."

"I know we have a problem. I don't know how to fix it, but Alika's a good boy and loves the work. There's a way through this. I know there is. I'll figure it out," Brent countered.

"I have no doubt you will. This is fixable. Now let's get out there and get that boy working."

"Aye, aye, Mark."

Brent turned away, paused, then faced Mark again. "And, Mark, thanks!"

"No issues, shipmate!"

Alika let out a long click string, announcing his anxiousness to get things moving.

Brent went back to work, but this time, he was beaming.

CHAPTER 9

THE HOME STRETCH

Besides being aware of themselves, dolphins experience basic emotions, engage themselves in some degree of abstract, conceptual thought, choose their actions, learn by observing, understand the structure of their environment, learn what works and what doesn't by solving problems and create new solutions to problems with which they are presented.

—Kevin Green, "Are Dolphins Intellectually Superior to Us Humans?"

False Positives

Friday, 23 November 2001
SSC, Pier 159, Sub Base, Point Loma, California

There were no new tasks introduced for the remainder of the recertification training. The final test would come on Friday, 30 November, one week away. But until then, Mark's team worked each day reviewing, practicing, and perfecting Alika's techniques and procedures.

The team moved to other training areas and ran similar drills to include one that had a known decoy: an old hubcap. The divers had

227

purposely set it in place so as to appear as a mine. Initially, Alika had returned to the boat and hit the forward disk; he reported the hubcap as a *mine*. Brent told him to verify.

Alika looked genuinely surprised but quickly dove, headed for the hubcap a second time. When he swam up to the port side of the control boat, he correctly hit the aft disk—*target is not a mine.*

Except for that initial miscall and the misadventure with the blue shark, Alika had a clean sheet, a phenomenal record of correct hits. As Mark explained, "False positives don't get anyone killed. It's the mine you miss that gets people killed."

A Bond Forged

Wednesday, 28 November 2001
SSC, Pier 159, Sub Base, Point Loma, California

Training continued with steady progress in the days following the shark incident. There were no further signs of a breakdown or so much as a flaw in Alika's conduct or performance. All were hopeful that the shark incident was a single event, one that would not be repeated.

Even in the complex scenarios of mine detection, discrimination, and marking, Alika's performance continued to impress the trainers, divers, and biotechs. Alika was—in all critical areas of certification: search rate, detection distances, availability, consistency reliability, detection, discrimination, and marking precision—hammering out new standards of performance. Mark's team was duly impressed.

The day before Thanksgiving and two days before Alika's final certification day, Friday, 30 November 2001, the training team headed for a location five miles southwest of Point Loma. It was a gray and gloomy day. A low-pressure system to the west was moving into the area, and the weather guessers promised cool temperatures, high sea states, rain, and if that wasn't displeasing enough, a twenty-knot wind from the south. The wind forecast promised to be an ass kicker as the low moved eastward.

It wasn't a long ride to the training area, but it was a bumpy ride. The wind was a steady blow and took off the tops of the waves, soaking everything and everybody in the boats. Only Alika and the two divers were prepared for this.

Once in the training area, Mark and Brent transferred to the eighteen-foot RHIB helmed by Tommy. Alika took his customary position: boat following. In their company in the Boston Whaler dive boat was the usual team: Colin Lang, coxswain; Big Ben, dive supervisor; and divers Dave and Malcom.

The divers had already laid a practice mine on the bottom in thirty-five feet of water. It was not a deep dive, but there were a number of outcroppings, ledges, and a steep drop-off into deeper water. An old fishing boat that had been sunk years ago lay just on the edge of the drop-off.

The practice mine was some sixty yards from the decaying hull, but with the engine amidst the wreckage, now a heap of rust and useless iron, it would present Alika with a discrimination challenge. The divers knew Alika would get return pings from his echolocation transmissions off the engine and other metal structures on the fishing boat, and he'd be forced to investigate the source of the returns to determine if it was a false reading or the real thing. The divers expected him to be able to discern these returns from an actual practice mine whose size, construction, and metallic composition was much different. If Alika did his job, he'd give the boat a quick look, determine the remains of the engine was not the target, and continue to search the area for the actual practice mine. When Alika detected the real practice mine, he'd assess it more closely, never actually coming into contact with it, and then dash to the control boat to notify them that he had something.

Tommy navigated to the target area and cut power. "We're in the right spot, Mark. The target mine should be within ninety yards of where we are now, pretty much due west."

Mark turned to Brent. "Send your boy out, Brent."

Brent leaned across the port sponson and called Alika over. "Alika, we're here. Go find that mine, big boy!"

Alika whistled once, and Brent gently eased his rostrum down.

Typical of Alika, he took off and swam in a high-speed orbit around the control boat with his echolocation system pinging constantly. He was building a mental grid of all the contacts in the area and orienting himself using the boats and bottom contacts to triangulate in order to establish a mental chart of his location.

Brent had to smile. Every time he watched Alika work, he was amazed at the process, the precision, and the efficiency of his actions. This was a dolphin technique humans just couldn't teach. They either had it, or they didn't.

When Alika was satisfied he had an accurate plot of their position in relation to the contacts on the bottom, he turned and dove, heading in a northwesterly direction. Typically, Brent hit the start button on his diving stopwatch as soon as Alika sounded.

Mark leaned against the center console, bracing against the ground swells and scanned the area just vacated by Alika. He pulled his Nomex rain gear tighter around his shoulders and neck. His demeanor was calm and relaxed.

Brent's comportment was a bit different. When his animal was out of sight, Brent always experienced a certain sense of anxiety.

"Looks like we're in for a bit of a blow," Mark said offhandedly, scanning the darkening western horizon.

"Looks like. And the temp must have dropped ten degrees in the last hour or so," Brent responded, never taking his eyes off the water.

He glanced at his watch. Alika had been down for three and a half minutes. A short time later, Brent stood and leaned against the gunnel to brace himself against the roll of the RHIB. "Coming up on four and a half minutes, Mark."

"He's fine, Brent. There're a few metal decoys down there. He's just sorting things out. He'll be up soon."

Brent was sure Mark was right, or pretty sure anyway. He remembered that it wasn't unusual for bottlenose to make dives of four to six minutes, and one of the old MK 7 veterans, a big moose of a bottlenose, often made dives lasting ten minutes. All that considered, Brent wouldn't start breathing normally again until Alika's big gray head broke water.

When his watch showed five minutes, Brent stood erect and glanced at Mark. Mark snatched up the VHF radio and keyed the mic, "Hey, guys, no visual for five mikes." He swiveled to look at the divers on the RHIB and raised both hands, palms up, as if in question, *What gives?* The divers returned the gesture. Not good.

"Collin," Mark transmitted, "do you show Alika on the DUKANE?"[46] And as an afterthought, he added, "Get me a cut to the Alika's pinger!"

After a short pause, Collin responded, "Yeah, he's right there in front of the control boat, about sixty feet northwest of you, pretty close to the old boat wreck...but he's not moving," Collin reported.

That was it. Anxiety had just turned to a growing sense of urgency for Brent. He went to the stern of the RHIB, grabbed a mask, snorkel, fins, and his dive knife.

"What do you think you're doing, sailor? We don't know that anything's wrong yet, so stand by!" Mark said, irritated but with concerned in his tone.

"If Alika isn't up in in the next thirty seconds, I'm going in after him."

"My ass, shipmate. You just hold your position. He's probably still searching. He'll be up soon."

Brent had already made his decision; now he was just waiting out the clock.

Brent slid his fins on, strapped on his dive knife, spat on the faceplate, rubbed it clean, and pulled the silicon strap over his head.

"No shit, Brent, DO NOT GO IN THE WATER!"

Brent looked at Mark, glanced at his watch, and rolled over the side.

Brent knew the general direction of Alika's vector: northwest. He swam as fast as his muscled legs could cycle the fins. He was on the surface sucking sweet oxygen through the snorkel and being pummeled by the ground swells.

Although the sky had darkened and light was poor, the water visibility was good. He could just make out the bottom thirty-five feet blow. He felt he was on a good line in the direction Alika had gone, but then a flash, a strobe of glittering movement, caught his attention to the left. Details were not clear, but there was something thrashing on the bottom of the sea in middle of a heap of junk.

Brent made an immediate turn in the direction of the strobing flash and redoubled his effort. Now, from forty feet away, Brent could more clearly make out the hulk of an old boat and finally saw the source of the flashing. His dolphin was entangled in a fishing net attached to the boat. His thrashing caused the reflected light to change from dark to light, depending on the light reflecting off his two-toned body—dark gray on his back to nearly white on his lower body.

Brent gulped one last lungful of air and dove with all the speed he could muster.

Alika was completely engulfed by the old net. He'd only managed to become further ensnared with his thrashing, but he was not giving up.

Brent had heard that a dolphin caught underwater and unable to surface often panicked. Death could follow in under a minute.

When Alika's eyes met Brent's, there was recognition and a new sparkle of hope. Brent stroked Alika's flank. Alika stopped thrashing, calm returning somewhat. Brent pulled out his dive knife, surveyed the net, and plotted the quickest way to free Alika.

Brent slipped the blade alongside Alika's rostrum and began to slice the lines leading down his flank. He severed the lines on both sides of his pectorals and over his dorsal fin.

The growing CO_2 buildup in Brent's lungs was almost incapacitating. More than anything, he wanted to break for the surface. His lungs screamed for air.

Alika was now showing signs of oxygen starvation also. He was holding still while Brent cut the lines, but rising panic was obvious in the gloss of his dark eyes.

Brent cut the lines wrapped around Alika's fluke, the final section of net ensnaring his dolphin, and then with a powerful thrust of both arms and back, Brent pushed Alika upward. Alika took off like a torpedo for the surface. Brent dropped the knife and began his own frantic strokes for the surface. His lungs were about to explode.

A dark-gray veil settled over him. He was having difficulty seeing. The urge to inhale was almost irrepressible. He seemed to be losing control of his diaphragm. He lost all sense of time.

Then something smooth—greased neoprene, soft and comforting—pressed against his abdomen from underneath. Brent was on the verge of passing out, but the contact with the softness and power of this thing brought him back from a black abyss and gave him new hope. He had a vague, veiled sense of rushing somewhere. He could feel the water flowing forcefully over his shoulders and down his back.

At Mark's command, the dive boat raced toward Mark and Tommy.

"Do you have Alika on the scope?" Mark yelled.

Colin studied the monitor then hollered, "Got him. He's right off your port bow."

"Go get 'em!" Mark yelled.

Dave and Malcolm were in the water before Mark completed his sentence. They swam hard toward the point of Brent's descent and soon had visual contact with Brent and then Alika. What they saw would forever be burned into their memory and become the topic of many a story among the Marine Mammal Program clan.

Brent, almost limp, was being hurdled to the surface much like a submarine making an emergency blow.[47] Underneath him, Alika swam with full force while carefully balancing Brent on his rostrum and melon. When they hit the surface, Brent was nearly launched into the air. Alika repositioned under Brent and then continued to push him toward the control boat with astonishing speed.

The divers were positioned between Alika and the control boat, but when they tried to intervene by taking Brent, Alika rammed through them like a Green Bay running back. He forced Brent forward the last few feet to the control boat and then, with shocking power produced from his massive fluke, almost lifted Brent up and over the gunnel of the control boat.

Mark and Tommy caught Brent under the arms and hauled him in. They laid Brent on his back and quickly checked his breathing and pulse. A coughing fit hit Brent. Seawater geysered from his nose and mouth.

Alika, still frantic, tail-danced for several seconds in an attempt to see Brent. A long click train and a whistle followed. It went unanswered.

The divers were closely behind and scrambled aboard through the transom. Brent was conscious but not quite fully aware of the situation. He looked dazed and was still coughing up great heaps of seawater. The divers shed their tanks and fins and huddled over Brent and Mark.

"How many fingers am I holding up?" questioned Mark. His look was serious.

"Three. Where's Alika?"

"Alika's fine. Never mind about him. How are *you*?"

"Mark, you want me to call it in?" Tommy asked urgently.

"Stand by," Mark snapped. "How do you feel?"

"Like"—cough, gag—"whew! Like I just swallowed the Pacific Ocean. Where's Alika? Is he okay?"

"He's fine."

Brent lifted himself and pushed his back against the pontoon. He raised himself slightly to see over the gunnel. When he saw Alika, he extended his hand over the gunnel. Alika wedged his rostrum into Brent's hand.

Tommy passed an oxygen tank and mask to Malcolm. Opening the valve and clearing the mask, Malcolm passed it to Mark, still hovering over Brent. Mark fitted the mask to Brent then turned to Dave and Malcolm. "What happened?"

"We only saw part of it, but I'll never forget it. Alika was headed for the surface, got a breath, then dove back down. Brent was trying to ascend too, but he was really slow," Dave explained.

"Yep!" Malcolm chimed in. "Alika dove back down, swam under Brent, and pushed him all the way to the surface. Crap, he was going so fast I thought they were going to land back at Point Loma."

"Okay," directed Mark, "fire up. We're outta here. Tommy, call it in. I want a medical team at the dock by the time we get there. And I also want our vets to take a look at Alika."

Brent repositioned his hand over Alika's melon and gently stroked him. Alika raised his head and whistled. Brent made a feeble attempt to respond, but his whistler was still out of order.

Mark tucked a blanket around Brent then did a quick central nervous system (CNS) assessment. Pupils were good, pulse rate, skin color, reflexes, and awareness to surroundings all seemed to be normal.

Then Dave asked of Mark, "Did you get a time on that dive?"

"Yeah. Over three minutes on Brent, about eight minutes on Alika."

Colin eased the dive boat against Tommy's control boat. Dave and Malcolm transferred to the dive boat while Sean positioned the transfer boat against the control boat. Mark and Sean assisted Brent aboard the transfer boat.

After they made Brent comfortable, Mark beached Alika in the transfer boat, making sure Brent was within easy reach of his dolphin; they seemed to be natural elixirs for each other. Mark took a seat near Brent so he could continue monitoring him. Brent wasn't out of the kimchi yet.

Sean moved to the console of the transport RHIB and made a quick visual sweep around his boat, ensuring they were clear of all lines. Then he gradually added full power, came on step, and turned for a course to Pier 159. Sean modulated the throttles to make it a quick but smooth ride to base, taking advantage of the tailwind and following seas.

Mark looked back at Brent, now resting against the sponson. His hand hadn't left Alika's big melon.

"How ya feeling, Brent?" Mark asked, elevating his voice to be heard above the roar of the engines.

"That sucked! I'm feeling better now."

"That was close. Too close, Brent. And stupid too. You broke every rule in the book. I'll have to write this up, you know."

"Do what you gotta do, Mark. I got Alika back alive. I don't care about anything else." As almost an afterthought, Brent coughed up a lug of seawater and added, "Alika was caught in a net, Mark. He would have died. What would you have done?"

Mark said nothing. He turned forward, scanned the horizon, and thought, *I would have done the same damn thing!*

Breaking Records

Friday, 30 November 2001
SSC, Pier 159, Sub Base, Point Loma, California

Brent was checked out by the corpsmen and found to have no adverse effects. The vets gave a thorough physical assessment to Alika. He also was determined to be good to go.

Mark wrestled with his dilemma the rest of the afternoon and evening. Should he or shouldn't he make a formal report? He knew how these things worked, and there was no way he could spin it to ensure upper management would take it for what it was: a gallant act of heroism to save his dolphin. The bureaucracy in the upper reaches of the stratosphere, untouched by the realities of the environment and unburdened by the physical and emotional connectivity between trainers and mammals, would find that Brent's actions were demonstrative of a Navy petty officer completely off his rocker. There would be hell to pay, and Mark was pretty sure upon whom the brown stuff would fall.

Finally, Mark concluded a report would do no good. In fact, in some ways, an incident report might cause great harm and shake the culture of the NMMP team. Of all the mammal handlers and trainers Mark had known, and there were many, none of those worth their salt would have reacted differently than Brent. It was best, Mark concluded, just to let this one die on the vine.

Die on the vine—not likely. By Friday afternoon, the day following Thanksgiving and the day of Alika's final fleet certification, all key personnel at Foxtrot Platoon were aware of the incident. Lieutenant Heinrichs, Command Master Chief Murphy, and Kahuna gathered in the OIC's office to discuss the episode and determine a viable course of action (COA).

A big factor in determining their COA was greatly influenced by a phone call Master Chief Murphy had received. Shortly after the trainers returned from Alika's certification test, Mark conferred with the divers about Brent and Alika's performance. He then called Master Chief Murphy and spewed forth high praise for Brent and Alika. Mark had seen quite a few certification trials and been in many real-world mine-clearing operations, but rarely had he seen a performance as precise, efficient, or as well executed as Alika's. While it was Alika's show, clearly, he depended on Brent for guidance, coordination, and affirmation. They were a team—a team whose actions and processes were a magnificently choreographed series of actions synchronized for maximum efficiency and success.

Mark's verbal report to the CMC described a near-flawless execution of all tasks: boat transfer, communication, location and identification of the bottom mines, and placement of the markers. Then Alika did something else unusual for a young dolphin with so little actual experience. He continued to look for additional bottom mines even after he had located and marked the several mines placed by the divers. Alika was not satisfied that he had found all the mines and conducted his own sweep to ensure there were no missed mines lurking beyond the designated target area. This demonstrated a degree of cognition, innovation, and thoroughness usually shown only in the older and more experienced mine-hunter dolphins.

Mark's glowing report, although not the official written fleet certification, was the tipping point for Lieutenant Heinrichs and the master chief. They couldn't very well celebrate Brent's and Alika's magnificent trials and then admonish Brent for an impulsive and ill-conceived response. They finally agreed instead to accentuate the positive publicly with the full command. At a convenient moment in private, they would then address Brent's near-terminal decision to save his partner. *Praise in public, punish in private.*

Homecoming

Friday, 30 November 2001
Foxtrot Platoon, Pier 40, Sub Base, Point Loma, California

Kahuna had but a few hours to make ready for Brent's and Alika's return to Foxtrot that afternoon. He headed down to the fish house to inspect the surprise concoction OS3 Dale Thompson was building for the returning heroes. And what a surprise it would be.

It was approaching 1500. Brent and Alika were supposed to be released by then. Kahuna checked out a seven-meter RHIB equipped with a beaching tray and headed to Pier 159. He arrived just as Brent and Mark were pulling the gate to allow Alika to exit his pen. Smiles, handshakes, and shoulder bumps were exchanged between Kahuna and Mark while Brent loaded Alika.

"Heard you had some exciting times, bro."

"More exciting than I would have liked, but I think you have a good MK 7 dolphin. He's impressed everybody he's worked with. I'm sure some of our biotechs would like to keep him here. He's quite a boy."

"We'd like to help. The fleet and Air Force are asking for more and more mine recovery services, and we're shorthanded as it is. Besides, Brent and Alika come as an inseparable pair, and I don't think you want a cowboy hanging around the place. It would drive the real estate prices down."

"We'd be glad to take him too. Gutsy guy. I'd take him into battle any day!"

Mark glanced at Brent and smiled as Brent finished securing Alika's tray.

"I'm taking them back to Foxtrot to see if they know anything. If they don't, you can have both of them."

"It's a deal, Kahuna!"

Kahuna released the painter lines and stepped aboard the RHIB while Brent leaned against the port sponson.

"Thanks for everything, Mark!" Brent said. There was more meaning in the tone in which it was said than in the simple spoken words.

Mark smiled. "Fair winds, shipmate. It was a pleasure. Take care of that boy and come see us anytime."

"Will do, Mark!"

Kahuna cranked the engines, and Brent beached Alika. With that completed, Kahuna double-checked all lines, eased the RHIB away from the pier, and swung it around toward home plate.

Kahuna ignored the five-hundred-pound gorilla in the room: the shark incident and the rescue. There'd be plenty of time for that. Right now, the important thing was that they both mastered their respective challenges, they were heading home, and there was a big surprise in store for them.

Fish Cake for One

Dateline, Friday, 30 November 2001
Pier 40, Foxtrot Platoon, Sub Base, Point Loma, California

As they approached the Foxtrot piers, Brent stood and peered ahead. What he saw was at first mystifying.

"What's everybody doing on the dock, Kahuna?"

"Hailing the heroes, bro."

"Hailing the...? Who's that?" Brent was genuinely bewildered.

"Alika and you. The way word came down, there was some life-saving going on out on the high seas. We're trying to keep that info down at the deck-plate level, but you and Alika did some pretty amazing stuff. The incident with the shark...well, we need to figure that out, but Alika saved your life, and you his. That's not something that happens every day."

"I didn't do anything that anyone here wouldn't have done."

"That may be true, bro, but the fact remains that you and Alika did it. That's big magic. Lieutenant Heinrichs and the master chief wanted to meet you at the pier, and I think all your shipmates are here for the comic relief and to knock down a couple of beers."

"Oh, cool!" was all Brent could muster.

Kahuna landed the RHIB, and some of the hands secured the docking lines. Brent started to ease Alika into the water, but Kahuna stopped him. "Leave Alika there. We have something for you."

Lieutenant Heinrichs proudly walked up to the center of the assembled crew. The lieutenant held a plate, and upon that plate was a concoction shaped in the form of a cake, but this particular cake held some ghastly-looking ingredients.

Dale had fashioned his famous seafood gumbo cake out of finely diced herring and shredded anchovies and glued everything together with pureed squid. It could not look worse than it smelled, and it looked frightening.

With all due ceremony, Lieutenant Heinrichs stepped to the side of the RHIB. "Special Warfare Combatant Craft Crewman Brent Harris, front and center."

Brent stepped to the dock and edged himself toward the lieutenant, eyes in horror fixed on what looked like a science-fair project gone bad. The smell was overpowering and made his eyes smart.

Brent finally figured out what this was all about. *They made Alika a cake. Very cool. And as bad as this smells, he'll love it. Jeezo, whew! That could gag a condor.*

The lieutenant continued, "For conspicuous gallantry on the high seas and under them, we, the mammals of Foxtrot Platoon, take great honor in presenting you with this fish cake."

"Ah, sir, I didn't really do anyth—"

"I think there might be some disagreement there. Anyway, here's your fish cake."

"Oh. Yes, sir. I'll give it to him. I'm sure he'll enjoy this."

As Lieutenant Heinrichs handed the cake to Brent, with a twinkle in his eye, he added, "I'm sure he would, but it's not for him. We can't feed Alika food like this. It might make him sick!"

Full understanding did not come right away. As Brent assembled the meaning of the lieutenant's statement, it finally hit him. *I'm supposed to eat this crap?*

Brent's jaw dropped open. The team raised their beers and cheered. Brent stared in horrified disbelief. Then he waited for the punch line—"Ah, we were just kidding"—but it never came. Quite the opposite.

"Eat! Eat! Eat!" The chant from the crowd crescendoed into a roar.

One look at Lieutenant Heinrichs and the master chief, and the finality of it hit Brent squarely in the face. *They're not kidding! Well, there's no getting around this.* And Brent opened wide and bit off a large chunk of the swirl and chewed vigorously. Somebody handed him a beer, which helped him get it down. It was horrible. *Even the jokers on the boat teams wouldn't do anything this bad.*

Brent turned toward Alika, who was wide-eyed and interested. Brent had another big swallow of beer. That helped with the remaining fish scales, squid tentacles, and the offending herring eye that didn't go down on the first try. It helped get it down, but it helped not at all to keep it down.

The first sensations felt as though there was a tectonic shift in the upper reaches of his GI tract and then painfully radiated to all points on the human compass. He dove for the top of the sponson and went down on his hands and knees. Sinusoidal convulsion took hold of him. It started with his feet. He felt as if giant hands grabbed him by the ankles and shook him out like a wet rag. He power-puked in the water. He looked like a fire hose. Everything for the last six hours that had been sitting in his upper GI track was ejected into the water. It formed a fan shape pattern and consisted of fish guts, brains, squid tentacles, and some things that would, thankfully, forever remain a mystery.

Everyone cheered, "Welcome home, asshole!"

Brent rolled on his fanny, back against the sponson, wiped off his face, raised his beer, feigned a smile, and said, "Thanks, team. It's good to be home!"

He then looked at Alika's big gleaming eyes and perennial smile. *The stuff I do for you, Alika!*

CHAPTER 10

ADVENTURES IN DOLPHIN LAND

In recent years, the public has come to appreciate the remarkable ability of service dogs to protect our military in the deserts, cities, and mountains. There is another animal group that has long gone unnoticed and underappreciated—the US Navy dolphins that have protected our military at sea for the past fifty years.[48]

—Terrie M. Williams
Professor of Ecology and Evolutionary Biology
University of California, Santa Cruz

The Mobile Unit THREE Boys

Tuesday, 8 January 2002
Foxtrot Platoon, Pier 40, Sub Base, Point Loma, California

With Alika's fleet certification and Brent's handler training[49] behind them, life settled down to a more predictable and routine pace. That is not to say that anything was mundane; on the contrary, each day brought new learning experiences, and each day held its own adventures as well.

Brent had been assigned to Foxtrot Platoon for four months. He'd assimilated well into the command and adapted to his new position as Alika's handler with impressive aplomb. So tight was the relationship between Brent and Alika that many of the Foxtrot personnel referred to Brent as *Alika's human*. And that was just fine with Brent—he'd been called worse.

Brent had anticipated a plateau in the excitement and interest in his new profession, but that never materialized. And why would it? The mission was important, therefore stimulating. He enjoyed his team, and the adventures with Alika were never dull. There was so much to learn from and about Alika. He was a complicated beast—loyal, loveable, gregarious, at times ridiculously funny, startlingly smart, and so very focused on the task when it was time. The true depths of his character and intelligence would take some time to plumb.

Brent was well aware that Foxtrot Platoon, whose mission it was to use MK 7 dolphins to locate and mark sea-floor mines, was only a small part of a much bigger NMMP mosaic. He was inquisitive by nature and often joined Kahuna to assist other commands within Explosive Ordnance Disposal Group ONE (EODGRU ONE).

On one such day, Kahuna invited Brent to accompany him during a visit to Explosive Ordnance Disposal, Mobile Unit 3[50] (MU-3).

Commissioned on 3 October 1983, the official mission statement read:[51]

> EODMU3 is a subordinate command of Commander, Explosive Ordnance Disposal Group ONE within the Naval Surface Force, US Pacific Fleet. Explosive Ordnance Disposal Mobile Unit 3 provides operational EOD capability as required for the location, identification, rendering safe, recovery, field evaluation, and disposal of all explosive ordnance including chem-

ical and nuclear weapons, up to the high-water mark of coastal and inland water areas and within the boundaries of naval activities in southern California.

MU-3 had two component missions in support of its primary mission, and both required marine mammals. One of those, the MK 5 mission, was similar and complementary to Foxtrot's MK 7 mission: to detect bottom mines. But where Foxtrot Platoon's animals detected, identified, and marked bottom mines, MU-3's MK 5 system attached recovery devices to submerged hardware the Navy wanted to retrieve.

Different from the MK 7 system that only used dolphins, the MK 5 "quick-find" system employed California sea lions. While there is some overlap in underwater detection capability, the sea lions have an impressive dive depth—exceeding five hundred feet. And like the dolphins, sea lions are smart, quick to learn, and work well with humans. Their underwater directional hearing and low-light visual acuity is phenomenal and greatly enhances their ability to detect submerged hardware in deep water. One MK 5 sea lion provided a demonstration of its prowess on November of 1970 when he detected and assisted in the recovery of an ASROC (antisubmarine rocket) in 180 feet of water, something human divers would have had great difficulty in doing.

Also assigned to MU-3 is a mission less talked about: the MK 6 Fleet Protection (FP), Swimmer Defense mission. This mission employs both sea lions and dolphins.

Hatching a Scheme

Tuesday, 8 January 2002
MU-3 at the Naval Amphibious Base, Coronado

It was a grand January day to be in San Diego: clear with a winter crispness in the air and a high overcast layer, temps in the mid-fifties with a light onshore breeze—just enough to ruffle the flags. In contrast to this perfect clime, Brent considered what the weather back on the Wyoming ranch would be like. *It's probably fifteen degrees and snowing like crazy, but I'll bet the entire gang is out there in the field working their tails off. If they only knew!*

Kahuna and Brent exited the duty truck and made their way to the MU 3's command master chief's office at NAB Coronado. It belonged to a salty EOD master chief whose initial enlistment in 1969 took him to Cam Ranh Bay during the Vietnam War. EODMC Jackie Quigley had been on the leading edge of the Navy's deployment of dolphins in the Fleet Protection and Swimmer Defense mission nearly since its inception.

At age eighteen, then Seaman Quigley and a small detachment of Navy marine mammal handlers attended to and cared for five bottlenose dolphins whose job it was to provide underwater surveillance and protection for Navy personnel, the ammo pier, base facilities, and vessels at Cam Rahn Bay, Vietnam. When his deployment ended in January 1971, Seaman Quigley applied for Explosive Ordnance Disposal and qualified as a Navy Diver.

His experience in Vietnam cultivated a calling for the sea and kindled a close relationship with both dolphins and sea lions. His thirty-three years of enlistment kept him deployed to overseas assignments for seventeen of those as an EOD diver.

Through diligence, commitment, and plain hard work, Quigley climbed up the EOD leadership ladder. His assignment at MU-3 was his swan song, and it was a good one. He was on the waterfront, responsible for the growth and development of scores of sailors, provided an important mission for the Navy and the Joint Services, and was surrounded by some amazing creatures.

Master Chief Quigley had met Kahuna a decade ago while on deployment. They immediately hit it off and stayed in contact with each other through the years. As luck would have it, they were once again assigned to sister commands under EOD Group ONE.

"Master Chief, I come in peace!" Kahuna hollered as he opened the CMC office door.

"Kahuna, you old bilge rat, I thought the fish ate you," Master Chief Quigley yelled back and flashed a big grin as he stood from a rickety wood chair. They grasped hands and bumped shoulders.

"Nope. I'm here in the flesh and ornerier than ever! Good to see you, Jackie."

"And it's great to see you. You're looking well. How's Foxtrot treating you?"

"All work, no play. The pay sucks, and we get no love. You know the life."

"I do indeed. But it's the life we chose. And who is this young gent?" he asked, indicating Brent.

"Master Chief, this is our new guy, SB2 Brent Harris, a Special Boat warrior we're trying to train as an MK 7 handler. We've hooked him up with Alika, and at this point, I think Alika is doing all the teaching."

"Brent Harris?" A pause. The master chief extended his hand with a quizzical look. Then his face brightened. "Is this the young SB2 Harris that jumped in the water to save a dolphin a couple of months ago?"

"The same, Master Chief, though we're trying to keep that story below the waterline."

"Understood. Still, that was a brave and maybe crazy thing to do, *crazy* being the operative word. The way I've always figured it, it ain't crazy if you do it for something important. Can't say I wouldn't have done the same crazy thing. Anyway, good to meet you, Brent."

"A pleasure, Master Chief."

"Grab a seat, guys. Want some coffee."

"Hell yeah. Why do you think we're here?"

"Well, let's fix that now." CMC Quigley stepped to the adjoining office and asked the yeoman to bring three coffees, hot and black.

The CMC took his seat behind a battered ancient wood desk. It looked as though it could have been assembled from planking from an old schooner. *Ancient, solid, and heavily weathered—not unlike Master Chief Quigley*, thought Brent.

"What brings you to God's country, Kahuna?"

"Mostly to catch up with you, Master Chief. But also, I'm hearing you're looking for a couple of talented dolphin handlers for an exercise up north."

This was news to Brent. He leaned forward slightly.

The yeoman entered the CMC's office and passed around heavy mugs of very black, very hot coffee, then excused himself.

Brent accepted the cup, blew the steam away, and sipped carefully. *Yep, giraffe piss here too.*

"Ahh, word gets out quickly on the waterfront. That's a true statement. We've got an exercise going on at the sub base at Bremerton, Washington. This is classified, Kahuna. Does Brent have a secret clearance?"

"He does, Master Chief."

"This is not a read-in program, but it is highly classified and still sensitive. Anyway, the sub base is conducting a physical security exercise to determine how well their security systems are at protecting their boomers,[52] piers, weapons storage areas, and other facilities. This is a big chance to test our MK 6 animals in the Fleet Protection[53] mission. We're taking four dolphins and four sea lions up to Bremerton to act as an augmentation force for the base's security team. I've got handlers for all the animals, but we're running the exercise for six days around the clock. I want two handlers for each animal. You interested, Kahuna?"

"I can't. I'm two-blocked with stuff, but I came to you to offer Brent here. Talked it over with Master Chief Murphy at NSCT-1, and he spoke with Lieutenant Heinrichs. Brent's not an MK 6 guy, but—not to blow smoke up his dress—he's a pretty savvy and talented MK 7 handler. With a little bit of work, I think you could use him."

"Hmm. Brent, you interested?" Master Chief Quigley scanned Brent's face.

"Ahh, yeah. This is kind of a surprise, but if I can find somebody to take care of my dolphin, I'd like to do it. Sure!"

"Let me give it some noodling. I'll work it out with Master Chief Murphy."

The rest of the visit was small talk, who did what to whom, but Brent's mind continued to circle back to the offer of working the MK 6 animals. He was dazzled.

The Phone Call

Tuesday, 22 January 2002
Foxtrot Platoon, Point Loma

Petty Officer Second Class Briggs was standing the command duty officer watch when a phone call came in. He'd been assigned to Explosive Ordnance Disposal Group ONE for nearly three years, and though he detested the watch, it was part of the job, which, in his mind, was still the best job he'd ever had. He relished the challenge and the prestige of being one of the sailors attached to the command that "provided the Pacific Fleet with the capability to detect, identify, render safe, recover, evaluate, and dispose of explosive ordnance which has been fired, dropped, launched, projected, or placed in such a manner as to constitute a hazard to operations, installations, personnel, or material."

This bold mission statement was posted on the bulkhead opposite the duty desk. Briggs had read it so many times he could recite it forward or backward. He also understood, better than most, that command tasking extended to all explosive ordnance, from Civil War era artillery (cannonballs) to terrorist devices, to nuclear weapons—particularly those that were the responsibility of the Navy or may be discovered in the ocean, including inlets, bays, and harbors.

The heart of the mission was to enhance ship warfighting abilities and survivability by integrating EOD capabilities into fleet battle groups and amphibious ready groups (ARG); conduct mine countermeasure operations; support US Secret Service missions; and operate and maintain the Pacific Fleet's various marine mammal systems that conducted mine countermeasures, port security, and underwater object-location operations.

No question that the mission, function, and task statement was a broad one with strategic implications and responsibilities. Because of that, he endured the duty without complaint.

Briggs answered on the third ring. "Explosive Ordnance Disposal Group ONE, Petty Officer Briggs speaking. How may I help you, sir or ma'am?" It had been a slow morning, but this call was about to change all that.

"Good morning, Petty Officer. My name is Katie Donovan. I'm a student at Florida State University. About six years ago, my brother and I found a little bottlenose dolphin on a beach in Florida. We helped the Florida rangers move him to Gulf World in Panama City. I spoke with the biotechs there, and they explained the Navy sent a team from San Diego to take him back and rehabilitate him. I think they took him to somewhere in Point Loma or Coronado. I'm not sure which. Anyway, they didn't know what organization had him, but they suggested I start with, ah…" There was a slight pause on the phone while Katie scrambled through her notes. "Here it is, EOD Group ONE. Is that where I've called, sir?"

"Yes, ma'am, it is. So, are you trying to find this dolphin, or are you just trying to find out if he's okay?"

"Actually, I'm in my junior year of marine biology at state. The university is organizing a research trip to Sea World in San Diego this July. Hopefully, I'm going to make the trip. I've always wondered what happened to that little dolphin, and I had hoped that while I was out there I might be able to see him. Is it likely that he came to ya'll's group?"

"Ma'am, it could very well be that he's here at one of our component commands, but I wouldn't know where to start. And to be honest, I'm not supposed to provide any information on our mammals even if I knew about this dolphin, which I don't."

"Oh. Hmm." A hesitation that clearly registered Katie's disappointment.

"I'd sure like to help, but…" Petty Officer Briggs could sense her distress. "You might want to call Navy Special Clearance Team ONE. Ask for Master Chief Murphy. He's the command master chief. He's been in the programs forever. If anyone can help you, it'd be him."

"Oh my gosh. Thank you so much. Do you have a number I can reach him at?"

"Yes, ma'am. It's …"

Katie quickly scribbled down the number for NSCT-1 and thanked the nice sailor.

Petty Officer Briggs hung up then immediately called the CMC's office and gave the yeoman a heads-up for Master Chief Murphy.

Katie was in her junior year of a four-year degree in marine biology, a very demanding course. Now nearly twenty years old, she'd grown into a tall and slim young woman. Thanks to several years of competitive soccer, she had shed herself of her girlish awkwardness but retained her blond hair, the adorable lilt of a pure Southern girl, and her sparkling green eyes. She was a head-turner for sure but ignored the come-on gestures, moves, and comments from her coeds. Hers was a busy life, and she had too much to do to become entangled in any romantic webs.

That one adventure in discovering a little baby dolphin in distress and the miraculous save by Matt Patterson, the tall good-looking ranger from Florida State Fish and Wildlife Conservation Commission, proved to be a cathartic moment, a pivot point in Katie's life, one that solidified her life's goals on the spot. She knew at that moment what she wanted to do in life, but she realized it would require a college degree. She knew her parents couldn't afford to fund the entire cost of tuition, books, room, and food, so being resourceful and pragmatic, she started working while still in high school, part-time initially. Later, she submitted an application to and was hired by the Florida State Fish and Wildlife Conservation Commission as an intern and then as a guide for two summers immediately following high school. In her first year at Florida State, she was offered a part-time job as a lab aide and then assistant to several faculty members in the biology department. This helped pay for the mounting education bills. It was no surprise that she dazzled the marine biology faculty with her work ethos and dedication.

Despite the many distractions—school, work, and soccer—Katie never forgot that mystifying adventure with the little dolphin and never forgot her small part in his rescue. She thought about him often. Now, with a few senior students selected to make a behind-the-scenes trip to Sea World in San Diego to observe and study their internationally acclaimed marine-life programs, she thought it would be a once-in-a-lifetime opportunity to see the little dolphin she had helped save.

It took two more calls to finally track Master Chief Murphy down. She wasn't disappointed.

"Team ONE. CMC Murphy speaking. How may I help you?"

"Is this Master Chief Murphy?"

"It is, ma'am. How may I assist you?" Master Chief Murphy knew at once that this was the phone call Petty Officer Briggs had mentioned.

"Yes, sir. I sure hope so anyway." Katie replayed the monologue she'd delivered to the sailor she spoke with at Group ONE.

When she finished, Master Chief Murphy responded, "Well, I may be able to help you. Let me make sure I have this right. You're a student at Florida State, you're in the Marine Biology Department, and a group of you are going on a research trip to Sea World in July, and while you're in the area, you were hoping to locate and visit a dolphin you helped rescue about six years ago on a beach in Florida?"

"Yes, sir. That's correct. But the way you said it makes it seem like it'll be impossible to find him."

"We may be able to help. Can I have your number? I'll call you back."

The master chief copied the number down, hung up, and called his admin assistant into his office. "Cahill, please contact the biology department at Florida State University and ask one of the faculty if they have a"—he looked at the name he had penned—"Ms. Katie Donovan registered there as an assistant in the lab or as a student."

"Got it, Master Chief."

"And, Cahill, please put some heat on this. I need to call her back."

The CMC wanted to be absolutely sure he was talking to the person she claimed to be. All too often, leadership in the NMMP was pummeled by people who were ostensibly interested citizens and ex-Navy compatriots. In reality, many were not who they claimed. Too many turned out to be reporters for liberal news agencies, members of animal-rights groups, or outright animal activists. The CMC wouldn't have an issue with these people if they were forthright about their identity and they reported the news accurately and honestly. Rarely did that happen, however. Sadly, the outcome of too many of those interviews was inaccurate, harmful for NMMP, and detrimental to the Navy.

Within five-minutes, Cahill had the information. "Master, Ms. Katherine Ann Donovan is, in fact, a student at Florida State University, enrolled in the marine biology curriculum, holding a 3.88 GPA, and is working as an intern within the department. She looks authentic."

"Excellent, Cahill. Thanks!"

"Hello. You've reached the Marine Biology Department at Florida State, Katie speakin'."

"Yes, ma'am, I'm trying to reach Ms. Katie Donovan. This is Master Chief Murphy with the Navy in San Diego."

"Mister, uhm, Master Chief Murphy, thanks so much for your call. This is Katie. Did you learn anything?"

"Maybe. Did this happen around September or October in 1995?"

"Yes, sir. It was a Sunday, September 10, 1995. I remember the date better than my birthday."

"Did the rangers tell you anything, or do you remember anything about the dolphin you found?"

"Yes, sir. I remember the ranger. His name was Matt Patterson, he said"—Katie closed her eyes and thought back to that desperate day—"he was a young male Atlantic bottlenose dolphin and about six to eight months old. That's all I can remember."

"Did he mention anything about marks, scars, or distinguishing features?"

"No, sir. Just that his mom had been killed by a shark."

That did it. Murphy knew exactly which dolphin it was. He remembered the story of the rescue, the probable loss of the dolphin's mother to a shark attack, and the dolphin's arrival at Pier 302. He connected those data points with the most recent issue with Alika during his recertification training. That was the clincher.

"I think we have that dolphin, Miss."

Katie could barely contain herself. It took all of her self-control to stifle a jubilant squeal. She went from reflective to anxious and spiked the excitement chart all in about two seconds. "Oh my gosh, thank you so much, sir. How is he? Is he okay? Where is he now?" Katie held her breath.

"He's fine, ma'am. He's a healthy seven-year-old Mark 7 dolphin...ah, that's a mine-locating dolphin, and he's not so little anymore. And by all accounts, he's a bit of a workaholic and tipping the scales at over five hundred pounds."

"Can I see him when we come out? Can we visit the base and see what you guys do? Do you let civilians on your base? Do you think he'll remember me?"

The master chief knew those questions were coming, and he thought deep and hard. "As a matter of policy and in consideration for our security regulations, we can't allow civilians within the confines of this particular facility." He could nearly hear the pop of Katie's hope balloon across twenty-five hundred miles of phone line.

"Oh. Darn," was her only comment.

"But—and I'm not saying this can happen—we occasionally provide briefs and demonstrations for government, supporting agencies, and educational groups. We may be able to gin up something along those lines for your group."

Katie's emotional state had just gone through the third sine wave cycle. She was hopefully ecstatic but tried to control her euphoria—it might only be temporary. "Oh, that would be wonderful. Thank you, sir!"

"Katie, this hasn't happened yet, and there are fair odds that it won't, but we'll give it a shot. I'm going to give you the name and contact information for your dolphin's handler. Do you have a pen?"

"Yes, sir. Go ahead."

"His name is Petty Officer Second Class Brent Harris, and the name of the dolphin you saved is Alika. Petty Officer Harris will be your contact point here, and he'll let you know how this is coming together. Also, our public affairs officer will contact the marine biology department to coordinate a visit, assuming, of course, we get approval. Please don't get your hopes up too high."

"Gosh, Master Chief Murphy, just to know he's okay makes me so very happy. If I could see him, even for just a little while…well, that's more than I could hope for."

"It's all good, Katie. You'll hear from Petty Officer Harris in the next couple of days."

"Thank you very much, sir. Goodbye!"

"Take care, Ms. Donovan."

Katie hung up. She spun on her toes and almost tripped as the telephone cord wound around her legs. Her excitement level soared.

Happy Days

Tuesday, 22 January 2002
Mobile Unit 3, NAB Coronado, California

Master Chief Murphy was on a high. It seemed like good things, as well as bad, came in packages of three. Today he had two important tasks—both good, and they both involved SB2 Brent Harris. First, he informed Lieutenant Heinrichs and Kahuna that NMMP leadership had approved Brent's temporary additional duty (TAD) assignment to Mobile Unit 3 as an MK 6 handler under training. Second, they had also approved the visit of the marine biologists from Florida State University to Foxtrot Platoon for a mission and capabilities presentation on the MK 7 system.

The point paper justifying support for the visit had the key words, "to improve higher education's understanding and appreciation of the NMMPs policies and practices for marine mammals." These were always powerful predicates to advance the public's understanding of what went on behind the green curtain at Foxtrot Platoon and the entire marine mammal program.

And there really was a third thing in the three-pack of good things: it was just a great day to be an American.

One phone call later, Master Chief Murphy had delivered the good news to Kahuna: SB2 Harris would be temporarily assigned to Mobil Unit THREE for three weeks of MK 6 handler training, and Foxtrot Platoon was assigned the prestigious honor of hosting and presenting a mission and capabilities brief to a contingent of marine biologists from Florida State University in July. He let on that the young lady he spoke with, Katie Donovan, was the same person who, seven years earlier, found and saved Alika.

The master chief wasted no time in calling Kahuna and giving him the good news.

"With that as kind of the nickel tour, Kahuna, what would you think of assigning Brent as the point man for the presentation?"

"Funny. That's who I was thinking of as you laid out the tasking. Yeah, let's do it."

"Perfect. Thanks for stepping up to the plate, Kahuna. I'll call the OIC to complete the comm loop. Then I think I'll hop on over to Mobile THREE and take that worthless Duffus for a walk."

With typical efficiency of word usage, Kahuna relayed the happy news to Brent: he was going to Mobile Unit 3 for three weeks of MK 6 training in April. And item two: he had been unanimously selected to be point for the mission and capabilities brief to several marine biologists from Florida State University.

Brent was so tickled with the first part of the news he almost crashed and burned during his mental victory cartwheel when the second part of the news hit him—*Mission and capabilities brief?*

"Chief, I don't know hooey about a mission and capabilities brief. I'm still new to the program, and I've never given a brief in my life. You sure you have the right guy?"

"Nobody's ever given a brief until they gave one, Brent." This response sounded eerily reminiscent of the words of Bill Washakie when he said, "No one ever rode their first rodeo until their first rodeo."

"Yeah, but I don't want to hose it up and make the command look bad."

"I'll be with you the entire time, and besides, you were Master Chief Murphy's first pick."

That last comment pretty well ended any further negotiations. Brent was clearly destined for this.

"Here's the number for your contact at the university." Kahuna passed him a slip of paper with a phone number scribbled on it. "Call that number. Talk to a lady by the name of Katie Donovan. Seems as though she and her little brother were the kids who found Alika and called the state rangers. She saved Alika's life, which is another reason I think the master chief picked you for this task. She'd be about twenty or so, and she's in the marine biology program. There are two great reasons you should be fired up to take this on."

"Copy all, Kahuna, but she's probably three hundred pounds, drives a Rambler, and has acne. When are they coming out?"

"In July. There's supposed to be about eight of them."

"That's about the same time that I get back from the security exercise in Bremerton. That won't give me much time to prep for this visit."

"Nope. Not much time at all, so quit wasting it talking to me."

"Yes, sir!"

And with that, Brent headed down the brow in the direction of the one thing that could shake him out of his crankiness. He whistled. Alika whistled back.

It came as no surprise to Brent that the cabal of the chief petty officers—Quigley, Murphy, and Chief Olopoto—tweaked all the behind-the-scenes gearing to get Brent temporarily assigned to Mobile Unit 3. Brent's assignment would be in two phases: first, to become cross-trained as an MK 6 dolphin handler under training; and second, to lend a hand in the upcoming security exercise in Bremerton, Washington, in June.

It always amazed Brent just how much could be accomplished when Navy chiefs got into the game.

The officer corps went by the book, so all the steps were according to procedures, processes, rules, and with due consideration given to political sensitivities of all parties including the media. The downside to this practice was the ridiculous amount of time it took to get anything done, if anything got done at all. And sometimes it just didn't.

The chief petty officer mafia, in contrast, had a formidable and clever unwritten system that circumvented the paperwork, red tape, and bureaucracy. The chief mafiosi actually got important things done and done quickly. It was a system embedded and refined within the Navy for over two hundred years—and it worked.

First Contact

Tuesday, 22 January 2002
Foxtrot Platoon, Pier 40, Point Loma Sub Base

When a chief petty officer gives a directive, Brent had learned from experience, a junior petty officer is to execute said directive immediately, if not sooner.

Brent found himself a rare quiet office space with a chair, a telephone, and a view of the magnificent San Diego Harbor. There, he prepared himself for what was to be the first of several phone calls to the fat girl who drove a Rambler and had acne.

He reviewed the primary objective: to host and provide a mission and capabilities brief and overview presentation on Foxtrot Platoon and the MK 7 dolphins. He then scribbled the questions he would ask on a scratch pad. Once satisfied that he had all the pertinent questions and comments down in an orderly flow, he picked up the phone and dialed the number, remembering only then that Florida State University was a full three-hours ahead of San Diego time. It was 1415 in San Diego, 1715 in Florida. He'd be lucky if anybody even answered the phone, much less have the good fortune to find Ms. Donovan on the other end of the line.

"Hello, Florida State Marine Biology Department, Katie Donovan speakin', sir."

Good fortune smiled upon Brent.

"This is Petty Officer Harris calling from Foxtrot Platoon in San Diego. You are Ms. Donovan?"

"That I am, sir."

Sir? Wow! What a great voice. Maybe she doesn't have acne.

"Ms. Donovan, I was assigned as the coordinator for a mission and capabilities brief on Foxtrot Platoon and our Mark 7 dolphins for a group of faculty and students in the Marine Biology Department of Florida State University tentatively slated for July. Are you the point of contact for this event?"

"Why, I'm as good as any, I reckon. And please, I go by Katie, sir."

"Great. I go by Brent. I'd like to ask you some questions and tighten up some of the details of your visit if I could."

Brent was about to ask for her e-mail address so he could just send her the list of questions and she could respond the same way. He wasn't sure why he didn't follow through with that plan.

Since his induction into the Navy, he'd built a rather jaded view of civilians and college students in particular, mostly because he had never been enrolled in a university—he had never been part of the academia elite. He viewed the vast majority of the collegiate membership as self-serving, self-indulging left-wingers enmeshed in a parallel universe that provided only a very narrow view of the real world and blinded them to the horrors and aberrations of that world.

Before he made the call, he was determined to spend as little time on the phone as possible, but in less than a minute on the phone with Katie, something changed his mind. It could have been the fact that it was after 1700 her time, and she was still at it, showing a certain degree of dedication, which he liked. It could have been the good ol' Southern hospitality and respect she'd shown him, something most uncommon to the California inhabitants. Or it could have been (and probably was) the crystal clarity and wonderful timber of her voice encased in that soothing honey-coated Southern twang. Whatever it was, he found himself wanting to keep the conversation going a while longer. *She couldn't possibly weigh three hundred pounds!*

Brent knocked out the questions he had scribbled down, gave a cursory overview of Foxtrot Platoon, and a very brief, brief on their mammals. When he ran out of information and questions, Katie posed several of her own.

They spent nearly twenty minutes on the phone, and Brent had run flat out of reasons to stay on the line—aside from the fact that he was captivated by the pitch of her voice.

When they finally hung up, they agreed that, unless otherwise reassigned, they would assume the mantel of the POCs for their respective organizations.

Brent oriented the computer keyboard and initiated an e-mail to Master Chief Murphy with a CC to Lieutenant Heinrichs and Chief Olopoto. This would capture the important details of that first contact with the Marine Biology Department at the Florida State University.

For a moment, before any fingers touched the keyboard, he reviewed his conversation with Ms. Donovan and tried to imagine the face of the girl with the sweet-as-molasses voice. *Maybe she doesn't drive a Rambler either*, Brent thought.

CHAPTER 11

THE MAKING OF A MARK 6 HANDLER

*Until one has loved an animal, a part of
one's soul remains unawakened.*

—Unknown

Short Time—History and Profile of the MK 6 System

Tuesday, 5 February 2002
Foxtrot Platoon, Pier 40, Point Loma Sub Base

Two weeks after Master Chief Quigley, Kahuna, and Brent had
met to discuss the assignment to Mobile Unit 3, Brent had verbal
orders for temporary additional duty (TAD) to become a handler
(under training) for the MK 6 system. Start date for this very abbre-
viated training was scheduled for Wednesday, 3 April 2002. The MK
6 used the same kind of an animal, a bottlenose dolphin, but the
dolphin's mission and temperament were worlds apart.

Brent didn't like walking into a new job cold, so he spent two
days at EOD Group ONE reading up on the MK 6 system. By the

time he finished the recommended reading, he'd learned a boatload: mission, training techniques, deployment, dolphin psychology, MK 6 handler protocols and responsibilities. But what fascinated Brent most was the history and operational deployment of Project Short Time embedded in the after-action reports.

This laid out the development of the swimmer sapper defense system—the forerunners to the MK 6 system.

In 1968, Admiral Elmo R. Zumwalt became Commander of Naval Forces Vietnam (COMNAVFORV). He was quick to recognize that the biggest threat to US Naval Forces and Joint logistics bases were the VC and NVA special operations forces: naval sappers. From February 1968 to August 1971, there were dozens of attacks on US and Vietnamese ships, Naval Support Activities, the Marine Base at Dong Ha, Mobile Riverine Forces (MRF) in the Cau Lon River, and at the largest deepwater port in the south—Cam Ranh Bay.

A primary US Joint doctrine precept is that a small, tactical-sized special operations force, properly trained, led, equipped, and placed can have strategic impact against a hostile nation. North Vietnamese military had their own version of special operations forces: *Dac Cong* or Special Tasks. These forces were divided into three types of specialized units: urban sappers, field sappers, and naval swimmer sappers. The swimmer sappers were the most effective and proved to be the most worrisome for Admiral Zumwalt and other service commanders due to the strategic effects on logistic bases, supply lines, and line of communications.

From the mid-1960s until war's end, though innovative and certainly motivated, US and South Vietnamese military fielded a number of different counter-swimmer sapper systems to protect logistic heads, facilities, naval vessels, operational forces, and personnel—both military and civilian. Defensive systems used to nullify and defend from waterborne attacks became a growing concern and not just to naval forces but to the unified effort of the field commanders as well. A persistent and reliable system to defend ships, harden port facilities, and protect personnel was haphazard at best. Success was nominal and inconsistent.

In the early stages of the war, the Dac Cong seemed to be as inexperienced in conducting successful attacks as US Naval Forces were in defending against them, but there was a difference: the swimmer sappers improved. From 1967 to 1968, sapper-mining attacks increased from 42 to 127.

Early defense systems against naval sappers included posting of snipers on ships and piers, stringing antiswimmer nets around vital facilities, tossing concussion grenades randomly near possible targets, sonar sensors mounted on an LCM-6[54] vessels, deployment of water dogs trained to locate the exhaled breath of swimmers, and combining an array of sonobuoys with a mortar team. None of these proved to be consistently successful, and too much was left to the innovation, skill, and awareness of the operators.

Midsummer 1969, Admiral Zumwalt directed the execution of Operation Sea Float/Solid Anchor[55] (CTG 116.1). This concept, developed by the admiral's chief of staff for operations, CDR "Dick" Nicholson, proposed construction of a collection of pontoon barges, which would be positioned off the beach in strategic areas. It would provide a floating Mobile Advanced Tactical Support Base or MATSB.

Sea Float was given the go-ahead. Construction was completed on 29 June 1969. The floating support base was anchored on the north shore of the Cua Lon River, which opened into Cam Rahn Bay. Once operational, it was temporary home to approximately seven hundred personnel to include underwater demolition team elements, a beach jumper unit, three SEAL platoons, and several Navy sniper teams. Riverine craft, two Seawolf attack helicopters, and the placement of M60 machine gun mounts and 81 mm mortars provided the teeth for the defense of Sea Float. Although built with the idea of providing a secure defense system against the NVN swimmer sappers and other water-borne threats, it became a high-value target for the Doc Cong.

In defense of Sea Float and other prime targets along the shore, nearly all the counter-swimmer techniques and systems were employed. What seemed to be the most effective were concussion grenades tossed randomly about the perimeters of likely targets. This practice was not without its drawbacks: it was imprecise, subject to the skill and accuracy of the operators, and, in that this procedure entailed round-the-clock activities, was not conducive to sleep.

For several months, Sea Float went unmolested. It wasn't until 21 April 1970 that it suffered its first major assault. Though successfully defended, the attack highlighted the vulnerabilities of Sea Float and the reliance exclusively upon alert human sentries and good karma. A better, more reliable system was needed.

Coincidently, during a sweep through Commander in Chief Pacific Fleet (CINCPACFLT) headquarters in Hawaii, Admiral Zumwalt asked about a new and, at the time, unfielded system to detect and mark swimmer sappers using dolphins. The admiral was told by a staffer that the then *secret* system, Project STROMAC, was not ready to go operational. The fact was, however, it had been ready to deploy seven months before the 21 April 1970 attack on Sea Float.

The admiral was on the horns of a dilemma. What they had wasn't working, and what they needed, Admiral Zumwalt was told, wasn't available.

Had the NVN military leadership expanded and better equipped and trained its Dac Cong forces, the US and the Joint Services could have easily succumbed to a strategic threat and possibly hastened the end of the war.

Navy research on dolphins began deep in the Mojave Desert, over one hundred miles from the nearest seaport. It was in 1960 when Dr. William McLean, the technical director at Naval Ordnance Test Station (NOTS) at Point Mugu, California, and developer of the air-to-air Sidewinder missile, became fascinated with dolphins. At first blush, an attraction to marine mammals might seem to be an unusual interest for an aeronautical expert, but Navy scientists and engineers had long been intrigued to discover if higher speeds could be achieved with Navy ships and submarines by adapting hydrodynamic attributes characteristic in marine mammals.

NOTS formed a collaborative effort with Point Mugu Naval Missile Center (NMC) to conduct research on dolphins. In 1960, the Convair Laboratory in San Diego purchased a white-sided dolphin named Notty from Marineland of the Pacific in Palos Verdes, California. Thomas Lang conducted a study on the dolphin's hydrodynamic characteristics using Notty as the test platform. They came to realize there were an abundance of additional non-hydrodynamic capabilities inherent in dolphins. The scientists discovered they had an amazing echolocation system that could not only detect and locate objects underwater but could also differentiate the physical makeup and shapes of different objects. And if that wasn't enough to whet the curiosity of the scientists, dolphins were off-the-chart smart, had their own communication system, and seemed to have an abundant proclivity to work with man. They were the perfect platform to research a number of possible military applications.

The studies with Notty in 1960 were the first key stepping-stones of the Navy's research program on marine mammals. Initial findings proved to be provocative enough to fund a complete research project.

In 1962, a construction project began at Point Mugu Bioscience Facility for a concrete pool to house dolphins the Navy planned on purchasing. With growing interest in the physical and cognitive capabilities of dolphins, the Navy purchased several Atlantic bottlenose dolphins. Initially, the task was to discover just how much capacity they had to learn new behavior and the best methods to communicate with and train their mammals.

In the early years of the Navy's research into marine mammals, one feisty and aggressive dolphin stands out. In 1964, Pacific Ocean Park (POP) announced it was closing. POP had a number of dolphins and agreed to sell one of them to the Navy. Tuf Guy, an emaciated, scared, but spirited male dolphin, was sold to the Navy for $150. He was delivered to the Point Mugu Bioscience Facility where a UCLA biology student, Debbie Duffield, began rehabilitation, socialization, and training. Tuf Guy's name was changed to Tuffy, and under Debbie's care, his confidence, trust, and skills improved dramatically. Tuffy was only the second open-ocean released Navy dolphin.[56] Partially for that reason, Tuffy was selected to assist in the 1965 SEALAB II experiment off the coast of La Jolla.

Diving to over 200 feet, Tuffy regularly carried tools and mail to and from SEALAB. He also was trained to rescue lost divers and locate specific objects on the seafloor. Tuffy also set a new observed diving record—a deep dive to 990 feet. Tuffy provided a breakthrough for the Navy Marine Mammal Program; he established a new frontier in man-dolphin communication potential and proved marine mammals could be a reliable extension of man in an environment for which he was not designed.

It was probably through the observations of Tuffy's remarkable and, as yet, unknown capacity to master new behaviors that Captain George Bond, SEALAB dive medical officer, suggested to Sam Ridgway, first full-time marine mammal veterinarian, that their dolphins might be used for other tasks including swimmer defense and detection. This was a new mission "in concept," and it was taken seriously by NMMP leadership. In short order, the concept caused a major pivot point that shifted focus to the swimmer defense and detection mission.

Early in 1966, NMMP received funding and tasking to train a dolphin to search for, detect, and report the presence of a human swimmer. When the NMMP leadership closely analyzed the mission elements, they began to realize that even successfully completing those elements really didn't accomplish the mission objectives. They also needed to know where the swimmer was.

Upon careful deliberation, it was agreed that *locating* and *marking* the swimmer were critical tasks within the set of mission elements. It was also agreed that the dolphins would be trained to avoid prolonged contact or hostile action against the swimmer. They were concerned that the program would suffer a quick death if Congress believed they were training *killer dolphins*.

This change in tasks—to search for, detect, *locate*, *mark*, and *report* the presence of a human swimmer—seemed a small change on paper, but it proved to be a huge change in training objectives. The mission and the training program suddenly became much more complex. Dolphin trainers had already developed a rudimentary behavioral training system based on *operant conditioning*. Their new task was to expand their communication and training techniques to meet the new specifications for the swimmer defense system criteria.

The physical act of marking a swimmer was done by placing a rostrum cup on the dolphin. The dolphin was trained to approach the swimmer from the rear and tap the rostrum cup against the backside of the swimmer, releasing a waterproof buoyant strobe light visible in daylight or darkness. The dolphin was also trained to avoid any confrontation or retaliation from the swimmer and return to his handler. This was an enormous set of tasks, and training would be difficult. They needed a bright stout dolphin to begin the training. Thankfully, they had just the animal.

Red Eye was a smart and energetic Atlantic bottlenose dolphin and the Navy's third open-ocean released dolphin. He was a quick learner and seemed to enjoy his association with his human handlers. After several days of focused training, Red Eye was successful in a historic swimmer detection and marking *proof-of-concept* test. He consistently searched for, detected, and marked swimmers in test environments and returned to his handler to confirm the presence of the swimmer.

NMMP engineers and trainers now had a proven set of behavioral training procedures in hand. They channeled their energies to improve and expand the swimmer-detection capability by training additional dolphins. The behavioral teaching techniques gradually improved, and the dolphins adapted well to their tasks.

It was about this time that the divers discovered some of the five trained swimmer-defense dolphins had different understandings of *marking* their targets. Three of the dolphins tagged the target just hard enough to release the strobe light. Two of them, however, Slan and Toad, were a bit more exuberant in tagging their targets. They were both female Atlantic bottlenose dolphins and the stars of the Short Time Program, but they both hit their targets hard. Toad reportedly broke a rib of one diver, and another diver refused to swim with either one of them.

Program development continued on schedule, but it was not without its hiccups. With marked progress in the development of the program, by December 1969, they were notified by higher authority that they were scheduled for their first operational evaluation.

In that same month at Kaneohe Bay on the Marine Corps Air Station, Navy SEALs were tasked to stage a mock attack against a temporary operations command center at the base of a small pier. The SEALs were to begin their assault along the shoreline opposite the pier and attack the command center's trailer at the base of the pier. A single defender dolphin and his handler would defend the pier.

The NMMP team should have been suspicious about the objectivity of the evaluation when they realized that the neutral observer from CINCPACFLT wore a Budweiser badge[57] over his left breast pocket, but they *weren't*. They were scientists, engineers, and veterinarians, not sneaky, snake-eating warriors.

In the wee hours after midnight, several SEALs bashed through the command center's door and announced to the NMMP personnel, "You're all dead!"

This was unfathomable. Their dolphin had not detected any intrusion whatsoever. How could that be?

During the debrief, it was explained that the innovative SEAL divers entered the bay from the shore opposite the command center as they should, but then hiked overland along the beach and through a swamp to reach the pier and attack the command center. They did not expose themselves in the water, which was patrolled by the security dolphin. Had it been a Belgian Malinois rather than a dolphin, the results would most certainly have been different. The SEALs did not actually test the system they were tasked to evaluate. They cheated, which is much their nature.

The evaluation was deemed by the "neutral" observer (wearing the SEAL Trident) as a failure—the dolphin system was *not* ready for operational deployment. This brought an all-stop to the dolphin swimmer defense system and a severe center-of-mass hit to the NMMP team.

Mark 6 First Operations

Wednesday, 1 April 1970
Pacific Theater/Pentagon, Washington, DC

Not all was lost. On 1 April 1970, Admiral Zumwalt shifted colors from COMNAVFORV to Chief of Naval Operations. While barraged with global concerns, he still had a vested interest in the progress of the Vietnam conflict, especially the disposition of the swimmer defense system. This time, when he asked about the swimmer defense system, he was correctly informed that it had been ready since December 1969. He then, not knowing that it had lost funding, directed that it be operational and in place "as soon as possible."

Wheels began to turn immediately, and the program was back on line.

Just to show the sometimes amazing capacity to make things happen when the right people get involved, by December 1970, five swimmer-defense dolphins and supporting personnel and equipment were in place and operating at Cam Ranh Bay (CRB)—eight months after the CNO's directive.

In the twelve months of the Short Time deployment[58] to CRB, there were several sapper attack attempts, but only one was successful. On 26 August 1971, the 226th NVA sappers assaulted the Tri-Service Munitions Storage Activity (ammo dump), adjacent ordnance bunkers, and POL storage tanks. Most probably due to the high state of readiness and the security provided by the Short Time dolphins within the bay, the sappers chose to cross the wire from the oceanside and approach the base from land—they avoided entirely the bay patrolled by the dolphins.

It was a devastating attack on a primary logistics center. The POL storage areas burned for days, and millions of dollars worth of ammo and equipment were destroyed.

To many, it would seem obvious that the sappers planned to attack from the ocean side precisely because of the presence of the swimmer-defense dolphins in the bay. Since then, MK 6 systems have been deployed to a number of areas, many of which remain highly classified, but at least two are not: Bahrain during the Iran-Iraq War and San Diego for the 1996 Republican National Convention.

Though the MK 6 system was not often deployed in the twenty-first century, it could have been in any number of hotspots. The fact remains that it is the most effective defense system available to protect ships, facilities, personnel, and equipment in the littoral environments. It is a unique and important arrow in the quiver of theater commanders.

The Vietnam experience and lessons learned from both a planning aspect and an operational perspective is twofold: all vital real estate and strategic emplacements must be defended regardless of the environment in which it occupies; and secondly, for littoral assets, there is no better in-shore/littoral defense system than the Swimmer-Detection and Neutralization dolphins, also called the Force Protection and Swimmer-Defense dolphins—the MK 6 system.

The Threesome—Roger, Bilbo, and Bruiser

Monday, 8 April to Friday, 26 April 2002
Mobile Unit 3, Navy Amphibious Base, Coronado, California

Brent's TAD orders came down the line and were delivered by Kahuna. Brent would report to MU-3 at the Gator Base and begin his training on Monday, 8 April. He was slated to train and work under the guidance of Explosive Ordnance Disposal First Class Petty Officer (EOD1) Roger Birosh and, in the course of three weeks, become a handler for the MK 6 dolphins.

The leadership at MU-3 had their doubts that anyone could even learn the basics in three weeks, let alone become fully qualified; but Kahuna, with the backing of Master Chief Murphy, assured the doubters at MU-3 that Brent was not just anyone. Besides, Kahuna had a case of beer on the line with Master Chief Quigley, and he was sure that if anyone would, Brent could get it done. Kahuna left that little data point out of the conversation, but what he did share with Brent was both dazzling and very useful information.

Kahuna and Brent sat on bait buckets next to Alika's pen, enjoying the warmth of the noontime sun and the antics of Alika and his pen mates.

"Now, you probably want to know something about the gent you'll be working with, EOD-1 Roger Birosh," Kahuna began.

"Actually, I've heard his name mentioned a few times, but never met him."

"Well, Brent, consider yourself a very lucky cowboy. Roger is top dog among both the dolphin handlers and the sea lion handlers, and not just for the MK 6 system. He's got a subtle knack for teaching and communicating with the mammals and, equally important, teaching handlers their jobs, which, according to him, is actually more difficult than training the mammals."

"I'm sure that'll be the case with me too," Brent interjected.

"I'm thinking you just might surprise yourself, Brent." Kahuna continued, "A bit about Roger. He's been in the mammal program for years and has cycled back and forth from EOD assignments to the NMMP outfits. He's worked several different mammal systems, but most recently, he's been assigned to MU-3 due to the mission overlap between Explosive Ordnance Disposal and the MK 6 system. Roger's assigned to both a big MK 6 hybrid male bottlenose dolphin named Bruiser and a sea lion named Bilbo. The sea lion was named after a hobbit in Tolkien's trilogy.

"You'll like Bilbo. I know you've never worked with the sea lions. Most of the MK 6 sea lions are pretty down to business and totally professional, but not all of them. Bilbo, or Blubber Butt to those who know him, is a rarity. Blubber Butt, BB for short, has worked with Roger for a long time, and despite the fact that Roger is one of the foremost authorities on MK 6 systems and one of the kingpin trainers, he met his match with BB. Blubber Butt is driven by two motivators: first, he believes that the entire ocean is his buffet table, and second, he is committed to the concept that a happy sea lion is a well-rested and a well-feed sea lion.

"I've got it on good authority that the story I'm about to tell you really happened. One day, during work-ups, BB discovered a school of little sharks on the bottom near an old boat hulk out at one of the training areas. All those little tasks an MK 6 sea lion needs to do like detecting and marking swimmers pretty quickly became priority two. Priority one became catching and eating as many baby sharks as he could. Don't know if you've ever seen a sea lion in full pursuit of anything, but they're very quick and agile, and not much gets away from them. Well, BB ate so many baby sharks he wasn't able to complete the training mission.

"As the story goes, when he finally came back to the boat, he could hardly jump aboard. And when he finally did, he crawled forward to the bow, rolled on his back, and went to sleep. Roger Birosh was pretty embarrassed and was heard to say, 'Well, I guess he's done for the day.' That's not to say that BB is not a dedicated and masterful MK 6 sea lion. He's all that and a lot more, according to Roger. It just so happens that, from time to time, BB has some issues in figuring out his priorities. Now, I wouldn't mention this story to Roger. Roger is completely loyal to the beast, and it would do no good to bring this little escapade up."

"I won't mention it, Kahuna, but thanks for the insight. It's good to know who you're working with," Brent said.

As often was the case with Kahuna, there was a pause in the conversation. Brent had been around Kahuna long enough to know when he took these short mental detours, it was best not to bother him. He was deep in thought.

Kahuna surveyed the azure sky, scanned the horizon, and then a big smile formed on his face as he returned his gaze to Brent. "You probably won't be working with Bilbo during the exercise. I don't think Roger is taking him up to Bremerton. But you will be working with the rock star of all MK 6 dolphins—Bruiser."

Kahuna began, "Bruiser is as different from Bilbo as anything could be. He's amazingly focused and completely professional. He's a hybrid, we think—half-Pacific and half-Atlantic bottlenose. And compared to the full Atlantic bottlenose dolphins, he's a monster. Word is that he weighs in at nearly one hundred pounds more than his workmates. Visualize a Green Bay tackle version of a dolphin, and you'll have the picture. He wasn't given the name *Bruiser* by chance. He earned it. By now, you know that nearly all the Navy dolphins have a lighter side. They're good-humored, playful, even mischievous at times. But Bruiser's all work. Unlike the other dolphins, he has no sense of humor. It just isn't part of his character.

"As near as the vets can estimate, Bruiser's about thirty-two years old. He's been in the Navy since he was rescued from a purse seiner's net by a Sea World mammal technician, Debra Harris, a truly wonderful and kindhearted young lady, and rehabilitated by the miracle workers at Pier 159. Even in his younger days, he was very serious and down to business. At one time or another, Bruiser's been trained in every mission in NMMP. The word at Group ONE is that he probably knows more about all the missions than any of the trainers. And his personality makes him perfectly attuned for the MK 6 mission.

"He's been around so long and done so much he's almost contemptuous of all but a few trainers and biotechs. Those he seems to like are Master Chief Murphy, Master Chief Quigley, Mark Cory, and his current handler, Roger Birosh. Roger and Bruiser are far more than an MK 6 team. They're like... well, like brothers. And they're hands-down the best MK 6 team we have in the fleet, which means they're the best in the world. Learn all you can about the MK 6 mission. I'm thinking you may need the experience in the future. But also, learn all you can about their relationship. It'll come in handy."

"I'll do my best, Kahuna. Thanks for the background. It's good to understand the personalities."

It was suddenly clear to Brent why he was assigned to Roger and Bruiser. And, as it turned out, it was one of those high points in his life and one that he would remember forever.

Class in Session

Monday, 8 April 2002
MU-3, Naval Amphibious Base, Coronado, California

Brent reported to Master Chief Quigley early on Monday morning, 8 April 2002. The master chief was jovial and informative as he escorted Brent down to the loading dock to make introductions to Roger and Bruiser.

Brent took it all in—the brows, the weathered storage areas and repair structures, rickety floating docks, the highly modified and well-used boats being prepped for the morning run. It was all so... invigorating. Brent just couldn't help but feel proud to be a part of it all.

"Hey, Roger!" Master Chief Quigley yelled at a well-toned and tanned sailor flat on his back under the steering console of a seven-meter RHIB. "I'd like to introduce you to your new assistant."

Roger crawled out from underneath the console and, wiping his hands on a dirty shop rag, stepped from the RHIB to the dock.

"Brent, meet EOD-1 Roger Birosh. Brent, Roger."

Roger extended his hand. "Good to meet you, Brent."

"My pleasure, Roger. Looks like I'll be working for you for the next few weeks."

"Well, now that you two are properly introduced, I've got places to go and people to be. Fight nice!"

Brent watched the master chief hike back the way they had come. The master chief had a genuine amiable personality, but Brent had heard stories of Master Chief Quigley and knew that he had been in some serious poop in his nearly thirty years of service, yet none of those horrors or stressors seemed to wear on him.

"Good man," Roger said reflexively.

"Just met him. Bet he has some stories to tell."

"I know he does, but damned if I can get any of them out of him. Maybe we'll have to take him to McP's and pour some truth serum down his gullet until he opens up."

"Count me in on that," Brent returned.

"I will! As soon as I get this throttle cable reconnected, we'll load up Bruiser and head out to our working area."

"You've also got a sea lion, if I was told right. Bilbo?"

"Yep, I do, Bilbo. He's a sweetheart, but he's not going to make the trip to Bremerton. And for now, I was told to train you for the MK 6 dolphin only." As an afterthought, Roger added, "I've heard about you and your work with Alika. Heard you saved his life, and maybe he saved yours."

"Seems like a century ago. And to be honest, I don't remember a lot about it," Brent explained.

"That can happen. Sometimes we subconsciously forget those really scary things. Point is, you had your heart and mind in the right place. I think Bruiser will warm up to you, but let him make the first move. He has a cantankerous side, and unlike most of our dolphins, he doesn't like to grab ass much. He's seriously serious."

"Can't wait to meet him!"

"Okay. For now, you can pass some tools so I can fix that cable. Then we'll go get Bruiser."

It took Roger ten minutes to finish the job. Brent felt like a third thumb; Roger needed no help. He certainly knew his way around the mechanical mysteries of small boats. Roger finished the task, buttoned up the steering console, and rubbed off most of the dirt and grease using the same dirty rag. "Okay, let's go get the big boy."

"Yeah. I need to see this guy."

They both hopped over the sponson to the dock, and Roger led the way to Bruiser's pen.

Bruiser shared a large pen with four other MK 6 dolphins, all males. Still a hundred feet away, Brent locked on the dolphins, who all had their heads out of the water watching the two humans meander down the dock. Brent was startled to see one dolphin whose melon was noticeably larger than his pen mates. In fact, aside from Brent's very first encounter with a dolphin years ago during his snorkeling adventure in Catalina, Brent had never seen a dolphin as big as this one. At the time, he really had nothing to compare it with; he just knew it was big.

"There's my boy." Roger whistled, and Bruiser quickly returned the whistle. Then Bruiser nodded his head up and down, spy-hopped, and elevated his upper body out of the water up to his pectorals. He was unmistakably very happy to see Roger.

"Good golly, he's a giant," Brent remarked.

"Yep. Some of the guys nicknamed him Bruiserilla. Pretty fitting name, I'm thinkin'."

As Brent came closer, he noticed the scars and areas of skin discoloration identifying old injuries. "Dang, what are all those scars from?"

"He's been around the block once or twice, and he doesn't suffer fools well or back down from anyone or anything. If you look just forward of his dorsal fin, you'll see a whole bunch of small scars, pretty well healed now, but when he was little, long before we got him, we think he got tangled up with a pretty fair-sized shark."

"I see it. My gosh. How did he survive?"

"Near as we can figure, he was attacked by something pretty big. We think he got hit by either a great white, a tiger, or a real big blue shark. He was much smaller when that happened, and as he grew and the wounds healed, the bite radius expanded to what it is today—almost twenty-four inches. Even now, as an equal-opportunity shark assassin, he hates sharks of any flavor. Sometimes I have a heck of a time keeping him from thumping them. At around eight hundred pounds, he packs quite a wallop. I've seen him lift a pretty big mako shark completely out of the water. Bruiser came right back to the boat on my call, but the shark was a mess…he probably didn't live."

Even before Roger and Brent reached the edge of Bruiser's pen, he had his giant melon out of the water with his chin resting on the edge of the dock.

"Have you been staying out of trouble?" Roger growled as he got on his knees, reached out, and rubbed Bruiser's melon and flank. Bruiser was clearly enjoying the contact and rolled on his right side, waving his left pectoral in the air, obviously begging for more caressing along his flank and tummy. A giant grin formed on Roger's face, and he complied.

Brent couldn't help but form one of his own. The trust and confidence of the bond was very obvious. Here is a man and his big dolphin completely enjoying the company of each other.

A long-standing canard is that people look like their dogs. Brent had no opinion on the validity of that adage one way or the other, but here in front of him was a dazzling example of a dolphin that looked a whole lot like his human.

Bruiser was a structurally sound—a stout, muscled dolphin. His partner, Roger, was a bit taller than Brent but much wider and buffed out. His head seemed to connect to his shoulders without the benefit of a neck. Brent took him for a wrestler or part-time guerilla. This was the guy you wanted to follow into McP's on some of those wild Friday nights when the civilians tried to claim what was rightfully Navy SPECOPS real estate.

Mk 6 Dolphin Handler—Under Training

Monday, 8 April to Friday, 26 April 2002
MU-3, Naval Amphibious Base, Coronado, California

Forty minutes later, Bruiser was secured in his beaching tray aboard Roger's seven-meter RHIB. Lines were cast, the engines were warmed up, and they pulled away from the dock headed northwest around the NAS North Island point toward the mouth of the San Diego Harbor.

"We're not doing any serious training today," Roger explained. "I wanted to take Bruiser for a ride and show you the fundamentals of handling an MK 6. There shouldn't be much difference in the commands between your dolphin and an MK 6. What you're going to find is that the only big change is what takes place underwater. The dolphin, for the most part, does all the work."

Brent had taken his regular position, sitting on an upturned plastic bucket where he could see both Roger and Bruiser. Brent now could view the full extent of Bruiser's scars and ancient injuries. He was missing a small piece of his dorsal fin on the trailing edge, his pectoral fins had several faint discolored areas, and the right side of his fluke had a number of deep indentations where he may have been hit by a prop.

As Brent scanned the big dolphin's amazing torpedo shape, he suddenly had the strange feeling he was being watched. Brent looked and locked eyes with Bruiser for a moment and then, not wanting to appear challenging, shifted his scan to the horizon. There were no outward tells that would give away Bruiser's thoughts, but he was most definitely evaluating this new human.

"He's really checking me out. What's he up to?"

"He's just trying to size you up. He doesn't take to many humans, and it may be a while before he warms up to you, if he ever does. Go ahead and talk to him so he gets used to your voice, but I'd keep everything you've grown fond of away from the front end of him."

Brent did just that. He muttered and whispered to Bruiser until they were a few miles offshore; then Roger smoothly pulled the throttles back and came off plane.

"All right, let's go ahead and lay the tray sides down and get Bruiser into the water. We'll let him run his recce pattern, and then I'd like you to beach him."

"I can do that, but wouldn't it be better if you did it? I mean, I just got here, and he doesn't know me from a sand crab."

"I realize that, but there's nothing gained if I do it. I'm pretty curious how he'll react to you."

"Okay, but I don't think he likes me. If he were a horse, his ears would be pinned back, and he'd be pawing the ground."

"Let's just see what he does. You're going to work with him a lot up in Bremerton. We might as well start this partnership now."

With that, Brent unfolded the sides of the tray, scanned the horizon to ensure there were no other boats near and no fins present, and then bent down and gently pressed against Bruiser's rostrum.

"Let's go check out the water, Bruiser," Brent half-whispered. Bruiser wiggled and slapped his tail to aid in the launch. In just a few short seconds, Bruiser was in the water and cutting a large arc around the RHIB.

"When he completes a circle or two, he'll make a couple of dives just to check things out, then he'll come back to the boat. When he does, go ahead and beach him. When you get him aboard, give him this." Roger offered a big herring. Based on its size, it could have been a bonito.

Still unconvinced this was the right time for this, Brent took the fish and turned to watch Bruiser. *What a magnificent boy. The war scars just give him more character, but he is beautiful,* Brent thought to himself.

Sure enough, Bruiser ran two large arcs around the boat and made three dives, then glided back to the hand station. Brent slapped the water and then motioned to the tray as he said, "Come on up, boy."

Bruiser, head out of the water and looking curiously at Brent, then shifted his gaze to Roger. Roger, in turn, nodded his head.

That must have been some kind of signal, Brent noted. There was a second's hesitation; then Bruiser made a single massive tail cycle and came aboard in a seemingly effortless jump onto the beaching tray. Brent rewarded Bruiser with the herring, avoiding any confusion between his hand and the fish. Roger moved to Bruiser's tray, took a knee, and gave him several strokes along his flank, talking to him all the while.

"Now, go ahead and get him back in the water. We'll just let him free swim, and you and I can talk about what we'll be doing up north."

"Sounds good to me."

Bruiser knew the drill. Brent gently pressed against Bruiser's rostrum and barely got the words, "Let's go swimming," out when Bruiser almost self-launched. "What a great boy," Brent said admiringly.

"No argument there. We've been together almost five years. I'd be a chief petty officer by now, but I had second thoughts about taking orders back to the fleet. Absolutely no regrets, though. It would be like leaving your wingman, or in your case, your brother snake-eaters in a firefight. Just couldn't do it."

"From what I hear, you aren't the first to make that decision."

"Yeah, well, all good things must come to an end. But it ain't happening today, so let's get down to business."

For the next hour, while Bruiser cruised the area and occasionally performed a few aerial leaps, tail walks, fin roles, and a few other acrobatics Brent hadn't seen before, Roger briefed him on the basics of the MK 6 system, the force protection and swimmer defense mission, handler procedures, tactics, techniques, equipment, radio communications and codes, dos and don'ts, and safety precautions. He also got an earful about the specific nature and mettle of Bruiser.

Brent was impressed with Bruiser's reputation before, but when Roger was done, Brent understood why everybody thought Bruiser must of have descended from Mt. Olympus.

Roger ended the brief with a reminder concerning the sensitive nature of the mission and the fact that the tactics, techniques, and procedures—the TTPs for the MK-6—remained classified. Roger cranked up the engines and cut a large semicircle, steadying up on heading back to the mouth of the bay. Bruiser was quick to slide into boat-following position without so much as a hand signal.

There were no practice target swimmers in the water this day, but Roger explained the different search patterns and how they ran grids in a patrol area while Bruiser boat-followed. When Bruiser was directed to take point or go forward to investigate a suspect area, he'd return and hit one of the two paddles, much like the MK 7 dolphins: the forward paddle indicated he had a positive hit on a swimmer; the rear paddle was a negative.

Usually, the handler would ask the dolphin to confirm the presence of a swimmer if he hit the forward paddle. If he returned to hit the forward paddle a second time, he was fitted with a marking device. Just as they did during Short Time in the early 1970s, the dolphin would approach the target from the rear hemisphere and press the marking device against the swimmer, which deployed the marker. The dolphin would then return to his boat. The handler and security crew would then further investigate the marked target and determine an appropriate course of action. In the real world, this might result in an apprehension or, depending on the rules of engagement (ROE), direct action.[59]

Learning the Ropes

Monday, 8 April to Friday, 26 April 2002
MU-3, Naval Amphibious Base, Coronado, California

Each working day of the first week, Brent spent most of his waking hours working with and learning from Roger and Bruiser.

The first week of Brent's training was focused on building the partnership and invigorating the trust and confidence with Bruiser. It wasn't until the end of that first week that Brent sensed a softening of Bruiser's demeanor toward him. There was an unmistakable easing of the tension and a definitive change in the way in which Bruiser studied him. Things were improving.

Roger explained something that was of great interest to Brent because it was precisely what Bill Washakie told Brent so many years ago—more sophisticated words, perhaps, but the meaning was the same.

As they sat in the RHIB and Bruiser swam large patterns around the boat one hazy day in mid-April, Roger explained, "Training is individualized for each dolphin. While initial stages of behavioral development are fairly standard, the more complex the training becomes, the more the trainer needs to adjust the behavior-modification process for the specific personality of his dolphin. The techniques, the rewards, and the speed that behavioral conditioning progresses is also based on age, time in captivity, prior training, intelligence, and mien. The training tools and processes we use are adjusted by the trainers to obtain maximum performance in minimum time, all the while reinforcing the bond of trust between the dolphin and the trainer.

"The interesting and really the impressive thing about Bruiser is, I don't know how much more the mammal trainers can teach him. He's been certified in every mission and task in the Marine Mammal Program. He's around thirty-two years old, and he actually socializes and teaches behavior to the younger dolphins. To put it another way, he has more history, more competency, and more experience in all our missions than any human currently in the program. He's like… like a combination of Zeus and Plato around here. And just between you and me, I love him to death. But don't tell my wife."

All Brent could do was smile and nod in appreciation. His admiration for Roger and Bruiser, pretty high to start with, had just soared off the charts.

The second week was even more interesting. Once Roger was confident that Brent and Bruiser were connecting and working on the same plane, Roger scheduled swimmers to exercise with the team. Just as it was explained to him, Brent was quick to realize that the bulk of the effort rested on the shoulders of the dolphin, and Bruiser was a thrill to watch in action. It was difficult to believe that an eight-hundred-pound dolphin could be as agile and as gentle as he was. Even when the divers knew Bruiser was on the search-and-tag phase, Bruiser was so quick and so maneuverable that they often didn't see the hit. Despite his size and the energy he could generate, none of the swimmers complained about working with Bruiser for fear of hard contact. Bruiser was a soft-touch dolphin. The only exception was if Bruiser happened to locate a top-tier predator—a shark. Results from these encounters were often fatal.

On to the Big Show

Friday, 26 April 2002
Mobile Unit 3, Navy Amphibious Base, Coronado, California

Brent's training during the third and final week was less about MK 6 handling and more about the TTPs. They didn't venture to the training areas to work with the swimmers during this time, but they did take Bruiser and Bilbo out each day and let them free-swim while Roger held class in the RHIB.

The classroom environment could not have been better. Southern California in early spring was a delight. Seas were calm, the sun bright, the water temperature a comfortable sixty degrees, and the seascape was absolutely opulent.

Brent was occasionally mesmerized by the antics of the seagulls and the hunting techniques of the pelicans as they performed their wingovers then folded their wings just before impact with the water. By Brent's appraisal, most of their dives seemed to be successful.

And then there were the visits by local seals. They were curious about the boat and cruised by, panhandling for handouts. They also seemed to be confused by the giant dolphin and fat sea lion—why would they hang around humans for hours at a time when they could be exploring the depths and taking part in seal capers?

Bruiser accepted their presence. He intermittently pinged them but showed no outward signs of either affection or aggression. For the most part, he ignored them even when the seals tried to entice him in a game of follow the leader. Bilbo was more interested in the undersea menu. He did occasionally snap at any seal who wouldn't take the hint, but they all seemed to know, he was no threat—he was too fat to catch anything but very slow fish.

Roger gave a comprehensive layout of the upcoming security exercise. He spoke in great detail of the objectives, the rules of engagement, the red team composition, likely SEAL tactics, and the MK 6 system's countertactics. Brent occasionally asked questions, but for the most part, Roger's delivery was well paced, logical, and descriptive.

On Friday, 26 of April 2002, the last day of his MK 6 training, Brent finally ran out of questions.

In less than two months, Brent's skills, experience, and capabilities would be put to the test. He had a thorough understanding of what to expect and what was expected. He was confident and upbeat about the upcoming exercise. The anticipation it generated was very much the same as the vibrant, dry-mouth tenseness of his first combat engagement. He was excited to get back in the action and completely ready to *git 'er done*.

For Brent, the coming exercise took precedent to all else. He had his reputation and that of Foxtrot Platoon on the line. He wasn't going to screw it up.

And Brent had a head-start. Roger's appraisal of Brent was all positive. Roger noticed immediately the gentle manner and patient approach in which Brent worked with Bruiser. Bruiser, in turn, eventually warmed up to Brent. Clearly, there was an element of trust, and the early stages of a foundational connection between Bruiser and Brent that was denied to most other humans. And when it came to grasping the elements of the exercise and the mission, tasks, tactics, techniques, and procedures of the MK 6 system, Roger was quite amazed at just how quickly Brent assimilated the information.

Bottom line, Roger was going to have to tell Master Chief Quigley he owed Kahuna a case of beer. Brent was going to be ready for the big show at Bremerton in June.

CHAPTER 12

THE BLUE TEAM

Never trust a species that grins all the time. It's up to something.

—Terry Pratchett, *Pyramids*

Mixed Emotions

Sunday, 16 June 2002
Mobile Unit 3, Gator Base, Coronado, California

Brent felt an enormous sense of accomplishment. How many Wyoming cowboys carried the credentials of a MK 7 dolphin handler and an MK 6 Handler (under training)? But as the days counted down for the flight to Bremerton, he also experienced an unshakable sense of guilt. He was anxious to put all his training to work in the upcoming security exercise at Bremerton, but he was going to miss Alika. He harbored no concerns about Alika's well-being. Chief Olopoto had almost adopted him as his own. Alika could not be in better hands. And that was the thing of it; Brent had some misgivings that Alika wouldn't miss him and maybe even accept Kahuna as his new handler. It was a selfish and unrealistic concern, but he couldn't deny the fact that the thought hovered over him.

Brent admitted to himself worrying about it was a waste of valuable time. He had a list a mile long containing things he needed to think about, plan for, and do in preparation for the trip to Bremerton, a.k.a. Naval Base Kitsap.[60]

At the top of that list was a solemn oath to himself to ensure he honorably represented Foxtrot Platoon when he joined forces with Roger, Bruiser, and the rest of the Mobile Unit 3 team. A popular axiom in the Navy fighter community seemed appropriate to Brent's situation, "Better dead than look bad."

Naval Base Kitsap Overview

Sunday, 16 June 2002
Naval Base Kitsap, Seattle on the Kitsap Peninsula, Washington

Naval Base Kitsap[61] is the third-largest Navy base in the United States.[62] The base provides operating services and support facilities for surface ships, Fleet Ballistic Missile submarines and other Navy vessels. It sets about twenty-five miles due west of Seattle, Washington on the Kitsap Peninsula. It is one of four nuclear shipyards in the United States, one of two strategic nuclear weapons facilities, the only West Coast dry-dock capable of handling Nimitz-class aircraft carriers and the Navy's largest fuel depot. Its mission is to serve as the home base for the Navy's fleet throughout West Puget Sound.[63]

It is the security for the ballistic missiles and the nuclear subs, the boomers, that are the big worry. The boomers represent the third leg of the *nuclear triad strategy*. The other two components are the long-range strategic bombers and the land-based intercontinental ballistic missiles (ICBMs). The nuclear triad strategy provides a tremendous deterrent effect and greatly reduces the enemy's ability to destroy the United States' nuclear forces in a first-strike scenario.

Conceptually, the United States would retain a credible nuclear capability even after a short response time, first strike by a nuclear-armed enemy in order to ensure an overwhelming and devastating response upon an aggressor nation. Security for the base, the facilities, and ships assigned is of titanic importance. To ensure security and defensive measures are effective, regular security exercises are scheduled.

Commander, US Fleet Forces Command (USFF), and commander, Navy Installations Command (CNIC), regularly test the force protection and antiterrorism posture of the Navy's bases and installations in the continental United States under an exercise called *Solid Curtain-Citadel Shield* (SC-CS).[64] SC-CS uses realistic scenarios to ensure US Navy security forces maintain a high level of readiness to respond to changing technologies and dynamic threats. Specifically, SC-CS assesses the physical, electronic, cyber, and intelligence systems set in place to guard against intrusion, surveillance, and physical attacks upon the facilities and fleet assets aboard Bremerton, Naval Base. It was this exercise to which Mobile Unit 3 was tasked as the Blue Force littoral security contingent, a.k.a. the *Blue Team*.

Gearing Up

Sunday, 16 June to Saturday, 22 June 2002
Mobile Unit 3, Navy Amphibious Base, Coronado, California

It was a typical *June gloom* day early on Sunday the sixteenth of June—low misty fog hung in the air, reducing visibility to less than one hundred yards. Typically, the fog would burn off by 1100, but there was no hint of that in the wee hours. At 0600, it was still pea-soup thick and damp.

The personnel assigned to the Mobile Unit 3 detachment to Bremerton included eighteen handlers, two veterinarians, and three medical techs. They'd all pitched in and had worked most of the previous day staging equipment, constructing the air transport carriers (ATCs) for the animals, positioning the support gear, and getting four MK 6 dolphins and four MK 6 sea lions ready for the flight north.

By midmorning on Sunday, all the equipment, animals, and personnel arrived by truck at Naval Air Station, North Island, in preparation for the actual load aboard the leviathan Lockheed C-5 Galaxy. The flight from San Diego to Bremerton was just under four hours, but the preparation, time to stage the equipment, load and offload usually took three times longer.

This was Brent's first exposure to the process, and while he pitched in where and when he could, for the most part, he felt as useful as a large nose wart. Still, he kept his eyes open, his mouth closed, and his hands at the ready throughout the load-up.

Master Chief Quigley was the officer in charge and therefore responsible for the load. Roger, the next senior enlisted person, ably assisted the master chief.

When time allowed, Roger and his new sidekick Brent hovered around the ATC containing Bruiser just to ensure Bruiser remained calm and quiet. The fact was, Bruiser was an old hand at these evolutions; in fact, he had more support flights than any of the handlers or biotechs assigned to MU-3. He took it all in stride and seemed to shut down one hemisphere of his brain and just settle in for the ride.

The gangly C-5 touched down at 1530 Sunday afternoon. The Air Force crew was efficient and courteous, but spent an inordinate amount of time admiring the animals. This was a shock to no one, though. How many times would one expect to encounter dolphins and sea lions aboard an Air Force heavy lifter?

For the next five hours, the Mobile Unit 3 team offloaded the animals and their gear and relocated everything to an old building adjacent to the submarine piers bordering Wyckoff Way on Bremerton Naval Base. It was a typical Navy maintenance building: functional, comfortable for the most part (but badly in need of paint), and smelling of mold, salt air, and seagull guano.

Roger and Brent led the team assigned to securing the animals in their new but temporary pens. This was close to the building they'd use for locker space, gear storage, operations, briefing rooms, and administration.

Things were finally coming together a bit after 2015. And though it was getting late in the evening, Brent was surprised by the persistent sunlight, not that he could actually see the sun. It seemed to doggedly hang above the thin clouds and produced a gauzy form of illumination on all horizons. He was reminded that due to the nearly yearlong overcast layers shielding the sun and moderate temperatures and high humidity, the Seattle residents didn't actually tan—they rusted.

Master Chief Quigley called an all-hands meeting set for 2100 in the administration space. This gave Roger and Brent one more opportunity to check on Bruiser and the rest of the animals. Bruiser was calm but alert. He knew something was up and gave every impression he was ready to go to work, whatever the task.

All hands were assembled in the admin spaces a few moments after 2100. The Mobile Unit 3 team, all twenty-three of them, sat quietly, some dozing, when the master chief positioned himself in front of a large archaic blackboard.

"Attention to brief, gang!" Quigley ordered. "First, nice job to all on moving the animals and gear. Doesn't look like we lost anything or anyone, and the animals seem comfortable. Does anybody have any issues so far?"

Heads swiveled, but there were no takers.

"Good! But don't be bashful about letting me or Roger know if something's going south. I want to correct anything before it breaks. The schedule for security patrols, watch teams, and the duty officer is posted on the sideboard to your starboard. Everybody is going to be double tasked with the patrols, fish-house duty, and other assignments. Each of the animals will have a primary and a secondary handler. The exercise, as you already know, begins early tomorrow morning and runs twenty-four hours a day until its secured—we think around eighteen-hundred on Friday. You'll all be running port and starboard twelve-hour patrols. Doc"—the master chief zeroed in on Major Brian Hamilton, US Army, who led the medical and veterinary team—"I'll let you set the schedules for your team. On top of that you'll be standing additional security and duty officer watches. Sleep, eat, and take care of your personnel business when you can. "But first and foremost, make sure your animal is healthy, fed, and calm. This is a new environment for many of them. The water temp is currently fifty-four degrees. That's about nine degrees colder than the water back home. Their schedule will be chaotic for a few days, but they'll adjust. Just make sure nothing rattles them. With us this evening is one of the White Team[65] members, Lieutenant Commander Steve Connolly. Sir, you have the floor."

"Good evening, gents," LCDR Connolly stepped to the podium and began. "On behalf of US Fleet Forces Command and Commander Submarine Command, Pacific, thank you all for making the trip and augmenting our security force for this exercise. In that we have both nuclear ships aboard the base and special weapons in storage, this is a *very* serious event. Your job, as part of the Blue Force,[66] is to patrol and maintain a high state of security all along the waterfront within the confines of the base. You'll all be issued base charts, and annotated on those are the high-priority and sensitive areas that you'll focus on. I don't need to remind you that while this is a real-world scenario, safety of your animals and our people is our number-one concern.

"All right then," he continued, "I'll do a deep-dive brief on objectives, procedures, point-of-contact information, the comm plan, area layout, first day schedule, rules of engagement, and safety. If you have any concerns or questions, ask them. I want this to be crystal clear in everybody's mind."

LCDR Connolly hit all the details for the next two hours. It was 2330, seven and a half short hours prior to the commencement of the exercise and six and a half hours until the first patrol launch. The lieutenant commander closed with, "If there are no further questions, I'll leave you with this—*don't do nuthin stupid!*"

The MU-3 team traded glances and giggled heartily. It was getting late into the night, but they still maintained a sense of humor.

Master Chief Quigley thanked the officer, reviewed the schedule and boat assignments for the first day of the exercise, and then secured the team. The men staggered to their vehicles and headed for their assigned bachelor enlisted quarters.

Brent reviewed the posted schedule just to make sure he had it right. He, Roger, Bruiser, and Sir Lancelot, one of the four sea lions, were slated for the first go, a 0600 launch. He had it on good authority that his team would take the 0600 to 1800 patrol for two days; then, with a short break in the battle rhythm, would switch to the second shift, 1800 to 0600.

It had been a long day, but Brent was all a twitter. This was exciting stuff; sleep would not come easily this night.

Day One—COMEX

Monday, 17 June 2002
Naval Base Kitsap

Brent woke himself on time, a few minutes before 0500, a trick he'd learned with the boat teams. He rolled out of the rack, pulled on his shorts and topsiders, and exited his room. He was about to tap on Roger's door when it opened. Roger was up, still tucking in his shirt, but nearly ready to go.

Brent greeted him, "Good morning sunshine!"

"Yeah, and to you. You wake the others scheduled for the first go?"

"Not yet. I wanted to make sure you were up first."

"Been up for a while. Hardly slept. It's going to be a busy day."

"Amen!"

"You wake Scott Sanders and Bear Watson. I'll shag a bunch of box lunches and meet you guys at the van at 0530. We'll get out a little early."

"Got it. See you there, Roger,"

Brent woke the others and then jumped in the shower. At 0520, he tugged on his shorts, deck shoes, a fresh T-shirt, his navy-blue thermal layer, and his Gore-Tex jacket.

A few moments past 0530, two seven-meter RHIBs left the dock: Roger, Brent, Sir Lancelot, and Bruiser in one RHIB; and Petty Officer Second Class Scott Sanders and Petty Officer 3rd Class Bear Watson, handlers for Zeus, an MK 6 dolphin, and Seymour, an MK 6 sea lion, in the second RHIB. They proceeded to their assigned grids and began their twelve-hour patrol.

The first day of ops went without incident—no reports of any activity, no contacts with the bad guys, and pretty much no excitement. But that would change.

Red Force Contact

Day two—Tuesday, 18 June 2002
Naval Base Kitsap

Tuesday was initially a repeat of the previous day, but shortly after 1500, nine hours into their watch, Bruiser, who had been running a large square search pattern near the submarine piers, came racing back to the boat, nosed the forward paddle, and looked anxiously at Roger and Brent. "You got one, Bruiser!" Roger queried, sensing Bruiser's excitement.

Bruiser's eyes, the intensity of his focused stare, his posture, everything said, *Yes. Now let's get this guy!*

"Give it to him, Brent."

Brent retrieved a marking nose cup[67] and held it just above the surface of the water. Bruiser, without hesitation, swam to Brent and fitted it on his rostrum. Upon a signal from Brent, Bruiser dove and swam toward his mark, pinging all the way.

At nearly 120 yards from the RHIB, Bruiser detected two divers—SEALs simulating diver sappers—the Red Force.

Based on the sonar returns, Bruiser calculated the position, direction, depth, and speed of the two targets. They were using rebreather systems that emitted no bubbles and were in a formation about ten yards abeam of each other. The diver farthest from the boat was slightly aft of the closest diver in twenty feet of water, swimming at two knots on a course that would take them directly to the sub piers.

Bruiser made slight adjustments to his intercept geometry so as to tag the diver farthest from him then reverse course and return to the RHIB to report. This intercept plan would mark the second diver and avoid detection by the forward diver, if things worked out.

As it unfolded, Bruiser swooped in and pressed the marking device against the back of the second diver and sped away, avoiding any contact. It was a perfect delivery. The floatation device inflated, the pinger began to transmit, and the strobe light to which it was attached ascended to the surface. The target diver felt the bump, but it came so fast that he never saw what delivered the hit. Bruiser was halfway to the RHIB by that time.

Within seconds of the hit, Roger spotted the strobe light bobbing on the surface. "He's got one," Roger excitedly blurted out. "Stand by..."

Bruiser returned to the RHIB and tapped on the forward paddle. Brent was ready with a big fat mackerel, which Bruiser completely ignored—he was too juiced up to think about food.

"Bring him aboard, Brent, and we'll go check the strobe and see what Bruiser caught."

The rules of engagement (ROE) specified that a diver simulating a swimmer sapper, if detected and marked, was to surface and wait to come aboard the patrol craft. He would be out of the problem for at least twelve hours. That was the rule anyway.

While Brent was busy beaching Bruiser, Roger grabbed the radio and notified Blue Force control that they had a hit on at least one Red Force diver sapper. Blue Force replied that a reinforced Blue Team was on the way to the most likely high-value target—the subs at the pier.

In seconds, Brent had Bruiser secured in his tri-mat. "Good to go," Brent reported and flashed Roger a thumbs-up.

Roger powered up and headed for the strobe light. He cut power and drifted up to the light while Brent recovered the float. He quickly coiled the lanyard half-expecting to see a SEAL connected to the other end. Quite suddenly, he came to the end of the lanyard. There was no SEAL attached. Brent inspected the line more closely, then turned to Roger. "It's been cut."

"Son of a..." Roger didn't finish, but the frustration was evident. "They're supposed to come to the surface and wait for the boat. They've done this before." Roger leaned his head against his forearms as they rested on the helm, deep in thought.

An uneasy silence fell upon them. Brent watched Roger for a moment and then shifted his gaze to Bruiser.

Seconds ticked by. Then Roger lifted his head, looked deeply into Bruiser's bright eyes, and then barked, "Okay, launch Bruiser with another marker."

With no enticement, Brent eased Bruiser back in the water. The tension and excitement was very evident in Bruiser's mannerisms. Brent fitted a second nose cup and signaled him to deploy. Brent watched the pro go to work.

Bruiser swam a tight fast semicircle in the vicinity of the RHIB, made one breach to gather a lungful of air, and then darted off as if shot out of a torpedo tube. He headed directly toward the sub piers.

Roger and Brent steadied themselves against a gathering cold breeze and waited impatiently for Bruiser's return. Hopefully, they'd soon see the glimmer of a strobe light rising to the surface.

Less than five minutes ticked by, and a translucent glow illuminated the water near the closest pier. A moment later, Bruiser appeared at the port sponson, excited and triumphant.

"Get him in the boat. We'll check this out. And those assholes better not have cut the line again!" Roger added.

With Bruiser aboard, Roger added full power to the two Mercs and sped to the strobe light. Twenty-five yards from the strobe, Roger eased back on the throttles and pulled the transmissions out of gear. The RHIB came off step and drifted toward the light. Brent leaned over the sponson, grasped the light, and tugged on the line.

There was no resistance. The end of the line appeared on the surface.

"They cut it again, Roger."

Even in the faltering afternoon light, Brent could see the tautness in Roger's neck and jaw muscles. "Those needle dicks." And then Roger added, "Wait until tomorrow night. We'll fix their wagon!"

"Tomorrow night?" Brent asked tentatively.

"To catch a SEAL, you need to think like a SEAL. They never do anything the same way or use the same tactics twice in a row. SEALs are very innovative, resourceful, and sometimes ruthless—but they need to be in their operational environment. They try to be very unpredictable, but knowing this sometimes makes them predictable. I think they'll keep everybody in tension in the evening, and then very early in the morning, maybe just after midnight, just when the security Blue Team is beat and distracted, they'll hit the sub pier again. But this time, we're changing our tactics, and we'll mod our ROE just a little bit. Besides, we have a secret weapon."

"Whatdaya mean a little bit? And what secret weapon?"

"You'll see soon enough."

A View to a Keelhauling

Day two—Tuesday, 18 June 2002
Naval Base Kitsap

The daily ops debrief was held in a classified conference room at Navy Region Northwest headquarters Tuesday evening. Representatives from all three forces were present: Blue Force, White Force, and Red Force. Several senior staff officers representing USFF were also present. Master Chief Quigley, Roger, and Brent represented the maritime security team for the Blue Force. They all knew they were about to get their lips ripped off, but they cowboy'd up in anticipation of the report.

Brent scanned the faces of the attendees and noticed six of the Red Force SEALs sitting in the back of the conference room, their chairs leaning on the back two legs and their backs against the bulkhead. They arrived in a montage of mismatched uniform and civilian garments. Most sported cargo shorts, flip-flops, and Hawaiian shirts; and despite the crispness of the evening, the mercury hovering in the mid-forties, none of them wore a jacket or a pullover. They seemed to be impervious to the Northwest weather.

Based on their lax posture, one might assume they were about to view a first-run movie rather than a classified debrief of the day's events. All that was missing was a keg and a popcorn machine.

One of the directors of the exercise, Lieutenant Commander Steve Connolly of the White Force, led off. He thanked the attendees for the day's work. He almost said *progress* but hesitated. He then introduced the Blue Team commander, who took no longer than ten minutes to address the day's successes and the major breach of security at the sub pier. The commander's gaze then lit on Master Chief Quigley. "Anything to add, Master Chief?"

Master Chief Quigley rose from his chair, shoulders square, back straight, head high. "No, sir. We screwed the pooch. Won't happen again, Commander."

The master chief purposely did not mention the violation of the ROE and that the SEAL swimmers cut the strobe light line. Unarguably, his team was responsible for a giant breach in security. The *why* of it was between the MU-3 team and the SEALs.

There was snickering in the back of the room. The SEALs could hardly contain themselves. Nothing could be funnier—to them.

LCDR Connolly let out a primal grunt then turned the podium over to the Red Force commander. The Red Force commander spent nearly twenty minutes in a monologue describing, in exquisite detail, their assault plan and—hardly mentioning those several failed attacks on other high-value targets—the successful hit at the sub piers. The SEALs were enjoying the show and seemed about ready to fall out of their chairs. When the master chief stole a glance over his shoulder, the SEALs suddenly regained their military bearing.

LCDR Connolly finished the debrief and thanked all in attendance. For the maritime Blue Team, their keelhauling was over.

Roger found a small classroom and ushered the master chief and Brent inside and closed the door.

"What do you have for us, Roger?"

"A way to tag the sapper swimmers so it won't matter if they cut the strobe light line."

Brent was all ears, but he had not a clue as to how Roger was going to pull this off, nor did Master Chief Quigley.

"Just how the hell are you going to do that? And a better question is, are you going to break the ROE? We're not messin' with the ROE, Roger."

"I'm willing to bet a case of beer that the SEALs won't go out again until tomorrow night. Get Brent, Sir Lancelot, Bruiser, and me scheduled for the eighteen-hundred go. We'll take up station in deeper water, but we'll still stay close to the sub piers."

"Okay, but you still didn't explain how you plan to stop the SEALs."

"You'll see tomorrow night, Master Chief."

A long stare followed. Quigley bored into Roger's eyes but couldn't get a read. "All right, Roger. Don't make us look bad."

Bruiser—Coloring Outside the Lines

Day three—Wednesday, 19 June 2002
Naval Base Kitsap

At 1800 the following evening, Brent released the painter lines from the dock, and Roger nudged the throttles forward slightly. He waited for the number two boat to clear the dock. The second RHIB, just as on the first day, was skippered by Scott Sanders, with Bear Watson attending to Zeus and Seymour. Scott flashed Roger a thumbs-up, and Roger eased on power. The RHIB smoothly came on step. Once joined, they headed for the sub piers.

It was in the low forties, with a low overcast layer and no wind. Dew covered everything on the boat and made movement aboard the RHIB a bit sporty.

Sir Lancelot, a big handsome California sea lion, was at the stern, head on a swivel, enjoying the outing. Bruiser, on the other hand, was alert but agitated. Brent had no way to explain it, but he sensed a great frustration building in Bruiser. Certainly, Bruiser couldn't understand Roger's words from the day before, but was it possible that Bruiser could read his comportment, sense his dark mood, or hear the mounting frustration in Roger's voice? Whatever senses were involved, whatever communications had taken place, it was abundantly clear that Bruiser shared Roger's frustration, and there became a new sense of urgency and determination about him.

En route, Roger briefed Brent on the night's activities and the engagement tactics. If the SEALs actually showed up, things would be different. And Roger was sure that they'd show up.

Roger had a visual on the offgoing MK 6 crew seventy yards off the port bow. He cut power and drifted to within one hundred yards of the sub piers. Over the radio, he received the handover.

"Any contacts?" Roger asked.

"Not a thing. It's like a cemetery out here."

"Who'd you bring?"

"We've got Keno and Slider."

Roger said in almost a whisper to Brent, "Keno's a good dolphin. Slider's a sea lion, a little young, still in that grab-assin' stage. But if you can keep his attention, he does great. If there was anything out there, they'd a found it." Roger keyed the mic, "Okay, guys, we got it."

"You got it. And kick their ass for us, will ya, Roger? We need to get on the scoreboard."

"We plan to do just that."

Roger turned to Brent. "Get Bruiser in the water and get a marker ready for Sir Lancelot but hold him on board. I don't want any distractions for Bruiser. We'll launch Lance as soon as Bruiser gets a hit."

Bruiser swam his routine circle around the boat, his click trains audible; then he cruised toward the sub piers.

The clouds thickened as twilight approached, and all was still for several hours.

That serenity was splintered when Bruiser burst out of the water and sped toward the forward paddle. He tapped the paddle then stared intently at Roger, awaiting a signal.

Roger rushed to the port sponson.

"I've got the marker ready. You want it now?" Brent asked excitedly.

Roger's response was puzzling. "Won't need it for Bruiser."

He then did something that Brent thought unusual. Roger opened his left hand and held it at chest level, palm open, facing to the right. He made a fist with his right hand and drove it into his open left hand. Then he pointed in the general direction of the sub piers and whistled. Bruiser returned a whistle, nodded his head up and down, then broke for the piers.

"Get Lance in the water and give him a marker," Roger ordered.

Brent complied, and Sir Lancelot took off after Bruiser.

Roger grabbed the radio mic and transmitted, "Scot and Bear, okay, we've got a hit. Get your boys in the water and stand by to recover swimmers."

"Copy! Zeus is in the water. We're launching Seymour now."

"Copy all," Roger responded.

Roger cranked up the Mercs, eased the transmission into gear, and began creeping toward the piers. "Now watch this."

It was well after midnight. The tension was palatable. Brent squinted into the darkness. Two minutes later, a large black shape appeared on the surface; seconds passed, then another appeared.

"Goddamn it!"

Then, "Son of a bitch! What was that?"

The RHIB was still sixty yards from the now-surfaced SEAL Red Force swimmers, but their outbursts carried easily over the still water.

A strobe light hit the surface. At the other end, a very disgruntled SEAL was attached and also appeared on the surface. "What in the hell just happened?"

Roger lit up and pointed the spotlight at the flustered SEALs.

"Nice evening for a swim. You boys all right?" Roger asked calmly. The RHIB inched closer to the swimmers.

"Something big just hit me in the ass. Hurts like hell," hollered the swimmer nearest to Roger's RHIB.

"Yeah, and I got tagged right on the back of both legs. I can hardly move them," a second diver added.

The third diver, the one connected to the strobe light, muttered a strong string of words—verb, adverb, and pronoun—all ingeniously derivatives of the "F" bomb.

As Roger brought the RHIB within reach of the swimmers, he said, "Come on aboard, boys. I'll take you ashore. You can hit the bar." And almost as an afterthought, he added, "Oh, and by the way, you're out of the fight."[68]

As the problem unfolded, when Bruiser returned to the RHIB and tapped the forward disk, he had not one but three contacts. The fist-into-the-open-hand gesture was Roger's signal to Bruiser to *play ruff.* No other dolphin-human team had developed that signal nor established the behavior for the signal. It meant Bruiser could bump a swimmer but could not injure them. There was wide diversity in the definition of "do not hurt" to a dolphin, but Roger had taken several bumps himself during the development of this behavior in order to calibrate what was acceptable and what was not.

During this specialized training, it was amazing to Roger that Bruiser never hit a human anywhere but the butt or posterior of the legs—he seemed to intuitively know never to hit a human in a vital area.

It was a sad fact that no human was witness to the choreography of the tactic on this night. A highly proficient fighter pilot attacking multiple bogies could not have achieved a more perfect line of attack. The geometry, timing, and unscripted synchronization between Bruiser and Sir Lancelot were a thing of immense beauty and tactical aplomb.

Bruiser processed the returns of his click stream and identified three humans: two swimmers about five yards abreast of each other and a third ten yards in trail. He plotted a line of attack and maneuvered from abeam and slightly aft of the two swimmers in front. He silently closed on the nearest swimmer at less than half his flank speed, about ten knots. He hit the first diver with his rostrum firmly on the butt just below the rebreather pack, then made a slight correction in track and walloped the second diver across the legs with his fluke as he passed.

Sir Lancelot, in close trail with Bruiser, carried the marker. The third diver to the rear of the leading divers became Lance's target. Lance approached from dead six o'clock and, none too gently, attached the marker to the diver's breathing gear. The flotation section inflated, rose to the surface, and activated the strobe light, successfully marking the diver.

Adding insult to injury, Keno and Slider arrived slightly late but entered the fray anyway and attached the marking device with the strobe lights to the first and second diver. Redundant but effective.

While Brent beached Bruiser and Sir Lancelot, Roger helped the three SEALs aboard. One of them rolled over the starboard sponson and came face-to-face with Bruiser's big melon, his perennial grin enhanced enormously this evening by the success of the mission.

"Is this the guy who tapped us?"

"Yep! Bruiser, meet the SEALs. Gents, this is Bruiser."

"Damn. Sure is a big guy. I'm not going to be able to sit down for a week." Then added, "Ya know, we could use this guy. Can we have him?"

Roger chuckled, positioned himself at the helm, and responded, "Yeah. Over my dead body!"

The SEALs, now seated on the deck of the RHIB and leaning against the sponson, stole a glance at one another. One whispered, "That could be arranged!"

The Debrief

Saturday, 22 June 2002
Naval Base Kitsap

Solid Curtain-Citadel Shield concluded on Saturday, 22 June 2002. There were no more busts of the ROE, there were no more breaches of security, there were no more SEAL shenanigans of any kind.

On Saturday morning, all the players on both sides of the exercise attended a plenum debrief. Prominently seated at the head table of the conference room was the coordinating authority for the exercise, Rear Admiral David Johnson from US Fleet Forces Command. He sat erect, fingers intertwined, and listened intently to the representatives from each of the forces as they summarized their debrief and lessons learned.

The team leader of the maritime Red Force—the SEALS—had a very succinct debrief. "We had two sappers who were successful in making it to two of the subs at the pens on the first day of the exercise. We assessed that attack as successful."

Master Chief Quigley leaned toward Roger and whispered, "You'll notice they conveniently forgot to mention they had been marked before they got to the pens."

"I noticed," Roger murmured.

The SEAL leader continued, "We were less successful the following nights. In fact, all simulated attacks on the subs were unsuccessful. We were intercepted every time. Although we've been doing these security exercises for quite a while, we were quite impressed with the Mark 6 team. The dolphins and the sea lions were most impressive and the most effective Blue Force we've seen yet. Bravo Zulu[69] to them and their handlers!"

The SEAL started to take his seat then stood again and concluded with, "Oh yeah, we learned a big lesson this time." He looked around the room, his eyes coming to rest on Roger. "Don't screw with the big dolphin!" The SEAL then gingerly eased himself into his chair and let out a stifled gasp as his butt made contact with the seat.

Nothing could have been more gratifying or more humorous to Master Chief Quigley. Roger and Brent, at this point, were only partially successful in keeping a big smirk off their faces—a definitive breach in professional protocol, but *well earned.*

The White Force commander made the final summation. "While not without an occasional stumble, we believe we successfully met all goals of this year's Solid Curtain-Citadel Shield. We drove decision-making at all levels of command through immediate analysis, fusion, and enunciation of threat indicators and warnings. Further, we tested and assessed our preemptive defense in depth measures based upon a variety of threats across the region. Except for the first day of the exercise, we had no assets or ships attacked. We learned a lot, played hard, and no one got hurt."

Two SEALs seated in the rear of the conference room looked at each other and silently lipped, "Well, not exactly."

Solid Curtain-Citadel Shield was deemed a success by the White Force commander and hailed for the many learning points by Commander Navy Region Northwest.

All was well in dolphin land.

Reflections

Saturday, 22 June 2002
Return flight from Kitsap to NAS North Island

The flight from Bremerton to NAS North Island was a bit of a blur. The load-up and departure went without a snag. The four-hour flight turned out to be a godsend to Brent. He planted himself near to Bruiser's ATC, close enough that he could keep an eye on him and well within reach.

The master chief strolled forward in the cargo area, checking the animals and speaking with each of his troops. Brent watched with admiration, and an age-old leadership maxim popped into his head, a leadership adage he remembered from his SPECOPS days: "Never rest, never eat, and never sleep until your troops are taken care of."

With the master chief's check complete, he plopped down next to Brent and strapped into the fold-down seat. He let out a long sigh of exhaustion then swiveled toward Brent. Over the roar of the engines, he said, "Brent, I just wanted to thank you for pitching into the exercise. I don't usually take anybody but trained and certified MK 6 guys, but Kahuna is a good friend of mine. He spoke highly of you, and he was right. You're pretty good with the animals. You listen up, learn quickly, and pull your own weight. That's big medicine around here."

He smiled and showed a straight line of white teeth and appreciation in his eyes. "You also impressed Roger, who is not easily impressed. And apparently, by all reports, you even impressed Bruiser. He pretty much ignores most of the trainers and handlers. He thinks they're rookies and unworthy, but for reasons better explained by Roger, you won him over. Impressive job, Brent. Mobile Unit 3 is in your debt!"

This came as a welcome shock to Brent. "Master Chief...thanks for the opportunity to do this. It was really an adventure and a learning experience I won't forget."

"I hope not, because I'll be sending a letter of appreciation and a recommendation letter to Special Clearance Team ONE. You're going to be recommended as an operational MK 6 dolphin handler."

Brent was flabbergasted. A full-fledged MK 6 dolphin handler qual was something he only hoped for. "Wow! I...ah...don't know what to say, except thanks a ton. I sure appreciated all the hands-on help from Roger. You got yourself a pretty impressive teacher and a master dolphin handler. I'm still trying to figure Bruiser out, though. It's almost as though he can read Roger's mind. I mean, what an amazing team."

"Bruiser's been around a long time. He's got this job nailed. Sometimes I'm not sure who's teaching whom. One more thing." Quigley crossed his arms over his chest and leaned into his seat. "If ever you want to come back here to the MK 6 program, let me know. We can make that happen, and we could sure use you."

"Thanks, Master Chief. That means a lot to me. It really does, but I really do like the MK 7 mission, and I know this is going to sound crazy, but I like my dolphin."

"Bring Alika with you. We can always use another rock-star dolphin in the program."

"I'll sure give it some thought, Master Chief. Thanks for everything."

"You did well, Brent. Again, thanks for the help."

And with that, Brent tugged his Gor-Tex parka close around his neck, bracing against the growing chill and snuggled back into his seat.

Brent knew that handlers didn't ordinarily sleep on a transport flight, too busy attending to their animal, but he was a spent round both physically and mentally, and soon his mind drifted to the remarkable bond between Roger and Bruiser. Maybe it was the kinship born in the affinity for the sea. Perhaps it was that Roger had much the same down-to-business mien, or possibly it was some delphian connection between the two—Brent didn't really know. But the bottom line was, Bruiser and Roger formed the perfect complementary bond.

Brent wondered if he would ever have that same type of relationship with Alika. And then…he was drifting in the warm ocean currents with his dolphin, and all was well.

It seemed as if only seconds later the landing gear squeaked onto the runway at Navy North Island. Brent was jarred awake but feeling far better than he did when they lifted off. For the next two hours, Brent assisted Mobile Unit 3 in returning the MK 6 animals to their pens at Naval Amphibious Base Coronado and offloading their gear.

Brent was exhausted. Heading back to his apartment in Imperial Beach was tempting, but he felt an urgent calling to see Alika first.

It was well into the evening when Brent went through the security gate. He stood at the head of the brow leading down to the pens and whistled. It was quickly returned. Brent smiled and saw Alika spy-hopping to see over the edge of the dock. He was obviously excited and whistled several more times as Brent closed the distance. Brent kicked off his shoes and sat down on the edge of the pen, his feet dangling in the water. Alika was with him immediately and rested his big melon across Brent's right thigh. Brent began to rub his rostrum, his massive head, and down his flank. Alika squirmed happily and emitted several squeals and click trains while Brent caressed his sides.

Brent began to ponder the near term. With SC-CS behind him, he could think about the next big event scheduled for Tuesday, 9 July 2002, just seventeen-days away—the visit by marine biologists from Florida State University and the mystery woman, Katie Donovan.

It was a strange feeling. He never met her, but hardly a day went by that he didn't think of her. He was still betting she was fat, had acne, and drove a Rambler, but her voice told another story, and he remained captivated by the possibilities.

Monday, Brent thought, *I'll get a pass down from Kahuna, maybe take Alika out for a swim if we're not already scheduled for a mission, and then get serious about the MK 7 capabilities presentation for the Florida State group. So much to do, so little time.*

And then he leaned down and whispered, "It's good to be back with you, Alika."

Alika nodded and then whistled.

CHAPTER 13

A FIELD TRIP TO FOXTROT

The happiness of the bee and the dolphin is to exist.
For man it is to know that and to wonder at it.

—Jacques Yves Cousteau

Prepping for the Visit

Monday, 24 June 2002
Foxtrot Platoon, Pier 40, Sub Base, Point Loma, California

Brent was back at Foxtrot before the Monday morning sun peeked over the horizon. He checked on Alika, stored his gear in his locker, and finally checked the schedule. No scheduled missions or training for the morning, but there at the bottom of the schedule was a footnote directing him to see Master Chief Murphy at his earliest opportunity.

Brent made a beeline for the master chief's office.

"Brent, get in here," the master chief bellowed as soon as he saw Brent standing outside his door.

"Aye, aye, sir. You wanted to see me."

"I did, indeed. Grab a seat."

Brent noticed Duffus sitting in his customary position near the door of the master chief's office, stone still as an umbrella stand.

"Good morning, Duffus," Brent said casually. Duffus rocked back and forth, unknowingly mimicking Charlie Chaplin's trademark walk. He finished off with a large smile, which forced his long whiskers skyward. Brent almost burst out laughing but, not knowing the nature of the meeting, thought better of it.

"Heard some good stuff about you from Master Chief Quigley. Seems like you carried your own water and did great with that maniac of a dolphin Bruiser. He didn't hurt anybody this time, did he?"

"Only the pride of a couple of SEALs who decided to play with their own rule book."

"I heard. He's really something, ain't he?"

"Yes, sir. I was mighty impressed with him and Roger. What a team."

"No argument there. You up for a cup of coffee? Made it myself this morning."

"That'd be great, sir."

Murphy yelled to his yeoman for two cups of coffee then returned to his rickety chair, propped his size 13 deck shoes on top of the ancient desk, and pulled his signature stubby cigar out of his mouth.

"I wanted to lay out the plan for the Florida State marine biology group visit. It's still on schedule for July 9. Chief Olopoto will oversee the event, but basically, Brent, you got it. You'll need to handle the visit request, notify base security, build the presentation, meet and escort the group from the main gate, and deliver the presentation."

The yeoman delivered two steaming hot cups of coffee and excused himself.

Brent reached for his coffee, blew some of the steam off the top of the cup, and took a careful sip. *Still tastes like giraffe piss, but this time, it's volcano hot.*

"Ah...yes, sir. I'm working on all that. I was thinking we can give them a PowerPoint presentation, walk them down to the pier, show them the fish house, the medical facility, and let them see a beaching and launch of one of our dolphins, and then answer questions."

"Okay. Good plan. We've got an older presentation that should work for this group. Just update it and make sure there's no classified or personal information in it. When you have a good draft, show it to Chief Olopoto. Make sure he's good with it. I'll review it a few days before they arrive."

The master chief shifted in his seat and took on a more serious note. "Also, this may come as a surprise to you, but not everybody is as enthusiastic about the Navy's Marine Mammal Program as we are. In fact, there are some people out there that would just as soon shut us down as piss on our shoes. So what I'm saying is, don't get yourself tangled up in any arguments. I'm not suggesting that any of these people are advocates to free Willy, but be careful. And don't let them trip you up. Keep your brief points simple, straight, honest, and at the unclassified level. Don't let them bait you and don't get into a head-butting contest. You follow?"

"Yes, sir, but I don't think any of this group would get into it."

"They probably won't, but just be careful. Kahuna'll be there to back you up, and I'll be available too if you need me. Questions, Brent?"

"None, Master Chief. Thanks for warning me."

"No worries, shipmate. And glad to have you back. Now get out there and do something for your country!"

Brent had his work cut out for him. On top of his regular training schedule with Alika, fish-house duty, watch standing, volunteer work for the medical facility, and the myriad of tasks associated with these, he had to spin up for something he'd never done before—prepare a presentation and set up a visit for the marine biologist group. It was daunting.

Brent joined up with Chief Olopoto. He was a treasure trove of information and assistance.

By week's end, Brent and Kahuna had the visit requests approved, base security notified, a playbook delineating the schedule of events, and a fairly spiffy PowerPoint presentation assembled.

Brent had coordinated with Katie several times over the phone to nail down their schedule and gather a list of participants. He could have easily communicated using e-mail, but then he'd miss the sweet essence of her voice. Occasionally, he'd call her under the pretense that he needed additional information when, in fact, he called only to hear her voice. If she had any suspicions that those calls were not what they seemed, she didn't let on.

The days were counting down to 9 July, and Brent was as jittery as a new colt.

Welcome to Foxtrot Platoon

Tuesday, 9 July 2002
Foxtrot Platoon, Point Loma

Brent hardly slept a wink through the night. He tossed and turned and fretted until the wee hours, then finally admitted that he wasn't going to get any sleep. He rolled out of the rack, took a quick shower, dressed, and was out the door before the clock struck 0300. He drove to Foxtrot, checked with the watch—no messages for him—then visited Alika. He spent half an hour with him then headed to the conference room, cranked up the computer, and ran through the slide set twice. He had the presentation down cold.

Kahuna arrived at Foxtrot just before 0700, and Brent met him at the security gate. Brent was anxious to go over the schedule of events again.

"One thing we haven't talked about much is Katie Donovan's reunion with Alika," Brent said. "And you know, that's the most important event for her. I'll bet she pretty much set this visit up with that in mind."

Kahuna weighed in, "I was thinking we might as well take the entire gaggle over to see Alika. We can probably do that first thing. Get that out of the way so Katie can think straight and everybody else will get to see a real Navy dolphin. Kinda kindle their interest.

Then we can set everybody down in the classroom and go over your presentation. How's that sound?"

"Perfect, Chief. Thanks." Brent, both hands in his pockets, looked down at his feet and thought for a moment. When he looked back at Kahuna, he asked, "What are the chances that Alika will remember Katie?"

"Chances are pretty good. It was a long time ago. Alika was just a baby, and he wasn't in contact with her very long. But it was a crisis, and sometimes those are burned into the long-term memory forever. Besides, dolphins have memories like elephants. They never forget."

"Well, it's going to be interesting all the same."

"Yep, sure will." Changing the subject, Kahuna asked, "Did you get wheels?"

"I've got two Ford crew cabs. I checked them out, and they're in the parking lot." Brent tossed Kahuna a set of keys. "Maybe we can head to the gate now, just in case they're early," Brent suggested, barely able to contain his enthusiasm.

"Easy, sailor. They won't be here until 0900, and it's only"— Kahuna spied his diving watch—"hell, it's only a few minutes after eight. What's with you, Brent? You been running around here for days now like a slow cat at a dog show. Does this have anything to do with that Donovan girl?"

"Huh? Ah, no…no. Nothing like that. I just want this thing to come off perfectly."

"And it will, shipmate. Just simmer down some. We'll head over to the main gate in half an hour. We'll still be early."

"Yeah. Okay. Good plan."

But Brent didn't simmer down, and a half an hour seemed like a week.

Twenty minutes before nine o'clock, Brent followed Kahuna to the main gate in the second vehicle. He was out of it and jogging to the main gate even before Kahuna exited his vehicle. Brent asked the gate guard if he'd seen anything of the group from Florida State and showed the guard the approved visit request.

"Nah, nothing yet," the guard responded.

Brent nodded then adjusted his cover, tucked in his shirt, checked his gig line, and wiped off his low-quarter black dress shoes using his only handkerchief.

"You look like a poster boy in your summer whites, Brent," Kahuna yelled as he approached the gate. "Now quit fidgeting."

Brent was just about to respond when he looked just beyond the guard shack and saw two yellow taxi cabs heading for the main gate.

"Looks like they're here!" Kahuna said then side-glanced at Brent. Brent still hadn't spoken.

The taxis pulled up to the gate and stopped. The guard matched names on the visitors list with ID cards of those in the taxis then cleared them through the gate and into a small parking area. The taxis stopped, car doors opened, and people exited. Kahuna was at the side of the first taxi through the gate, and as people climbed out of the cars, he introduced himself, shaking hands with each guest. As he started to introduce Brent to the group, he pivoted and found that Brent was still at the gate, staring at one of the members of the group—entranced, or so it seemed.

Brent watched as a young lady exited the rear seat of the first taxi. She was rather stout, with short brown hair, a bright smile, but ordinary in every way. *Well, she's doesn't have zits, but I bet she does drive a Rambler*, Brent said to himself. He was almost relieved, but he just couldn't match this girl with the voice he had spent so much time listening to over the phone.

Kahuna broke the spell, "I'd like to introduce Petty Officer Brent Harris." Kahuna looked over his shoulder, elevated his voice, his exasperation evident. Brent seemed to regain his composure and walked toward the group.

"He'll be your host for today's events. And I believe he's coordinated this entire presentation with your Ms. Katie Donovan."

"That would be me, sir."

To the rear of the second taxi, a tall, slender young lady, hair the color of summer straw with luminescent green eyes that sparkled in the morning sun, spoke and raised her hand. Brent hadn't seen her initially; she had exited the second taxi from the opposite side.

The voice, Brent thought. *That's the voice I've been listening to. Katie Donovan.*

She walked around the rear of the taxi then made a beeline toward Kahuna. The closer she got, the better she looked.

Wow! I'm in trouble!

She wore a white cotton golf shirt with the Florida State logo embroidered on the left upper chest. Knee-length cargo shorts encased perfectly sculpted legs, obviously the owner of which ran, biked, or vigorously played a field sport.

Katie lugged her purse and a soft satchel as she walked up to Kahuna and extended her hand. "Thank you so much for lettin' us visit, Chief Olopoto. We've been lookin' forward to this for a long time." Katie smiled. Her sweet Southern drawl flowed like honey.

"You can call me Kahuna. And you're welcome, Ms. Donovan."

"And I go by Katie, sir."

"Okay, Katie. And this gent"—extending his arm toward Brent—"standing in the back is the petty officer you coordinated with, Brent Harris."

Brent stood still as stone, mouth agape, beguiled. Then the trance broke, and he realized they were waiting for him to respond. "Brent, ma'am. A pleasure to meet you."

Katie's muse face squinted into a magnificently bright grin. "Good mornin', Brent. And thanks for the hard work makin' all this happen."

"You're welcome, ma'am...ah...Katie."

"Chief Olopoto." A man on the short side with thinning brown hair and a patchy beard extended his hand. "I'm Dr. François Dubois. I'm the department head for the Marine Biology Department and in charge of this visit. Thanks for hosting us, but we do have a rather pressing schedule to keep, so I'd like to get things going."

"Certainly, Doctor," Kahuna returned. "If you'll all pile in the vehicles, we'll take you to Foxtrot Platoon and get started."

As luck would have it, Katie and the doctor climbed in the rear seat of the big Ford crew cab Brent was driving. One of the young male students crawled into the passenger seat in front.

Kahuna led the way back to Foxtrot; Brent followed in the second vehicle.

There was some quiet talk in the rear of the vehicle. Brent glanced in the rear-view mirror and noticed that the good doctor was sitting nearly in the center of the rear seat, forcing Katie against the right side, pressed against the door. They were the only two passengers in the rear seat. Something was not quite right.

They parked the vehicles near the security gate. The guests exited the trucks and gathered expectantly around Kahuna and Brent. A quiet hush came over the group; when Kahuna began to speak, all were intent on listening.

"First, on behalf of Navy Special Clearance Team ONE and Foxtrot Platoon, we thank you for your interest and your support in the Navy Marine Mammal Program. We've scheduled about two hours with you today. We'll give you an overview of our mission, our mammals, the equipment we use for the mission, then we'll take you to the medical clinic, the fish house, and to the pens to visit with some of our dolphins. Finally, you'll get to watch a demonstration of a beaching and launching of one of our dolphins. Before we go to the classroom for the overview, I need to remind you that you're going to enter a secure area. You'll be given visitor badges at the duty office. Please wear these at all times and stay with the group. If you need to use the head—ah, that's a bathroom for those less nautical—please let Brent or me know, and we'll escort you. If you have any questions, please don't hesitate to ask. We'll do our best to answer them. Now I have a short story to tell you, and then we'll go do something that isn't on the schedule."

Brent opened the gate, and Kahuna said, "Please follow me. And watch your step. There are quite a few lines on the dock, and occasionally, our local sea lions will use the docks as their personal bathroom."

As Kahuna walked down the brow, the group following, he began, "Almost seven years ago, a little dolphin was stranded on a beach in Florida."

Katie stopped in her tracks. She slowly lifted her left hand to her chest, brought her right hand to her mouth, and took in a huge lungful of air. She knew immediately where this story was going. And she waited.

With the initial shock over, she hustled to catch up with the group.

"He was a little Atlantic bottlenose dolphin, we think just a couple of months old. Reports from the Florida State Fish and Wildlife Conservation rangers indicated that he'd spent several hours stranded in a mudflat and in the sun. He was dehydrated, weak, and understandably stressed. A young lady and her little brother found the dolphin, covered him up, kept him wet, and tried to calm him. She sent her little brother to contact the rangers while she cared for him. The rangers came on scene and rushed him to Gulf World in Panama City. There, he was treated and stabilized, but he was still in critical condition. The Navy Marine Mammal Program was contacted. The Gulf World bioteams have worked with us for years. Their vets and marine biologists believed we would be able to better rehabilitate the little guy. We had the facilities, the experts, and the budget to do just that."

Kahuna had led the group towards a big dolphin pen containing several working animals. One in particular, head-up, sky hopping, watched the activity as the group walked towards him—Alika.

Kahuna continued, "The short story is, the Navy sent a C-130 from San Diego to Florida to bring him to Point Loma. He was paired with a surrogate mother for more than a year. Her name is Emily, and she is the best, most loving and protective mother dolphin in the Navy. The baby dolphin spent several months in recovery and several more being rehabilitated, evaluated, and socialized with adult bulls so he knew how to act like a dolphin. When the vets and the biotechs gave him a clean bill of health, he began training as a Mark 7 dolphin. When he completed his certification, he was transferred to Foxtrot Platoon. For the last several years, he's been performing training, support, and operational Mark 7 missions. And now, seven years later, he's one of our superstars."

Kahuna had timed the walk perfectly. The group was now at the edge of the pen, and four dolphins were surveying the group with great curiosity, no doubt thinking a snack was somehow involved.

"I'd like to introduce you all to Brent's dolphin, *Alika*, a Navy Mark 7 dolphin. This is the little boy that was saved from certain death, and this"—Kahuna's hand swept to Katie—"is the young lady who saved his life."

Tears of joy gushed from Katie's luminous eyes. She quickly pushed to the edge of the pen, kneeled on the edge, and gazed into the eyes of Alika.

She wouldn't have recognized him, obviously; and though he returned her gaze, he gave no indication that he remembered her. That is, at first.

There was a moment of tension as gears engaged and memories were jogged, and then Alika did something unusual—he whistled. Katie paused and then, in almost a reflexive action, mimicked his whistle.

A moment passed. Alika glided closer and stared deeply into Katie's eyes. No one spoke. No one moved. Katie held her breath.

Alika emitted a second whistle. Katie returned the whistle and then followed with, "Do you remember me, Alika?"

That was it. Alika elevated himself in a tail stand, did a backflip into the water, nearly soaking all present, and swam a tight fast circle around the pen. He came to a wave-producing stop in front of Katie and glided to the edge of the pen close to her.

"Katie," Brent said, kneeling next to her, "extend your hand, palm up, just above the water."

Katie, cautiously at first, extended her arm toward Alika. The back of her hand hovered just above the water. Alika looked at her hand, glanced into her eyes, then slid his rostrum into her hand.

Tears tumbled from her eyes, and she fought to contain the squeal she feared she would involuntarily emit.

"He remembers you," Brent whispered. "Amazing!"

Clapping erupted from behind them.

It was a moment of indescribable elation and exhilaration for Katie, of jubilance for Brent, and clearly complete and utter joy for Alika. He squealed and whistled several more times but maintained physical contact with Katie.

There was much muttering within the company.

"Katie, we had no idea you rescued a dolphin," Dr. Dubois injected.

"It was a long time ago. And it was only important to me and Alika," Katie returned, barely keeping the tremor out of her voice.

"Well, I am duly impressed. And ergo, the selection of marine biology as your major, no doubt, a wise choice. You have much to tell us, young lady."

The company asked a battery of questions of Katie, Kahuna, and of Brent concerning the rescue, the therapy, and the rehabilitation. Katie reluctantly stood and moved aside, giving everyone a chance to stroke Alika and the other three dolphins. Some were more eager than others to meet with the group, but Alika couldn't get enough and kept maneuvering to be near Katie.

"Unless there are any more questions, let's head up to the classroom."

The crowd followed Kahuna, leaving Katie at the side of the pen with Brent. She kneeled again and extended her hand and spoke to Alika in hushed tones. Alika, eyes sparkling and nearly buzzing with glee, relished the touch of her hand along his flank.

"Katie, we can come back later, but we better catch up with your group."

Katie reluctantly stood, turned away from Brent, and raised her hands to her eyes.

"Katie, you okay?"

She hesitated then spun around. Tears steaked down her checks. Her eyes were red. Her lower lip trembled slightly. She had the sniffles. She was a hot mess. And she was the *most beautiful* thing Brent had ever seen in his life. Even more wonderful than a spring colt, if that was even possible.

He could hardly contain himself as his gaze dove deep into her mesmeric eyes. He was so close now he could definitely see that her luminous green eyes were specked with gold. The glitter only amplified their radiance.

"Katie, we should—"

Katie threw a big hug on Brent, wrapping her arms around his shoulders and burrowing her head into his neck. She sniffed and trembled, took an enormous breath, then suddenly tensed and stood back, releasing him.

"I'm so sorry. I don't know what came over me. I've never done that before, and I sure never felt like this before. I don't think I've ever been so happy, so completely overcome. I'm acting like an emotional little schoolgirl, and I do so apologize." She pushed the heels of her hands against her eyes, squinting. Tears spread across her pink cheeks.

"Here. Use this." Brent handed her his one clean handkerchief.

"Thanks, but I'll mess it."

"Keep it. I've got lots of 'em."

"Gosh. Thanks."

She dabbed her eyes, blotted her brow, and blew her nose. Brent watched her every move. Every nuance of her actions was graceful and adorable. He was entranced and wanted to freeze this perfect moment forever.

Seconds ticked by.

Katie broke the silence. "We better git goin'. The others are gonna be wonderin' what's become of us, and you know how people can talk, so…"

Much to the dismay of Alika, Brent and Katie caught up to the group as they entered the classroom. Dr. Dubois held back slightly and watched as Brent and Katie walked toward the classroom together. He scowled, turned, and walked into the classroom.

The Grand Tour

Tue, 9 July 2002
Foxtrot Platoon, Point Loma

Brent led off with the PowerPoint slide show. He'd practiced it so many times he could speak to each slide without notes. The group seemed to be intrigued by the overview. No one raised their hand or spoke until Brent was finished. Only then were questions asked. Brent and Kahuna thoroughly answered these.

Then a young female student raised her hand. Brent nodded to her. "Ma'am?"

"Brent, I really don't know much about your dolphins. In fact, until today, they always seemed to be on cruise ads to faraway tropical places. I had no idea they had a personality and were so amazingly friendly, at least based on Alika's response to seeing Katie. I was just blown away."

"I come from a ranching family in Western Wyoming. We've had a lot of animals: horses, dogs, cows—well, you can just imagine the number and kind of animals we had. But until I met Alika, I've never known such pure devotion between two different species and—well, lacking a better word— loyalty. Now, not every handler or biotech has the same experience, but many do. It's pretty amazing! And for the record, not every dolphin is cute or friendly as the ones you see here. Each dolphin has his own personality, and some can be flat mean, so don't assume since it's a dolphin, it's automatically chummy with humans."

"I can imagine. Well, what I was going to ask is, now that you've been working with these dolphins for a while, is there anything you would change about them? You know, if you were like God or something, would you make anything different?"

"Ah…let me turn that one to Chief Olopoto. Chief?"

Kahuna was in the back of the classroom, leaning comfortably against a table with his arms crossed. He stood and clasped his hands behind his back, looking quite military. He looked at the deck for a moment as he formulated his response. When he brought his eyes back up to the students, all looking expectantly at Kahuna, he began.

"That's a question with two components. First, an operational component: would we change anything, if we could, to make them better at their job? And second, would we change anything to make them better at what God designed them for? Let me touch on the second part of the question first. Now, this is not a dodge, but I think only God could answer that. But I could say from my experience in working with these animals for many years, they are perfectly designed and adapted for their habitat and environment and perfectly suited for the job in which God intended for them: hunt, populate the species, and protect the pod.

"From an operational perspective, the second part of the question, a design function and an engineering aspect—when it comes to doing their Mark 7 job—I really can't imagine a way to tweak their architecture to allow them to do what we need them to do any better. Well, with one slight exception. It would be helpful if they could drive the boat. That gets old after a while."

There was scattered laughter about the room.

"But surely, Chief," Dr. Dubois interrupted and didn't bother to raise his hand, "you must agree that they aren't that smart, and wouldn't it be grand if they were intelligent enough to be able to communicate with us? I mean, even dogs understand a few words."

Kahuna rubbed his chin in thought. "A fair question. Let me say this. You would be astounded to see how truly brilliant they are in a task. They think and problem-solve and have remarkable powers of deduction. Honestly, Doctor, I don't want them much smarter. I'd kinda like to think I'm in charge."

Laughter erupted all about the room.

"No doubt, Chief," Dubois replied with a slight twist in his tone. "But what about communications? Surely, you must agree that it would be more convenient if they understood some basic commands?"

Kahuna nodded. "Ah, but they do. Most of our commands are hand commands, but they understand scores of voice commands too, as long as the handler keeps his voice at a frequency within their hearing spectrum. And for the record, dolphins can associate at least fifty words with specific actions. Humans can understand *zero* whistle communications. So, who's really the smarter of the species?"

Laughter again.

Dr. Dubois leaned back in his chair then folded his arms across his chest and crossed his legs, pondering the chief's response.

Kahuna, who was always in tune with his surroundings, studied the good doctor. He'd been attentive and courteous so far, but something in his mannerisms, something in his conduct, was just a bit off. Kahuna just couldn't put his finger on it, and it troubled him.

When all the questions had been asked and answered, Kahuna walked to the front of the classroom. "Thanks, Brent. Good job. We're just about on schedule, so unless there's more questions, we'll head to the veterinarian clinic and then on to the fish house. I think you'll be very impressed with the high standards we conform to for the diet and health requisites for our dolphins. I think you'll agree our feeding program and the cleanliness of our fish house are probably more stringent than those of most restaurants. When we're done there, we'll take you over to the far dock and let you watch one of our Mark 7 dolphins beach and launch a few times. Anybody need a head break?"

There were no takers.

"Good. Now please follow Brent, and we'll head to the vet clinic."

Only the lead veterinarian, Major Brian "Doc" Hamilton, US Army, was available when the group arrived at the clinic. The rest of the vet team, veterinarian technicians, and biologists were out at the pens and docks assisting handlers and checking the dolphins.

"Doc Hamilton, meet our group of marine biologists from Florida State University," Kahuna said as he walked up the brow to the clinic.

The doc, wearing a white lab coat over shorts and a T-shirt, was drying his hands off with a towel as he approached the troop and extended his hand. "Heard you were coming. Thanks for your interest, and welcome to Foxtrot Platoon's medical clinic." He continued, "We have many Navy Mark 7 dolphins here. My staff consists of three other certified marine mammal veterinarians and four specialized marine biologists and vet technicians. According to our mission statement, we're supposed to keep our animals healthy and fit for duty. The term *healthy* is kind of squishy thing here. Our interpretation means that they are physically, mentally, and yep, *emotionally* healthy. As you probably know based on your own work, dolphins are very complex mammals, and like humans, they can be a perfect specimen *physically* and a complete wreck *emotionally*. Here, we treat the whole mammal."

As the doc spoke, he led the group around the clinic. They were enthralled with the equipment, electronic monitoring systems, medicine cabinets, specially designed tables, and the overall cleanliness of the clinic.

"We comply with a rather stringent set of requirements and standards set by the federal government, the state, Department of Defense, and even our Navy department. These dictate care requirements and techniques for immunology, virology, epidemiology, microbiology, toxicology, vaccination compliance, and a bunch of other 'ologies' too abundant to list.

"Sometimes it's tough just to try to keep up with all the legislation, regulations, and laws pertaining to marine mammals. And often, I am proud to say we are the pioneers in treatment, medicine, and the behavioral sciences for both dolphins and sea lions. Unfortunately, we don't have a dolphin in the clinic, or we could show you firsthand the kind of care we provide. But in a way, that's good. It means all our animals are healthy and out doing their job."

Katie raised her hand and asked, "Doctor, do they really like doing their job?"

The doctor thought, then said, "Let me answer that this way. Early in the morning, when the handlers do their morning checks on their dolphins and get the boats prepped, many of the dolphins line up at the edge of their pens, waiting to be the first ones selected to go out. They all can't go out at the same time, we don't have enough boats. But the ones that stay back actually sulk. So yeah, they like their work. They like the adventure. They like the excitement. And they really like their handlers."

Kahuna took a quick look at his watch. "Thanks, Doc. If there are no other questions, we'll let the doctor get back to his doctor stuff, and we'll head down to the fish house." Kahuna raised his arm and ushered the group out the hatch and down the gangway.

OS3 Dale Thompson stood at the entrance to the fish house. He wore deck shoes, shorts, a clean T-shirt and topped it off with an ear-to-ear grin that conveyed his pride in the condition and cleanliness of his fish house. As Kahuna led the troop the last several yards to the fish house entrance, he gestured to Petty Officer Thompson and made introductions. "Dale, this is the group of marine biologists from Florida State University we talked about. Ladies and gentlemen, this is the petty officer in charge of our fish house, Dale Thompson."

Greetings were exchanged, and Dale's smile brightened.

"If you would, Petty Officer Thompson, please tell our guests a little about your fish house."

"Well, if you'll step inside, you'll see that we have a state-of-the-art facility…"

The tour of the fish house was an eye-opener. The group had the same image that most people had with the term *fish house:* blood, scales, unrecognizable fish parts, all accented with a bouquet of decaying smudge that was once swimming in the ocean. Quite to the contrary, Foxtrot's fish house shined like a like an operating room. When OS3 Thompson had completed his tour of the fish house, the guests were clearly impressed.

The next and final event was the beaching and launching drill. BM2 Rick Turner had been volunteered for this demo by Master Chief Murphy for the simple reason that Kona, Rick's dolphin, was the kindest and gentlest of all the MK 7 dolphins. True, he had a deep animosity toward Peter Schultz, but there was a legitimate basis for that: Peter was just mean. But now Peter was gone, and Kona was his old self—happy, responsive, inquisitive, and most sociable. Why, Kona even played with the local sea lion population when he wasn't dragging his boat bumper around.

Rick had anchored one of the seven-meter RHIBs about thirty feet from the edge of the dock, now the viewing position for the marine biologists. Rick wanted to avoid any possible contact between his dolphin and the dock. But the other reason for the separation was to keep the guests relatively dry. Kona had no reservations about soaking humans. It was great fun, and to him, it was just part of the game.

"Please be careful, and don't step too close to the edge of the dock. I don't want anyone to go swimming today, especially me," Kahuna said to the group as they gathered around him on the dock. "BM2 Rick Turner, in the seven-meter RHIB, will demonstrate beaching and launching."

Rick smiled and waved. The group eagerly returned his wave. "Hi, Rick," they said almost in unison.

"So, we have a handler, we have a boat rigged for dolphin transport, all we need now is a dolphin. If you look about forty feet to the aft of the boat, you'll see a white boat bumper looking as though it's being self-propelled through the water. Now, look closely underneath and slightly in front of it. You should see a large gray-and-white thing pulling the bumper. That's Rick's dolphin, Kona."

The group elicited a series of *oh*s and *aww*s.

The timing couldn't have been better. Between the boat and the guests, Kona breached well into the air; a stout rotation of his head catapulted the bumper nearly twenty-five feet in front of the boat. Kona slid back into the water but then, with a strong cycle of his fluke, elevated his head and spy-hopped to survey the pod of humans standing on the dock. He took in the scene, then seemed to remember his bumper, dove, and, at flank speed, headed for his toy.

"And that, ladies and gentlemen, is Kona, a certified Mark 7 Navy dolphin with a sense of humor. As a footnote, he was not trained to toss and retrieve his bumper. That, he learned all on his own.

"Rick, why don't you call him back and show us a beaching and launch?"

"Glad to, Chief."

Rick knelt down, leaned across the sponson, and slapped the water several times. The bumper changed direction and headed back in the direction of the RHIB. Suddenly Kona popped up within arm's reach of Rick. He looked excitedly at Rick.

For the next twenty minutes, Rick and Kona completed several beaches and launches while Kahuna described the signals being used and the function of the fore and aft disks suspended on the port side of the RHIB. He explained the significance of *operant conditioning*, the teamwork required on a mission, and the around-the-clock relationship between the dolphin and the handler.

Things were wrapping up. Rick launched Kona out of the RHIB a final time, and Kona made a beeline to retrieve his bumper, now drifting toward the channel, headed for the San Diego Bay. Brent called Kona over to the dock while Rick moved the RHIB about one hundred feet from the group and lashed it to the dock. Kona came hesitatingly to the edge of the dock, bumper in tow. The group, now on their hands and knees, immediately swarmed around the dolphin and extended their hands, hoping to stroke the slippery flank of the big dolphin.

Kona weighed the situation, saw no lurking threats, just humans being human, and sidled up to the edge of the dock.

There was much conversation among the group, most of which was undecipherable as one would expect when humans decide to speak to a dolphin. The conversations, however, must have had some settling effect on Kona because, in just a few moments, he was caught up in all the attention and mutterings. He positioned his eight-foot body alongside the edge of the dock, rolled slightly, left pectoral fin in the air, and exposed his tummy to eager hands. This may have been the highlight of the day for the members of the group. Most certainly it was for Kona, who joyfully ate it up.

Kahuna surveyed the scene. A smile came to his face, but then it faded when he noticed one in the group who took no part in stroking Kona. Interestingly, the doctor stood apart from the rest of the group on their hands and knees, reaching with giddy excitement for physical contact with a real dolphin. The doctor watched but remained aloof, disengaged, showing no real interest.

Kahuna, at first, wrote it off. *Not everybody wants to crawl around on a dirty dock just to pet a big dolphin*, he thought.

Touché

Tue, 9 July 2002
Foxtrot Platoon, Point Loma

Kahuna glanced at his watch. It was coming up on 1100. "We'll need to pile in the trucks in a few minutes, but if you have any questions, please ask away."

Reluctantly, the group slowly stood and brushed off their hands and knees, but before anyone else had a chance to speak, Dr. Dubois raised his hand.

This is where the wheels come off the cart, Kahuna thought to himself.

Dr. Dubois was a slight man but elegant in all respects. He had perfectly quaffed hair, preened fingernails, and sported a carefully groomed goatee. He carried himself erect, and his mannerisms were delicate, if not dainty. Aside from his personal appearance, Kahuna sensed something disingenuous, an underlying rancor. Why and at what was a big unknown. There was nothing from his outward mannerisms that would cue anyone, but cloaked below the exterior of his character, something dark was lurking. Kahuna just felt it.

"Chief Olyphoto, a question, if I may."

Kahuna just smiled at the obvious mistake, but Brent was quick to correct the doctor. "That's Chief Olopoto, Dr. Dubois."

"Yes. Of course, it is. A question, sir?"

"Ask away, Doctor."

"Isn't it true that the Navy uses both dolphins and sea lions on very dangerous missions and that up to 20 percent of the mammals escape from their horrible treatment each year?"

Kahuna listened intently to the question, but before he could respond, Brent, probably emboldened and annoyed by the doctor's inquisition, took lead.

"I think that's actually two questions, but I'll answer both. Chief Olopoto, if I goof up, please correct me."

"Go for it, Brent!"

"To the first question, both the dolphins and the sea lions are trained for wartime operations and peacetime missions. Both environments have their own set of risks and dangers, but their wartime tasks are noncombat related. The animals do not take part in any form of direct action or combat. They operate in support of forces. They detect, identify, mark, and in some cases, assist in removal of mines, undersea weapons, and other wartime and sometimes peacetime systems. In terms of risk, yes, there are risks, but they are minimal. And it's important to remember, their actions greatly reduce the risks to civilian ships, combat vessels, and other friendly forces.

"To your second question, the horrible treatment of our animals...I'm new on board and don't have a lot of personal history with the mammal program. I come from horse country, and from day one, my father and all our hands taught me to never punish, demean, or harm an animal, any animal. That mind-set, not surprisingly, is precisely at the core of the training and behavioral development protocols throughout the Navy's mammal program.

"It's true, there's been a lot of interest as far back as the 1950s in the cognition, communication, echolocation capabilities, and culture of the dolphins, and that has invited a ton of studies and, in some cases, experiments on captive dolphins. All too often, those have led to abuse and even the death of dolphins."

Brent was cooking, and Katie was mesmerized. *So, this young man is something more than just a pretty face*, she thought.

Brent continued, "A man named John Lilly abused and even killed many dolphins. He performed brain surgery, experimented with hallucinogens, he even used dolphins in sensory-deprivation tests—all in the name of science. Mr. Lilly was completely disassociated from the Navy. We don't work that way. Doctor, are you familiar with the Association for the Assessment and Accreditation of Laboratory Animal Care International?"

"I'm very familiar with AAALAC," the doctor responded. "They are a nonprofit group. They are supposed to promote better standards of animal care, enhance laboratory animal well-being, and improve life sciences research through accreditation. It's a good group. I, in fact, on occasion, have been asked to review and validate their research. What do they have to do with the Navy Mammal Program?"

"Recently, the Navy received an accreditation letter for the conduct and management of our mammal program. That's not something AAALAC would just hand out."

"That might be true, but I bet AAALAC didn't see this animal," Dr. Dubois challenged, pointing at Kona.

"I'm sorry. What about this animal?"

"I saw his back. He's got deep scars across his back and down his side, and he's got nicks in his dorsal fin. It doesn't look like you have been taking very good care of him. Those are the signs of abuse and neglect. It's a wonder he hasn't escaped from your cruelty." Dr. Dubois crossed his arms across his chest and lifted his head. He gave the appearance that he had just delivered the Gettysburg Address.

Brent was caught off guard with that assertion.

Kahuna came to the rescue. "Actually, Doctor, if you look closely, the scars across his back are from a shark attack. Near as we can figure, it happened when he was very young. Other scars and the notches in his dorsal also happened long before the Navy got him. The background on Kona dates back quite a few years. He was rescued at the age of about two. He was caught in a fisherman's net and nearly died. Sea World rescued him. They spent weeks and a lot of money on medical treatment and therapy. It was still touch and go when they called us. We had more resources and some of the best mammal veterinarians and biotechs in the world. We provided him with a surrogate mother, nursed him back to health, rehabilitated him, and then, when he was fully recovered and emotionally and mentally ready, we started training him as a Mark 7 dolphin.

"He can leave anytime he wants. The fact is, he likes it here. He likes his job, he likes the other animals, he likes all the perks, and he really likes his handler. What we didn't mention is, he'll probably live ten to fifteen years longer here than in the wild, and he'll be a whole lot safer and happier here. I've been assigned to Foxtrot for quite a few years. Care to guess how many dolphins have escaped or tried to escape from any of the San Diego facilities, Doctor?"

"Why don't you tell me?" The doctor snickered.

"Exactly none."

This counterargument should have shut the doctor up, but no, he wasn't done quite yet.

"There are many validated reports that describe how the Navy is using their dolphins and sea lions as *kamikaze* attack animals. Navy personnel strap explosives on them and make them deliver the devices to enemy ships and submarines. Others are fitted with hypodermic lances and are trained to attack and kill enemy divers. How do you explain that?" the doctor finished, looking quite satisfied with his delivery.

Kahuna retorted, "You call them validated reports. The experts, those that are experienced in the real world, call these reports assertions, speculation, and fantasy. There are many papers and articles published insinuating these things, but none that I'm aware of offer any proof. And certainly, none have been validated."

Kahuna continued, "Since the initiation of the program in the early 1960s, it's been highly classified. Irresponsible reporters, critics, and well-meaning activists often made fictitious reports similar to the accounts you just mentioned. The Navy couldn't counter the assertions because of the classified nature of the program. In fact, they could neither confirm nor deny even the existence of such a program. This was fresh meat for the activists. With no evidence that the assertions were false, the stories, some that would rival Jules Verness's tales, became more ridiculous and irresponsible but, at the same time, seemed to be self-validating because the Navy couldn't air the truth.

"It wasn't until 1992 that the program was declassified. Finally, the Navy could counter the arguments. But lies told often enough and loud enough sometimes take on a life of their own, despite all evidence to the contrary. In 1990, President George Bush directed the Marine Mammal Commission to investigate these claims, some of which you've mentioned. After many months of research and thousands of dollars expended, the commission's report stated that the allegations were not only untrue, but the Navy's Marine Mammal Program was exemplary in all regards.

"Yes, we do have a swimmer-defense capability. It falls under the force protection mission. It is the Mark 6 system and uses both dolphins and sea lions. They detect and mark—notice, I didn't say dispatch or eliminate—swimmers, divers, swimmer-delivery vehicles, and suspicious objects. They also protect piers, ships, and anchorages. And they don't use lethal force or devices to do their job for the simple reason that—as smart as they are, with all their echolocation abilities or, in the case of the sea lions, their incredible vision—they still can't distinguish the good guys from the bad guys.

"I can tell you that the Mark 6 systems have been officially employed three times. In 1971, they were used in Cam Ranh Bay, in Bahrain during the Iran-Iraq War in the late 1980s, and in 1996 for the Republican National Convention right here in San Diego. And please know that no one, especially not one of our mammals, has ever killed or injured anyone. In the interest of full disclosure, I do need to mention that one of our dolphins did leave us in December 1971 during the Vietnam War, but that is a very rare thing."

Kahuna ended the discourse on that note.

Dr. Dubois seemed to want to come back with a *Yeah, but...*; however, he wisely kept his comments to himself. He looked humbled.

Departing

Tuesday, 9 July 2002
Foxtrot Platoon, Pier 40, Sub Base, Point Loma, California

Kahuna and Brent piled their guests in the two crew cabs and deposited them at the front gate where two taxi cabs waited.

The guests were clearly impressed with the presentation and the tour, and they all seemed to enjoy the verbal cage match at the end. Thank-yous were lavished on the chief and Brent, and except for the doctor, it was a very happy group.

Brent was delighted just to get through the ordeal, but at the same time, he was suffering the very emotional effects of finally meeting Katie and not knowing what to do next. He recognized that something way down deep was amiss—and it wasn't indigestion. The thought of not seeing her again was causing Brent some issues he didn't know how to handle. He still had her number at the university, but he was at a complete loss as to what he might say now that the tour was over.

While he struggled with a way to approach her before she returned to her hotel, he saw Katie hesitate at the rear door of one of the taxis. A wry smile formed on her dazzling face, and she strolled over to Brent. "Thank you, Petty Officer Harris, for the incredible morning and for letting us meet Alika."

"It's Brent, ma'am, and it was our pleasure."

"Okay, Brent."

There were several seconds of uneasy quiet while they both grasped for something to say; then Katie broke the silence. She dug into her pocket and retrieved a small piece of paper. "Here. It's got my cell number on it. We're here 'til Sunday, if you want to do something." She held it out to Brent, and like a dope, he stood there and stared at it.

Katie reached out with her other hand, took Brent's wrist, stuffed the note in the palm of his hand, then curled his fingers around it. "There. Call me, and don't lose it." Katie spun on her heels and nearly skipped to her taxi.

Finally, Brent got his mouth to work. "I will. I mean, I won't. I mean…thanks, Katie."

Katie was about to enter the taxi but turned back toward him and smiled. It was a smile that seemed to brighten the day, make his heart flutter like a hummingbird's, and weaken his knees.

The taxis rolled away from the base heading down Rosecrans Street.

Brent stood there watching them drive away, mouth still agape. *What the hell just happened?*

Much to Brent's surprise, Kahuna suddenly materialized next to him, Kahuna's arm across his shoulders. "Oh, Brent, you're in trouble deep, shipmate."

And Brent knew it.

Rhapsody Under Starlight

Saturday, 13 July 2002
Foxtrot Platoon, Point Loma, California

Brent did not lose Katie's number, and he did call her—several times. Each time, Katie, with all sincerity, explained that she was wrapped up with research and administrative duties involving the trip. Finally, the mystery unfolded—the hubris and annoyance of Dr. Dubois came into clear focus. He was purposely tasking Katie with school-related work to prohibit her from going out with Brent.

It was already Wednesday, and Katie said they were departing from San Diego on Sunday morning. Brent was running out of options and time. He decided to play a last-chance roll of the dice.

"Hello."

"Katie! Hey, this is Brent. Sure glad you answered!"

"Brent. Thanks so much for calling. How's Alika, and how're you?"

"Well, that's what I was calling about. I thought—"

"Is Alika all right?"

"Yeah, he's fine. I was just kinda wondering if you were free on Saturday afternoon. I know you're leaving Sunday morning, but I thought we might be able to get together for dinner or something Saturday."

"I'd love to, Brent, but Dr. Dubois has me pretty well locked into writing the field-trip report. I'm 'spose to have it to him Saturday."

All the helium just went out of Brent's balloon.

"Ah...," Brent stammered and tried to think of something witty, but nothing came.

"Brent?"

"Yeah, Katie!"

"Okay, let's do this. Come and pick me up at eight o'clock at our hotel. That's the Marina Inn and Suites near the airport. Do you know where it is?"

"I'll find it."

"Brent."

"Yeah, Katie?"

"Don't come to my room, and in fact, don't even come inside the hotel. I'll be waiting for you just outside the entrance. What are you driving? Not that beat-up ol' Navy truck we were ridin' in?"

"I wish! No. I'll be in my pickup. It has Wyoming plates, but you'll hear it before you see it."

"Can't wait! And, Brent."

"Yeah!"

"Give Alike a big hug for me."

"I'll give him two."

The next three days passed as if Brent were hanging by his thumbs. He had trouble concentrating, had no appetite, sleep came in spurts, and occasionally he found himself in places he had no memory of going. He was a mess and just couldn't quite figure it out.

Friday evening, just after sunset, he sat on the edge of Alika's pen with his feet dangling in the water. Alika had his big melon resting on Brent's right thigh, his left leg draped across Alika's back. Alika was in typical full glow, joyful of all Brent's attention. But Brent was worried and shared his dilemma with Alika. *What the hell is wrong with me, Alika? I can't think. I'm making mistakes. I have no account of time, and all I can seem to do with any consistency is think of Katie. This sucks. I wonder if I'm coming down with something. Well, I have one more day. I'll take Katie out. We'll have good time, and then she'll fly back home, and I can get back to work and be normal again.*

But that wasn't going to happen—and Brent knew it.

Saturday came with glacial slowness. Brent was wired up and, partly to make the day go faster, actually washed his truck, something rarely done in Wyoming. He knew a clean pick-'em-up wasn't going to impress Katie, but at least she wouldn't be riding in a rolling dirt clod.

By seven o'clock, Brent couldn't stand the tension any longer. He jumped in his truck and headed for Katie's hotel, knowing full well it was only a thirty-minute ride with traffic. He found her hotel with no difficulty and made two complete recce passes around it just to get oriented. At seven-forty, he parked about half a block away from the entrance and waited...and waited...and waited.

Seconds ticked by. *What the hell is going on? This is the right hotel. It's three after eight. Maybe she changed her mind.*

Brent just started to dial her cell phone when he saw a dazzling girl step out of the hotel and move to the sidewalk, looking both directions as she did. Brent tossed his cell phone in the seat next to him, cranked up the monster pickup, and rolled down the street toward Katie. She snapped her head in the direction of the thunderous roar of the big Detroit V8. A big smile formed on her perfect face, unveiling sparkling white teeth. Brent's heart skipped a beat, he was sure of it.

He pulled to a stop in front of Katie and was about to jump out of the truck to run around and open the door, but she pulled it open, jumped in, and said four words, "Let's roll, big boy!"

Brent put his beast in gear and rolled down the street. Then she did something completely unexpected. She leaned across the seat and gave Brent a peck on the cheek. It was nothing romantic, no suggestion of anything to follow, just one of those greetings one might lavish on an aunt or cousin...or a close friend. The effect on Brent, however, was prodigious. His mouth dropped open, he stopped breathing for a moment, and he almost ran a stop sign. *Wow!*

"Wow, Katie. Thanks!"

"Well, thank you for being so persistent. Sorry I couldn't get out earlier, but Dr. Dubois was really pressing for the report fer some reason. Now I thinkin' I understand why."

"You okay, Katie?"

"Yeah, fine. I just didn't want Dr. Dubois see me leaving. He's been actin' mighty strange lately, and I think it might have sumthin' to do with you."

"Me? Is there something I should know about?"

"Nope! Nuthin' to know about. I think he has a kind of crush on me, but believe me, it is not reciprocated. Anyway, what are we doing?"

"Big surprise."

"Big surprise, huh? What does that mean?"

"It means I have no idea. It'll be a surprise to me too.

"Thought we'd start out at McP's in Coronado. It's a SEAL and Special Boat Team hangout. I'd like to introduce you to some of my old team buds and some of the dolphin handlers. Then I'll take you to dinner anywhere you'd like to go. I mean, it's your last night here, and I want to make it count."

"Well, we'll just see how things unfold and take it from there."

It was nearly eight-thirty by the time they walked in to McP's. It was popping, standing room only. Brent had just stepped through the patio-side entrance, closely followed by Katie, and half a dozen voices rang out, "Yo, Brent. Over here, brother!"

Brent turned to Katie. "These are Special Boat Team guys. Don't believe a thing they say. If their lips are moving, they're lying." And as an afterthought, Brent added, "And don't dance with them. They've been out to sea for a while."

Katie just giggled that wonderful girlish giggle.

Brent and Katie stepped through the sea of customers to reach the boat team throng, and strangely, the clamor of the room diminished somewhat; heads turned to follow Katie's movement.

As Brent approached the knot of tan, lean young men, he was pulled into the center of the group and slapped on the back several times. Three other boat team brothers surrounded Katie and laid their best lines on her. She was smiling, but as a student at Florida State, she knew their moves and handled herself with complete Southern decorum.

A beer was handed to Brent and one to Katie.

"Brent, long time, brother," a big guy, tan with a barrel chest, one of the older men said, smiling.

"It's been a while, Chief O'Dell. Great to see you."

He grabbed Brent's hand and bumped shoulders.

"How's the team?" Brent asked.

"Never better. Just got back from seven months in the Philippines and Korea and other points west. Lots of fun. Some action. Wished you could have been with us. Coulda used you on the fifty a few times. But enough about work. Who the hell is that goddess?" Chief O'Dell nodded toward Katie. "Did you kidnap her 'er somethin'? We all know you're too ugly to get a girl by yourself. Besides, I thought you only liked fishes."

"Believe it or not, Chief, she was in the group of marine biologists from Florida State. We hosted them earlier this week. Took me all week to get her to go out with me, and I've already lost her to those nimrods."

Chief O'Dell looked at the three sailors surrounding Katie. "Hey Puppy Breath, Hawk, and Lizard, stand down and let the lady through," Chief O'Dell bellowed. He then leaned forward, reached between them, gently took Katie's hand, and pulled her out of the envelopment.

"Chief O'Dell, this is Katie Donovan, a student in the marine biology program at Florida State," Brent proudly said. "Katie, this is Chief O'Dell, one of the old guys at Special Boat Team TWELVE."

"Chief O'Dell"—Katie extended her hand—"I'm mighty glad to meet you, sir."

A big smile formed on the chief's face, creasing the lines at the corners of his eyes. He took Katie's hand in both his massive paws and said, "A Southern girl. I love you already. Come with me. You're too good for this fish lover." And then he gently kissed her hand.

Katie beamed and, without missing a beat, said, "He's got a few rough edges, sure 'nough, but I think he'll polish up quite nicely with a little buffin'."

Brent didn't know what to think of that, but he had a deep suspicion that it was good.

The evening continued. Beers, sea stories, and good cheer were passed around liberally. Chief O'Dell had posted himself next to Katie and fended off every approach by the boat team guys, all of whom seemed to have an eye for her. Katie giggled and smiled and flirted and had the time of her life.

Brent was enjoying the company, glad to be among his brothers and catch up with the team, but he was never relaxed, never off guard, for fear that someone would swish Katie away. He glanced at his diving watch and realized that it was nearly midnight, and way after a respectable dinnertime.

"Katie," Brent yelled over the noise of the bar, "we better go. It's almost twelve."

"Holy smokes, Brent. I gotta get back. I haven't even packed."

"Chief O'Dell, thanks for standing sentry duty, but I need to get Katie back to her hotel. They're leaving at the crack of jack tomorrow morning."

"Roger! Understood."

Chief O'Dell turned to Katie, wrapped his big bear arms around her, gave her a kiss on the forehead, then whispered in her ear, "You take care of Brent. He's one of the most kind, decent, courageous, and unselfish men I know."

"I plan to, Chief. Thanks for watching over me."

"It was the most fun I've had all week. Thanks, Katie. Fair winds!"

Brent grabbed Katie's hand and made a run on the bar. He secured two cans of soda and rushed out of McP's heading for his pickup with Katie in tow.

"Well, that was fun! How you gonna top that one, sailor?" Katie asked impishly.

"Got an idea. You in?"

"Count me in, big guy!"

Brent pointed his truck east on Orange Avenue and headed for the Coronado Bridge. He went over the bridge—a breathtaking view any time—and merged on to I-15 north. He exited I-15 and joined North Harbor Drive.

"This looks familiar. Where we goin'?"

"You'll see soon enough," Brent returned.

Brent stopped at the security gate at Point Loma Naval Base, showed his military ID, and was waved through.

"Don't tell me…we're gonna see Alika?"

"Naw. You already saw him. He remembers you, and I think he has a big crush on you. No more visits for you. I'm going to take you to the classroom. I have a swell presentation I need you to see."

"Hey, I already saw your swell presentation. It needs some work. I want to see Alika."

"Hmm. We'll see," Brent chided.

Brent parked, grabbed the two soft drinks, and rushed to the passenger door. Again, he was a little late. Katie was already out of the truck. She slid her arm through Brent's, and together they headed for Foxtrot's security entrance.

"Wait here. I've got to get you a visitor's pass. I'll be right back."

"And I'll be right here."

Brent wasn't gone five minutes. He jogged up the brow, unlocked the gate, and let Katie through.

"You're not really going to make me sit through that brief again, are you?"

"Depends."

"On what?"

"On how nice you are to us."

"Us? You mean Alika and you?"

Brent led Katie toward Alika's pen. There was no longer any mystery. Katie already knew where they were heading, and her heart beat a little faster with each step. Still nearly a hundred feet from his pen, and Alika realized something was up. He spy-hopped to see over the railing and equipment, saw two humans approaching, and whistled. Brent was about to respond, but Katie was quicker and whistled back. Alika immediately dove and raced around his pen, building speed, and then came straight out of the water into a perfect backflip.

"That is some dolphin," Katie roared with delight.

"I told you he has a crush on you."

Alika had his big head out of the water as soon as they arrived. Brent sat down, pulled his deck shoes and socks off, and dangled his feet in the water. Katie followed his lead. Alika snuggled in between Brent and Katie and just begged for attention. This pushed Katie into another round of tittering.

Brent pulled out the two sodas and popped the tops, handing Katie one. She stopped laughing long enough to bump cans with Brent. "To God's great beasts," she said.

Without missing a beat, Brent followed, "And the people who love them."

They stroked Alika, who just couldn't seem to get enough fondling.

The wind had blown steadily all afternoon, rendering the sky clear without a wisp of a cloud. The bright lights of the city were well to the east, which cast the stars glimmering against a perfectly black heaven. A half-moon rose in the eastern sky.

Brent would normally have been more captivated by the skyline and brilliant collage of stars, but there was someone seated next to him who was far more magnificent than the night sky and more dazzling than the twinkling stars.

They talked and looked at the stars and relished the comradery, dolphin and all.

Brent pointed out several of the constellations and explained that for hundreds of years, the stars were a reliable navigation system for sailors; and even today, with all the technology leaps in navigation, on small boats, knowing the constellations was a good backup.

Katie snuggled under Brent's arm and tilted her head up. Brent was immediately captured by the glitter and sparkle of her gold-flecked eyes. Even in a half-moon, on a cloudless night, her eyes were effulgent. They gleamed up at him. He leaned down and kissed her softly on the forehead, the nose, the cheek, the neck. And when she leaned her head back, she accepted a long, deep, wet kiss on the lips. For the fourth time since Katie arrived, she took his breath away. It was mystifyingly perfect.

After a time, Katie snuggled her head into Brent's chest. She breathed slowly and deeply, and then became perfectly still.

With Alika nestled against his legs and Katie bundled into his chest, Brent came to the realization that he had never known such utter joy, such serenity, such blissful enchantment.

I wish this moment could last forever, he thought in a half presleep haze. *Forever. Forever. Fore—what time is it?*

Brent stole a glance at his watch. *Holy smokes, it's nearly three!*

"Katie girl…," Brent whispered to her.

"Yeah?" she murmured sleepily.

"We need to go. It's nearly three."

She shook herself out of her sleep-induced reverie. "Oh my. We surely do. What happened?"

"You fell asleep. I lost track of time, and Alika didn't wake me."

"Oh, goodness!"

There was a rushed goodbye. Katie leaned down and kissed Alika on the rostrum. She stood, turned toward Brent, and hooked her arm through his. Together, they walked up the brow toward Brent's truck. Katie stole a last glance over her shoulder where she had left Alika. She let out a long sigh.

Brent was quick to recognize the mood. "You'll see him again, Katie."

"Sure hope so. And you too, of course."

Twenty minutes later, Brent rolled to a stop in front of Katie's hotel. Katie gathered her things as Brent opened her door. She slid to the sidewalk and stood close. She leaned into him and kissed him lightly on the neck. A tingling ran from under his ear to the end of his toes. And there it was again, that involuntary deep breath.

"Katie, I know this comes kinda sudden like. Believe me, I haven't been myself for the last…well, since you came…and I don't know exactly how to put it, but I think I…"

"Brent…it's not sudden at all. I've been waiting for this for a long, long time. I thought I'd never see Alika again, and you made it all happen. This has been the most wonderful day of my life. And…"

"Katie, what I was trying to say was—"

Katie extended her right arm and pressed her index finger against his lips. "This is perfect just the way it is. Don't say nuthin' more. I'd hate to have to pop you one and break that cute nose of yours. If you ask me, and I can break away from work and school, I'll come out again. But for now…"

Then she stood on her toes and kissed him lightly on the cheek, and she was gone.

CHAPTER 14

STORM CLOUDS

I feel at ease and, in an indefinable way, at home, when dolphins are around. I now know when they are nearby before they appear. I dream after they leave.

—Virginia Coyle

Tough Sledding

Early Sunday, 14 July 2002
Foxtrot Platoon, Pier 40, Sub Base, Point Loma, California

Brent stood there, dumfounded for some time. She walked through the swinging doors of her hotel, and she was gone. Just like that. He didn't know what to expect, maybe a wave, maybe one of her sky-lighting smiles, maybe even a blown kiss. What hurt him most was that she didn't even look back all the while he stared at her and tried to telepathically send her a message to come back or at least turn around, but nothing came of it.

Brent stood there another five minutes like a faithful Labrador still believing she might come back out. It was nearly four in the morning with no indications of any such miracles.

There's only one solution for this predicament. If anything can take my mind off Katie, it would be Alika.

Brent slid into the driver's seat and, with a peal of thunder, fired up his truck.

Brent checked with the duty officer just to let him know he was aboard. "Hey, Gavin, I'm going down to see how Alika's doing."

Petty Officer 3rd Class Gavin Slater was an Aviation Electrician's Mate that had made the commitment to jump from the aviation community to NMMP. He was a new kid on the block, even newer than Brent.

"Shouldn't be more than an hour," Brent said.

"Good grief, Brent, don't you ever go home?"

"I do," Brent responded, "but just thought I'd go visit my boy for a while."

"No issues. Let me know if I can help with anything."

"Will do, Gavin. Thanks!"

Brent walked quietly to Alika's pen. He'd already shed himself of his deck shoes, hoping to be quieter and stealthier. He just hoped he wouldn't find any squishy sea lion bombs as he made his way. He was still twenty yards from Alika's pen when he saw Alika's head pop up over the edge of his pen. There was a moment's pause, and then Alika whistled. Brent smiled then returned the greeting. *Doesn't that guy ever sleep?* Brent wondered.

Brent spent nearly an hour with Alika. He confided in him everything, and while Alika didn't understand one word of Brent's predicament, he was a patient and caring listener.

The sun was just lighting up the eastern horizon when Brent finally called it quits. He was exhausted both physically and emotionally, and though he knew sleep was an amorphous thing and was sure to elude him this day, he also knew he needed to try to recharge his body and his spirit.

Today will be a great new day, Brent thought...and hoped.

Caught Off Guard and Taken by Surprise

Tuesday, 3 September 2002
Foxtrot Platoon, Pier 40, Sub Base, Point Loma, California

It was a great new day as Brent so optimistically divined, as was the day after and the day after that. In fact, the rest of July through August and into September, the days and evenings were picture post-card perfect—blue skies, comfortable temperatures, cooling onshore breezes, and an enormous ocean of sparkling blue water. It was all there, the California dream, but for all its magnificence and splendor, it was mostly lost on Brent.

Brent went about his work and spent an inordinate amount of time with Alika. He found that while his mind was occupied with tasks or working with Alika, he could keep his deep feelings for Katie at bay.

It was in the evenings when those warm, gentle twilights with a color wheel of soft pastels chased the setting sun westward that turned Brent's involuntary thoughts to Katie. These were too much like the one that he and Katie had spent together. It was then that his mind became preoccupied with memories of her, and the gloominess would set in.

Kahuna took note of the long hours Brent spent at Foxtrot and the change in his mood. He was sensitive to Brent's disposition despite Brent's attempts to hide it.

It was early in September. Brent was cleaning up the RHIB he had just used in a training mission while Alika frolicked near the dock. Brent felt the presence of somebody close and then noticed Kahuna standing on the dock near the RHIB, arms crossed and casually looking at him.

"Hey, Chief. How's it going," Brent said with much more cheer in his voice than he actually felt.

"Better question, brother, is how's it going with you?"

"Never better, Kahuna. Just living the dream."

"Bullshit, Brent!" Kahuna took a knee next to the RHIB, his brown eyes boring into Brent. "Really, what's going on with you? Is it that Katie girl from Florida State?"

Kahuna had just pushed the magic button.

Brent set the hose down, stared at his deck shoes, and leaned against the control console. "It's that obvious, huh?"

"Yeah! To just about everybody who knows you. Even Master Chief Murphy is kinda concerned about you. So what shakes?"

Kahuna came aboard the RHIB and plopped down on the starboard sponson. There was a long pause as Brent tried to cobble together the thoughts and feelings that were assaulting his system. Finally, he just let it flow.

After five minutes of spilling his guts, something he had never done before, Brent was a spent round. And the funny thing about it was, he actually felt better. Not that his situation had improved in the least, but he had it all out in the open, and he felt a certain catharsis about it.

Kahuna stared at Brent a moment longer. Then, much to Brent's amazement, a large smile spread across Kahuna's face. "You sucker, Brent. You're in love, ya big dope."

"I kinda figured that out, but why do I feel all out of sorts all the time, and why do I have so much trouble focusing? I'm a wreck, and I don't get it. We only went out one time!"

"That's the way of it, Brent. You've never been in love before, I'll bet."

"If this is love, then nope, I've never been in love, and I don't think I like it much either."

"Well, shipmate, welcome to heartbreak hotel!"

For the next hour, while Alika rollicked alongside the dock and cavorted with the local indigent sea lions, Kahuna and Brent talked. At first, it was about everything but that most euphoric and paradoxically most painful of all human emotions—love. Eventually, they came back full circle. Kahuna asked, "Well, Brent, what are you going to do about it?"

Brent thought for a moment. "I don't know what I can do about it. Katie's in Florida. I'm in California."

"Have you asked her to come out? Have you asked her if you can come out?"

Sheepishly, Brent said, "Nope."

"Brent, one of the things about you that I admire most is you never quit. Don't quit on this. Talk to her. You've got an ace in the hole."

Brent thought about it; then the light came on. "Alika?"

"Yes. Alika. He's a good icebreaker, and though I think she'd come out just to see you, this way, she has an excuse. Invite her out."

Brent stared off to the distant horizon, a smile forming on his lips.

"And before you get all giddy on me, EOD Group ONE is holding a situation summary on Iraq tomorrow, 0700 at the head-quarters auditorium. I want you to come with the master chief and me. Meet us at 0600 at his office, and we'll go over together. Oh yeah, you're nominated to bring four breakfast sandwiches."

"Four? There's only three of us."

"Yeah, you're forgetting Duffus. He loves ham, egg, and cheese biscuits."

That elicited a broad grin from Brent. "Okay, 0600 at the master chief's. I'll be there with four breakfast sandwiches."

Kahuna gathered himself and stood up. "See ya then, shipmate."

"See ya then, Kahuna. And, Kahuna…"

"Yep?"

"Thanks for the talk. I guess I needed that."

"No sweat. And for the record, I wouldn't wish love on any-body. I fell in love once. I was sixteen. She was a wahine nani—a beautiful island girl. Her father refused to allow her to see me. It was a bad time. I grew up on the wrong side of the coconut trees, I guess. That's when I decided to join the Navy. Nothing like inducing a crisis in your life to take the love pangs away. Anyway, that's what shipmates are for."

The Short Road to War

Wednesday, 4 September 2002
Foxtrot Platoon, Pier 40, Sub Base, Point Loma, California

Just before 6:00 a.m., Brent arrived at the master chief's office. Kahuna, the master chief, along with his security detail, Duffus, were already there. At the sight of the McDonald's bag, Duffus waddled up and leaned against Brent, expecting a handout. He was rather pushy about it too. Brent had hardly got the egg, ham, and cheese biscuit unwrapped when Duffus unceremoniously snatched it out of Brent's hand. Brent glanced up at the master chief. "Master Chief, you sure this is good for him? I mean, nothing in that breakfast sandwich is natural to him."

"Don't know the answer to that, Brent, but I'm sure not going to be the guy that tells him he can't have any more. Are you?"

"No, sir. Don't think so."

The rest of the sandwiches were passed around and consumed, along with liberal quantities of the master chief's private reserve coffee, the horrible taste of which was disguised only by the ridiculously high temperature at which it was served. The idea here, Brent presumed, was to make the coffee so hot that it scorched the taste buds, and ergo, the drinker couldn't discern just how bad it really was.

Master Chief Murphy stood, reached for his cover, and asked, "You guys ready to mount up?"

"Good to go, Master Chief," Kahuna replied.

They made the trip from Point Loma Sub Base to Naval Amphibious Base (NAB), Coronado, barely beating the main rush of traffic over the Coronado Bridge—a nightmare traffic jam reliably beginning just before 0700 every weekday.

They entered the auditorium and, with the master chief leading the way, moved toward the seats forward and centered on the stage. This was not where Brent would have chosen to sit, but the giant linebacker of a CPO seemed to know where he wanted to go, and Brent obediently stayed close in trail.

As they took their seats, Master Chief Murphy leaned over and asked, "Brent, do you know what this brief's about?"

"Just that it's a SITREP on Iraq, but I don't know any specifics."

"You been following the progress there, or should I say, the lack of progress there?"

"Just the message traffic, but we haven't had any operational or intelligence assessments for a while."

"Well stand by, son. I think you're about to get an earful, and it's not going to be good news."

"Yes, sir."

The lights dimmed, the chatter stopped, and those standing took their seats. A lanky lieutenant commander in khakis walked across the stage and positioned himself behind the podium slightly to the left of an enormous projection screen.

"Good morning. I'm Lieutenant Commander Frank Baum, your Group ONE intelligence officer. This morning, we'll be delivering the situation summary for Iraq based on CENTCOMs[70] assessments. This brief is classified SECRET. Nothing shown or addressed will be discussed outside the confines of this auditorium. This brief will be presented in three parts. A chronology of events starting at the end of Desert Storm. Second, our N-5 plans officer, Commander Monty Kendrick, will provide an overview of where we think this is all heading. And finally, Commander Pat Nolan, our force readiness officer, will discuss what it means to us at Group ONE and our subordinate commands. Let me begin. First slide, please.

"Combat operations in connection with Operation Desert Storm and the First Gulf War officially ended on 28 February 1991. But it wasn't until the third of March 1991 that Iraq accepted the conditions for their surrender and a permanent cease-fire. In the aftermath of Operation Desert Storm, the United Nations Security Council issued Resolution 687. That was the third of April 1991. This resolution allowed Saddam to stay in power. This was a big win for him, but it also placed a burning burr under his saddle, for it mandated a halt to all chemical, biological, nuclear, and long-range missile programs. It further stipulated that all such weapons be turned over to UN Special Commission Control (UNSCOM) for destruction. This resolution also established an in-country team to continue to monitor and verify Iraq's compliance with the provisions of that resolution and those that would come after.

"It was about this time that the Voice of Free Iraq, a Saudi Arabia–based radio station run by the CIA, began transmitting broadcasts inciting an insurrection against Saddam and his Ba'ath government. Almost at once, believing that the United States would support or, at the very least, defend them against Iraqi military forces, the Sha'aban insurgency of Arabs in the south and the national uprising of the Kurds in the north boiled over, and a full-fledged insurrection was in play.

"Initially, bolstered by encouragement from the Voice of Free Iraq, the rebel forces gained the upper hand. Their single common objective was to take out Hussein. Unfortunately, that single bonding agent did not compensate for numerous detractors. Disorganized forces, lack of command and control, lack of military training, an unstructured leadership chain, ineffective weaponry, internal rivalries, and many religious and cultural differences, however, doomed the insurrection from the start.

"The March 3 cease-fire agreement forbade Iraqi's use of fixed-wing aircraft. However, in that so much of the bridges and highways had been destroyed, the coalition negotiators at the 28 February cease-fire conference approved of Iraq's request to continue flying military helicopters ostensibly for humanitarian support missions. This was to prove far from the case.

"Iraqi frontline security forces responded to the insurrection with quick and brutal military attacks. Iraqi forces annihilated the rebels often using women and children as shields. Saddam's forces entered cities held by rebels and indiscriminately slaughtered rebel bands as well as civilians. Using tanks, artillery, helicopter gunships, and infantry, tens of thousands were killed, wounded, and displaced.

"Coalition forces, primarily the US, UK, and France, did not turn a blind eye to the mass slaughter of the innocents. As early as 3 March, the Iraqis were warned by General Norman Schwarzkopf that coalition aircraft would engage any Iraqi military aircraft flying over the country. Saddam tested the water, and by the end of the month,

USAF F-15C Eagles had shot down two Su-22s and claimed a kill on an Iraqi PC-9 trainer. The story goes that the pilot jumped out when he realized he was being approached by a US fighter.

"Kurds in Northern Iraq continued with their own insurrection though March. The movement was joined by Peshmerga and defecting Iraq military members. More than fifty thousand fighters formed to engage Iraq's military. By the end of March, the Iraqi government had lost control of every town and enclave in North Iraq. Fourteen of the eighteen provinces were controlled by the Kurds and other fighters who had joined them.

"But even with air support by the coalition, the successes of the Kurdish forces did not last long. Remnants of Iraqi troops and loyal Ba'athists counterattacked and pushed against the Kurds with mechanized forces, helicopters, and infantry. Outgunned, outmaneuvered, and using the nerve agent sarin and CS gas dispersed from helicopters, the Kurd rebels were decimated. By early April 1991, the Kurd forces were rolled back as far as Kore, a strategic and narrow valley near Qaladiza.

"That month, the British mounted Operation Haven, and the US began Operation Provide Comfort. Both initiatives were designed to provide humanitarian assistance and defend the Kurds from the ruthless attacks by the Iraqi military. Operation Provide Comfort and Operation Haven provided much-needed medical aid, supplies, water, food, shelter, but most importantly, it kept Iraqi aircraft from pounding the Kurds and refugees in Northern Iraq. The USS *Forrestal* (CV-59) also added her great military might to the operations. She arrived on station to ensure airspace supremacy and gather intelligence, surveillance, and reconnaissance (ISR) for coalition commanders.

"On 24 July 1991, Operation Provide Comfort was terminated, and Operation Provide Comfort II began. The chief difference between the two operations was the shift in focus to military operations, primarily to prevent actions against the Kurds and other refugees in the north.

"For those living in Iraq's southeast, the Marsh Arabs, retaliation was equally swift and vicious. But Saddam's response this time also caused an ecological catastrophe. From March through April 1992, Iraqi military using fixed-wing aircraft, helicopters, and supported by ground forces poisoned the waters and drained the swamps in and around Hawizeh on the Iranian border. When the Marsh Arabs scrambled from the villages to seek sanctuary, Iraqi military torched their homes and destroyed their infrastructure.

"The Iraq government announced on 5 April 1991 that all rebel forces involved in sedition and revolution had been crushed. In response, the UN Security Council passed Resolution 688 that same day, condemning Iraq's attacks and the oppression of the Kurds. Additionally, this resolution required the Iraq government to respect the human rights of its people. This, of course, was a laughable demand to Saddam Hussein.

"The insurrections and the aftermath were a human tragedy and a catastrophe of biblical proportions. Deaths on either side are impossible to count. Tens of thousands of lives were lost. Add to this the carnage and chaos of human suffering when nearly two million people fled from Iraq to Turkey, Iran, Syria, and the northern-border mountains.

"Operation Southern Watch commenced on 27 August 1992. It was a US initiative supported by UK, France, and Saudi Arabia designed to ensure Iraq's compliance with UN Security Council Resolution 688. Among other specifics, Operation Southern Watch was put in place to enforce the no-fly zone in the south. The Iraqi military largely ignored this and continued their attacks on Shi'ite Muslims in Southern Iraq through 1992. Consequently, the Iraqi military continued to lose equipment and lives.

"The plan for a visit to Kuwait in April 1993 by then President George W. Bush was cancelled when it was discovered that Saddam had plotted to assassinate him. In retaliation, on 26 June 1993, President Clinton ordered a massive cruise missile strike on the Iraqi Intelligence Service building in downtown Baghdad. Twenty-three Tomahawks were launched targeting the IIS facilities and C-3 networks. Again, Hussein's plot demonstrated the utter lack of understanding of our determination, the capability of our intelligence networks, and the range of our reach.

"In 1994, it appeared that Iraqi military aggression had subsided for a time, and the US began to pull troops out. In October of that year, Saddam demanded that the UN lift sanctions then ordered two division of the Iraq Republican Guard to the Kuwait border. The US response came quickly. US troops redeployed into theater executing Operation Vigilant Warrior. This enormous buildup of American military might forced Saddam to pull his forces north and away from Kuwait.

"Then in August 1996, when Iraqi troops pushed into the Northern Kurdish areas, Operation Desert Strike was unleashed. This op targeted military assets and forces in Southern Iraq with the objective of sending an indelible signal to Saddam that we were quite serious about protecting the Iraqi people and the Kurds.

"With the cease-fire agreement of 3 March 1991, additional conditions were placed upon Iraq. In regard to UNSCOM Weapons Inspections, Iraq was to grant 'immediate, unconditional, and unrestricted access to suspected production, storage, operational, and special security sites as determined by the UN.' What the inspectors received was altogether different.

"Initially, with the assistance of Iraqi official's, UNSCOM inspectors were successful in discovering and destroying a considerable number of weapons of mass destruction and materials that allowed for their production under Resolution 687. In the course of UN oversight and coalition military control, tensions increased dramatically, and Iraq's compliance and assistance with UNSCOM's weapons inspections suffered radically.

"In June 1997, Iraq officials went so far as to threaten the safety of UNSCOM's helicopters and their crews. Then on 20 October 1997, Deputy Prime Minister Tariq Aziz directed that all US personnel on the UNSCOM staff leave Iraq. Sensing the building tension in Iraqi's leadership chain, the UNSCOM executive chairman pulled the majority of the weapons inspectors out of Iraq. After a full month of negotiations, the inspectors were allowed to return to Iraq to continue their work.

"The frequency of military engagements in both northern and southern Iraq continued through 1998. These skirmishes had a direct impact on the UNSCOM weapons inspectors—they were getting nowhere. Access to suspected WMD-manufacturing facilities, material storage areas, supporting sites, and 'sensitive sites'[71] were delayed, restricted, and often denied entirely. Clearly, Iraqi officials were violating the terms of the resolutions by not granting UNSCOM teams 'immediate, unconditional, and unrestricted access to all sites designated for inspection.'"[73]

"The tipping point came on 14 December 1998 when Saddam accused the UNSCOM weapons inspectors of espionage. Saddam terminated the inspector's access to all military and weapons sites. In reality, the timing for this order was fortunate. On 15 December, the UNSCOM chairman, Richard Butler, pulled all the inspectors out of Iraq, citing Saddam's accusations and demands but also because of high-level intelligence that the US was planning a major strike against Iraqi military installations. This action would clearly put Butler's team in extreme peril.

"From 16 to 19 December 1998, Operation Desert Fox, ordered by President Clinton, struck ninety-seven targets. In the four days of attacks, US forces flew over six hundred missions, released over six hundred weapons, ninety air-launched cruise missiles, and fired over three-hundred Tomahawk land-attack missiles. In four days of strikes, Iraqi forces suffered the loss of scores of radar sites, SAM emplacements, command and control centers, and caused severe damage to the development of their missile program. It was the largest, most destructive sustained air strike since Desert Storm.

"Unfortunately, it seems that it did nothing to bring sanity or reality to Saddam. Apparently lost on Saddam was the fact that he continued to lose aircraft, SAM sites, command and control networks, and people as a result of aggressive actions against coalition forces. Unfortunately, one of the primary objectives of Operation Desert Fox was to force Iraq to allow the weapons inspectors to continue tasks specified in UN resolutions. That did not happen. On 11 February 2000, despite the sanctions and sustained military punishment upon Iraqi forces, Saddam declared that UN weapons inspectors would not be allowed back into the country.

"US and coalition response had been swift but measured. Between the end of Desert Fox and May of 2000, it has been reported that Iraqi military units had violated the no-fly zones in the South 150 times and had been involved in over 450 antiaircraft engagements. Now I'd like to turn this over to Commander Monty Kendrick, our plans officer, who will give us a look into the man Saddam Hussein."

Commander Kendrick, an EOD warrior of some acclaim and who had seen action as a junior officer in the First Gulf War, stepped to the podium. "Thanks to all for attending this brief. I think you'll get a sense of the seriousness of the situation when I give you a close look into the man that is Saddam Hussein—also known as the Butcher of Baghdad. Next slide please."

"Many believe that Saddam is crazy, and by Western metrics, he might be. But according to a well-known professor of psychiatry at the Elliot School of International Affairs and an advisor to the House Armed Services Committee, Dr. Jerrold Post, Saddam might be considered a megalomaniac, but he is quite rational. He is not psychotic, but his conduct shows strong signs of paranoia.

"In some ways, he is the worst of all opponents. He is not impulsive and instead carefully plans his political, media, and military strategies for maximum effects. From a psychological aspect, he has a rational mind, but paradoxically, he seems to be completely unaware of the international outrage and consequences of his actions. This, when put into the context of his experiences, is not so hard to understand. He has had very little contact with the international powers, especially with nations outside the Arab web of influence. He had some interplay with Russian military advisors but has had only one, we believe, short trip to France in 1976. This would suggest he has very little understanding of the cultures, history, and character of the leaders of nations of the Western hemisphere. This isolation has put him at a distinct disadvantage when it comes to being able to understand what makes us and the Western world 'tick.'

"He rules with incredible brutality and likens criticism with disloyalty. And this is not directed solely at his enemies. Early in his presidency, he ordered the execution of five hundred Communist party members and directed his senior advisors to form the execution squads. He once asked his cabinet members for their opinion on the conduct of the war with Iran, which at the time was going poorly. The minister of health recommended that he temporarily step down from office until peace was restored with Iran. Shortly after the meeting, body parts of the minister were delivered to his wife.

"This rule by fear has deprived him of otherwise sane and rational counsel from his most-experienced and worldly advisors. Saddam's quest for power and prestige seems unconstrained. He has proven on many occasions that he will use all sources of power at his disposal, including weapons of mass destruction, to attain his objectives, regardless of the pain, suffering, and the lives lost. Said differently, to our knowledge, he has never held in reserve a weapon that he has had in his arsenal. Therein lay the great concern to all nations in regard to the development of nuclear weapons and other WMDs.

"To quote Dr. Post, 'It is this political personality constellation—messianic ambition for unlimited power, absence of conscience, unconstrained aggression, and a paranoid outlook which make Saddam so dangerous.' This then makes it easier to understand that the only thing that Saddam understands, the only power that he respects, is military force. No better example of that is the Operation Vigilant Warrior in August of 1994 of which Lieutenant Commander Baum spoke.

"So, what does all this mean, and where do we think this is heading? Assessments from Joint and national sources indicate that while Hussein remains in power, political, social, and humanitarian conditions will continue to degrade. Hussein is still of the belief that the three controls he has over us and the UN coalition is a military-strike capability, albeit considerably diminished; the media, which have not been all that friendly to him; and his terrorist connections.

"Putting this in broader terms, we believe that Hussein would strike us or members of the coalition if he thought he could get away with it. But he is not an idiot. He now understands, to some degree, that we have the capability and the determination—the will—to respond with all forms of national power if attacked, and that includes diplomatic, intelligence, military, economic, and cyber force. That said, there is strong evidence that Hussein will likely either directly or indirectly support and encourage a high-visibility terrorist attack on American soil or on our assets and people wherever and whenever he can. Remember, he is a patient man whose cruelty, lack of conscience, and struggle for power is unfathomable by Western standards. Next up is our force readiness officer, Commander Pat Nolan, who will discuss what all this means to us at Group ONE and our subordinate commands. Commander?"

Commander Noland walked to the podium as Commander Kendrick exited the stage.

"As Commander Kendrick mentioned, I'll try to bring this back closer to home and explain what this means to us in the group. You'll be happy to know that my part in this presentation will be the shortest. After my delivery, we'll take questions.

"We know that Saddam Hussein will use any type of force or action against us. He has attempted to assassinate an American president, he's fired SCUD missiles into Israel and Saudi Arabia, he supported the Khobar Towers bombing in Saudi Arabia, he's used WMDs against his own people, and if he could, we believe, he would readily use them against us. The battlefield for him is not confined to the perimeter of a war zone. To Saddam, a kill is a kill, and if he could strike at the heart of America in a terrorist attack, even using WMDs against innocent civilians, he would in a New York second.

"Now let me shift to the source of much speculation and see if I can clear the air concerning a possible link between Saddam and the 9/11 terrorist attack. Nearly a year ago, when the terrorists struck, all fingers pointed at Saddam Hussein as the likely miscreant backing the attack. But since then, all intelligence sources that I am aware of seem to have come to the same conclusion. While Saddam was probably doing the Muslim version of the Irish jig in celebration of the attack, there is no evidence that he had any part in the planning, organization, or funding of the attack. That horrible event rests squarely on Osama bin Laden, who, no doubt, will be ushered into the next world as soon as we figure out where he's hiding.

"So, bottom line, we at EOD group believe that another conflict with Saddam Hussein is inevitable. It may be on the battlefield, it may be against soft civilian targets, but directly or indirectly, we believe another battle is brewing. What can you as leaders, supervisors, and combat-support people do? You can take this threat seriously. You can go home and take care of things, put your home in order, and hug your family. You can maximize every training opportunity, ensure your equipment is running at peak, get your gear ready, and take care of your people and your animals. The war with Iraq is not over. Now we'll take a few questions."

The master chief and his entourage stayed for the questions-and-answer session, but if Brent was hoping for resolution or some form of comfort, it did not come. And now, on top of a wounded heart, Brent had serious concerns with what the experts believed was another war in the gulf.

When It Rains, It Pours

Wednesday, 4 September 2002
Foxtrot Platoon, Pier 40, Sub Base, Point Loma, California

Brent was slightly dazed by the brief as they exited the auditorium and headed back to Foxtrot with the master chief and Kahuna. The brief painted a picture of an international crisis swirling dangerously out of control. Brent had been in combat before, not nearly as much as Master Chief Murphy or Chief Olopoto had seen, but Brent knew it was nothing he wanted to see again.

And then he remembered the words of Chief Olopoto: "Nothing like inducing a crisis into your life to take the pain away."

The fact was, the brief portended a new war in the Mideast—a crisis, to be sure—but this only added to the confusion Brent suffered in regard to Katie. *I have no idea if this is going to blow up or not, and not a clue as to when, but I need to see her before anything else pops. I need to talk to her again.*

"Hello."

"Katie, thank goodness I got a hold of you. I—"

"Brent? Brent…where have you been, and how come you haven't called me? It's been days, and I haven't heard boo from you."

"Katie, I…ah. I just didn't want to bother you. I know how much you work and study. I didn't want to intrude."

"Well, sailor, you kinda got yourself in some hot water, ya know."

"That's kind of what I was calling about. I'd like to make it up to you, if I could."

"Well, this is interesting. Just how do ya intend to do that?"

"Remember when you said you'd come out if you could get away from work and your studies?"

"Yep. Sure do."

There was a short pause on the line while Brent mustered his courage and got his words straightened out. He'd only have one chance to do this, and he had to get it right the first time.

"So…can you come out, or if that's too hard, I can come out and visit, and that may be easier since you wouldn't have to travel." When he got started, he was so flustered he just couldn't turn it off. "And there's an Air Force Base at Panama City. I might be able to get a military lift out there, and I could get a rental car and drive out to see you, and that's only about two hours away, and I could take you to dinner, and we could go to the beach and—"

Suddenly Katie broke out in her cute girlish giggle, and Brent had no idea where he was in his delivery, but he sensed it was not going well.

"Slow down, Brent. I'll come out."

Brent wasn't sure he heard her right.

"Wait. You said…you'll come out? You mean, out to see me and Alika?"

"Yeah. Out to see you. And seeing Alika would be a big bonus, but yeah, I'll come out."

Brent felt like he had the wind knocked out of him for a moment.

"Ya still there, Brent?"

"Yes. I'm still here. I'm just trying to get my pulse rate back to normal."

"Well, don't die on me, Brent."

"I'm far from that, Katie. Okay, how's this sound? I'll send you the tickets for a round-trip airfare, and I'll book you a room in Imperial Beach? That'll be real close to where I live."

"Do you have roommates?"

Without thinking it through, Brent said, "Yeah, but they're boat guys and both deployed."

"Great. How 'bout if I just stay with you and we use the money we save just to have some fun?"

For the second time in two minutes, Brent had to force himself to take deep breaths.

"Stay with me…at my apartment?"

"Sure! No hanky-panky, ya understand? But it'll save you from driving that gas-guzzlin' behemoth truck of yours all over the place."

"Gosh, yeah. That sounds like a great idea. Okay, I'll send you the tickets. When can you come out? This weekend?"

"Hold your horses, cowboy. It might be a month or so. I'll have to look at the schedule and get somebody to work for me. Dr. Dubois is not going to like this, but that makes it even better. And, Brent, I work, remember? I can pay my way."

"Katie, I don't mind at all paying for your tickets."

"Okay, we'll split the cost. Now I gotta get back to work. I'll let you know when I can get out there."

"One more thing, Katie."

"Brent, if this is gonna get gushy, tell me when you see me."

"I don't think I can wait that long, Katie."

"You can do it, Brent. Just cowboy up!"

CHAPTER 15

XANADU IN THE EYE OF THE TEMPEST

Cultures have long heard wisdom in non-human voices: Apollo, god of music, medicine and knowledge, came to Delphi in the form of a dolphin. But dolphins, which fill the oceans with blipping and chirping, and whales, which mew and caw in ultramarine jazz—a true rhapsody in blue—are hunted to the edge of silence.

—Jay Griffiths

Bouquets and Carousels

Wednesday, 9 October 2002
Foxtrot Platoon, Point Loma, California

The reunion between Katie and Brent had been delayed for a number of reasons, but the setback had only created more excitement, more anticipation. Katie was wound up tighter than a cheap watch. The landing gear came up and locked at 05:30 a.m. on Wednesday, 9 October. It was a seven-hour and forty-five-minute trip from Jacksonville, Florida, to San Diego with a single stop in Atlanta—she would have plenty of time to unwind before she landed. Her two favorite boys in the whole world would be waiting for her when the 737 touched down at 10:15 a.m. She had to get some sleep. She didn't want to look like a Halloween ghoul when Brent picked her up.

Hours later, she was jolted out of a light sleep when the wheels squeaked onto the runway at San Diego. She gathered her things and waited impatiently for the plane to dock at the terminal.

"Hello. Katie, is that you?" Brent answered his cell phone on the first ring.

"Yeah. We just landed and should be pulling to the gate in a few minutes."

"I'm here. Been here for almost an hour in case you were early. I'll be the guy with the biggest grin."

"And I'll be the girl that looks like she was in a hurricane."

"Doubt it. See ya in a couple of minutes."

"Bye!"

Katie had to suppress the urge to make a mad dash to the front of the airplane as soon as they opened the exit doors. Once off the plane, she was in full flight headed for the baggage carousel. As she approached the security checkpoint, she noticed a young man holding the biggest bouquet of flowers she'd ever seen. She shifted her glance from the flowers back to the handsome young man and, at once, realized it was Brent. And true, he was the one with the biggest grin.

She had hardly slowed down when she plowed into Brent, nearly scattering the bouquet.

The compression of their two bodies held the flowers in place, and with some tricky maneuvering, they were awarded with a long, deep kiss.

When they came up for air, Brent whispered, "Katie, thanks so much for making the trip. You have no idea what this means to me. I—"

"Shush! Now help me get my bag, and we'll blow this popsicle stand!"

Katie gathered the flowers with both arms as Brent took a step back to admire the girl he'd been dreaming about for weeks. She wore khaki cargo pocket shorts and a blue Florida State University golf shirt. Brent wasn't the only man studying her long, lean legs. She had some other admirers who strolled by and casually glanced back. But what captivated Brent's attention was her incandescent gold-speckled green eyes. He couldn't ever remember looking into those glistening eyes without taking a deep breath. An enormous grin came over him.

"What?" Katie lit up her muse smile.

"Just...oh gosh," he returned.

And with that, Brent draped his arm across Katie's shoulders, and Katie eagerly put her left arm around his waist, trying to avoid crushing her beautiful flowers. It felt completely natural and very comfortable. They walked slowly, savoring every step, as they headed for the carousel.

Katie pointed to her bag as it wound through the carousel, and Brent grabbed it on the first pass. Katie wrestled with the flowers while Brent toted her carry-on and roller suitcase and headed toward the parking lot and Brent's truck.

"Wow!" Katie exclaimed in amazement. "You didn't wax that big beast of a pickup, did ya?"

"I did. I wanted to make this perfect. Surprised you noticed."

"And it will be perfect, Brent, but it's got nuthin' to do with a shiny old pickup with a loud motor. Can we go see Alika?"

"We can. I cleared it with Chief Olopoto. He's expecting us."

"Oh, this is going to be so much fun." She leaned across the seat and gave him a peck on the cheek. "Thanks so much for invitin' me out here, Brent. This is like...a dream come true."

"More than you know, Katie. I don't think I slept more than a couple of hours a night for the last week."

Twenty minutes later, they pulled through the Point Loma Navy Base security gate and parked in front of Foxtrot Platoon. Katie was dancing on clouds.

Kahuna met them at the security gate leading to the pens with Katie's visitor's badge in hand. "Welcome back, Katie."

"Ah, Kahuna. Thanks so much." Hugs were exchanged. "Good to see ya. How's Alika?"

"Why don't you and Brent go find out for yourselves?"

"Thanks, Chief," Brent said and led Katie toward Alika's pen.

Katie, at first, suppressed the urge to run to Alika. She didn't want to make a big commotion, though.

It was uncanny. Brent and Katie were still more than a hundred feet away, and a big handsome dolphin popped up, studied the two humans approaching, and whistled. Katie, at first, giggled then whistled in return. Alika's immediate response was to spy-hop and emit a string of whistles interspersed with a number of chirps. It was all too much for Katie. She ran flat out the last fifty feet to his pen.

By the time she got to the side of his pen, Alika was up against the railing, waiting for her. Katie got down on her knees and, with both hands, hugged Alika's melon and kissed his forehead. Alika couldn't get enough attention from this kind human.

Brent sat down cross-legged next to Katie and savored the moment.

"Don't get too excited, Katie. He did the very same thing with the last girl I had here."

Katie lifted just enough to drive her elbow into Brent's solar plexus. It was nearly a complete surprise, but he managed to partially tighten his abs to lessen the blow. Still he found himself involuntarily gasping for air in between his chuckles.

"Okay, okay. Just kidding!"

"You better be, sailor. I didn't come all this way to play second fiddle to a local beach hottie."

"You gotta know, Katie, you're the only girl in my life. Actually, both of our lives."

"Better be, big boy! That goes for you too, Brent!"

Brent almost doubled up in laughter, and Alika, knowing full well something special was happening, blurted out another string of happy whistles.

Chivalry 101

Wednesday, 9 October 2002
Imperial Beach, California

Brent and Katie spent the better part of two hours with Alika. He seemed to never tire of the attention from his two favorite humans.

It was already past noon. "Can I take you to lunch?" Brent asked.

"Sure. I'm starved."

"What would you like?"

"You pick."

"McP's?"

"Perfect. Maybe we can just have a hydraulic lunch."

"That'll work for me. I have five days of leave starting this morning. I still need to go in every day to see Alika, but you can come with me, and I know he'll flip to see you."

"This keeps getting better and better. Thanks, Brent."

Lunch was a rushed thing. Brent and Katie slid into a rare parking place on Orange Avenue, right in front of McP's. Katie ordered a Reuben sandwich, and Brent went with fish and chips and a pitcher of Stella to wash it down.

There was very little eating going on. Between sipping their beers, talking, and just staring at each other, they had hardly dented their lunch. An hour later, Brent paid the bill and walked Katie to the truck, opened the passenger door, and connected her seat belt—anything to be near her.

Brent couldn't wait to get Katie back to his apartment. The timing couldn't have been better. His roommates, both with Special Boat Team TWELVE, were deployed for another five months. Brent and Katie had the place to themselves.

Brent pulled into his parking spot and grabbed Katie's bags out of the truck while Katie gathered her giant bouquet. As they walked to the front door, Katie asked, "Don't 'spose you have a flower vase handy?"

"Vase, no, but we have plenty of beer pitchers. That should work, ya think!"

"That'll be fine!"

It was an exciting but tense moment as they entered the three-bedroom apartment. Brent would honor Katie's wishes as she explained them on the phone, *no hanky-panky*. But in truth, he had hoped and prayed that she had changed her mind on the sleeping arrangements. He led Katie to the room closest to his. "This is Ty Olson's room. Ty's on Team TWELVE. He won't be back for months. He said you're welcome to stay here but not to leave any stuffed animals or girly things."

"Where's yours, Brent?"

"Right next door."

Katie smiled brightly. Brent knew he had made the right call. He had just passed a major test in chivalry 101.

She looked around Ty's small room and said, "Not bad. And you can tell him no girly things. I promise!"

Katie busied herself placing the flowers in several beer pitchers and then went to her room to unpack. Brent pulled two old bikes out of the garage, checked the tire pressure, and then returned to the apartment.

"Hey, Katie, want to take a ride down to the pier and see the sights of Imperial Beach?"

"Heck yeah. Be right with you."

Katie popped out the front door, skipped across the porch, and threw a long, tanned leg over the bicycle seat. "Where to?"

"Follow me. I'll show you downtown Imperial Beach. It'll take about ten minutes."

They rode down to the pier, toured the area, then reversed course and headed north, up the bike path paralleling Highway 75 toward Silver Strand State Beach.

It was a gorgeous day to be out. Katie was dazzled by the number of sunbathers on the beach at the state park on a workday and in early October. After riding around the RV park, they dipped through a tunnel heading east and cruised through the bay side of the park.

Then without stopping, they rode south on the bike path and headed back to Imperial Beach.

By the time they walked into Brent's apartment, signs of fatigue were showing on Katie.

"How'd you like to relax and watch some TV?"

"Sounds great to me. Mind if I collapse here on the sofa?"

"Heck no. Make yourself to home."

Brent hustled to his room, grabbed two pillows, stripped the top cover off his bed, and hurried back to Katie. She was already curled up on the sofa and paying no attention to the TV. Brent spread the blanket over her, eased her head up, and scooted his legs and the pillows under her head. She was out like a light and would stay that way for nearly two hours. Brent's legs and butt went numb in an attempt to keep still.

The TV played on, but Brent spent most of the time just admiring this blonde-haired goddess. It was the best two hours he'd had in a long, long time.

The To-Do List

Friday, 11 October to Sunday, 13 October 2002
Imperial Beach, California

On their agenda was the beach, long bike rides on the strand, a trip to the Wild Animal Park, and booming at McP's. But the thrill, the apex of the four-day visit, was frolicking with Alika.

On Friday, 11 October, Chief Olopoto received verbal permission from Master Chief Murphy to allow Brent to take Alika and Katie out on the San Diego Bay in a seven-meter RHIB. This was carefully cloaked as an indoctrination demonstration of the capabilities of the MK 7 mammals for possible recruiting of a marine biologist for the NMMP intern program.

Brent answered the phone a little after 7:00 a.m. "Good morning."

"Brent, what are you doing?" Chief Olopoto responded.

"Hey, Chief. Just getting the day going. What's up?"

"Well, we have an RHIB here for you. Thought you and Katie would like to take that big dolphin of yours out in the bay. Pretty nice day for a boat ride."

"You're kidding, right? I mean, you are kidding, aren't ya?"

"Serious as a snakebite. Come on down. We gotta get the boat back on the schedule by noon, though."

"We'll be there in half an hour. Chief, I owe ya a beer or two!"

"I'm not letting you off that easy, Brent. But you're all paid up."

"Whatdaya mean?"

"Your performance here and with Mobile Unit 3 at Bremerton earned you a few perks. Master Chief Murphy okay'd this. We're billing it as a recruiting demo. Maybe you can talk Katie into an internship with NMMP."

"I'll give it a try, Chief. See you in half an hour."

"Katie," Brent yelled on the other side of her bedroom door, "rise and shine, sweetheart. We're going for a boat ride!"

It took Katie fifteen minutes to get rousted, showered, and dressed. Brent made the trip to Foxtrot Platoon in twenty-five minutes, and upon arrival, Brent and Katie stopped by Kahuna's office to thank him. Katie greeted him with a big hug and one of her dazzling smiles.

"No thanks necessary. You two have a great morning, but we need the boat back by noon," Kahuna said.

"Got it, Chief. See ya then."

Brent and Katie hustled down to the pier. Brent threw their gear on the boat, helped Katie aboard, did several checks on the boat and the equipment, and started the engines. Brent then brought Alika out of his pen. He was excited and carried on quite a conversation between his whistles and chirps, but when he saw Katie waiting in the boat, he made a graceful arcing jump out of the water and rushed to the side of the boat.

Show off, Brent thought and then ran to catch up.

Brent prepared the beaching tray and signaled Alika to come aboard. With the beaching tray secured and the engines warmed,

Brent tossed lines, slipped the RHIB into gear, and slowly headed into the San Diego Bay.

Brent dropped anchor in an area just west of the submarine base—a small natural cove less traveled and better protected from the wakes of the ships and larger boats transiting the bay. Brent launched Alika, who did his customary reconnaissance circle around the boat. He quickly returned to the side of the boat in front of Katie and, with squeaks and whistles, beckoned her into the water.

"Brent, I think he's asking me to go for a swim. Is that allowed?"

"Today, it is. Go ahead."

"Oh my gosh!"

She stripped down to her bikini and slipped into the water and was instantly greeted by a playful dolphin push by Alika.

Having tested the anchor line, Brent dove in the water and was rewarded by Alika's version of a tug boat ride. Brent was pushed through the water like one of Alika's toys. They swam and gamboled in the blue-green water, played tag with Alika, and tossed the bait bucket cover for Alika to fetch. And Alika was very eager to tow them around. He was surprisingly fast, even with both passengers clinging to his dorsal and pectoral fins. He couldn't get enough of all the attention and contact, and clearly the feeling was mutual. To her recollection, Katie had never had so much fun. In fact, they almost had too much. They nearly lost all sense of time.

Brent glanced at his diving watch. "Katie, it's nearly eleven. We gotta get the boat back."

"Ahhhh, dang it! Okay. Let's go."

Alika made one more orbit around the boat with Brent and Katie in tow. They released Alika, and for a long moment, they treaded water and gazed at each other. Katie, hair sopping wet and smeared across her face, was simply dazzling. Her green eyes made the brilliance of the water they were immersed in pale by comparison. Brent stared at Katie in complete wonderment. He recalled that first phone call, how it sparked this romance that seemed only to grow stronger. And now he finally admitted to himself he was in a perpetual state of, *Oh, wow!*

Katie's interest, by contrast, was tempered by a cautious, pragmatic outlook. She watched Brent, listened to his words, began to understand his character, his true self, and recognized the abundant good in him. Hers was a slow crescendo that piqued all her senses and emotions, and though her feeling for Brent overshadowed all previous relationships, Katie was not quite ready to call this wonderful awakening *love*.

She silently glided to Brent. Brent wrapped his arms around her and kissed her deeply on the lips. It seemed so natural—she fit his hug perfectly. She returned his kiss and embraced him, giving him her all.

She pulled back slightly, looking deeply into his eyes. "Brent, I have never been so happy in such complete bliss. I wish we could hold this moment forever."

Brent almost blurted out the *L* word but, after having been cautioned twice now, attempted to interject a little humor. "Me too, but we're going to both look like prunes if we don't get out of the water pretty soon. And I gotta get the boat back, or Kahuna'll skin me."

"Okay, but I need another kiss."

Brent was quick to comply. And if it was possible, this second kiss was even deeper and more impassioned.

But the embrace was short-lived when a large wet rostrum wedged in between them. Alika whistled and chirped; his smile seemed to grow. Soon his entire body had wiggled in between Brent and Katie. Refusing to release each other, their arms encircled the big dolphin. Even after having their embrace interrupted, they laughed and laughed—and Alika whistled excitedly.

Brent had the RHIB back to the pier slightly before noon. He and Katie returned Alika to his pen amid some initial stalling. Brent reached for Katie's hand and walked toward Kahuna's office. Katie looked over her shoulder just in time to see Alika do a tail stand, looking completely forlorn. She whistled, and Alika quickly returned it.

The rest of the day included a long bike ride from Imperial Beach to Hotel Del in Coronado. Brent ordered two Mai Tais, walked to the beach, and stretched out in the warm sand. They slowly sipped their drinks and admired the panorama—Point Loma defining the northern parameter of San Diego Bay and the Coronado Islands well to the southwest. Lost in their own thoughts, they relished in the early moments of an electric-pink sunset for which Coronado was famous.

Later in the afternoon, they mounted their bikes and headed back to Brent's. It had been a long day and an emotional one. They were both exhausted by the time they got home. They took a short nap together bundled in each other's arms. Much to Brent's disappointment and honoring his word, there was no "hanky-panky." He loved this girl, and just to be with her was enough.

Beer Call

Friday, 11 October to Sunday, 13 October 2002
Imperial Beach, California

Friday night at McP's was hopping. Brent and Katie had no trouble finding the Special Boat Team brothers and SEALs gathered in the back of the main bar, laughing, telling stories, and consuming copious amounts of beer. Chief O'Dell spied Brent and Katie as they entered and pulled them into the group. Several other boat team gents recognized Katie and received her with big hugs. Those who had not met her before stared in quiet admiration, hoping for an introduction. Chief O'Dell reclaimed his duty as Katie's personal security team. The beer flowed, and the sea stories were retold and embellished.

"Well, Brent, how's your big fish doing?" SB1 Clint Johnson, an old and dear friend of Brent's from Boat Team TWELVE, asked.

"Pretty boring compared to what you guys have been doing, I hear. But I have a great boy and love the job. And now no one shoots at us. Can't beat that!"

"Maybe nobody's shooting at you," Chief O'Dell broke in. "But the word is, you had a little trouble a while ago, and your fish saved your bacon. What's with that?"

This caught Katie's immediate attention. She stared at Chief O'Dell then shifted her eyes to Brent questioningly.

Brent was shocked that this story strayed from the reservation, but he shouldn't have been. Nothing stays a secret on the waterfront for long, especially when the snake-eaters are involved.

"Nothin' much, Chief. Had a little trouble in the water, and Alika towed me back to the boat. I was kind of tired is all."

"That's not the story we're hearing," the chief interjected.

"Yeah, well, you know how things get blown out of proportion. And besides, it was months ago."

"Gotcha, Brent. We're just glad you're still with us. You need to give me the details sometime."

"Yes, sir!" Then Brent tried to revector the conversation. "How're the boys on Team TWELVE?"

Chief O'Dell smiled, took a big swig of beer, and began a detailed account of the most recent goings-on of the team.

Brent took a side-glance at Katie. Her eyes bore into Brent with an intensity that was palpable. Brent quickly took a sip a beer and watched the chief as he continued his story.

Katie sidled up to Brent and whispered in his ear, "I think you have some 'splainin' to do, big boy."

"It happened before I even knew you, and it was nothing. Honest!"

"Uh-huh!"

Brent and Katie, in the company of his snake-eater clan, chatted most of the evening away. It was late. The bar crowd was thinning when they headed home.

As soon as they walked through the door of his small apartment, Katie wrapped her arms around Brent's neck and laid a big kiss on his lips. Brent put his hands around her narrow waist, and just as he was about to up the ante, Katie whispered, "Big day, Brent. The best day I ever had, in fact. And I'm pooped." She kissed him lightly on the neck, turned, walked to her bedroom, and shut the door.

Brent stood there at a loss for words. The battle between chivalry, involving his honor as a gentleman, and human physiology, involving the most incredible sexual attraction he had ever experienced—raged within him. *I love her far more than my need for sex. I can live without it, but I'm not sure that I can live without her, or would even want to try.*

Warning Order

Saturday, 12 October 2002
Brent's apartment, Imperial Beach

Brent's phone rang at 0530 the next morning. It was Saturday.

Out of a deep sleep, Brent found his cell phone and fumbled for the right button. "Hello." The sleepiness was not quite out of his voice.

"Petty Officer Harris?"

"Yes. Who's this?"

"This is the duty officer at Group ONE. I know you're on leave, but we have a mandatory classified briefing for all hands at 0700 in the auditorium. Are you local, and will you be able to make it?"

"Yes, sir. I'll be there."

"Very well. See you here at 0700."

Brent hung up, planted his feet out on the floor, put his head in his hands, and rubbed his eyes. *What the hell is going on?*

He quietly took a short shower, dressed in fresh BDUs, and made a big pot of coffee. He poured at cup for Katie, doused it with cream and sugar, then tapped on her bedroom door. There was a peep that sounded much like, *Come in.* He carefully opened the door. "Katie?"

A squeak, "Yeah?"

"Can I come in? I have coffee."

He stepped into her room. She wore a blue Florida State T-shirt; her golden hair was in complete disarray and fell across her face in waves. Katie had gotten nutmeg brown from their days at the beach. Her skin tone only magnified those luminous applesauce-green eyes. She was stunning.

She sat up against the headboard and rubbed her eyes as Brent approached.

"It's awfully early for a Saturday. Why are you in uniform? What's up?"

"Got a call from the Group ONE duty officer. I gotta go in for a brief. Should be back by eleven."

"Wow. Wonder what's going on."

"I guess I'll find out. Figure out what you want to do today. I know you have to fly back tomorrow, so we'll do anything you want."

"Yeah, I almost forgot. How depressing. Okay, go save the world, and I'll think of somethin' fun to do."

"See ya soon." Brent bent down to kiss her. She embraced him and pulled him closer. It was a very long and impassioned kiss. Brent's conflict between honor and human drive was thoroughly reignited.

"I better go before this gets out of hand."

Katie giggled like a little girl then said, "I trust you. Get back here quick."

The drive to Group ONE was a short one but long enough for Brent to puzzle over the unusual call he took from the duty officer.

When Brent arrived at Group ONE, the parking lot was nearly full. *Strange! I've never seen these many cars here on a weekend.*

Brent hurried to the auditorium. He had no clue as to the subject matter of the brief, but the atmospherics of the collected group was one of intense sobriety. Gone were the backslapping comradery normally enjoyed by this congregation. *I guess I'll find out what all the hubbub is about in a couple of minutes,* Brent said to himself.

Thirty minutes later, the brief was over, and it wasn't good. Brent drove back to the apartment. He had lots of questions, few answers, and a heavy heart.

Brent walked through the door, tossed his cover on the table, and was charged by Katie. A big hug and a kiss were exchanged.

"Well, how was the brief? Did they make you the CMO?"

"That's CNO, Chief of Naval Operations. And no, I still have a ways to go."

"So, what was it all about?"

Brent had already made the decision not to give anything away, despite the fact that the news could and probably would change everything.

"Ah, nothing. Just a security update. Nothing to worry about. So, what do you want to do?"

"If it was nothing, why are you lookin' so glum?"

"I am? Well, you're leaving tomorrow. Who wouldn't look glum?"

"That's tomorrow. And it ain't here yet. Today we're going to have a grand old time."

"I'm up for it. What are we doing?"

"Okay, here's the plan. We're gonna go to Wild Animal Park and look at all the animals. Then we'll go to McP's where I'll buy *you* dinner. Then we'll get a bottle of the cheapest wine made and go see Alika and drink our troubles away."

Brent smiled, but it was all for show. "Sounds like a great plan. I'm up for it." *But*, Brent thought, *I don't think we'll be able to drink our troubles away. Alika and I are probably going to war, and I don't think there's enough wine, cheap or otherwise, to make my troubles go away.*

Katie's plan was executed as briefed. They spent nearly four hours at Wild Animal Park.[73]

Brent had seen a lot of wild animals in Wyoming: grizzly bear, moose, buffalo, elk, bald and golden eagles, even a mountain lion on occasion, but never had he seen the array of exotic and rare animals as was cared for at Wild Animal Park. Katie was completely taken with the beasts and wanted to be everywhere and see everything at once. Brent shared her enthusiasm, but the warning order brief kept nagging at him and sapped much of the joy from their adventure.

A bit before 5:00 p.m., they headed back to Coronado and their second event—an early dinner at McP's.

On the ride to Coronado, Katie asked, "I'm thinkin' 'bout fish and chips at McP's? How 'bout you?"

There was a penetrating silence as Brent looked straight ahead, then, "I have a better idea. How about Mexican food at Miguel's? If we go to McP's, you'll get surrounded again, and all I'll get to do is look at you and BS with the guys. Miguel's is quiet, and I'll have you all to myself."

"I thought you liked McP's because all your friends are there."

"I do, Katie, but I'd rather spend our last day with you...just you."

"Ahh, you're so sweet, Brent. Sure. We can do that."

They were seated near the back of the patio area at Miguel's and surrounded by hanging plants and foliage that looked like it was fresh from the Amazon jungle. Mexican fare was ordered and delivered in fine fashion. Katie ate heartily and excitedly. Between bites of chicken enchilada, she reviewed their day at the park. Brent smiled courteously and nodded occasionally.

When dinner was over and the bill paid, they left Miguel's and, arm and arm, walked to Brent's truck. Katie never missed a beat. She was so enthusiastic and so excited about their visit with Alika Brent figured he must be doing a spectacular job cloaking his melancholy.

They stopped at a small liquor store on Orange Avenue and bought two plastic cups and a bottle of wine that actually had a cork. Twenty minutes later, Katie had her visitor's pass, and they strolled down the pier to Alika's pen.

There was just no sneaking up on Alika. Supersensitive hearing or supernatural intuition, he seemed to know when Brent was approaching. He spy-hopped, saw Katie and Brent, and the whistles and chirping began. Katie giggled wildly.

Alika was in a tail stand at the side of the pen when they arrived. They wiggled out of their shoes and dangled their feet in the water, which gave Alika four sets of knees on which to lay his big melon.

Halfway through their bottle of wine, Katie's tone changed completely. "Brent, you've been about as much fun today as a train-wreck. You just haven't been you. So, what's going on? Was it your brief this mornin'?"

Brent set his plastic cup down, rubbed Alika's melon, then turned to look deeply into Katie's luminous green eyes.

"You're right. It's the brief this morning."

"I don't get it. What could be in a silly ol' brief to make you so sad all day?"

Another pause as Brent carefully picked his words. "The brief was secret, so I can't give you much content. I can tell you that the subject was a warning order."

"A warning order. Okay, what's that?"

"In military lingo, it's a preliminary notice of action that usually follows a crisis-action planning directive. It also starts the development of courses of action and requests a commander's estimate," Brent spewed forth this definition from rote memory.

Katie stared at Brent—puzzled. "I have no idea what you just said. Is that a bad thing?"

"Yeah, Katie. It means we're probably going to war."

"War. With who? About what? I didn't even know we were mad at anybody. When's this suppos'd to happen? Does that mean you and Alika are going?"

"Katie, I can't tell you much. The brief was highly classified, as I said. I can tell you it shouldn't be a surprise to anybody. We've been on a war footing with this country for years, and it looks like we're going to go back to the woodshed with these guys again."

This hit Katie like a freight train. She was dazed. She looked away, her mouth slightly agape; and if Brent saw correctly, her lower lip trembled slightly. Suddenly she looked down at Alika. "Now I get it. Now I know why you were such a big poo all day."

She turned back to Brent. Her eyes glistened with moisture, but she didn't cry.

Brent was sure her mind was racing around as rapidly as his, trying to grasp what all of it meant.

"Ya know," Katie began, "ten minutes ago, I was the happiest girl on earth, and suddenly everything comes tumblin' down on us. How can that happen?"

"I don't know, Katie. They've been preparing us for this possibility for months now, trying to push us to get our crap together, get our minds wrapped around this contingency. And I thought I was good to go. And then I met you and discovered how vulnerable I am. I had Alika, you, and the Navy, and I was on top of the world...and then...the warning order hit the streets, and everything changed."

Katie glanced at Brent, scanned the horizon, picked up her cup, and slammed down the remainder of her wine. "We got any more of that cheap stuff?"

"Half a bottle. You want some more."

"Fill 'er up, Brent. I think we need to git lit up tonight...our last night for a while, I'm thinkin'."

Brent filled both cups. The bottle was empty.

Brent had his arm around Katie's shoulders, and with her head resting against Brent's chest, they sat in silence, slowly sipped their wine, and stroked Alika.

Suddenly Katie took a huge hit from her cup, downing the remainder. She leaned down to Alika, kissed him on the forehead, then said, "Let's blow this place. I still have to pack."

They walked slowly back to the truck, and although there was only a scattering of light, Brent couldn't help but notice the moisture forming around her luminescent green eyes.

Rapture

Early Sunday, 13 October 2002
Imperial Beach, California

Brent helped Katie out of the truck. He gently wrapped his arm around her and eased her to the apartment, partially for stability but mostly just to feel her lithe body next to his. He held her supportively while he fumbled for his keys then tenderly lifted her and carried her through the front door and into her room. Clothes and all, he tucked her in, kissed her lightly on the forehead, took a knee, and just stared at this flawless muse and thanked God for that first day when she smiled at him. Life was good.

Brent went to his room, stripped down to his shorts and slid under the sheets. Between the morning's brief and realizing in just a few hours Katie would be heading east and, once again, out of his life, he accepted the fact that there would be no sleep this night.

As he lay there staring at a darkened ceiling, hands behind his head, and thinking of the inevitable deployment, he heard his door open. A splash of light from the living room silhouetted Katie in all her glory. She was Raphael Sanzio's Madonna di San Sisto. Exquisite!

"Brent, can I come in?"

"Yeah! Of course, Katie. You all right?"

"I'm dizzy, depressed, and I need some huggin'."

Brent scooted to one side of the bed and laid the covers back.

At 6:00 a.m., Brent rousted himself and kissed Katie tenderly on the neck and continued down her shoulder. She stirred slightly.

"Katie, we should probably get up and get you to the airport."

"What time is it?"

"Six o'clock."

"We have time. Just hold me for a few more minutes."

Which he did—happily.

On Silver Wings

Early Sunday, 13 October 2002
Imperial Beach, California

Brent and Katie raced to the airport and arrived at the Delta counter with less than an hour before Katie's flight departed. He parked at the curb and, risking an expensive parking ticket, escorted Katie to the Delta counter.

"No sad goodbyes, Brent. No tears. No promises."

"Katie," he started and was quickly admonished with Katie's now-familiar index-finger-on-the-lips routine.

Katie started to say something then quickly stopped, took a deep breath, stood tall and straight, then wrapped her arms around his neck and kissed him hard on the mouth. It was an intense, moving, and exhilarating kiss, the kind that poems are written about. When she pulled back, her eyes glistened with delight…or was it something else?

"I'll call you when I get in. Take care of yourself, Brent. And give Alika a kiss for me."

Brent was just about to say something when Katie gripped the handle of her roller bag, spun away, and headed for the Delta counter.

Brent's eyes followed her to the counter, then remembered he was illegally parked and stepped quickly for the exit.

Brent sat in the truck for a moment and stretched his hands over the top of the steering wheel and just thought. He pondered the last several days with Katie, the brief yesterday morning, and the unexpected lovemaking early this morning—just a few hours ago. He tried to make sense of all that had happened and how it would change his future, for certainly these events would change everything.

Jumbled thoughts. Mixed feelings. A kaleidoscope of emotions: passion, sorrow, excitement, uncertainty…love?

In troubled and uncertain times as these, there was only one place to go. Brent cranked up the old Ford and headed to Foxtrot.

CHAPTER 16

DEPORD

Man has always assumed that he was more intelligent than dolphins because he had achieved so much...the wheel, New York, wars, and so on...while all the dolphins had ever done was muck about in the water having a good time. But conversely, the dolphins had always believed that they were far more intelligent than man...for precisely the same reason.

—Douglas Adams

Spinning Up

Friday, 24 January 2003
Foxtrot Platoon, Pier 40, Sub Base, Point Loma, California

There's nothing like a hard copy SECRET warning order message issued by the Chairman of the Joint Chiefs of Staff to get everybody's attention. In effect, the warning order said, "Hey, y'all, we're thinking about going over the other side of the world and kick some raghead ass. Let's all get together and figure out how to do that. And, by the by, come up with a couple of different courses of action we should consider."

And while the warning order, the precursor for several follow-on actions, was a four-alarm fire-in-a-match-factory attention-getter, it was the deployment order, or DEPORD, that gave everybody wearing the uniform that "come to Jesus" moment. That moment had varied effects on different people.

There are generally three groups in the military faced with deployment to some far-off theater of conflict. The first group is made up of those who refute the obvious, those who choose to ignore the implications and the facts. They hope that, at some point, before things get totally crazy, the hand of God would crash through the heavens, squash the bad guys, and make all things right again.

The second group consists of those who joined the military for the thrill of it. The glory hounds who imagine the gallantry, prestige, and the grandeur of war. Few in this group have ever fired a shot in anger and, therefore, are unaware of the horrible cost of combat—the physical, psychological, and spiritual toll it exacts. This toll is not just laid upon those brave hearts who go into the hell of a battlefield but also on the families, loved ones, and close friends.

The third group contains the professionals. Those who have joined the ranks to fulfill a commitment, a patriotic calling to do *the* job. These are the pros who would much rather stay at home with their family, loved ones, and friends rather than travel to some rotting third world country and put their lives on the line. But they do it willingly, with humility and reverence for their country and because their teammates need them. Most of those in this third group have been in the crucible of battle, tasted cordite, seen the suffering and loss of a close friend, and yet they return to the killing fields and do their job without protest. This was the group of professionals—the warriors—to which Brent was bonded.

Regardless of the group, all anxiously awaited word of a possible deployment order.

It was not long in coming.

Deployment Order

Thursday, 20 February 2003
Foxtrot Platoon, Pier 40, Sub Base, Point Loma, California

By early 2003, the United Nations levied a number of demands upon Saddam Husain in an attempt to avoid another costly war in the Gulf and the loss of life that would accompany it. Yet despite the thrashing he received by the coalition of forces in the first Gulf War, Saddam persistently displayed an enormous parallax error: there was a huge abyss between the reality of the unfolding situation and the illusion seen by Saddam.

The strategists, planners, and combatant commanders knew that he was not a madman, not a lunatic. He was a calculating, petulant dictator who was willing to sacrifice his military, his country, and his people in a vain and irrational roll of the dice to save himself and what was left of his dignity.

The US and the UN levied four primary demands with which Saddam had to comply: cease-fire on UN forces (primarily US and British military aircraft), end program research and development of weapons of mass destruction, terminate the massive and brutal genocide of his own people, and the immediate compliance with all UNSC (United Nations Security Council) sanctions.

If all conditions were not met, US coalition forces would engage the Iraqi military in a second Gulf War. This time it would be different, however. This time, one of the primary objectives for the operation was *regime change*. This time, Saddam would lose his country and, most probably, his life.

Owing to the dynamic nature of the atmospherics and politics in the Mideast, the deployment order (DEPORD), with appropriate addendums for EOD Group ONE, was released several weeks following the warning order. The DEPORD provided an updated list of units, assignments, and projected deployment dates in accordance with the Time Phased Force Deployment Data (TPFDD) for OPLAN 1003—Operation Iraqi Freedom (OIF). This was a clarion call to arms. It had the effect of shaking the lives of all those wearing the uniform.

The DEPORD laid out a number of details of the operations plan, or war plan. Chief among them was the command and control structure of the various task organizations. The DEPORD for Task Force 55, the mine countermeasures (MCM) command, identified RADM Barry Costello[74] as the operational commander. Assigned to him in supporting roles was an array of world-class mine hunters and Fleet Force Protection units that would be the envy of any MCM commander.

Special Clearance Team ONE, would lead tailored elements from all component commands under EOD Group ONE. EOD divers, SEALS, and Marine recon divers formed the dive teams. SWCC platoons would man the RHIBs and support boats while Unmanned Underwater Vehicle platoon (UUV) would operate the REMUS systems.

Also joining the effort was Fleet Diving Unit 3 from the United Kingdom and a clearance dive team from Australia. Both units would assist in conducting deep- and shallow-water mine countermeasure operations to clear Umm Qasr harbor, a small port facility on the southeastern end of Iraq.

On the Foxtrot deployment list, Lieutenant Heinrichs and Master Chief Murphy would lead the team. A handful of administrative types would make up the headquarters staff, but the core of the Foxtrot Platoon, the operators, included Chief Petty Officer Engineman Malakai Olopoto, who was teamed with a twenty-one-year-old Atlantic bottlenose dolphin named Kekoa; Special Operations (SEAL) Chief John Sebastian and his dolphin Thor; Petty Officer Rick Turner with Kona; Brent and Alika; and several other teams, totaling nine mine-hunting dolphins.[75] Caring for them were eighteen handlers, biotechs, and medical personnel. In all, about one hundred and twenty personnel deployed to form the task element from NSCT-1.

Considerable thought went into selecting the teams for their combat experience, versatility, leadership, composure under fire, and mission competency. It was not a stretch of the imagination to understand why Brent and Alika were on the list.

As anxious as Brent was about the prospects of going to war with a bottlenose dolphin as his partner, when Brent surveyed the deployment list, he was at once relieved. He would be traveling with bad company, the dream team, a phalanx of warriors and professionals—unquestionably the best group of mine hunters ever assembled.

NSCT-1 and the supporting units would deploy, and due to the nature of their mission—detection and elimination of sea mines—they would be among the first to arrive in theater.

Stressing the Heartstrings

Friday, 21 February 2003
Foxtrot Platoon, Point Loma Naval Base, California

For Brent and Katie, their affair had become a bit brittle. It had been many weeks since they had last seen each other, and though during those times they spoke on the phone several times a week, it just wasn't the same.

Brent hadn't lost one bit of interest in Katie. His heart throbbed for her. His primary concern was that she would lose interest in him. And although he had an ace in the hole in the form of an Atlantic bottlenose dolphin, he didn't pin all his hopes that it was enough to perpetuate a lasting future together.

It was impossible to get a read on Katie's heart. On the phone, she always seemed genuinely excited and interested in what he and Alika had been doing, but he didn't know if that was her natural good-natured sweetness, or she really had strong affections for him.

Emotions ran high as Christmas approached. One long phone conversation in early December brought home the fact that their relationship was strained. Brent broached the topic he'd been wrestling with for the past two weeks and, finally, in a fit of boldness, asked Katie if she could visit him or if he could make the trip out to her over the holidays. Brent remembered the long edgy silence on the end of the phone, and he knew at that moment something had changed.

Katie gently explained that the idea just wouldn't work. School, work, family demands, and personal business left her with no free time on her schedule. It was this "personal business" that captured Brent's imagination and festered his concern. *What kind of personal business? A new boyfriend, an old boyfriend, Dr. Dubois?*

Unfortunately, Brent was programmed with a most active imagination at birth. It had served him well through life, but it had a serious drawback. The more he thought about distressing things, the worse he imagined them to be. His relationship with Katie was now in doubt and at the mercy of that overactive imagination.

To counter that, Brent was also gifted with a remarkable ability to compartmentalize. Usually, the mental gymnastics of putting bothersome things in a box, taping it up, and storing it in the back of a seldom-used shelf worked wonderfully. But not always.

Trying to break into Katie's most guarded secrets represented a perennial conundrum for Brent. There were two diversions, however, that kept Brent from fretting more over his relationship with Katie—Alika and the incredible deployment preparation schedule.

Preparation and Staging

Monday, 24 February 2003
Foxtrot Platoon, Point Loma Naval Base, California

Although few knew for sure the date of the deployment, Navy Special Clearance Team ONE leadership were betting on mid to late March. They had but a few weeks to organize their command structure, pack up all the equipment, deploy into theater, and in-chop to Task Group 55.4 under Central Command.

From the get-go, it was a frenetic effort. All the air transport carriers[76] had to be inspected and repaired. The dolphin's harnesses and locating equipment were tested, and if not in working order, were repaired or replaced with new. The deploying animals underwent complete physicals, shots, and a panel of other tests.

The heavy equipment, tools, and support equipment were inventoried, packed, and secured on large pallets for easier transportation and loading on the transport aircraft. The RHIB's engines and transmissions were run through overhauls and modified for operation in the Persian Gulf.

The tasks, schools, and projects they were scheduled for prior to the deployment were utterly staggering: small-arms refresher training, schools and planning meetings, medical requirements including a battery of shots and vaccinations, field-gear issue, physical training, open-water survival training, refresher survival, evasion, resistance escape (SERE) course, first aid training, custom and language indoctrination, security reviews, fitting for MOPP gear, and a long list of administrative requirements to include an update of their personnel records and a review of their wills.

New camouflage uniforms and boots were issued, which created something of a stir. Foxtrot personnel took great pride in their less-formal T-shirts, khaki shorts, and deck shoes. That said, their beloved "uniforms" were anything but and would aid in blending in with the surrounding terrain not at all. Everybody was issued and happily wore their camo gear.

But the single-most sobering activity, the event that brought full clarity to the reality that they were headed to the far ends of the earth to bring death and destruction to a sworn enemy of the United States and, in fact, most of the free world, was the day personal weapons were issued. Brent and all the personnel on the "go" list were issued a Beretta M9, 9mm pistol with five magazines and a Colt M4 .223-caliber carbine with ten magazines.

It was a sobering day. Now there was no one still clinging to the fragile hope that this was somehow a big misunderstanding or another Navy drill. They were headed for war.

The date of the flight over remained something of a mystery, and still only a few knew where they were going or what the mission specifics were. That is, until Wednesday, 5 March.

The "Go" Brief

Wednesday, 5 March 2003
Foxtrot Platoon, Pier 40, Sub Base, Point Loma, California

"Good morning, gentlemen," Lieutenant Heinrichs addressed the gathering of Foxtrot Platoon handlers, trainers, vets, and administrative personnel. "Go ahead and charge your coffee cups and then grab yourself a seat. We need to get this show on the road."

Except for a few chairs scraping the deck, the room got deathly quiet. Brent stood near the back of the room next to Chief Olopoto.

"I'm going to turn this brief over to EOD Group ONE's lead planner, Commander Monty Kendrick. I remind you, this brief is classified SECRET. There is going to be a great temptation to let your family in on our little secret, blurt out our destination, or mutter important dates. Your life and the lives of your team are at stake here. Zip lip is the word of the day. Commander Kendrick, the stage is yours, sir."

"Greetings, team! As you probably surmised from the pack-up activity, the message traffic, and the hectic meetings, this is no drill. Our brief this morning will give you the latest poop on four pieces of information: where we're going, what we're doing, who we'll be joined with, and when all this is going to happen. And as Lieutenant Heinrichs said, this is classified SECRET. First slide please.

"There is a deep waterway on the southeastern side of Iraq. It leads to Iraq's only deep-water port—Umm Qasr. You probably never heard of it. I never did until this tasking came down from on high. It's on the western edge of the al-Faw Peninsula where the Shatt al-Arab waterway flows into the Persian Gulf just across the border from Kuwait. It's strategically significant because we're going to use it to off-load war material, food, medicine, and other humanitarian relief goods."

The commander looked up from his notes and across the room to let the news settle in.

"Slide two please. Our intelligence assessment indicates that the Iraqis have laid mines—tethered, bottom, and floating mines—in the waterway and at the port. I don't need to remind the old-timers the havoc that rained on us when they crippled the amphibious ship *Tripoli* and the missile cruiser *Princeton* in 1991. We'll have better intel on the number and types of mines later, but you can guess that, in keeping with the Iraqi military mentality, when it comes to destruction and death—money is no object. So, our job is to clear the mines, make the Khawr Abd Allah waterway and the Umm Qasr Port safe for coalition cargo ships, and maintain security in that region.

"Slide three. Now, we're not doing this alone. We'll be joining up with a number of elements to make sure this op is successful and everybody comes home in one piece. The Marine Force Recon boys and assessments from the intel weenies suggest that there will be a fairly large contingent of Iraqi military in the town and around the port of Umm Qasr. We hope they scurry on home when they see the concentration of forces we plan on putting ashore, but their perseverance in combat is an unknown. Should they actually stick around to fight, they'll be knocking heads with some really bad guys. The Royal Marines of the British Third Commando Brigade augmented by our Marines from the Fifteenth Marine Expedition Unit and the Polish GROM[77] force will spearhead the assault. We'll also have close air support provided by Marine Harriers and on-call naval gunfire support courtesy of HMAS *Anzac* and HMS *Marlborough*.

"The water temp in the north part of the Arabian Sea this time of year should be in the low sixties. That's only a few degrees warmer than the water here. You guys, Foxtrot Platoon, have already built your deployment list. You'll be initially embarked aboard the USS *Gunston Hall*, LSD-44, moored at Manama Harbor in Bahrain. It's an amphibious dock-landing ship with a well deck for landing craft. For those that don't know, it's a combination amphibious assault ship, troopship, helo platform, and has a medical detachment aboard. It's been modified to accommodate your dolphins and all your support equipment. It's not a cruise ship, but word is, it'll have everything on board you'll need to do your job. As soon as they can, they'll move north and helo you, your animals, and your gear into Umm Qasr. There, you'll be housed in several warehouses right on the pier.

"Your team, Lieutenant, will be part of act one—part of the first operations of OIF. If this thing goes off as advertised, your team will make history as the very first marine mammal team to take part in mine-hunting operations in an active combat zone. And *no*, we're not going to issue your dolphins M16s and have them storm the beaches. We have Marines for that. They're harder to train but a lot cheaper."

The humor was not lost on the audience, but it was the previous statement, the one concerning the first to take their animals into a combat zone, that caused everyone to pause and take note. No one had even considered the historical significance of the upcoming operations. And that said, it would only mean something to those who survived the action.

"Your MK 7 dolphins will be supported by our dive platoon composed of EOD, SEAL, and Marine Recon divers. You'll be glad to know that we'll also have several MK 6 sea lions and a couple of dolphins in the area for additional force protection and swimmer security. Included in the MK 6 team is Scott Sanders with Zeus, and Roger Birosh with Bruiser. And God help the raghead bastard who's found swimming in water patrolled by Bruiser. All we'll find is a bunch of broken bones held together by a bag of skin."

The humor injected by the commander had the assembly roaring. Everyone was familiar with Roger and his assassin Bruiser.

When the laughter died down, Chief Sebastian, one of the few snake-eaters in the audience, raised his hand. When the commander called on him, he asked, "Sir, you said there were four points you were going to brief us on. *When* are we going?"

Commander Kendrick looked down at his notes, cleared his throat, and took on a sobering sense of seriousness. This would not be easy news to pass.

"Saturday."

Ears popped to adjust to the reduced air pressure in the room as oxygen was sucked into lungs of about everyone.

"Eight March. Three days from now. You'll be loading up on three C-5 Galaxies and heading east."

There were many looks around the room and side-glances with inquisitive eyes, wondering if they really heard the commander right. *Saturday?*

"Leadership was very concerned about OPSEC[78] and didn't want to put the word out any sooner. Can't blame them. This is serious stuff. You'll depart on Saturday morning and arrive at Bahrain airport around eleven on Monday, the tenth of March. You'll be chopped into Task Group 55.4 in a supporting role under Commander, Mine Countermeasure Squadron THREE.

"One more point, and I know I don't need to mention it to this august group of warriors, but for the sake of clarification, I'll say it anyway. You handlers are a part of a two-member team. You are the supporting element. Your dolphin is the operational element. We can't do our job, we can't complete this mission, unless your system—that's you and your animal—are intact and functioning at peak. So take care of each other. Watch over your brothers and come back alive. Are there any questions?" Commander Kendrick looked soberly around the room, his eyes casting a *no-bullshit* message.

There were no questions.

"One more thing…GO, DOLPHINS!"

At this, the Foxtrot team opened up and yelled, "Go, dolphins!" at the top of their lungs.

It was this type of jovial insertion that was welcomed at high-tension gatherings, and in this case, it was well received.

Breaking the News

Wednesday, 5 March 2003
Foxtrot Platoon, Pier 40, Sub Base, Point Loma, California

It was Brent's second attempt to call Katie. His hands were so uncooperative he aborted the first try. He didn't know if his nervousness was caused by the brief earlier in the morning or the anticipation of talking to Katie. Maybe it was a bit of both.

"Hello," Katie answered on the third ring. Her voice was honey-coated in a Southern drawl that, no matter how often Brent spoke with her, sent him head over teakettle.

"Hey, Katie, it's Brent. How are you?"

"Oh gosh, Brent. I was hopin' you'd call. And a better question is, how are you? And how's Alika?"

"We're both doing pretty good, but we miss you a lot."

"And I miss you guys too. Been listening to the news, and it sounds like things are getting real serious. Have you heard anything about all the hoopla over in Iraq? Sounds like the UN's losing patience."

"I have, Katie. We just had another brief, and that's what I called about."

Brent expected a barrage of questions from Katie and was surprised when she didn't follow up with one. In fact, there was utter silence from her end.

"Ah…Katie, it looks like we're headed to the Mideast. Alika, Master Chief Murphy, and Kahuna are all on the 'go' list, and I wanted—"

"Wait a second. You mean you and Alika are going over there?"

"Yeah, Katie. That's what I was trying to tell you. We're heading out, and pretty soon."

This started a stream of questions from Katie he expected seconds earlier.

"You better not be joshin' me, Brent. This ain't funny!"

"I wouldn't do that to you, Katie. This is serious stuff."

"Okay…when are you leaving? Where are you going, and when're you coming home?"

"I can't tell you much. They warned us that all that information is pretty highly classified. I can tell you we're leaving soon, and we're going to the area you probably heard about in the news."

"I don't get it, Brent. You and Alika just find ol' mines and stuff. What does this have to do with you and Alika? I mean, you're not going over there to shoot anybody, are you?"

"No, we're not going over to shoot anybody. We're going over to do our job. Remember, we hunt and clear mines, and I guess they're going to need us to do just that."

"Hunt sea mines…in a desert? Well, that's just crazy talk, Brent. And what's Alika going to do while you're out stompin' around in the sand?"

"Iraq has a very small coastline and a deepwater port. That's where we're going."

Brent just realized he disclosed classified information. He had no intention of doing that. Katie just had this way of getting information out of him. Just proves a point, he was pretty helpless and malleable around Katie.

"And, Katie, don't breathe a word of what we were just talking about. It's classified."

"Well, you haven't really told me anything of importance, or actually answered any of my questions."

"And I can't, Katie. I'm sorry."

For the next ten minutes, they talked about small stuff and purposely avoided any more discussion about the deployment. Brent tried to wrap things up. "Katie, I have to go. Things are pretty crazy here."

"Brent, I don't want you to go. I need to talk some more. I just feel so…so…sad!"

"Katie, I gotta go. I'll call you back, and we can talk tonight."

"Brent, I feel all hollow inside. Now I have two boys to worry about. This is a really crappy feeling. I just don't know how wives can do this. I only saw you twice, and now you and Alika are going to some far-off place, and I feel like hammered dog doo."

"I feel terrible too, Katie. And for the record, I didn't volunteer for this. Alika and I were picked to go."

"Knowing you didn't volunteer to go over doesn't make me feel any better, Mr. Harris. You and Alika are going, and I guess I gotta get used to it. But I really don't like this feeling…at all!"

Again, a painful silence on the phone. Brent clumsily searched for soothing words to console Katie, but all he came up with was, "You okay, Katie?"

"No, I'm not okay, Brent. You're going halfway around the world where all the bad guys live, and you're taking my dolphin with you. No, I'm not okay!"

"Katie, we're going to be okay. We're going to be surrounded by Marines and SEALs and other special ops guys. We'll get in there, do our job, and come home. No issues!"

"Brent...I've been doing a lot of thinking, and I'm having trouble dealing with this right now. How do spouses and kids and girlfriends cope with this kind of separation? I just don't know how to handle this kind of...a life. And I'm not sure I even want to."

"I...ah...don't know what to say, Katie. This is my job. I don't want to go either, but it's what Alika and I have been trained to do. We're trying to help save lives and win a war against a real bad man."

"Yeah, I got all that. I just don't understand with the millions of people in this country, why it has to be you and my dolphin. Why don't they send some of those idiot politicians over there to fight? Maybe we wouldn't get into so many wars if they had to do the fighting. It's just not fair, Brent."

"Life sometimes isn't fair, Katie, but it's what we're stuck with."

"Any chance I can see you and Alika before you go, if only for a day or so?"

"No time, Katie. We're outta here soon."

There was a chilly pause in the conversation that was palpable.

"Okay, Brent, call me tonight. And take care of Alika and yourself, okay?"

"Sure, Katie. I'll do my best!"

There was a *click* and then silence. "Goodbye, Katie."

Brent called Katie that evening. The discussion was short, but Katie's disposition had not improved.

"Katie, me again. You okay?"

"Look, Brent, we'll put this...this...whatever this relationship is on hold until you come back. I've got school and work and all types of other pressures, and I don't want to have to worry about you and Alika on top of all that. Okay?"

Brent could hear the sound of Katie sniffling. That, in combination with her last words, made him feel like he just took a kick in the gut from a big Morgan stallion.

"Okay, Katie."

"Brent…take care of yourself and Alika, and don't do nuthin' heroic or stupid. I want you both back in one piece."

The line went dead, and Brent just stood there, thinking. *Well, that's that, I guess. I'm too damned busy and have too much stuff to do to let this conversation get the best of me.* He turned and jogged to Alika's pen.

There was much to do and only three days to get everything done.

Climbing to Flight Level 230

Saturday, 8 March 2003
Aboard a C-5 en route to NAS Rota Spain and Bahrain

Early Saturday morning, all hands from the Foxtrot Platoon and dozens of NSCT-1 personnel were completing the final load on three leviathan C-5 Galaxies. Pallets were secured to hard points on the deck of the cargo area, and personal gear was secured along the bulkheads. The last to load were the animals in their ATCs.

Most of the old-hand dolphins had made long trips in aircraft before, but the new kids on the block shared a mix of enthusiasm for the adventure blended with a big dose of anxiety.

One by one, the Galaxies took the runway and throttled up a few minutes after 9:00 a.m., Saturday, the eighth of March. The third C-5 carrying Foxtrot Platoon began its takeoff roll and, owing to the high payload and light wind, used most of the eight-thousand feet of runway before it staggered into the air. It was a fifteen-hour flight from NAS North Island to Bahrain airport with one refueling stop at NAS Rota Spain.

Gear up and all systems functioning properly, an Air Force major in the left seat obtained clearance to flight level 230, almost four miles above the earth, and put the GPS heading indicator on the nose.

The dolphins and sea lions were relaxed and calm in their repose, safe and secure in their ATCs. And why wouldn't they be with a group of handlers, veterinarians, and biotechs seeing to their every need?

Brent threw his pack into the seat next to Kahuna but for most of the trip, he hovered over Alika's ATC. Alika was one of those new kids. He'd never made a trip of this duration before, but as long as he could see Brent, he was at ease.

Fifteen hours later, a few minutes before 10:00 a.m., the Galaxy touched down at Bahrain International Airport. The plane taxied to a remote site for offload. If anyone thought for a second they weren't suddenly in a combat zone, the sight of the armed-up HUMVEEs and Air Force security personnel forming a protective perimeter would have changed their mind very quickly.

No sooner had they landed than Lieutenant Heinrichs organized his team into task units. Master Chief Murphy was to coordinate the offload, Chief Sebastian would direct transportation, Major "Doc" Hamilton would oversee the offload of the animals, and Chief Olopoto would check in with the USS *Gunston Hall*, now pier side at Manama, Bahrain. He would join with the ship's coordinator, survey the ship, and secure space assignments.

Lieutenant Heinrichs grabbed one of his junior officers, gathered their gear, and headed to the coalition headquarters to check in and get a quick SITREP. The mammals, men, and all their equipment would be trucked to the *Gunston Hall* and loaded aboard.

Two hours later, NSCT-1 and all attached personnel to include the Foxtrot Platoon detachment assembled in the well deck of the USS *Gunston Hall*. Five dolphin pools, large circular pools that would become the dolphins' homes, were still being erected and filled with water. The "Doc" had determined that salt had to be added to get the correct salinity.

Each of Lieutenant Heinrichs's senior petty officers reported their progress. He was more than satisfied with the work they'd accomplished and indeed proud of his men, especially knowing no one had much sleep for the last several days. He gathered a handful of his people together. "Okay, gang, great job. Remember to set your watches. It's 1530 in this time zone. So here's the plan—get your animals secured on board the *Gunston Hall*. Doc Hamilton, you supervise that. Also, let's get a quick medical assessment by their handlers and get them fed."

"Got it ell-tee," the Doc responded.

"When that's complete, everybody secure your gear in your assigned quarters. Master Chief…"

"Yo!"

"Please get with the stewards and see if they can get our guys an early dinner. I want them to hit the sack as soon as they can so we are fresh as daisies tomorrow morning."

"Hooyah!"

"Tomorrow," Heinrichs continued, "we're going to start putting our boats and equipment together. We'll give our dolphins a day to get acclimated. We're going to have an intel assessment and a rules-of-engagement brief tomorrow midmorning. The day after, we'll start running some recce missions to get oriented with the operating environment and stand by for tasking. I remind you, war has not been declared, but don't for a second assume you're in a safe zone. They just don't exist over here. These guys are sneaky bastards, and *do not* follow the Queensberry rules. If you go off the ship, take your weapon, make sure you have a round in the pipe, and wear your body armor.

"Any questions?"

There were none. The exhaustion was taking its toll.

With the brief complete, Foxtrot Platoon personnel made final checks on their animals, stowed their gear, and headed for the mess decks prior to securing in their assigned bunks.

Brent checked on Alika, carried his gear to his bunk, and then found a quiet nook aboard the ship from which to call Katie. He was tired—no, he was exhausted. He tried to figure out the time difference between Iraq and Florida. After several failed calculations, his mark 1, mod 0 BB counter was just not hitting on all cylinders. He gave up and just called Katie. The time zones be damned!

The call ended on a positive note. Katie sounded much more in control, much less concerned, and she didn't ask a bunch of questions he couldn't answer. And as luck would have it, the time worked out. It was 1:15 p.m. Katie's time and 10:15 p.m. Brent's time.

It was at this time it occurred to Brent that, tangled in all the tasks and short-fused projects as he was, he still hadn't eaten.

Time for chow and the rack, Brent thought. *Tomorrow is going to be a butt-kicker and full of challenges.*

CHAPTER 17

RIDING TO THE
SOUNDS OF GUNFIRE

*If in shark infested waters, don't assume the fin
coming toward you is a dolphin.*

—Mary Russel

Recce Runs

Monday, 10 March 2003
Aboard USS Gunston Hall, Manama Harbor, Bahrain

The challenges and knee-knockers were in abundance, and
some seemed insurmountable. But in the end, solid leadership, innovation, team spirit, and a profusion of energy won the day. In a matter of several days, NSCT-1 had reasonable accommodations aboard
USS *Gunston Hall*, decent comm networks; and most important, the
mammals were safe, in good health, comfortable, and in fact, most
were eager to explore their new surroundings.

The first swimming sessions for the dolphins began on
Wednesday, 12 March. The *Gunston Hall* pulled out of Bahrain and

sailed north up the North Arabian Gulf. When the ship found suitable deepwater and no Iraqi threat, the handlers loaded their dolphins in the RHIBs and launched them from the stern gate.

These first outings were designed in equal measure for exercise, to acclimatize them to the new environment, become orientated with some of the underwater reference points, and allow them to do what dolphins do best—grab ass.

Brent and Alika were teamed up with Kahuna and Kekoa for an afternoon mission. Ordinarily two dolphins wouldn't occupy the same RHIB, but these were not ordinary times and boats were scarce. Their RHIB was jury rigged to bring aboard both Alika and Kekoa. The two dolphins had worked together for some time. As was their habit as savvy MK 7 dolphins, as soon as Alika and Kekoa were released into the water, they ran a large reconnaissance circle together with their echolocation systems pinging at full tilt. They bonded like brothers and had an unusual nexus to each other. When they swam, jumped, or maneuvered together, it was as if the moves were pre-scripted, choreographed. It was a delight just to watch them in action.

Kekoa was twenty-one years old, quite a bit older and more experienced than Alika, but he often let Alika take lead on many outings. Perhaps that was the dolphin's way of allowing the youngsters to take on greater roles and responsibilities. After launching Alika and Kekoa into their new environment, getting them both back aboard the RHIB was, at times, a bit of a chore. They were so interested in their new surroundings—the different terrain, the exciting new sounds, new and unusual sea inhabitants. They showed little interest in rushing to get back in the RHIB. If there was anything Brent needed to learn from his Hawaiian teammate, it was patience.

Brent leaned against the port sponson and huffed a few times in between hand slaps against the side of the RHIB.

"Brent...," Kahuna said as he leaned against the starboard sponson and soaked up the sun, give them a few minutes. They're just doing what nature programmed them to do, exploring their environment and having some fun. They'll be back before you know it."

"Easy for you to say, Chief. I've never had Alika outside of San Diego. I don't know if he'll decide just to take off on his own. You know, maybe go look for his own little wahine nani."

"You should know by now, Brent, you are his family, and they never leave their family. He'll be back in a while. Just hang loose."

Brent emitted another impatient grunt then, recognizing the wisdom of Kahuna's words, sat down on the bait bucket and leaned against the port sponson.

"Kahuna, what do you think it'll be like? What exactly are we going to do?"

Kahuna glanced at Brent for a moment then shifted his vision to the sky and surrounding terrain.

"I think it's going to be like the lieutenant said it would be. We're going to sail up the Khawr Abd Allah waterway after HM-14 starts their minesweeping and then let us do our job in and around Umm Qasr. Piece of cake, shipmate."

"Think there'll be any shooting?"

"I think there'll be lots of shooting. That's what the Marines, the Brit Commando unit and the Polish Spec Forces are here for. But the important thing to remember is that most of the fire is going to be outbound, not in bound."

"Sometimes, Kahuna, I think the worst part about a firefight is the waiting. When things get going, everything calms down. Everything becomes clearer to me, but it's the time before the shooting starts that always gets me jumpy."

"I know the feeling, Brent, but it's wasted energy. We're either going to live through this or be killed. If you get killed, we'll go to our fathers and our family already in heaven. And if we live, we'll either be just fine, or we'll be injured. It's the injury thing that sometimes bothers me. There are a whole lot of physical casualties that trouble me a whole lot more than dying, so I just don't think about it. Sometimes I live in the beauty of the moment and try to think about all the good things in life, like dolphins. And I'm happy."

"Gezzo. That's heavy. I gotta hang around you more often, Kahuna. You're chicken soup for the soul."

Kahuna smiled then straightened up and looked well beyond Brent. "Looks like our boys are coming back from their recce mission."

Brent stood and looked across the glistening water just in time to see two magnificent dolphins spring from the sea in unison, arc high in the air, and return to the water with barely a splash. *How do they do that?* Brent wondered.

Kahuna fired up the engine, and Brent beached the two boys in their tri mats. He was about to haul in the anchor when he looked more closely at the two big mammals. They both had their customary permanent smiles, but he noted they were today more pronounced, more prominent. *They live for the beauty of the moment,* Brent pondered. *They have no idea what tomorrow will bring. Lucky them.*

Brent pulled the anchor up. Kahuna dropped the transmissions into gear and spun the helm to head north up the Khawr Abd Allah waterway. For the next two hours, aided by their charts, compass, and GPS, they surveyed the coastal waterway, becoming familiar with the traditional landmarks and making note of a few prominent visual reference points that would aid in their navigation efforts. Alika and Kekoa were launched twice more during this first orientation sortie. They stayed fairly close to the boat and, this time, came quickly when called.

In the early afternoon with the temperatures in the midsixties, Kahuna came about, headed south, back to the *Gunston Hall,* and for now, home.

"Foxtrot base. Foxtrot base. Foxtrot 5-Mike," Kahuna transmitted on the radio.

"Foxtrot 5-Mike, go."

"Foxtrot 5 Mike with two MK 7s is returning to base. Kahuna and Brent are inbound with ETA of 1530. All systems up."

"Kahuna, base, bring her on in, but keep Alika and Kekoa on board. The doc wants to check them out before they go in their pools. He's looking for any parasites, infections, and stress."

"Copy. See you in a few," Kahuna signed off.

"Pretty standard stuff on these deployments," Kahuna said to Brent.

"Kahuna, you ever get the feeling that our dolphins are treated better than we are?"

"Yeah, but that's the way it should be. They can't tell their docs when they're not feeling well. We can. And besides, like it or not, they're the critical piece of the machinery in this business. They do all the important stuff."

"No question in my mind," Brent agreed.

The Foxtrot team ran more orientation and reconnaissance sorties in the several days that followed, each time venturing out a bit farther up the Shatt al-Arab waterway and closer to the Umm Qasr port. The port, although quiet at this time, was still reported to be held by a small company-sized combat unit of about 150 personnel and composed of general-purpose ground forces backed up by a handful of Republican Guard troops.

As the days of March continued to count down, everyone sensed the tension in the air—war was just days away.

Despite the talks of compliance and peace, the endless negotiations of the UN, and the patience and fortitude of the weapons inspectors, Saddam Hussein continued to goad and provoke the coalition. If he fully understood that this time one of the primary objectives of the looming confrontation was regime change, it didn't seem to bother him. This time, however, there would be no hole small enough into which he might slither.

The *Gunston Hall* returned to Bahrain. The military buildup at the Manama port and international airport continued unabated. All manner of hardware, heavy equipment, supplies, medical gear, food, water, and weaponry, ammo, and fuel were off-loaded in what seemed to be a steady stream. Brent and most others had never seen such a huge supply base. There seemed to be no end to the logistics tail. At all hours of the day and night, trucks rolled in, emptied their load, and departed for another resupply run.

On the twentieth of March, USS *Gunston Hall* departed the port at Manama. She proceeded up the Khawr Abd Allah waterway and into the port of Umm Qasr. En route to the port, all the dolphins and most of the personnel were helo'd off the ship and deposited pier side. Temporary housing facilities were set up in two adjacent warehouses, just yards from the pier at which the *Gunston Hall* would birth.

Foxtrot Platoon went to work immediately, first setting their own security perimeter and then erecting the dolphin pools and all the facilities necessary for their mine-hunting operations. After security was set, priority one was to devise a system to lift the dolphins from their pools and place them in their RHIBs, at times nine feet below the edge of the pier due to the large tidal changes. An abandoned forklift—heavily modified, hot-wired, and rigged with a sturdy sling—was just the thing to move the dolphins from their pools to the boats and back again.

Tensions ran high. And although there seemed to be no current interest in Foxtrot Platoon by Iraqi forces, everyone wore body armor and carried their weapons—locked and loaded.

The Battle for Umm Qasr

Thursday, 20 March 2016
Umm Qasr, Iraq

It was a few minutes past midnight, Friday, the 21st of March 2003. A slight breeze came whispering from the southwest and a waning gibbous moon just two days past full was high overhead, providing good illumination of the terrain and the enemy troop emplacements down range.

A young Marine staff sergeant sat cocooned in his MA1A Abrams main battle tank and glanced at his watch. He'd verified they had weapons-release authority, ensured there were no blue forces in the frag area, confirmed the elevation and windage calculations, triple-checked the load and fuse, and reviewed the target coordinates half a dozen times. He was absolutely sure that the Iraqi soldiers manning an artillery piece eighty-five hundred yards distant were now just seconds away from receiving their seventy-two virgins. The sergeant was only too happy to facilitate the rendezvous.

With only seconds to go, the sergeant checked the sweep secondhand of his watch, then calmly keyed the ICS and said to his gunner, "Send it!"

The 120 mm smooth-bore cannon roared, belched fire, recoiled violently, and spat an antipersonnel round true on course. The battle for Umm Qasr had begun.

About the same time, US and British airpower began the *shock-and-awe* bombing campaign, the US Third Infantry Division started its drive north through the Arabian Desert headed for Baghdad, the First Marine Expeditionary Force pushed easterly along Highway 1, and coalition forces conducted a midnight amphibious assault to secure the oil fields on the al-Faw Peninsula.

The Battle of Umm Qasr was a synchronized and unified effort to overwhelm over one hundred Iraq Republican Guards and regular infantry soldiers dug in at the port city. The Fifteenth Marine Expeditionary Unit troops spearheaded an attack as part of the British Third Commando Brigade of the Royal Marines,[79] reinforced by Polish GROM special forces troops, and backed up by the heavy ordnance from HMAS *Anzac* and HMS *Marlborough*. They had taken station on the Khawr Abd Allah waterway seven miles from Iraqi-held territory and provided indirect naval gunfire support. To add to the carnage, British Harrier AV-8 jets provided close air support.

The battle raged for five days, but even before Umm Qasr was declared secure, units under Task Group 55.4, Commander Mine Countermeasure Squadron THREE, began mine-hunting operations.

HMS *Bangor* and HMS *Sandown*, led by HM14's monstrous MH-53Es, made sweeps from the confluence of the north end of the Persian Gulf and the Khawr Abd Allah waterway north to the point where the waterway made a left-hand dogleg turn to the west. The responsibility for the remaining three miles into the port of Umm Qasr belonged to EOD Group ONE's unmanned sonar undersea vehicles, REMUS,[80] and Foxtrot Platoon's MK 7 dolphins.

The REMUS systems surveyed and mapped the bottom terrain, searched for bottom and moored mines, and charted suspicious objects on the seafloor. The MK 7 dolphins worked in grids, primarily in the shallow waters where the unmanned vehicle capabilities were very limited. The dolphins located, identified, and marked any buried mines and investigated other suspicious objects charted by REMUS and other assets.

While the Battle of Umm Qasr was being fought, the REMUS systems and MK 7 dolphins[81] investigated over 230 suspected mines, aided in the clearance of over 100 mines,[82] and surveyed in excess of 913 nautical miles of water.[83]

Into the Lion's Den

24 March 2003
Umm Qasr, Iraq

On the fourth day of the op, 24 March 2003, the British Third Commando Brigade with the Marine Fifteenth Expeditionary Unit and GROM combined allied task units were mopping up the remaining resistance throughout the city of Umm Qasr. There was still the burning stench of cordite and sulfur in the air and the far-off staccato of automatic weapons, but the outcome of the battle had, days ago, been decided.

The mine countermeasures teams had cleared a two-hundred-yard channel leading into the port, and the word down the chain of command was that the task group commander was about to declare the port and waterway secure. This declaration would allow RFA *Sir Galahad* to tie up and off-load hundreds of tons of food, water, and medical supplies badly needed by the Iraqi people.

Even with the end in sight, EOD Group ONE still worked a rigorous schedule, as were all the MK 7 teams. They were all eager to get on the water and get it done. They were at war, and the harder they worked, the more mines they could find, and ergo, the more lives that they would save.

On that forth day, Brent and Alika were teamed with Kahuna and Kekoa in a RHIB. A second MK 7 RHIB with Chief John Sebastian and his dolphin, Thor, and Petty Officer Rick Turner with Kona were assigned to an adjacent grid. They were escorted to their search grid by a dive boat with a helmsman and two Navy EOD divers aboard. In the previous several days, they had made vast headway in locating and identifying mines. In fact, it was becoming harder and harder for the MK 7s to locate possible mines. The pickings were becoming scarce.

It was in the late afternoon. The sun, now a blurry orange ball behind an eerie smoke-filled sky, was just touching the western horizon. Kekoa was in his assigned search grid while Alika was on the port side of their RHIB. Alika repeatedly tapped the forward disk on the port sponson, chuffed, then glared at Brent: the double whammy signaling serious agitation.

"He's pissed," Brent said to Kahuna. "Don't blame him, though. He's tapped the forward disk four times now, and he wants us to hook him up with a transponder."

"Won't do any good. We still have to wait for the EOD guys in the dive boat. They're looking at another possible mine. They'll be back here anytime now. Tell Alika to chill."

"Already did…a couple of times. He's anxious to get this mine cleared. So am I. It's going to be dark soon."

Kahuna leaned over the port sponson and looked squarely into Alika's eyes. "You're just gonna to have to hang on, Alika. They'll be here soon."

Alika responded by several clicks and his signature whistle. Clearly, he wanted to get on with the mission.

Brent thought for a minute then turned to Kahuna. "I know the divers are still on another site, but while we're waiting, we could give Alika a pinger, let him place it, and I could dive on it to see if it's a real mine or a piece of junk. That would help the EOD boys, and we might even get this thing done tonight. I'd hate to wait until tomorrow morning. We might lose it."

"We could do that, Brent, but that's not our job."

Brent thought about that and then retorted, "In the Special Boat Teams, sometimes we had to do things we didn't want to do and weren't our job, but we were all taught to be flexible, innovative, and do what was necessary to get the job done."

Kahuna came off his seat at the helm, stepped to the port sponson, and stared at Alika, impatient as ever, then glanced at the setting sun. "Okay, Brent. It's against my better judgment, but go check it out and get back soon."

Brent was digging in the gear bag for his mask, snorkel, fins, and dive knife even before Kahuna finished his sentence.

"And I don't want to be trying to find you in the dark, so do it quick."

"Be right back, Kahuna. Thanks!"

By this time, Alika had everything figured out and approached the sponson with his head elevated. No sooner had Brent fitted a transponder to Alika's rostrum than the big dolphin spun on his tail and dove, heading west by northwest in the direction of his find. Brent grabbed the transponder receiver then slipped over the sponson and into the murky water.

Brent followed the director on the receiver in roughly the same direction that Alika had sped to.

The water was not clear, but it was workable—visibility was ten to fifteen feet. He was swimming on the surface, using the receiver as his primary navigation device, and had covered about fifty yards when, suddenly, he was startled to see Alika swimming in the opposite direction with good speed. *He must have already positioned the transponder and is returning to the boat*, Brent surmised.

Then the most unusual thing occurred. Alika turned away from Brent and emitted a series of clicks and chirps. Then sped away heading south.

Strange. Brent considered the incident but maintained course to the transponder. *He's never done that before. Always before, when we're in the water together, he won't leave my side.*

Brent returned his concentration to the receiver, but he could still hear the barrage of Alika's clicks and buzzing. He sounded frantic. It forced him to rethink Alika's strange behavior. Only once before had he heard such a wild concentration of clicks, and that was when Alika saw the...*shark*!

Alika had just placed the transponder near the mine and then turned to head back to the boat. He pinged en route but quickly realized there were three echo returns when there should only have been two: Brent and the boat. Now there was something else—big and moving in the direction of his human. It took Alika only a few seconds to associate the shape and echo return composition with the form of the thing that had killed his mother long ago. Alika knew almost at once what it was—it was death.

There was panic in his heart but fight in his spirit. He emitted a staccato of pings and swam as fast as he could, passed Brent, then made a hard turn to the south, to Brent's left and in the direction of the threat. He closed with more speed than at any time in his life. He made a powerful leap in the air, timing it so he would land just on the other side of the form. He came down hard, and with one mighty cycle of his mighty fluke, he walloped the shark just behind the dorsal fin. Alika was terrified and in full flight.

Alika changed direction and made a direct line to the boat to alert his other human.

Brent instantly snapped out of his concentration with the receiver. At the same time, he heard a loud splash off to his left. He pivoted in that direction, saw frothy white water maybe ten yards away, then began to roll on his back to see behind him. That's when a 280-pound, eight-foot female bull shark tore into Brent's left leg.

Brent was hit hard. The shark's gaping mouth completely encircled Brent's lower left leg. The big bull shark bit down and savagely shook his head from side to side, tossing Brent around like a party pennant.

Brent lifted the receiver, cocked both his arms above his head, and brought the box down squarely on the shark's snout. Startled, the shark released his hold on Brent and dashed away. Brent released the receiver and grabbed for his left leg. It wasn't there, at least not all of it. Brent realized at once that he was touching mostly bone. The tibia and fibula were intact, but most of the tendons and muscle mass was missing.

Brent could feel the rise of icy panic in his chest and struggled to maintain control, to maintain discipline, for that was the only thing that would keep him alive.

Okay…deep breaths. I've got to do three things all at once: stop or slow down the bleeding, keep from panicking, and keep from going into shock.

What initially caught Kahuna's attention was Alika's amazing leap out of the water, then his reentry. But what was strange was that Alika slapped the water hard when he reentered. Most unusual!

Halfway to the boat, Alika spy-hopped and whistled loudly in a clear attempt to get Kahuna's attention.

Kahuna stood, pushing off from the helm chair, grabbed the binoculars, and focused on the area he had last seen Brent. Fifty yards away, he saw a great disturbance in the water and—if his eyes were not playing tricks on him—Brent was entangled with a large gray form. The water around Brent was being churned to a pinkish froth. In the blink of an eye, Kahuna pulled his sheath knife, cut the anchor line, fired up the engine, slammed the throttle full forward, and spun the helm in the direction of Brent. He was only seconds away from Brent, but every second counted.

With both hands, Brent squeezed his leg just above the knee. He spun in a tight 360 looking for the shark. He saw no speeding dorsal fin headed his way, but he did notice that the murky water had turned an unusual shade of crimson. He'd lost a lot of blood. Brent knew all too well that most of the top-tier predators will hit their prey once, injure it, and return for the kill and the feed later. Brent was not out of the fight yet, and he would prepare himself as well as he could for the second round.

As quickly and coolly as he could, Brent released the straps of his diving knife and restrapped it to his left leg, just above the knee. Strangely, there was little pain associated with so much carnage. That is until he pulled the straps tight—then the whole world seemed to flash white.

He dared not look at his leg, or what was left of it, but he did strain to see the blood flow. It was still seeping, but the massive pulsing had been stemmed. He pulled his dive knife from the sheath and thought, *Okay…where is that shark, and shit…where's my dolphin?*

Brent spun in a tight circle. He saw no sign of the shark but did get reoriented with the position of the RHIB some fifty yards away. He couldn't be sure, but he thought he heard the sound of the engine firing up. He began to backstroke toward the boat.

The pain level became excruciating, and he suddenly felt the onset of nausea, dizziness, and cold—shock was setting in.

He'd only swam about fifteen yards when, out the corner of his left eye, he saw a horrifying sight. The unmistakable sight of a large gray fin closing on him. Brent had two choices: roll over and let the bull shark finish him or take a little hunk out of the shark as a last desperate and terminal effort to fight. Brent, at this point, held no illusions about his chance of survival. He was bleeding like a stuck pig, he was fighting off shock, he was on the teetering edge of panic, and his big dolphin was nowhere to be seen.

Alika, believing he had gotten the attention of his other human, spun and dove. His first inclination was to head away from the threat, as fast as his fluke could propel him. But something deep inside him—a growing fury, a supercharged rush of rage—displaced any sense of fear. He emitted several click trains and quickly reacquired Brent and the bigger form's position. It was again closing on his human. With a series of enormous cycles of his massive fluke, Alika put on a burst of speed.

This time, there would be no mistake. This time, there would be no retreat. This time, he would utterly obliterate the monster racing toward his human. This time, vengeance would be exacted in full—or he would die trying.

Brent swallowed hard. He aligned his body in the direction of the oncoming threat, now just yards away, cocked his hand holding the knife, and readied himself for the attack. Then, almost in slow motion, Brent saw an enormous gray-and-white shape launch from the water, climb high in the air, then rotate slightly to reenter the water, nose first and just ahead of the dorsal fin of the shark.

In a fit of rage, Alika pushed himself to over twenty-five knots and closed on the large form from the rear aspect. Nearly five yards away, Alika leapt a good eight feet out of the water, lowered his head at the apex of his trajectory, then aimed just behind the head of the form now just a few feet away from his human.

The collision was shocking. A colossal crack reverberated through the water. Brent felt it deep in his chest. The shark lost speed almost instantly. All swimming motions ended, and the shark glided smoothly past Brent. There was not even the slightest attempt to turn on Brent. As the shark passed him, Brent took one long look into the shark's flint eyes now staring into endless nothingness. The shark rolled and began to make a slow descent to the bottom, but not before Brent clearly saw that the shark's head was curiously tilted up nearly 30 degrees from his longitudinal axis. His neck, although made of cartilage instead of bone, had obviously been cleanly snapped.

Then things for Brent began to turn various hues of gray. With the exhaustion of his adrenaline and loss of blood, he remembered little.

Kahuna was in a hurry. Still nearly twenty-five yards from Brent, Kahuna saw a sight that he would never forget as long as he lived. The shark's dorsal fin was on a direct vector to Brent. Suddenly Alika made a tremendous leap from the water, hung in the air for a moment, then began a speedy descent back into the water. But instead of a clean entry, Alika's descent hesitated as he made contact with the shark. Even over the roar of the engine, Kahuna heard a loud crack, sounding much like a two-by-four being broken in two.

The shark's long tail lifted in the air then slid under the water with no tail action. He was headed for the bottom.

Just as Kahuna cut the engine so as to avoid overshooting Brent, he saw Alika circle around Brent once, make a slight dive behind him, and much to his amazement, Brent seemed to elevate by some magic levitation power and move toward the boat. Alika had carefully balanced Brent on his rostrum and melon and pushed him toward the RHIB.

As soon as he was in reach, Kahuna, with all his colossal brute strength, hauled Brent out of the water, over the side of the sponson and carefully laid him in the bottom of the boat. He looked ghostly white, but he was still conscious and breathing. Kahuna quickly pulled his khaki belt off and wrapped it around Brent's leg just above the knee to help stem the blood loss.

Alika lifted himself high enough to rest his head on the sponson. He looked first at Kahuna then at Brent.

"I can't bring you aboard, Alika. I gotta move quick," Kahuna said. Kahuna moved behind the helm, dropped the engine into gear, and made sure Alika was clear of the props then threw the throttle to the stop and spun the helm toward home plate.

"John, Kahuna," he said over the radio.

"Go, Kahuna."

"I'm making an emergency run back to the *Gunston Hall*. Brent got hit by a shark. He's in bad shape. I didn't have time to load Alika or Kekoa. Bring them aboard your boat and head back."

"Did I hear you right?" John asked. "Brent was attacked?"

"Affirm. Take care of Alika and Kekoa. Gotta go."

Kahuna then switched frequency to the command center aboard the *Gunston Hall* tied up at the pier.

"Elbow Quebec control. Elbow Quebec control. This is Navy Foxtrot 5-Mike." He waited for the tactical control center aboard the *Gunston Hall* to respond.

"Navy Foxtrot 5-Mike, this is Elbow Quebec control, go ahead."

"Elbow Quebec, I'm inbound with an emergency. Requesting a medical team on the dock to respond to a severe laceration in ten mikes."

The Elbow Quebec controller acknowledged the transmission. "Copy all, Navy Foxtrot 5-Mike. Say nature of injury."

"Shark attack. Victim is type O negative and has lost a lot of blood."

"Copy 5-Mike. We're rolling the medical-response team now. They'll be on the dock to meet you."

"Thanks, Elbow Quebec. Five-Mike out."

Now all Kahuna had to do was learn how to make the RHIB fly.

He pushed harder on the throttle, but he was already getting every knot possible out of the boat. He turned to check Brent. He was white as new snow. The deck was slick with his blood, but he was still breathing.

Nine minutes later, Kahuna sped into the dock area still under full power. He saw at once the medical-response team and set a course to the dock close to them. Several members of the medical team noted the closure of the boat and started to back away from the edge of the dock.

Fifteen yards from the dock, Kahuna pulled the throttles back, popped the gear into reverse, then pushed the throttle full forward again. The motor screamed in protest. As the engine arrested the boat's speed, Kahuna gradually reduced power. When he had an acceptable closure speed to the dock, he shut the engine down and tossed the corpsmen a docking line.

"He's right here. Help me get him out."

A big Navy chief in green surgical scrubs yelled, "We got him, Chief. My guys know what they're doing. You relax. We'll have him out in a second."

Kahuna reluctantly moved forward to let the team of five corpsman aboard. In less than five minutes, they eased Brent onto a stretcher, had gotten Brent's vitals, put an additional tourniquet on, and had run an IV line, feeding Brent with much-needed expanding fluids. In another minute, Brent was in a medical Humvee racing for the *Gunston Hall*.

"You okay, Chief?"

The big chief in the scrubs had stayed aboard to check on Kahuna. Kahuna hadn't even noticed him.

"Yeah. I'm fine. Just take care of the kid. Took me a long time to break him in. I'm kinda fond of him now."

"I won't lie to you, Chief. He's lost a lot of blood, but he's in good shape, and he's young. If it's within the reach of modern medicine, we'll save him."

"Thanks, Doc. I know you will."

"Okay," the chief corpsman said and took a last look at Kahuna. Not liking the pallor of Kahuna's skin, he said, "You sure you're good to go? I can stick around a while if you want."

"No. Thanks. I'm good. I'm just trying to sort things out."

"I understand. If you change your mind, call Elbow Quebec control. They'll get a hold of me."

"Thanks. I will."

"Take care, Chief."

"You too."

The chief corpsman stepped to the dock, took one look over his shoulder at Kahuna, lowered his head, then began to jog toward the *Gunston Hall*.

Kahuna scanned the gore in his RHIB. Vinyl gloves, tape, gauze, rubber tubing, and packing materials lay all about the deck, and all of it seemed to be coated with Brent's blood. Suddenly Kahuna went to his knees. The big islander leaned on the port sponson, held his head in his hands, and for the first time in his memory, openly wept. "Please, God. Not Brent," he whispered to himself. "*Not Brent!*"

Above his sobbing, he heard a rush of air: the unmistakable exhalation of a large mammal. It jolted Kahuna out of his dark cloud. He looked over the sponson and came eye to eye with Alika. Kahuna had a long moment of disbelief. A moment passed, and it finally occurred to Kahuna that he needed to bring Alika aboard. He set up Alika's tri mat, and even before he could signal him to beach, Alika was gracefully sliding onto his mat.

Kahuna took a seat close to Alika. He stroked his big melon and rostrum and tried to be reassuring. "He'll be okay, Alika," Kahuna whispered, knowing full well Alika would not understand. "We'll get him back, and he'll be as good as new."

But Kahuna wasn't so sure. He had never felt such depression, such overpowering sorrow.

It was my fault. I should never have let him go. The fault rests with me, Kahuna thought.

Sorrow was a new thing to the big tough Hawaiian, and he wasn't sure he knew how to deal with it. He looked deep into Alika's eyes and suddenly realized that this was the first dolphin he had ever seen in his life who wasn't smiling.

THIS DAY SHALL GENTLE HIS CONDITION

We few, we happy few, we band of brothers; For he to-day that sheds his blood with me shall be my brother; be he ne'er so vile, this day shall gentle his condition; and gentlemen in England now a-bed shall think themselves accurs'd they were not here, and hold their manhoods cheap whiles any speaks that fought with us upon Saint Crispin's day.

—St. Crispin's Day speech
William Shakespeare's *Henry V*
Act IV, Scene 3

The Black Maw of Despair

Sunday, 20 April 2003
Foxtrot Platoon, Pier 40, Sub Base, Point Loma, California

It was Sunday, and to those in San Diego and most of the nation, it was just another day.

Brent sat with his right leg dangling in the water and his prosthesis resting along the edge of the pen. Alika pressed up against

Brent, resting his large gray melon on Brent's good leg. Occasionally, he'd emit a chirp, as if to remind Brent that his stroking was slacking. Mostly, though, Alika was quite content with just the warm, reassuring contact with his very favorite human.

They sat under a brilliant cerulean-blue sky, and Brent tried to convince himself he had no right to be in the grips of the despair he was experiencing now. He was grappling with perhaps the lowest point in his life. By his measure, he was a gimp now: a one-legged man. He was twenty-two years old, and in the span of his young life, he had gained so many things—some through hard work, diligence, and good decisions, but most through the grace of God. He had completed a spiritual oracle, a mystical calling that beckoned him five years earlier. He had been to the seventh level of Maslow's triangle of hierarchy—self-actualization. And now it seemed, one by one, all those wonderful things he was blessed with, his life's greatest treasures, were being systematically stripped from him.

He tried desperately to count his blessings, take stock in all that he had, but it seemed as though the more he fought the mental anguish, the more he slipped into its clutches. Still…he tried to make sense of it all.

Brent stared off into the blue horizon and pondered the blessings heaped upon him over the past several weeks. At the top of the list of good things was that he was still alive, not whole, perhaps, but still functioning and fully cognizant; and for that, he could thank a host of people. He had had the good fortune of having the best medical care probably in the world. His physical condition and the fact that he was still alive was the successful result of a carefully designed, properly managed, and combat-tested set of procedures known as the Forward Resuscitative Surgical System (FRSS).

The objective of FRSS was to reduce the time and the confusion often associated with providing critical medical treatment to injured personnel coming off the battlefield and thereby save lives and minimize injuries. Six Forward Resuscitative Surgical teams (FRSTs) were formed in order to increase the speed and the quality of surgical intervention for US and other injured personnel during Operation Iraqi Freedom.

At the core of FRSS were some remarkable, dedicated doctors, nurses, and medical specialists. It was the people, those on the front lines, in the operating rooms, those providing post-op care and therapy, and the scores of devoted professionals behind the scenes that kept Brent and so many other injured military personnel alive and put them on the road to recovery.

The enormous effort to save Brent's life began with the medical team aboard the *Gunston Hall* who met Kahuna when he pulled the RHIB to the dock at the port of Umm Qasr. Brent remembered none of it, but based on Kahuna's replay, the medical team was where they needed to be when they needed to be there and came with the right mind-set. They stemmed the bleeding, filled Brent full of life-saving fluids, and made him ready for an emergency medical helo lift.

The helo delivered Brent to damage control orthopedics (DCO) phase I—the first of four FRSS phases. This first phase was a quick stop but a very necessary step in the process. As soon as Brent completed this phase, he was quickly flown to the Navy Regional Hospital at Kandahar. There, he completed phase II: debridement and follow-on care.

Brent had been sedated through most of the initial treatment, and while he struggled to divine reality from a thick-fog-induced dreamworld, for the most part, he was unsuccessful. But things became clearer, and his memory improved at the end of phase III. He distinctly remembered a full evaluation by a medical team, being pumped full of antibiotics and fluids, stabilized, and flown to Landstuhl Regional Medical Center in Germany.

Brent was admitted at Landstuhl to begin further evaluation and final stabilization. This was Brent's last stop prior to being flown back to CONUS.

In a phenomenal example of synchronization, dedication and management, within two days of the shark attack, Brent was then transported to Walter Reed Hospital, Bethesda, Maryland, for phase IV of FRSS. This was the final phase of the process: reconstructive surgery and rehabilitation.

By this time, unfortunately, Brent's memory was quite good. He remembered clearly how hard the doctors and medical personnel worked to save his leg. As Brent came out from under the anesthesia of what would become his last surgery, the chief of orthopedic surgery sat patiently by his side. Brent remembered how the doctor, as delicately as he could, explained that they were unable to save his leg. It was a traumatic shock to Brent when the truth finally settled in, but the pain was shared by others. A petite young Navy nurse attending the surgeon was hit hard. Her eyes misted over, and her lips trembled. It was perhaps Brent's second-most traumatic day of his life, and the young lieutenant junior grade shared Brent's pain.

Brent had one additional flight, a nonstop medical sortie from Walter Reed to NAS North Island, San Diego. He was delivered to Balboa Naval Hospital where he spent nearly two weeks for follow-on medical treatment, reconstructive care, fitting of his prosthesis, and additional rehabilitation.

Forward resuscitative surgical system cared for hundreds of wounded and sick military personnel coming from the combat zone. It saved countless lives and provided counseling, which greatly reduced the number of post-traumatic stress disorder cases and consoled and assisted scores of family members. The entire process, from the first phase in theater to the last, took between seventy-two and ninety-six hours.

Brent could not have had better treatment nor more dedicated medical technicians caring for him. For these medical professionals, Brent was eternally grateful and humbled. Yes, he was a very lucky man. By any measure, the medical personnel were extraordinary in their skills, acumen, and empathetic to Brent's new physical and emotional challenges.

That didn't change the reality that this day, and every day for the rest of Brent's life, would be tougher.

Brent thought back on his time while recovering at Balboa Naval Hospital. He remembered getting the news that Master Chief Murphy, Kahuna, and much of the platoon had returned to Point Loma from Umm Qasr. He was very grateful for the many visits from the team. And although Brent was very anxious to hear about Katie, for fear of being disappointed, he didn't ask about her, nor had he tried to call her. Too much emotion, too much pain. He just couldn't deal with any more letdowns, not at this point.

Foremost on Brent's mind was news of Alika. Kahuna had explained in vivid detail that Alika was an emotional train wreck after Brent had been injured and flown home. Even in the company of his other humans to attend to him and provide emotional support, Alika ate little and lost all interest in working.

The vets and biotechs were quite concerned about his mental health. They described Alika as inconsolable and recommended that he and Kahuna return to Point Loma on the first available airlift. Surrounded by his dolphin friends and in familiar surroundings back at Foxtrot Platoon, Alika's depression improved somewhat, but it was still clear to everyone who knew him that he wasn't the same happy-go-lucky dolphin he had been when Brent was with him.

Now, days later after being released from Balboa, Brent sat on the edge of Alika's pen and pondered the future. Within the next week, he expected he'd have definitive word on his medical discharge now in the works at Balboa Naval Medical Hospital. And while he cringed at the thought of leaving his beloved Navy, he took great stock in the fact he had a home to return to, a family who loved him deeply, horses and puppies who missed him, and friends he could count on. *See,* he thought to himself, *I have all these wonderful things going for me. How could anyone be depressed with all that?*

Then he made the mistake of looking deeply into the bright, shimmering black eyes of the one soul to whom he owed his very life and knew deep in his heart that their odyssey would not end well.

Although he resisted the pull into the dark depths of anguish, he had no counterargument for the fact that, in the course of several weeks, he had lost his leg, his girlfriend; and next he would lose his job and his dolphin.

It was truly phenomenal just how close he had grown to the big beast. Alika had unwittingly wiggled deep into Brent's heart with his antics, his spirit, his loyalty, and—if it was possible for a dolphin—his courage and gallantry. Alika was all that and so much more. Leaving this guy was going to cause some serious hardships for both of them.

And then there was Katie.

He was a certified idiot if ever he thought he, a simple cowboy, could ever win over such a stunningly beautiful and kind, young woman. It was incalculable just how quickly he fell for her and uncanny just how deeply. He was a man beguiled. There seemed to be no way out of his predicament. He was in love, a love that just wasn't meant to be.

Katie's Promise

Sunday, 20 April 2003
San Diego International Airport, California

Katie rushed to the luggage carousel and saw Chief Olopoto almost at once. Her face lit up like a Christmas tree; Kahuna smiled brightly. When she approached him, he opened his arms wide, and Katie fell into them.

"Thanks so very much for pickin' me up, Kahuna."

"It's the best part of my day. And if everything goes right, today may be one of the best days of my life."

"How is he? I wasn't sure I should come since I hadn't heard from him in weeks."

"He's a trooper, but even Brent is having a tough time of it. He's gone through a lot, and there's a lot more he's going to have to get through."

Katie pointed to her bags as they came around the carousel, and Kahuna grabbed them.

"The truck is just outside."

Kahuna placed Katie's bags in the rear seat while she skittered to the right front door of the truck and jumped in the passenger seat.

Kahuna hopped in behind the wheel, fired up the truck, and announced, "We're twenty minutes out, and we're not sparing the horses."

"Can't wait to see him, Kahuna."

They had just entered North Harbor Drive when Kahuna broke the silence. "You know about his leg. He's going to be very sensitive about it. But the triple whammy is, he'll be discharged from the Navy, he'll lose Alika, and he thinks he's lost you too. It's a lot to cope with all at one time."

"I can't imagine the depression he's goin' through right now." Katie raised both hands to brush away the tears that had misted her eyes.

Kahuna pretended not to notice. "He's a tough kid, but the news we're about to bring him, and the fact that you're here…well, I think this might be the stuff that miracles are made of."

"So he has no clue I'm here?" Katie questioned.

"None. And to top it off, I think Lieutenant Heinrichs has a proposition for you, but I'll let him talk to you about that."

"Hey, Kahuna, you can't leave me danglin'. What is it? Give me a hint."

"It's not my information to pass, darlin'. You'll just have to gut it out."

"That's not fair. Are all the Navy's chiefs as impossible as you?"

"Yep! Every one of them."

The rest of the trip was completed in silence. It took all of Katie's willpower not to whittle her fingernails down to nubs.

Kahuna pulled the truck to a stop in the parking spot near the Foxtrot piers. Katie noticed a sizable crowd had formed near the security gate. There were twenty-five to thirty men in Navy working uniforms and parts of uniforms. These were young men, hard, arrow-straight, and deeply tanned. Almost at once, her eyes came upon Master Chief Murphy, whom she had met on her first trip, easily recognizable by his dark features, well-used cigar protruding from his teeth, and his towering figure. Next to him, she saw a lieutenant she did not know and Chief O'Dell, her self-appointed bodyguard when she was in town.

"What's going on, Kahuna? Who're all these people?"

"Well, Lieutenant Heinrichs and the master chief thought, since you were coming anyway, it would be a big boon to Brent's recovery if we just got a couple of his friends to come over and have a welcome-home celebration. You're, of course, the main attraction, but these guys are some of his brothers from Pier 51, the Special Boat Team, Mobile Unit 3, and of course, Foxtrot Platoon. Brent will be mighty happy to see all of them."

Katie said nothing but instantly saw the good of it.

Kahuna and Katie exited the truck and approached the gathering crowd. Master Chief Murphy saw the two as soon as they stepped through the security gate. His voice boomed across the expanse of open ground, "Ms. Donovan, front and center, dear."

Like the parting of the Red Sea, the crowd opened a pathway leading to the master chief and the lieutenant. Katie tenuously followed Kahuna. She didn't know what to expect but knew that, in a moment, everything would soon become clear.

As Katie approached the master chief, he reached out and caught Katie's hand. "Katie, I'm Master Chief Murphy." The master chief motioned to the large sea lion at his side. "And this is Duffus, a certified Navy MK 5 sea lion and one of my best friends."

Katie was at once shocked then amused when she saw the enormous grin form on Duffus's face. *He's actually smiling…isn't he?*

Master Chief Murphy continued, "We met once last summer when you brought your group from Florida State University out for a tour of Foxtrot. It seems that the visit may have started something special."

"I think it just may have, sir. Thanks for havin' me!"

The master chief stepped to one side. "Ms. Donovan"—he gestured to the lieutenant—"this is Lieutenant Heinrichs, the officer in charge of Foxtrot Platoon. Lieutenant, Ms. Katie Donovan from Florida State University."

The lieutenant was quick to reach out to Katie and took her hand in both of his. "Katie, thanks very much for making the long trip out here. This is for a very good cause. Your presence will do wonders for Brent."

Katie gave one of those big light-up-the-room smiles and said, "Thanks, Lieutenant, for keeping me up on Brent, and thanks for inviting me out here. That means more to me than I can say."

"Katie, if you look around, you'll see just a handful of his ship-mates and brothers."

Katie took only a few seconds to scan the faces of the group surrounding her. She was duly impressed.

Lieutenant Heinrichs continued, "We've joined up to officially welcome him back home, but I gather from the master chief and Chief Olopoto that he has a bit of a thing for you. We think with you here, it would be a pretty big morale boost for him."

"Actually, I have a bit of a thing for Brent too. And ya'll know I'd do anything I can to help."

"Excellent, Katie. This will be great. And after you two have had a chance to catch up, please stick around. I think we have a job offer you're not going to be able to refuse."

Katie just stared at the lieutenant for a moment, believing she had heard incorrectly. *A job? Here?*

While she tried to make sense of it, Lieutenant Heinrichs yelled, "Okay, gents, listen up. We're about to head down to Alika's pen. Brent's there with him. The master chief, Duffus, and I will lead this gaggle. You guys follow, and behind you, I want Kahuna, Chief O'Dell, and Ms. Donovan."

The lieutenant looked directly at Chief O'Dell and added, "I understand you're already checked out on bodyguard duties for Ms. Donovan."

"I am indeed, Lieutenant!" Chief O'Dell responded and smiled proudly.

"Okay, gang, any questions?"

There were none.

"Roger. Let's roll!"

Brent was head down staring at his big dolphin and doing his very best to shake himself out of his depression with little success. Alika fixed his big black eyes on Brent with obvious concern. To Brent, it almost appeared that Alika could sense his sadness.

Suddenly Alika's head snapped up. He pushed away from Brent and glided toward the center of his pen. Much to Brent's surprise and without any reason, Alika spy-hopped and looked toward the security gate. Brent spun around and could see, off in the distance, a large throng of men marching down the brow headed his way. At the head of the column, Brent saw Lieutenant Heinrichs and next to him a huge black man. If the size of the man didn't give him away, the large waddling sea lion by his side did. Brent recognized them both at once: Master Chief Murphy and his best friend, Duffus. *What the hell's going on?*

Brent quickly grabbed his crutch and scrambled to get on his feet. He still hadn't mastered the prosthesis, and it took a moment to steady himself. He stood tall facing the progression, his mind working at high revs trying to figure out what this was all about. Alika whistled several times then swam to the side of his pen and looked over the edge at the approaching humans.

The last time Brent saw this many people at Foxtrot was when Petty Officer Schultz was escorted to the gate to be turned over to the NCIS agents. Brent considered everything he might have done to deserve a similar fate but came up empty. The way his luck was going, however, anything was possible.

He was slightly relieved when he noticed the wide grins on everybody's faces.

Still twenty feet away, Lieutenant Heinrichs hollered, "Stand easy, young Brent. We come as friends."

Whew. Thank goodness. I don't need anything else to go wrong, Brent thought.

"Brent," the master chief began, "we wanted to welcome you home. And we sure wish it was under better circumstances."

Brent couldn't stifle the urge to look down at his prosthesis, but he tried valiantly to hide his hurt.

Lieutenant Heinrichs stopped a few feet away from Brent, the master chief at his side with Duffus braced against him.

Master Chief Murphy began, "We gathered just a handful of your brothers, Brent. Most of your team is still deployed, as you know. And just to let you know our hearts are in the right place, we invited another person to welcome you home. Lieutenant…"

In the corner of his eye, Brent saw the lieutenant raise his arm and signal someone. There was movement at the back of the group.

The men cleared a path forward: Kahuna and Chief O'Dell came into clear view. They were both smiling brightly as they came forward. Then they stopped. They took a step away from each other, opening a space between them, and there stood Katie. Green eyes sparkling, her wondrous, twinkling smile lit up the sky.

"Hi, Brent!"

Brent's mouth dropped open. He stopped breathing, and for a moment, he wondered if this was all a dream, some cruel hoax cast upon him to taunt and torture him as if his life wasn't already enough to bear.

"Katie! What...why..."

"The master chief and Kahuna called me. They explained things and thought you and Alika might want to see me. Of course, as soon as they mentioned Alika, I just knew I had to come out."

"Oh!"

"Just kiddin', ya big dope!"

At that moment, Katie rushed him, threw her arms around him, and almost knocked him into the water. When they finally caught their balance, Katie kissed him hard and squarely on the mouth, a long, deep, passionate kiss.

The crowd rallied. Shouts, hurrahs, and whistles shattered the silence. When Brent and Katie finally came up for air, Katie saw Alika. He had heard her voice and recognized her at once. He swam to the edge of his pen and whistled several times, desperately vying for her attention. Then he lifted his body and leaned on the edge of his pen to be closer to Katie. She released Brent and bent down, hugged her dolphin, and kissed him solidly on his rostrum.

Most of the dolphins realized that something was going on and stared in confusion at the rowdiness. Gray melons bobbed up and down, and chirps and whistles pierced the air. With all the commotion, they just didn't know if the humans were engaged in a good thing or a bad thing.

Katie stood again and, more carefully this time, embraced Brent.

Master Chief Murphy paused for a moment then signaled the crowd to stand down. He took a deep breath and said, "Brent, there's no way of getting around it. You suffered a terrific loss, almost died doing your job, but you and Alika saved a lot of lives. We just wanted to thank you for your sacrifice to your shipmates and for your service to our great nation."

The master chief let that settle in then added, "Apparently, the secretary of the Navy also thinks you did a fine job because he awarded you both the Purple Heart and the Meritorious Service Medal, probably the first citation of its kind to be given to a sailor for intrepid combat against an enemy shark."

That sparked boisterous laughter from the crowd.

Lieutenant Heinrichs raised his hand, and the laughter subsided. "I will now read the Purple Heart citation. Attention to orders." With his booming voice echoing off the nearby bulkheads, Lieutenant Heinrichs began, "To all who shall see these present, greetings. The President of the United States has awarded the Purple Heart, established by General George Washington at Newburgh, New York, on August 7, 1782, to Special Warfare Combatant craft Crewman Brent Scott Harris, Foxtrot Platoon, while assigned to Task Force 55.4, for wounds received in action on or about the twenty-fourth of March 2003 at Umm Qasr, Iraq."

Master Chief Murphy retrieved a six-by-three-inch richly constructed blue-and-gold box from his pocket and handed it to the lieutenant. Heinrichs opened the box and held it high so all hands might see it. It sparkled, and sunlight radiated from the Purple Heart award. He handed it to Brent, who held it in both hands and marveled at it.

"Brent," Lieutenant Heinrichs said with complete with total reverence, "your life will never be the same, but we think we have a way to make it a little less devastating. Petty Officer Harris, you'll be discharged from the Navy in a few weeks, and no doubt your family and friends back in cowboy country USA, the great state of Wyoming, will be excited to get you home and back in the saddle."

"Sure hope so. They tell me there're a few colts to be trained," Brent said, putting on his best act to look cheerful.

"Well, son, we've done a little horse trading, and we've got the powers up the EOD chain of command convinced we can't continue our mission without you. So...I've been authorized to offer you, upon your separation from naval service, a position here with Foxtrot Platoon as a civilian government service employee doing pretty much the same damn thing you've been doing, except you won't be going to war anymore. Sorry."

There was instant bedlam. The assembled men hooted and hollered and whistled and thrust their fists in the air.

Brent tried to replay the lieutenant's words, wondering if he actually heard what he thought he heard. *Remain at Foxtrot? Keep my dolphin? Stay with my brothers?*

If ever there was a bolt from the blue, a stroke of good fortune that came raining down from the heavens and would magically help mend the tragedy in Brent's life—this was it. He was at a total and complete loss for words. He blinked and tried to keep his head straight and his mind clear.

When the clamor receded, Brent, back straight, head high, looked across the field at his best friends and teammates. "Ah…I… just don't know what to say, sir. I've been lucky…no, I've been privileged…beyond expectations. I've been allowed to serve my country and fight alongside you men. I lost my leg. Okay, it's not the end of the world. It was a small price to pay to be able to do something important, something that saved lives, and I think something that might even help win the war. It was a small thing in exchange to be able to work with the best, most dedicated, the most courageous men I've ever known."

All was quiet on the pier. Each of the men was taking stock of Brent's words and realized at that second this was one of those moments in time, one of those poignant, indelible points in their lives, that they would remember forever.

With sober clarity, they glanced at one another, each suddenly realizing the significance of this moment. They were among their brothers, doing a job that they were both called for and proud of. They were the lucky ones.

"Well…" Brent looked again at his Purple Heart and finished, "I just wanted to thank you for your trust and for the opportunity to serve with you guys. Thanks!"

It was a good time to break things up. Lieutenant Heinrichs hollered, "Okay, you bilge rats, pay your respects to Brent and Katie and go do something for your country!"

Each of the men moved to the front of the line to shake Brent's hand. Katie was surprised but shouldn't have been when she also was so warmly greeted by so many sailors. Over the close scrutiny and scowl of Chief O'Dell, they gave her a hug and a friendly peck on the cheek.

When the last of the men departed, Lieutenant Heinrichs stepped toward Brent and Katie, their hands intertwined. "We have an offer. This one's for Katie. I hope it comes as good news. Since it was mostly through the magic of Master Chief Murphy and Kahuna, I'll let them explain."

The master chief stepped a little closer to Brent and Katie and cleared his voice. Duffus, realizing his human had moved, shuffled closer and leaned against the master chief. The master chief looked at Brent and Katie and, with his well-chewed cigar wedged between his lips, said, "Katie, we want you to come work for us."

A moment of tense silence followed.

Katie stared unblinking at the master chief then looked at Brent, who returned the look, confusion in his eyes. Then, in unison, Katie and Brent both turned their gaze back to the master chief, both wondering if they had heard him correctly.

"Let me get this straight, Master Chief," Katie said. "You want me to come and work here at Foxtrot Platoon with all these dolphins?"

"You heard right, Katie."

Another pregnant pause ensued while Katie weighed his words. "I'm not in the Navy, and I still have two months to go before I graduate."

"You don't have to be in the Navy. We'll bring you in as a civilian under the intern program. We don't advertise it much because we're very selective. You won't make much at first, but after you graduate, we'll hire you under the government services pay scale, which ain't that bad. So, what do you think, Katie?"

"Well...I think I'd be crazy as a hoot owl not to say yes. But I still need to graduate from Florida State."

"Yep. We know, and that's not an issue."

Katie was getting misty-eyed, but she fought the impulse to become emotional. "I just don't have the words to tell you how much this means to me."

And then she released Brent, turned to face the master chief, stood on her tiptoes, and tried to get her arms around the master chief's enormous shoulders. She looked much like a child's doll when he hugged her back—she was completely engulfed.

When he released her, she pivoted toward Kahuna and the lieutenant, still smiling but wet-eyed and sniffling. "I just don't know what to say. You guys are the best!"

Kahuna reached out and held her shoulders to steady her. "Just say yes, Katie, and we'll make it happen."

"Well then—YES!"

Kahuna hugged her and quietly whispered in her ear, "Just take care of Brent, Katie. He's a good man, one of the best I've ever known. He's got a lot of adjustments to make in the coming months. You and Alika can ease the trauma and help in the transition."

"I'll do whatever I can Kahuna...whatever it takes."

When Katie eased away from Kahuna, the master chief realized she was on the verge of letting the dam break. She took several deep breaths, looked deep into the sky, and mumbled what Kahuna thought was a prayer. She wiped her tears away with the heels of her hands and sniffled. Her eyes were lined in red, but the flash of her emerald-green irises and award-winning smile melted the hearts of the three tough guys.

"Don't mind me. I'm just a Southern girl who's having the very best day of her life. I never get this emotional but..."

Lieutenant Heinrichs realized the sensitivity of the situation. "Well, let's let them get reconnected, and we'll go do what we get paid for."

"Great idea, Lieutenant. This calls for a celebration. Let's head to my office. I think I know where a bottle of single-malt Scotch might be hiding."

"I'm up for that," the lieutenant said.

"Count me in on that. I love free whiskey," chimed Kahuna.

The master chief added, "You like free anything, Kahuna!"

As the three walked up the brow with Duffus waddling in close trail, Katie snuggled into Brent's hug and kissed him lightly on the neck. It was a small act of intimate tenderness, but Brent felt the fire, as if a bolt of electricity arced through his body.

Now for the six-hundred-pound gorilla in the room, thought Brent.

"Katie, you didn't say anything about my leg. I don't want you getting into something you're not fully prepared for. I mean, I'm not a basket case. I can get along without the pity or the help."

"Brent," Katie began, her forehead wedged into the side of Brent's neck, "you know what Kahuna just told me?"

"Not a clue. What?"

"He said to take care of you, that you were one of the best men he ever knew. Well, sailor, I knew that the day I met you."

"But my leg…you know this is not going to be easy."

"Brent, even with part of your leg missin', you're more man than anyone I've ever known."

This time, it was Brent who had trouble keeping back the floodgates. His eyes reddened, and tears threatened to stream down his cheeks. "Katie, I've got to get this out now. I—"

She snapped her right hand out, index finger pressing against his lips. She snuggled up to him, pressed her lips against his ear, and whispered to him a solemn promise.

Brent was nearly overwhelmed by joy. His hand covered his eyes, and his breaths came unsteadily.

And then Katie whispered, "Brent, I love you…with all my heart!"

And Alika whistled.

NOTES

Prologue

1. "Defining Culture." Retrieved from https://www.dolphins.org/culture.

2. Dell'Amore, C. "Dolphins Have 'Names,' Respond When Called" (July 23, 2013). Retrieved from http://news.nationalgeographic.com/news/2013/07/130722-dolphins-whistle-names-identity-animals-science/.
   "Dolphin Anatomy" (April 17, 2017). Retrieved from http://www.dolphins-world.com/dolphin-anatomy.

3. *Melon*: a round organ located in the head, filled with special fats and used for echolocation ("Bottlenose dolphin," retrieved from https://en.wikipedia.org/wiki/Bottlenose_dolphin).

4. *Fluke*: horizontally mounted triangular tail structure and used to both propel the animal forward and for steering in conjunction with other fins (ibid).

5. *Rostrum*: The rostrum is roughly akin to snout or beak. It is very sensitive to touch, and used to feel objects and for contact in social interactions (ibid).

6. Most research in this area has been restricted to the North Atlantic Ocean. "Bottlenose dolphins typically swim at 5 to 11 km/h (1.4 to 3.1 m/s), but are capable of bursts of up to 29 to 35 km/h (8.1 to 9.7 m/s). The higher speeds can only be sustained for a short time" (ibid).

7. "Birth and Care of Young." Retrieved from https://seaworld.org/en/animal-info/animal-infobooks/bottlenose-dolphins/birth-and-care-of-young.

8. Sharks do not have an air bladder and rely on the liver to provide some amount of positive floatation.

Chapter 1

9. "Bottlenose dolphin." Retrieved from https://en.wikipedia.org/wiki/Bottlenose_dolphin.

Though the true name is bottlenose *dolphin*, much of the Southern population refer to them as *porpoise*.

Chapter 3

10. Population of Alpine, Wyoming, was 828 in 2015.

11. "Born in the early 1800s, Chief Washakie earned a reputation that lives on to this day as a fierce warrior, skilled politician and diplomat, great leader of the Shoshone people, friend to white men. His influence on this part of the West lingers not just at our nation's Capitol, but also in the names of hot springs, historical centers, a county, and the small town named in his honor in northwest Wyoming." ("Chief Washakie: Great Leader of the Shoshone people" [June 21, 2011], retrieved from https://www.yellowstonepark.com/park/chief-washakie-a-voice-for-the-people)

Chapter 4

12. An adult male horse, if left intact, is called either a *stallion* or a *stud*. If castrated, he is called a gelding. In some cases, particularly informal nomenclature, a gelding under four years is still called a colt.

13. The canter is a controlled three-beat gait that usually is a bit faster than the average trot but slower than the gallop. The average speed of a canter is 16–27 km/h (10–17 mph), depending on the length of the stride of the horse.

14. *Cow sense*: a term to mean a horse's ability to anticipate a cow's next action or move. It implies that a horse can (to some extent) almost read minds of the cattle being worked.

15. *Draw cattle*: a horse's capability to cause cattle to look at them, draw the attention of a cow to the horse.

16. *Dry work*: initial cutting horse training without introduction of cattle.

17. *Brindle*: cow with a dappled, speckled, or mottled coat.

18. *Baldy*: a cow with a white area covering the head and face.

19. "SEALs and SWCCs go through separate specialized training programs that emphasize special operations in the maritime environment. SWCCs are trained extensively in small combat craft, weapons and tactics, techniques, and procedures. Focusing on clandestine infiltration and exfiltration of SEALs and other special operations forces, SWCCs provide dedicated, rapid mobility in shallow water areas where large ships cannot operate. SWCCs must be physically fit, highly motivated, combat-focused, and responsive in high-stress situations." (https://en.wikipedia.org/wiki/Special_warfare_combatant-craft_crewmen)

20. "Special warfare combatant-craft crewman insignia is a military qualification badge of the United States Navy which was first conceived in *1996*, though the design was not approved for wear until *2001*. *On time! On target! Never quit!*" (Retrieved from https://en.wikipedia.org/.../Special_warfare_combatant-craft)

Chapter 5

21. WESTPAC: Western Pacific Theater

22. INCONUS: Within the continental US

23. TACAIR: Tactical aviation. Shooters and those aircraft/crew deploying aboard aircraft carriers

24. SPAWAR: Space and Naval Warfare Systems Command

25. OIC: Officer in charge

26. EOD: Explosive ordnance disposal

27. OPLAN TPFDD: Time phased force deployment data for theater warplans—OPLANs details end-to-end logistics plan for war materials and forces.

28. SOC: Special operations chief petty officer; SO is the rating for SEAL; *C* is the abbreviation for "chief."

29. WARCOM: Commander, Naval Special Warfare Command stationed at AMPHIB Base Coronado

30. DEVGRU: US Navy component of Joint Special Operations Command. Although DEVGRU was created as a maritime counterterrorism unit, it has become a multifunctional special operations unit with several roles that include high-risk personnel/hostage extractions and other specialized missions.

31. Navy SEALs from the Naval Special Warfare Development Group (DEVGRU). Task Force Ranger—which consisted of an assault force made up of US Army Delta Force operators, Army Rangers, Air Force Pararescuemen, Air Force Combat Controllers, four Navy SEALs from the Naval Special Warfare Development Group, and an air element provided by the 160th Special Operations Aviation Regiment.

32. ADM Jay Johnson: Admiral Jay L. Johnson, USN, (born June 5, 1946) served from 1996-2000 as 26th Chief of Naval Operations (CNO). Naval Aviator with extensive operational experience, including combat operations in Vietnam flying the F-8 Crusader, command of an F-14 fighter squadron, and command of a carrier air wing.

33. CDO: Command duty officer

34. BM2: Boatswains mate second class petty officer

35. EN3: Engineman third class petty officer

36. Disposition of stranded dolphins would be decided by National Marine Fisheries Service, part of National Oceanic and Atmospheric Administration (NOAA) in the Department of Commerce who has cognizance over the enforcement of the Marine Mammal Protection Act.

37. VR-57: A reserve logistics squadron based at North Island flying (at the time) C-9s on logistics and fleet support missions. Dolphins, however, need a C-130 or larger for transport.

38. NASNI: Naval Air Station, North Island, two miles north of Naval Amphibious Base Coronado

Chapter 6

39. RHIB: Rigid hull inflatable boat, used extensively by Navy SOF and the Marine Mammal Program operators.
40. OS rate is an operations specialist: plotters, radio-telephone and Command and Control sound-powered telephone talkers and maintain Combat Information Center (CIC) displays of strategic and tactical information.
41. Carl von Clausewitz (1 June 1780–16 November 1831) was a Prussian general and military strategist/theorist generally acknowledged as one of the most important and influential minds of modern warfare.

Chapter 7

42. "September 11 attacks." Retrieved from https://en.wikipedia.org/wiki/September_11_attacks.
43. General Schwarzkopf's Left Hook: Bypassed the entrenched Iraqi Army along the Iraq-Kuwaiti border, enveloped, and then cut off the Iraqi Army and Republican Guard divisions still stationed in Kuwaiti, isolated supply, communications, and severed lines of retreat. Coalition forces were then able to make short work of the surrounded Iraqi armies.

Chapter 8

44. *Spy-hop*: When *spy*-hopping, the dolphin rises and holds a vertical position partially out of the water, often exposing its entire rostrum and head. It is visually akin to a human treading water. Primarily, it used to extend the viewing distance of the dolphin. Spy-hopping can last for minutes at a time if the dolphin is sufficiently inquisitive about whatever it is viewing.
45. *Operant behavior*: "Operant conditioning (also, "instrumental conditioning") is a learning process in which behavior is sensitive to, or controlled by its consequences. For example, a child may learn to open a box to get the candy inside, or learn to avoid touching a hot stove. In

contrast, classical conditioning causes a stimulus to signal a positive or negative consequence; the resulting behavior does not produce the consequence. For example, the sight of a colorful wrapper comes to signal 'candy,' causing a child to salivate, or the sound of a door slam comes to signal an angry parent, causing a child to tremble. The study of animal learning in the 20ᵗʰ century was dominated by the analysis of these two sorts of learning, and they are still at the core of behavior analysis." ("Operant conditioning," https://en.wikipedia.org/wiki/Operant_conditioning.)

Chapter 9

46. Dukane system: "Underwater acoustic locating systems/localizer" ("Dukane Seacom Locator Beacons," retrieved from http://www.radiantpowercorp.com/product-families/instruments-sensors/dukane-seacom-locator-beacons/).
47. Submarine emergency blow: a procedure used aboard a submarine that forces high-pressure air into its main ballast tanks. The high-pressure air forces ballast water from the tanks, quickly lightening the ship often resulting in a surface breach.

Chapter 10

48. Goforth, Jr, Harold, Captain, US Navy (Ret), PhD, *Defender Dolphins*, Adducent, Inc, 2012.
49. Marine Mammal Systems Operator and Maintenance Course
50. At the time of this story, research indicates that MU-3 was in existence (as of 2000). Documents (Marine Mammal Program) state that in 2004 a realignment took place and resulted in the MK 5 sea lions being assigned under SSC Pacific. The MK 6 system was assigned to EODMU THREE.
51. http://www.globalsecurity.org/military/agency/navy/eodmu3.htm

52. Third leg of the nuclear triad, the Nuclear Ballistic Subs.

53. *Force protection*: Preventive measures taken to mitigate hostile actions against Department of Defense personnel

54. *Landing craft mechanical*: a landing craft designed for carrying vehicles. They came into prominence during the Second World War when they were used to land troops or tanks during Allied amphibious assaults.

55. SEA FLOAT/SOLID ANCHOR: platform built by the US Navy and Tran Hung Dao III by the South Vietnamese; a joint US/Vietnamese attempt to inject an allied presence into An Xuyen Province, 175 miles southwest of Saigon. Its purpose was to extend allied control over the strategic Nam Can region of the Ca Mau peninsula. Heavily forested, the area sprawled across miles of mangrove swamp. The site selected was on the Cau Lon River, which connected to the Bo De and Dam Doi rivers. The entire area had been solidly held by the Viet Minh against the French and by the Viet Cong against the Saigon government (and its American ally).

56. Pegasus (Peg) was the first Navy open-ocean releasable dolphin, released at Port Hueneme Harbor on 13 August 1964.

57. Budweiser badge: common Navy terminology for SEAL pin.

58. Short Time was operational in Cam Rahn Bay from December 1970 to December 1971. Goforth Jr., Harold, Captain, US Navy (Ret), PhD, *Defender Dolphins*, Adducent, Inc, 2012.

59. *Direct action*: short-duration strikes and other small-scale offensive actions conducted as a special operation in hostile, denied, or diplomatically sensitive environments. In the context of close combat, this generally means lethal action.

Chapter 12

60. Naval Base Bremerton was retitled Naval Base Kitsap in 2004 at the time of the consolidation.

61. Naval Base Kitsap was created in 2004 by merging the former Naval Station Bremerton with Naval Submarine

Base Bangor. The mission of Naval Base Kitsap is to serve as the host command for the Navy's fleet throughout West Puget Sound and to provide base operating services, including support for both surface ships and submarines homeported at Bremerton and Bangor.

62. "Naval Base Kitsap." Retrieved from https://en.wikipedia.org/wiki/Naval_Base_Kitsap.

63. "Naval Base Kitsap also provides service, programs, and facilities to meet the needs of their hosted combat commands, tenant activities, ships' crews, and civilian employees. Naval Base Kitsap is the largest naval organization in Navy Region Northwest, and it is composed of installations at Bremerton, Bangor, Manchester, Indian Island, and Keyport, Washington. Naval Base Kitsap was the recipient of the 2005 Commander in Chief's Award for Installation Excellence—the Best Base in the U.S. Navy." (Ibid)

64. "Solid Curtain-Citadel Shield (SC-CS) is a force protection and anti-terrorism exercise conducted by Commander, U.S. Fleet Forces Command (USFF) and Commander, Navy Installations Command (CNIC) on most Navy installations in the continental United States. The annual exercise uses realistic scenarios to ensure U.S. Navy security forces maintain a high level of readiness to respond to changing and dynamic threats."

65. *White Team*: the officiating team and those who conduct and evaluate the exercise

66. *Blue Force*: the US and allied forces, the good guys

67. Marking nose cup is a part of the swimmer detection system.

68. Meaning they had been neutralized

69. *Bravo Zulu*: a congratulatory declaration in effect meaning a job well done

Chapter 14

70. "CENTCOM: United States Central Command (USCENTCOM or CENTCOM) is a theater-level

Unified Combatant Command of the U.S. Department of Defense. The CENTCOM Area of Responsibility (AOR) includes countries in the Middle East, North Africa, and Central Asia, most notably Afghanistan and Iraq." ("United States Central Command," retrieved from https://en.wikipedia.org/wiki/United_States_Central_Command)

71. Sensitive Sites: specific sites which Iraqi leadership defined as having legitimate security concerns.

72. "UNSCOM Chronology of Main Events" (December 1999). UN.org. Retrieved from http://www.un.org/Depts/unscom/Chronology/chronologyframe.htm.

Chapter 15

73. Wild Animal Park was renamed Safari Park in 2010.

74. RADM Barry Costello: Rear Adm. Barry Costello, the US officer overseeing mine-clearing, said floating and bottom-hugging mines have been found in stranded boats, intercepted barges and captured warehouses in Umm Qasr and the Khawr Abd Allah. Both kinds of mines were blamed for explosions that crippled the USS *Tripoli* and USS *Princeton* in the 1991 gulf war. (Commander Task Unit (CTU) 55.4.3

75. There were five MK 7 dolphins and four MK 4 dolphins for a total of nine dolphins.

76. ATC: Air transport carriers

77. GROM: (English) Military Unit GROM named in honour of the Silent Unseen of the "Home Army" is Poland's elite counterterrorism unit. GROM, which stands for *Grupa Reagowania Operacyjno-Manewrowego* (English: *Group [for] Operational Maneuvering Response*), which also means "thunder," is one of the five special operation forces units of the Polish Armed Forces. It was officially activated on July 13, 1990. It is deployed in a variety of special operations and unconventional warfare roles, including antiterrorist operations and projection of force behind enemy lines.

78. OPSEC: Operational security

Chapter 17

79. "Battle of Umm Qasr." Retrieved from https://en.wikipedia.org/wiki/Battle_of_Umm_Qasr.
80. REMUS: Remote environmental monitoring units
81. Per firsthand accounts from those who were on scene, no mines were recovered.
82. Kreger, N. "Putting Sea Mammals to Work: Dolphins Help Coalition Forces in Iraq" (7.2: August 2003). Retrieved from https://www.jmu.edu/cisr/journal/7.2/features/kreger/kreger.htm.

GLOSSARY

Ampullae of Lorenzini. Special sensing organs called electroreceptors arrayed linearly along the snout forming a network of jelly-filled pores. They are mostly found in cartilaginous fish (sharks, rays, and chimaeras). These sensory organs help animals sense electric fields in the water. They provide an additional capability to detect electric and magnetic fields as well as temperature gradients. *Ampullae of Lorenzini.* Retrieved from https://en.wikipedia.org/wiki/Ampullae_of_Lorenzini

Carcharhiniformes. Ground sharks; the largest order of sharks—over 270 species; characterized by the presence of a nictitating membrane over the eye, two dorsal fins, an anal fin, and five gill slits. The Tiger shark is a member of this group. *Carcharhiniformes.*
Retrieved from https://en.wikipedia.org/wiki/Carcharhiniformes

Chirps. Common vocal tones of varying frequency in marine mammals. Their purpose is not entirely understood.

Chuff. Slapping the water with the fluke often associated with an audible grunt; a dolphin is usually signaling dissatisfaction, agitation, or frustration.

Clicks. Generally used for echolocation by many marine mammals. Echolocation functions similar to radar. High frequency sound energy, "clicks", are emitted by the dolphin (marine mammal). The sound travels through the water, bounces off objects, and the echo returns to the source for analysis.

Click-train. A series of high frequency clicks; burst-pulsed sounds. The clicks are directional in nature and are used for echolocation often occurring in a short series of bursts called a "click train". The click rate increases when approaching an object of interest. Dolphin echolocation clicks are amongst the loudest sounds made by marine animals. *Dolphin*. Retrieved from https://en.wikipedia.org/wiki/Dolphin#cite_note-87

Echolocation. Echolocation is a process that permits dolphins to send out sound waves that are bounced back allowing them to identify the range and bearing, shape, size and composition of objects in the water. Used to navigate, locate prey, hunt, protect themselves from predators in murky or low-visibility waters, and to communicate with other dolphins. Most odontocete cetaceans can emit very high-frequency sounds. The frequencies vary according to the species, but these are general characteristics in all dolphins. For example, they always communicate with low-frequency signals, which include whistling or chirping, but they emit high frequencies when using echolocation. The sounds vary according to the circumstances and the purpose. (2017, April 27). *Dolphin Echolocation*. Retrieved from http://www.dolphins-world.com/dolphin-echolocation/

Manipulandum. A small disk, approximately six inches in diameter. Generally, two disks are hung on the port sponson or pontoon of a control boat. A dolphin returning from an assignment to identify an object will press with the rostrum either the forward disk (object confirmed) or the aft disk (not confirmed). In this way the dolphin can communicate with his handler and team mates.

Navy Enlisted Paygrades:

United States Navy enlisted rates define the pay grade of an enlisted person in the Navy and/or Coast Guard. An enlisted member's rate is similar in concept to a naval officer's rank. Only naval officers carry the term "rank", however. The word *rate* refers to an enlisted sailor's pay grade, while the word *rating* refers to one's area of occupational specialization within the enlisted ranks. Associated with the enlisted pay grades is a numbering system identifying the most junior enlisted sailor (E-1) to the most senior enlisted sailor (E-9). This enlisted numbering system is consistent in all five branches of the U.S. Military. In the Navy, E-1 through E-3 are known as Seamen; E-4 through E-6 are called Petty Officers. E-7s are called Chief Petty Officer; E-8s, Senior Chief Petty Officer; and E-9s, Master Chief Petty Officer. Rates are displayed on a rating badge which identifies the individual's rate and rating.

List of United States Navy enlisted rates.
Retrieved from https://en.wikipedia.org/wiki/List_of_United_States_Navy_enlisted_rates

Chief Petty Officer Structure—Non-Commissioned Officers:

Chief Petty Officer (CPO; E-7). Often referred to as simply "Chief". As a traditional naval grade, CPO is senior to a petty officer and is the third highest enlisted naval rank in the US Navy and US Coast Guard. *Chief petty officer.*
Retrieved from https://en.wikipedia.org/wiki/Chief_petty_officer

Senior Chief Petty Officer (CPO; E-8). A senior chief petty officer is the eighth highest of nine enlisted ranks in the U.S. Navy and U.S. Coast Guard, just above chief petty officer and below master chief petty officer. They are addressed as "Senior Chief" in most circumstances, or less formally, as "Senior". *Senior chief petty officer.*
Retrieved from https://en.wikipedia.org/wiki/Senior_chief_petty_officer

Master Chief Petty Officer. The ninth, and highest, enlisted rate (pay grade E-9) in the U.S. Navy and U.S. Coast Guard, just above senior chief petty officer. Master chief petty officers are addressed as "Master Chief". They constitute the top 1.25% of the enlisted members of the maritime forces. *Master chief petty officer.* Retrievedfromhttps://en.wikipedia.org/wiki/Master_chief_petty_officer

DOLPHIN ANATOMY

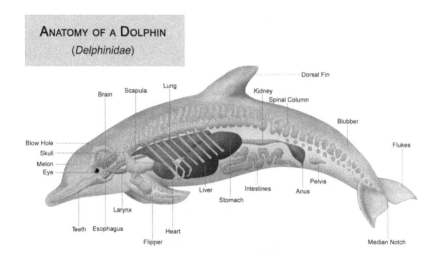

Anatomy of a Dolphin. Retrieved from https://commons.
wikimedia.org/wiki/File:Dolphin_anatomy.png

Brain: The brain of cetaceans is quite large; its mass is slightly greater than that of humans. It is 15-60 times bigger than the brain of a shark of similar body size. The human EQ, or encephalization quotient, is 7.0. The EQ for great apes, elephants, chimpanzees and whales is about 1.8-2.3, meaning they have smaller brains for their body size than do humans. The dolphin's EQ is 4.2, the closest EQ ratio to humans of any animal. *Dolphin Brain and Intelligence - Understanding Dolphins.*
Retrieved from http://understanddolphins.tripod.com/dolphin-brainandintelligence.html

Dorsal fin. Positioned on the longitudinal centerline on top of the dolphin. They have only one dorsal fin which gives them stability when swimming. It is filled with fibrous connective tissue.

Eyes. Located on each side of the head, they provide a broad field of view and are very sensitive despite the inability to identify colors. The eyes can move independently of one another, but they are not able to look directly up or down. The dolphin eye is relatively small for its size, yet they do retain a good degree of eyesight. Their vision consists of two fields, rather than a binocular view like humans have. When dolphins surface, their lens and cornea correct the nearsightedness that results from the refraction of light; they contain both rod and cone cells, meaning they can see in both dim and bright light, but they have far more rod cells than they do cone cells. *Dolphin.* Retrieved from https://en.wikipedia.org/wiki/Dolphin#cite_note-87

Fluke. Horizontally mounted triangular tail structure used to both propel the animal forward and for steering in conjunction with other fins. *Bottlenose dolphin.*
Retrieved from https://en.wikipedia.org/wiki/Bottlenose_dolphin.

Pectoral Fins. The pectoral fins are used for steering and movement. In the lower part of their body, dolphins have two pectoral flippers which are curved, useful for directing and controlling movements and changing speed when swimming.

Melon. Spherical organ located in front of the skull, the forehead, of the dolphin. It is filled with special fats and used for echolocation. It acts like an acoustic lens, aiding in sound recognition and direction finding. *Bottlenose dolphin.*
Retrieved from https://en.wikipedia.org/wiki/Bottlenose_dolphin.

Teeth. Located in the front area of the head, dolphins have several teeth whose number varies according to the species. The teeth are also used to secure food, but they also play an important role in echolocation and in the sensory system of the dolphin. The jaws are elongated and the teeth are arranged in a configuration that functions as an antenna to receive incoming echolocation sound energy allowing the animal to pinpoint the exact location of an object. *Bottlenose dolphin.* Retrieved from https://en.wikipedia.org/wiki/Bottlenose_dolphin.

Rostrum. The rostrum is roughly akin to a snout or beak. It is very sensitive to touch, and used to feel objects and for contact in social interactions. *Bottlenose dolphin.* Retrieved from https://en.wikipedia.org/wiki/Bottlenose_dolphin.

Blowhole. The blowhole is the external airway to the lungs. Dolphins both breathe and communicate through their blowhole. These sounds are generated from air sacs below the blowhole A slightly recessed, crescent-shaped muscular flap is located on the dorsal side of the animal in the center of a swollen part of the head, the melon. The opening and closing of the blowhole is controlled voluntarily by the dolphin. Muscle contraction causes the flap to open, and relaxation of the muscle allows the flap to close in a water tight seal. *Blowhole and Breathing.* Retrieved from http://understanddolphins.tripod.com/dolphin-blowholeandbreathing.html

Genitals. Dolphins' reproductive organs are located on the underside of the body. Forward of the anus are either two or three slits aligned with the animal's spinal column. Males have two slits, one concealing the penis and one further behind for the anus. The female has one genital slit, housing the vagina and the anus. Two mammary slits are positioned on either side of the female's genital slit. Dolphin copulation happens belly to belly; though many species engage in lengthy foreplay, the actual act is usually brief but may be repeated several times within a short timespan. *Dolphin.* Retrieved from https://en.wikipedia.org/wiki/Dolphin#cite_note-87.

Epidermis. The skin of dolphins feels soft to the touch although it has a thick epidermis covered with a thin layer of cornified cells. Despite this, it is extremely sensitive due to a large number of nerve endings on the exterior. Given this fragility, it damages very easy with any contact of a rough surface and even human fingernails The healing process, however, is fast and develops a dark scar in the tissue which later turns white. Beneath the skin, there is a thick layer of fat that dolphins use as an energy reserve in periods of food shortage, as insulation to prevent heat loss in cold environments, and as a resource that helps maintain the hydrodynamic shape of their body. Dolphins-World (2017, April 25). *Dolphin Anatomy*. Retrieved from http://www.dolphins-world.com/dolphin-anatomy/.

Lateral line. Sensory organ on the snout that extends down the flanks on both sides of the bodies of both sharks and fish. The lateral lines, situated just under the skin (subcutaneous), are canals that are filled with fluid. Tiny modified hair cells line the walls of the canals. The lateral line is instrumental in sensing vibrations and movement in the water. Meyer, A. (2014). *Sharks, Lateral Line*. Retrieved from http://www.sharksinfo.com/lateral-line.html.

Navy Marine Mammal Program (NMMP). The U.S. Navy Marine Mammal Program (NMMP) is a program administered by the U.S. Navy which studies the military use of marine mammals, principally bottlenose dolphins and California sea lions, and trains animals to perform tasks such as ship and harbor protection, mine detection and clearance, and equipment recovery. The program is based in San Diego, California, where animals are housed and trained on an ongoing basis. NMMP animal teams have been deployed for use in combat zones, such as during the Vietnam War and the Iraq War. *Navy Marine Mammal Program*.
Retrieved from https://en.wikipedia.org/wiki/United_States_Navy_Marine_Mammal_Program.

Signature whistle. A form of dolphin vocalization emitted by bottlenose dolphins. They are used in communication within the species and have specialized functions and properties. Researchers define it as a whistle with a unique frequency curve that dominates in the repertoire of a dolphin. Each dolphin has a distinct signature whistle that no other dolphin duplicates. They are typically used for locational purposes, however they also provide dolphins with identity information and behavioral context. Signature whistles also play an important role in group cohesion and social interaction. *Signature Whistle.* Retrieved from https://en.wikipedia.org/wiki/Signature_whistle

Sloughing. Shedding of the outside layer of skin. The top layer of epidermis layer sloughs off easily and is quickly replaced. This process of skin sloughing provides a continuous "smoothing" process so that the dolphin's body is less resistant to contact with water molecules as it swims. Micro dermal ridges are present on the dolphin's skin surface. These small ridges trap water molecules as the animal swims. Thus, the liquid trapped on the skin surface allows the animal to pass through the water more easily than if the same animal had a dry skin surface. Dolphin, *External Features.*
Retrieved from http://understanddolphins.tripod.com/dolphinexternalfeatures.html.

Sponson. Inflatable hull of a RHIB

Spy Hop. An action by a dolphin/whale of standing on his tail to improve its view.

Tapetum lucidum. A reflective layer behind the retina of many sharks, called the tapetum lucidum. This allows light-sensing cells a second chance to capture photons of visible light, enhancing vision in low-light conditions. *Tiger Shark.* Retrieved from https://en.wikipedia.org/wiki/Tiger_shark

Turciops truncaus. Atlantic Bottlenose Dolphin; members of the Cetacean order. Owing to a highly developed cognitive process, dolphins, porpoises, and whales are fully sentient beings and considered to be some of the most intelligent of all mammals.

ABOUT THE AUTHOR

Donald E. Auten, a native of Southern California, graduated from Long Beach State University, Salve Regina University, and the Naval War College, where he earned a Master of Arts in national security and strategic studies. He retired from the Navy following a twenty-seven-year career and completed two commanding officer assignments and several staff postings on both coasts. Although originally trained as a light-attack pilot, he graduated from TOPGUN fighter and adversary courses and became an adversary instructor pilot in four adversary commands. In the course of seventeen years of operational flying, Donald completed six squadron assignments and logged nearly five thousand hours. He makes his home in Etna, Wyoming, with his wife, Katherine Sullivan Auten, and their yellow Labrador Retriever, Heather. Donald is the author of *Roger Ball!* and soon to be released, *Black Lion ONE*.

CPSIA information can be obtained
at www.ICGtesting.com
Printed in the USA
LVHW031639291220
675339LV00001B/47